Praise for Nandini Bhattacharya's

Love's Garden

* * *

"Wonderfully dense and wise, with a narrative sweep recalling the work of Dickens, *Love's Garden* conveys both characters and ideas with impassioned intelligence. The garden of the title is India, gorgeously portrayed in all its complexity through the personal travails and occasional triumphs of one fragmented family centered on Prem, who struggles to hold her fragile clan together. Bhattacharya's love for her subjects and for India shines through in her lyrical prose, creating a compelling saga of broken people navigating through a broken world, its brokenness illuminated by beauty and heart, and by the courageous human individuals trying to survive."

—Laura Catherine Brown, author of *Made by Mary*

"A gripping historical novel set in India in the first half of the twentieth century, *Love's Garden* is about a young mother's deal with the devil that sets in motion extraordinary sacrifices, atonements, and twists of fate in three generations of "mothers," during a time when women struggled to have a say in their lives and that of their children. The novel astutely examines what women will do to protect those they love, and how they survive after devastating loss."

—Sybil Baker, author of *While You Were Gone*

"*Love's Garden* is a fascinating and well-crafted journey into India's complex past with characters that will entice you, fill you with indignation, and sometimes break your heart. I particularly enjoyed the stories of the women, who are complicated, brave, headstrong, and impetuous—in other words, deeply human."

—Chitra Banerjee Divakaruni, author of *The Forest of Enchantments*, and *Before We Visit the Goddess*

"From the first chapter of Nandini Bhattacharya's novel, one recognizes the urgent, unflinching voice of an author who lays bare the political and cultural barriers towards choice faced by women in Ango-Indian society as the subcontinent struggles with the weight of imperialism at the turn of the 20th Century. We follow the lives of women, sobered by the limits class, money, and color play as they navigate their world as best they can."

—Indira Ganesan, author of *The Journey* and *Inheritance*

"In *Love's Garden*, Nandini Bhattacharya weaves a lush and beautiful and complicated landscape, a 'not-good-enough love.' The prose is lyrical and smart. The lens, critical and human."

—Danielle Rae Bryant

Love's Garden

Nandini Bhattacharya

Aubade Publishing
Ashburn, VA

Edited by Joe Puckett

Cover design and book layout by Cosette Puckett

Library of Congress Control Number: 2020938782

ISBN: 978-1-951547-08-0

Published by Aubade Publishing, Ashburn, VA

Printed in the United States of America

Dedication

To All My Mothers, For All They Made Possible

Contents

Part 1:
The Village, 1898–

CHAPTER I

In the year 1898, in a corner of Britain's far-flung empire where the imperial sun is still rampant, a train snakes through a vast plain checkered by bronze, green, and ochre fields of wheat, corn, and millet. A woman stumbles through the train, passing compartments, peering into some, trying to reach the engine at the front. Her name is Saroj and she wants to stop the train. Stop the train. Get off.

How can this be happening? Why hasn't Munia come? She promised she would come, without fail. Munia knows the stakes. She swore on her honor and her love.

People are sleeping—seated, slumped, stretched out—some with their entire bodies and heads covered with makeshift sheets, others in ugly positions that bring no shame only to the utterly oblivious. The train is completely dark. Here and there Saroj hears a moan, a whimper, even a low droning. Is that an infant crying, though? Saroj freezes for a long second. No, it's a little girl who has fallen off a bunk. She is lying sprawled on the dirty floor, sobbing, as if getting up without her mother's remorseful help is out of the question. Saroj can't wait, can't stop, can't step into the compartment and help her up. No time to lose. Saroj lurches on, forward.

The engine shrieks—again and again—as it shreds the night. Saroj begins to think she will not be able to reach that engine compartment where the driver and the stoker are busy urging on the machine like a trained beast. Her legs are giving way. The spirit billows out of her, like smoke from an extinguished fire. All is burning. All has burned.

She should have burned too. It was her fate. But she erred. She sinned. Had she sinned? Had she erred? The old agony of that dilemma stops her as if someone has just punched her in the gut. She doesn't even try to break her fall to the floor.

On the gritty floor of the snaking train taking her away from everything she has ever known or loved, Saroj dies that night, inside.

In Patna, Bihar-Bengal Province, a man called Manohar Mishra who has promised to marry her is shocked and distressed to see her being supported out of the train by two or three other passengers. There's a deep gash on her forehead where she says her fall broke when she slipped in the sewage-slicked train bathroom. She looks at her husband-to-be but can't see him. Just a blur. Because another face glows before her eyes.

When she is a little recovered with cool water and a shard of bread, she steps into the tonga Manohar Mishra has brought for her, adorned with flowers and bells. They go to his house, many miles in the interior, set deep within leagues of cracked fields and dry gullies. Here she will find love, indeed she will, even if it is her new husband's not-good-enough love. Her new husband is fortyish, round, and docile. Practically old enough to be her father. She will throw away that love.

It isn't as if she says all this to herself. But because she can see so clearly into the future and sees herself doing all these things, they will all happen.

Saroj reaches her new husband's Bihari-Bengali home when she's only twenty. At first she tries to put her mind to her duties as a wife. There are accounts to check, cattle to count, fields to visit, crops and harvest to oversee, servants to scold, a kitchen to supervise—this in part is the reason why her childless, widower husband has remarried—and a guileless, elderly boy-man to take care of. Only when she stands at night at her bedroom window—fog rolling and parting over the fields stretching before her—she feels the weight of the boulders crushing her back and her chest, threatening to pull her down under waters of oblivion. A face swims before her eyes, brighter in the dark.

Yes, she left voluntarily. But the empty place inside her doesn't know that.

One day she asks her husband if he can send someone back to her old village to look for a woman called Munia. He asks why, and she says she'd promised to take her with her when she left. Munia was her personal maid. Somehow they got separated during the flight and the night train journey to her new home.

Manohar Mishra does try. He's a good man and a good husband. He wants to please his pretty young wife, see a smile on her pale, withdrawn face. One night he tells her in how many ways he's tried. "I'm more than willing to spend money, if I only knew where to look. I sent three people to your village. They couldn't find out anything. Some people said there used to be a young maid-servant called Munia there, but she's gone, they say. She just vanished one day, they say . . . right after you left. Some people even say she may be dead. I'll keep looking but . . ."

Saroj listens quietly, her eyes on the floor at her husband's feet.

Dead or alive, Munia, may you burn in hell. Burn, Munia. Burn in hell.

That's all that's left now. All is burning. All is afire. Saroj burns. In eternal hellfire herself. Can she tell anyone what she's lost with Munia? Can she? Like lightning the thought—almost injunction, almost temptation—flashes in her head: tell him. Tell him what you were going to reveal later, begging for kindness, had Munia come. Can she confess to her husband? Can she ask him to look again, to send men to ask where and how and if Munia died?

No. This man has done enough This man has done more than enough—more than most men would do. And Saroj? She has done an unspeakable thing.

Then, like a thunderbolt, a girl is born to her. She's twenty-one. In the two years of marriage to Manohar Mishra she has used every available contraceptive—ayurvedic, folk, homeopathic, and hearsay—as well as douched and scraped herself raw, after every visit from her husband. But it seems there will be no forgiveness for her.

CHAPTER 2

Fifteen years pass. That's a long time. Saroj doesn't quite know how they passed. She spent most of the time building a fortress around herself.

Prem, daughter of Saroj and Manohar Mishra, is now nearly fifteen, the same age as this new century. Some time ago Manohar Mishra began entertaining proposals for Prem from Delhi, from Ajmer, from Allahabad, from Kolikata. His wife's growing remoteness troubles him. He worries for his daughter. She's uncharacteristically withdrawn and weary of late. She doesn't leave her room much. He's asked her what has made her lose her appetite, her glowing fair skin paling into an unhealthy sere. Why are there shadows under her eyes? Why doesn't she tease him, pleasantly torture him, anymore? He asks her where she would most like to live as a married woman. His daughter says, "Doesn't matter."

Saroj simply looks blankly at Manohar Mishra when he brings this up. When asked about Prem's marriage she says, colorlessly, "Whatever you think best."

Saroj has always seemed strange to the people in this village and her own household, and remains a stranger. Do people tell tall, fantastic tales about her? Do people merely imagine things? Old nurse Shyampiyari, the crone who has raised Prem and given Prem all the mother love the girl ever knew, always says snappishly, "No, they don't." Prem grew up hearing this. A small, puzzled Prem would cock her head to look into Shyampiyari's bleary eyes. Shyampiyari—like the crafty harridan of old epics—would tell Prem tales that modern folk say children shouldn't hear. About demons and giant monkeys and whole islands burning, and great sea monsters rising, holding the world on their crowns and horns. About women who were really witches and demons and married good men and fed off their blood—and even their own children's with these poor men—at night. Strange women. Shameless women who'd stop at nothing. From strange, uncharted places. Such things happen all the time, she'd grunt; not at all tall tales, not at all.

Without this Shyampiyari, whom she calls Dhai, Prem would likely have died in babyhood. Her mother couldn't, wouldn't, or didn't give her the breast. Seemingly she had no milk. An unnatural calamity. It was Shyampiyari—retainer from the time of the dead first wife of Manohar Mishra—who carefully received, boiled, skinned, strained, and spooned cow's milk into Prem's distended, bawling mouth. It was she who wiped up the green muck the baby expelled for the first week from drinking cow's and not mother's milk, crying desperately and incessantly all night, her little face blue, her tiny fists clenched. Faded memories of the burrowing of men and children into her own body setting withered dugs and folds of her skin zinging one last time, Shyampiyari cuddled and nursed the baby girl whose mother couldn't nurse or even hold her. Yes, Prem would certainly have died in babyhood without Shyampiyari. When Prem was older, it was still Shyampiyari who babied her, put her to bed, did her hair, sang her to sleep in the croak that Prem knew as love crooning.

No one understands it, but Saroj avoids her daughter at best and looks at her when forced as if the girl is a speck very, very far away. Shyampiyari has never understood a woman like that calling herself a mother. Shyampiyari has never forgiven Saroj and never will. In Prem's head, for as long as she can remember, Shyampiyari, grinding sweet *paan* in her jaws to the rhythm of combing Prem's hair, has been saying, "If only your *Mai-ji* would behave like any good, respectful, man-fearing woman, *Bitiya!*" Her voice has always quavered with unbridled anger when talking about Saroj.

Manohar Mishra worries a lot that at Prem's age her mother's always strange indifference—neglect, even—torments Prem beyond endurance. She is turning into a woman, his little girl. For her mother, this is apparently of no special import. He's had to arrange the marriage himself.

So Prem is about to be married. Her husband-to-be is Brown Baron Rai Bahadur Sir Naren Mitter. He is the sort of Indian gentleman the British once derided as an effete *"Babu"* who now harrumphs as mandarin of the British *Maibap*. Maibap means mother and father in Hindi, and that is what the British are to their Indian subjects. And knighthood is something the British Maibap bestow only on their most loyal Indian subjects. This is how Narendranath Mittir has become Sir Mitter and Rai Bahadur, or Brave Lord.

Sir Naren Mitter has made a fortune in military and food supplies during this Great War that's going on. How much exactly, who can say. But those who claim to know say that in this war a sixth of the British forces are Indian men. Hapless fathers, husbands, sons and brothers from bleary villages. Of them, they say, at least thirty thousand have already died fighting, and another thirty thousand have returned home maimed, penniless, and without a future. Thousands are missing. No one will look for them.

Sir Naren supplies jute, cement, iron, steel, ammunition, garments, and provisions to the British war effort in India. They say he makes a thousand rupees a day. That's a lot of money. Like the fifty million British pounds that Indians have already paid in taxes to save civilization from the Hun. Even four-legged Indians are going to war for England. All hundred thousand of those patriotic cattle need provisions, so grain and supplies have had to be diverted to them from starving villagers by enterprising men, brave lords, like Sir Naren.

A perfectly natty, nut-brown *sahib*—a brown version of his sahibs, India's white masters—Sir Naren Mitter strives to be. Saroj believes such a man will not beat his wife, or lock her up. Such men—especially the city-dwelling ones—vaunt their ceremonious, if grudging, tolerance of women. This Brown Baron Babu will take care of a wife as she ought to be maintained. Prem—Premlata Mishra—will learn and master the ways of that brave, strange world where entry is prohibited without permits like beauty and money, or servility and cunning. And she will live in Kolikata—British India's capital, eclipsed only by London, it is said—no less. Far from these capricious harvests, rogue dust storms, treacherous earth, and ancient customs. There, Prem will dazzle and rule. Better that way. No one sees these orphan dreams scatter like glowing sparks off the hammered smithy of constant pain that is Saroj's heart. People doubt that she has a heart.

For the first time in decades, Saroj remembers a dream. In her dream, a towering, swaying man says—as she lies in her room, flat on her back, on the still-unchanged linens of her marriage bed, eyes nakedly open—"What's wrong with our ancient customs? You see now, even the English Maibap understand the benefits. Otherwise why this law?" Peering through the blaze of a funeral fire that always licks at her, that calls out to her in dreams and in waking, Saroj places an unspoken blessing on Prem. *May fearless sway be your fate, beautiful Prem.*

It is, indeed, and naturally, a sybaritic taste for beauty that has drawn Sir Naren Mitter to provincial Bihar-Bengal, to a fifteen-year-old village girl quite out of his usual beat. Saroj understands. What is love, after all? Saroj would agree. Love doesn't mean a thing. Better that way. Much better.

CHAPTER 3

Love is an enigma, but marriage is serious business. Girls can only leave home when they marry. This is well known. Any girl or young woman who does otherwise is, of course, ruined.

Before marriage girls have to wait somewhere between bliss and hell. All girls. Prem and the raggedy girl who once loved her included.

There hadn't been many cozy spots for Prem between hell and bliss in the village in 1914, in the days before all the marrying started, except in the love and the loving of that raggedy girl. This girl's name was Kanan. Prem and Kanan would meet and daydream as often as possible by the placid, stagnant pond behind Manohar Mishra's farmhouse. Though this was a community pond, it only came alive at midday for about two hours when women came to wash and bathe. The last bathers left only an echo in the air and a ripple at water's edge. The rest of the time the pond was quiet, shaded by the spreading and interweaving branches of banyan, mango, and saal trees.

One afternoon—all bathing and washing ended for the day—Prem and Kanan set their heist of stolen fruit on the pond's crumbly edge. Beetles and ants hurried away in frenzy. No one would see, so the girls loosened their saris around the waist, to ease the bruising from the petticoat cord, and hitched up the hems. The saris, which they had to wear tucked into petticoats tied tightly at the waist and covering the legs entirely, made them sweat and itch. Boys could just run around and shimmy up trees anywhere, anytime, clothed or bare-bodied.

They didn't really know any boys. Something called a "Great War," they heard, was taking some village boys to faraway places, but generally boys were as much a part of their daily lives as enchanted forests and flying horses. Aimlessly, they rooted up tufts of grass. They soaked their feet, shivering and squealing lightly with pleasure as inch by inch they lowered them into the chill water. The water was like cool, green limeade. Their pale feet unhitched from them under water. Prem fiercely bit into a whole mango—they never let her do that at home—and juice streamed down her face, chin, neck. It was bliss, that lawless afternoon, Kanan with her, by the pond.

Kanan's mother had shown up at the farm from nowhere one day, years ago. No one ever learned her real name, and few ever saw the face which she kept covered by a burlap of a veil that extended almost to her hips. When mother and daughter had arrived, they were completely caked in fine yellow-brown dust. Maybe dust from months of trekking, wandering, meandering; kicked up by calloused, bone-weary feet. Everyone settled on calling the woman "The Dusty One." They called the raggedy girl "Hey." Until Prem said her name would be Kananbala.

Which means Garden Lady in sentimental romances with dreamy, easily fainting heroines. But Kanan wasn't garden-lady material. She was tall, big-boned and quiet. She wouldn't dream of standing out, taking away air and space from her betters. So, secretly, Kanan didn't like her name. It was the only secret she had from Prem. Could you really be called Kananbala if your mother was a shabby, dust-caked maid in a great farmhouse? The name could be thwacked down a little. Girl of the Garden. Flower Girl. Didn't matter. It was stupidly ostentatious. Meaninglessly pretentious. Kanan felt it couldn't belong to someone like her. She should have a more common, normal name. But she'd never do anything about it; Prem, daughter of Manohar Mishra's dotage, had decreed that she would be Kananbala. Within weeks, Prem had adopted this other practically motherless girl who was being called "Hey," or *Bhikharin,* which meant beggar maid. Prem didn't have any friends. Prem was four and the beggar maid was six. Prem forgave the beggar maid for being a beggar; for dirty hands, feet, and black nail rims; for pale lemony dried snot sometimes streaked across her broad, flat-nosed face. And the beggar maid made it obvious that she would love Prem—no, already loved her. Prem gave her the name Kananbala: a refined, school-going, English-learning sort of name, like her own. "My self Prem which means Vine of Love, so my best friend is Kanan or Garden Lady." The gavel fell; Bhikharin was henceforth Kanan. All decided. By Prem. As to Kanan, opposition wouldn't have occurred to her. The princess and the beggar maid. Old story, new names.

Prem didn't think this was vain. Prem didn't know that some might call this imperious, oppressive, controlling. All she knew was that Kanan loved her if Mai-ji didn't, and she loved Kanan if The Dusty One didn't, so their two names cemented these loves and failures to love: Premlata's Kananbala, or Love's Garden; Kananbala's Premlata, or Garden's Beloved Vine. Prem felt her name for Bhikharin or "Hey" was a warm gift, a token of love. Also, that this was a stroke of genius, and Bhikharin meekly agreed.

That afternoon in 1914 by the pond, like most other afternoons, Prem was wearing a dazzling silk sari with a thin gold lace border. She was a striking, petite beauty. Her long, dark hair was well oiled, combed, and plaited into a thick long braid down her back that ended in a gilded red tassel. Prem's eyes were almond-shaped and flecked with tinges of auburn. Fish-shaped solid gold earrings climbed her delicate earlobes; a string of tiny rubies dangled from the fish's mouths like droplets of fresh red blood. Her delicate complexion was what the English called peaches and cream. Small feet, small hands, and pink-tipped tapering fingers and toes further marked her genteel bloodline and gentle breeding.

Kanan, like most days, was wearing a frayed cotton half sari—inappropriate for her age—someone had handed down to her.

But unlike other afternoons, that time Kanan told her dearest friend and young mistress a secret. Not the one about the name, certainly, but important. This important secret had been promised recently.

Kanan was going to be married. She was fifteen. Someone had found her a husband. Maybe another maid who worried more for the gangly, springy daughter of a feckless, unkempt mother than the mother herself. Or, maybe a maid who didn't like the way her round-the-clock opium-dazed husband or teen son had started looking at the budding Kanan. The Dusty One hadn't said anything when asked if she agreed to the match. She'd rubbed her tobacco leaves between palm and thumb and stared out at the fields spreading away from where she sat on her haunches under the shade of a spreading saal tree. After a few minutes, the messenger had considered her task concluded and gone to the matchmakers to say that the girl's mother consented.

That afternoon, Kanan said to Prem, "*Issh*, now I'll be free. I'll go make my own home, in my own way." In that new home her mother wouldn't be allowed. Girls' mothers didn't go live with their married daughters. Only boys' mothers could and did live with their married sons.

"*Issh*, and you'll come and live with us?" Kanan said. It was a question and a plea, a promise and a hope. Unlike here, in her own house Kanan would be mistress of all, of course. She could do whatever she pleased. So whatever she or Prem said would be law there. Prem nodded. Though Kanan's habit of saying *issh*—which really meant nothing but just loosely sort of "Ooh! Ah!"—annoyed Prem; it was so childish and bumpkin-like.

"Of course, of course I'll come."

Was it Kanan or Prem who'd slowly dreamed up a husband as a man who was loving, a kind provider, and a slave to his wife's wishes?

A little like Prem's father, but young and handsome.

Who had few desires or wishes of his own, if any.

And never, ever scolded or punished.

However it happened, this was the future and those were the husbands they planned on. These husbands, when they materialized, would be generous and unobtrusive. Most of the time they would be engrossed in worldly affairs in any case, and when they came home—late—they'd be avuncular, mild-mannered, and extremely pliant. Also, most evenings they'd fall asleep early, exhausted from embarking on worldly affairs very early in the day. They would never complain when Kanan and Prem went on long trips and pilgrimages together. Or when Kanan and Prem went shopping and bought whatever they wished. And they would shower Prem and Kanan with sparkling jewels and gorgeous saris every birthday, holiday, and festive day.

No, at this point Prem wasn't yet thinking beyond the feast of idyllic freedom in Kanan's new home, where Kanan's husband would do whatever he was told. However, when she did marry, it would be the same for her, naturally. It was pretty simple. In the sentimental literature Prem read, husbands were always like that. Or old and ill, and soon died leaving their wives all their money and property so that their wives could become great social workers and reformers.

Kanan gushed on, "*Issh*, so wonderful! And I won't have to put up with a co-wife. So lucky!" Even generous, avuncular, drowsy, and unobtrusive husbands sometimes had first wives whom, of course, they loved a lot less than their second ones. But Kanan's guardian angel had fixed her marriage with a forty-year-old man who'd never married. He worked as a "clerk" in a government office. The girls pronounced it "Clark."

"*Issh*, this will just be so fabulous, Prem!" Kanan said.

They didn't speak for minutes after that. No need to. A cozy spot. Only one. But enough. But then Prem felt an unexpected anxiety succeeded by not-quite-unfamiliar irritation. After all, this husband fellow was being recruited sight unseen. What if he wasn't the right sort? What was a "Clark"? What did he do? Why did Kanan want to get married without knowing anything about her husband? What and whose was the rush?

"*Issh*! Lucky! So lucky!" Kanan was still saying, waving her large sunflower-like head from side to side. But Prem was suddenly having trouble being or acting enthusiastic about the news. Something stuck in her throat, making swallowing hard, quickening her heartbeat and hurting around her ribs. She didn't know what it was. But Kanan, oblivious, went on with the celebration: "Besides, he's also *Kuleen*!"

Prem stiffened. What was this now? She'd never heard the word Kuleen. Kuleen. Clark. What were all these things? She didn't have to wonder long. Kanan went on: "You know what Kuleen means, Prem? Kuleen means very high-caste Brahmin. And I'm Kuleen myself. *Issh*, it's very sad but it's hard to find us Kuleen girls husbands, because men worthy of us are dying out. Even a few years ago, men like my 'him' went around marrying as many Kuleen girls as they could actually get to because there were so few men to go around. If they didn't arrive on time, the girl had to marry a banana tree."

Really? Please.

"Then I think the Bitish"—Kanan's illiterate version of British. *Oh, such country cuteness!*—"passed some law against that. What amazing luck I have!" An abstruse allusion here to the forehead as in "my good forehead"—which is how one might say "my good luck" in the half-Bengali, half-Hindi dialect the girls spoke—had allowed Prem to unhang her head and glance at Kanan's forehead. Wide, bony, with a chalk-white childhood scar on the right temple.

Kanan—Bhikharin once. Always so easy, always so happy with whatever she got. Like this disgraceful, moth-eaten old sari she was wearing. Like this sudden marriage of hers. What was wrong with her? Why was she still behaving like a beggar?

"But what else do we know about him? Is he kind?"

Kanan shook her head. She didn't know.

"Do you know if he's rich and handsome?"

Kanan shook her head again.

"Will he give you lots of gold and jewelry?"

And again, Kanan had no answer. Prem became nearly speechless.

That afternoon by the pond Prem would also realize that her family life was a worse puzzle than she'd thought. While Kanan went on about her marriage like she was speaking from the window of a slow train moving away, Prem's fists clenched and unclenched for that reason too.

Why was her *Babu-ji*—who must be Kuleen too—not such a crowd-pleaser? Mai-ji especially acted like he didn't exist. All the household and the village knew. Anything related to Mai-ji darkened Prem's sky, and for this stupid reason, among others. Growing up, Prem had watched forever the black farce: Babu-ji's futile pursuit of Mai-ji's attention.

Babu-ji would say, "Saroj dear, won't you take the head of the fish?"

Silence.

"Dear, look at this pearl, wife! The size of a parrot's egg. Well, almost."

Silence.

"Would you like to go to the musical opera coming to the village, Saroj dear?"

Silence.

What had happened between them? When? Why?

Sometimes Mai-ji walked out even before Babu-ji finished his question. Prem carefully avoided looking directly at her father then. His unraveling in her mother's presence was the daily drama she'd watched since babyhood. Adulthood, lost and going the wrong way, stumbled upon her childhood many, many times. She felt that she wanted to comfort her father as if he were the child. Actually, no, she didn't. Babu-ji was weak. High caste, but weak. His weakness revolted her. She wanted to yell at him for being so weak.

Like when Mai-ji had just walked into this very back pond. Just like that, wading in, as though nothing remained for her to do. She'd walked into cold water, muddy and ankle deep, then knee hugging, then thigh slapping, then waist high, and then she must have forced her arms down by her side as the water rose above her neck and chin, entering her nose and eyes with a gurgling laugh. Must have forced her arms down, clenched fists that wanted, of course—by the force of nature and being—to explode out of the water and bring the body back to air and light with them. And Babu-ji never scolded her even for that.

Choosing to die, and how. That was freedom? Someone had caught a glimpse of something floundering and bobbing, and the maids had pulled the strange fish called her mother out of the pond, frustrating Mai-ji's apparently proud ambition to end her life her own way. After that, she'd been watched almost constantly for a while. She met the eyes upon her as a rough stone meets an iron blade. After that her skin—though she was still young—grew leathery, and then hornlike. Her beauty petrified. *Served her right.*

Maybe Kanan was getting married first and not she, Prem, because no one wanted to marry her when they heard about Mai-ji. A bitter, cold humiliation permeated Prem at this thought. Maybe Kanan would get married and reign over her husband's household, and Prem would become a wizened, whiskery spinster, not by choice. What kind of disgrace would that be? Would it have killed Mai-ji to wait just a year or two longer before she walked into the water, until Prem could have been safely married off and in her husband's home? So she could be where she belonged? Not having to depend on Mai-ji's mercy to notice, love or protect her? And so Mai-ji's crazy doings couldn't ping off her skin and leave welts of shame and humiliation. That afternoon the madness and sadness of mothers and their grotesque, grimacing mysteries floated on the water for a minute but held no real clues to the mysteries, no reasons for the wickedness.

That afternoon should have been dream drenched. But the future that had seemed a neatly fitted puzzle fell apart that afternoon and never got put back right again. Different worlds for different people, Prem saw. She saw at her feet the very crack in the earth that made possible her supremacy, and found both crack and rule nauseating and world ending. Kanan and her *issh, issh* on the other side. And Kanan's bending over backward in everything, to anyone. Her lack of . . . what? Prem didn't exactly know but she knew it was an important, indispensable thing. And then she felt unsettled by anger and affront, for the first time but not the last. Why did people always disappoint? Why did they betray your trust? Why couldn't they live up to expectations? Why did Dhai smell old and poor? Why did Kanan always grin like a born fool? Why did her Babu-ji waddle? Why did Mai-ji avoid and ignore him?

Why was Kanan allowing herself to drop into the world-ending crack willingly when she had Prem on her side?

Kanan, don't marry. Not yet. Please.

There were no words for what she was feeling. So she said, "I hope when you are properly married and everything you will stop saying *issh, issh* with everything you say, like a fool. Don't you know it doesn't mean anything?"

CHAPTER 4

Prem relented eventually. She forgave. Kanan, herself, every girl she knew, was waiting, dreaming, hoping. Till men came like loose cannons and picked them off. Then, free at last.

Well. Marriage then. Even if to a Kuleen clerk in Kolikata. Twenty-five years older. Poor high caste Kanan. Raggedy, rangy, and no Garden Lady after all.

Time then to get on with the practicalities. The next time they were alone Prem asked, "Children?"

Kanan nodded vigorously, blushing.

"How many?"

"Oh, five, six. One's for you, silly! Who's going to be good enough for you, oh insane one!" Premlata means Loving Vine. Garden Lady and Loving Vine laughed then. Loving Vine

wanly. Still, it was a relief. They were at the pond again. The light had thinned. The pond looked like a dead fisheye but the sad-faced pasts had gone bottom feeding. Prem glanced again at Kanan. Kanan was staring straight ahead, swinging her long, strong legs, unconcerned about the rope of mango juice running from mouth to chin.

It wasn't so bad, was it? After all, she and Kanan would always be together. Kanan, who loved her. Who loved only her. Who would always love her. She impetuously threw her arms around Kanan then, Kanan reciprocated, and the two girls rocked a while, their bodies fitting into one another's curves and hollows in that great, tight hug.

Kanan was married in the late summer of 1914. At Kanan's wedding Prem excitedly pored over the few blobs of gold Kanan would wear at her own wedding. She fingered Kanan's wedding sari, a hand-me-down moth-nibbled purple silk from generations of women in Babu-ji's family, with mixed pleasure that Kanan had at least this faded silk but also that Kanan had nothing better. She watched—equal parts seriousness and amusement—various intense womanly rituals that went on in the servants' *zenana* quarters, in tandem with men's hoarse bustle outside.

She was so overwhelmed, so excited, that she forgot a few details. After the wedding, Kanan would become a wife. Would belong to one man. Would leave the village. Must. And would.

At the wedding, Kanan wore her smatter of gold. Raw-knuckled hands lay bare on her lap like skinned rats rather than the gold-leafed fans one expects in a young bride. No one was talking about how much gold her Kuleen Clark had given her: none. Her smile was brilliant. The future was brilliant.

Prem had worn her hair up in a high mignon with a thick braid swishing down her back—an adventurous style favorited from fashion plates in an English magazine another landholding family's daughter had smuggled into school, quite modern for the village—the fanciest of mirror pins handed down by generations of her father's womenfolk stuck in the precarious arrangement. These pins served the useful function of small hand mirrors at a pinch. Her mother couldn't have been bothered, probably didn't even know where all her own load of jewelry was. She'd given Prem nothing to wear, nor a glance, nor a scolding appraisal. But other women long dead had made up for Mai-ji so Prem was wrapped in gold, practically head to toe.

All girls knew this one thing: mothers through time have prayed, begged, fought for gold for their daughters. If all else fails, gold remains true to its woman. Husbands may take mistresses, or drink, or die. Sons may bring home intolerable wives, enemies of their first loves, their mothers. Mothers-in-law may devise a hundred ways to break another woman's daughter who's become their terrible fate. Gold stands fast by its woman.

Gold, gleaming in locked boxes lined with soft red muslin. Wrapped in dreams of power. Waiting for the call to battle. In cabinets, secret chambers, wardrobes. Under piles of silk, brocade, cashmere. A woman whose man covers her in gold must really love her.

And despite being the richest landowner's daughter for leagues around, it was only thanks to those responsible, farsighted foremothers long gone that Prem was top girl at the wedding. Behind her—Prem imagined standing before her mirror—a long line of women stood quietly, watching. They'd prayed for gold, love, and miracles for the infant girls they'd had to everyone's disappointment or displeasure. They'd raised them, protected them as much as they could, saved for their small hands, tucked away for them secrets and treasures—golden, the best pieces—they'd scraped together. She, Prem, was that miracle. She was their miracle. She decided to forget Mai-ji for that moment, that day.

She enjoyed herself thoroughly.

Kanan's wedding was the bridge Prem crossed to step into young womanhood and the power of her genteel birth and fierce beauty. Who wasn't, wouldn't be, swept away by her? Buoyed by something new and nameless, Prem bossed and bullied and preened at every opportunity, glimpsing at fourteen in small, tarnished mirrors in low-ceilinged, dark vestibules a lady of a great mansion. The future.

She led, vigorously, the charge against the horsey, rawboned, gap-toothed groom, hiding his shoes until he gave each girl a paisa for rescue of his shoes. But in a secret drawer of her mind she'd begun fingering an unfortunate, unforeseen problem, slowly metastasizing into dismay: Kanan leaving the village.

To dispel the webbing fear, she'd laughed loudest at the humble, greenish copper paisa too. "What is this? A horse's egg! Look Bini, Chameli! Look, Kanan's 'He' can lay eggs. A horse's egg! One whole paisa!!" Bini, Chameli and others hadn't dared not to laugh uproariously—but not louder than Prem—at the joke. A horse didn't lay eggs! A horse's egg was a "nothing."

Kanan's "He" got stuck with the name "Kuleen Horse."

But the Kuleen Horse was still taking Kanan away.

Prem didn't want to tell anyone about her helpless terror. She stole many long, revulsed looks at the hollow-cheeked—was he toothless?—cratered face of the forty-year-old man. She decided to lock away in that same secret drawer of helpless terror every crevice, every pit, every jawless, chinless angle as ransom, as needed. She put her own paisa away in her precious tortoiseshell jewelry box to save towards a trip to visit the married Kanan in Kolikata, whether the Kuleen Horse wanted it or not.

She said to herself that this was all very "jolly." "Jolly" was a word her young village schoolmaster—his name was Jagat Pandey—sometimes used when in his poetic excitement he forgot to be nationalist and hate the English, because secretly he adored the briny brawn of the English language. She hadn't considered that she may have retained the word because the schoolmaster sounded so . . . so adorable using it.

Sometimes the heart's legerdemains at fourteen presage a lifetime of casting blind dice. Prem, no stranger to sadness, facing another world-ending moment, was meeting it—would meet it again and again—in the disenchanting forms that, sooner or later, escort most children by hand into the world of adults.

A few days later, Kanan was leaving for Kolikata. When the village came to see her away to Kolikata with her horsey husband, Kanan didn't carry on. Unlike the expected—that leaving her girlhood home and her soulmate Prem would seem to flatten, nearly kill her—she didn't cry or whimper.

At all.

Someone whispered: *"Hai Hai!* Unnatural! Like mother like daughter. Both touched in the head." Few had noticed the change in Prem, though. Prem's face had visibly shrunk and paled. In the last few days she didn't seem to have combed her hair, washed her face, or changed her clothes. Impassive, she resembled Saroj strikingly at the moment.

Kanan turned just before she reached the waiting carriage, but she didn't go to her mother. It was Prem she moved back toward.

"Prem . . . ?" she said.

Standing among a knot of women, Prem should have stepped up. Met ardor with ardor. She didn't. The Dusty One, silent, expressionless, was among the knot of women in the background. When Kanan called, Prem did an incredible thing, everyone would agree later. She moved back and stood behind The Dusty One.

Kanan said nothing more. Her eyes remained dry but her mouth trembled uncontrollably. Between the two girls The Dusty One stood, stolid as always.

The Kuleen Horse was standing a little distance away, looking at the knot of folks while taking quick, sharp drags on his *beedi*. But suddenly he made a long, rattling sound of impatience and mounted the tonga carriage, as if he were about to take off alone, if it came to that. This roused one of the elder servants to a sense of the rightness of things. The old man took the newly married Kanan gently by the elbow to lead her forth. Soundless and steady-eyed, Kanan turned around and entered the rickety wooden box. The galled horses tumbled forward with a slight skip and lurch, shaking their mangy manes, glad to move anyhow, anywhere, rather than stand harnessed under that fireball sun.

And that would be Prem's last view of Kanan.

But no one would ever know that the evening before Kanan left the village forever with the Kuleen Horse, the young Schoolmaster Jagat Pandey heard a knocking on the rickety door of the hut he shared with his widow mother.

He was very surprised; who would visit in such weather? He was alone that night. His mother was visiting her distant cousin three villages away; he'd accompanied her there and returned to prepare for his wars, big and small. Yes, Jagat Pandey was going to the Great War. To fight for Empire, somewhere unimaginably far away.

He opened the door. Prem stood there, hair and sari plastered to her form. Unadorned. Her eyes—wide, almost rolled up in her head as if from shock—landed, settled, and fixed on his. He couldn't imagine what had happened. He couldn't speak for seconds that felt like years. He was terrified and ecstatic.

Prem walked in, past him, as if in a trance. She shivered uncontrollably—the late-spring rain was cold—but walked across the room as if familiar with it, and sat on the sagging cot where Jagat slept. He could see, though, through vision blurred by a heart hammering, that she hardly knew where she was. He hurried to get her a dry towel, forgetting to feel ashamed of his threadbare home in his heartache for her condition. He too shivered as if he had that condition. As if he'd walked in cold rain for a long time. When he dried her hair gently, painstakingly, feeling the tremor passing through her seismically—this wasn't something he'd ever done for anyone else, not even his mother whom he loved deeply—she looked up at him finally.

He almost recoiled at her swollen, purplish eyes.

She didn't say anything at first; she didn't explain her arrival, her state, her strangeness. After minutes she said, as if still in a trance: "Can I stay here? I don't want to go home."

And poor Jagat stood before his dream like a man struck by lightning. He wasn't able to move or speak. He was barely able to breathe for fear of disturbing this frail, fabulous vision. He was only twenty, after all. The person sitting on his bed was only a girl. He'd been alone with her only once before and that had been farewell. He'd never expected anything other than maybe her pitying recollection of him if—or when—he was gone.

Because he'd told her one surprise Friday afternoon some months ago—school was done and she was waiting only for her father's carriage to take her back home—that he'd signed up with the British Army. She wasn't curious in the least. He'd poured it out. He sorely needed money. His schoolmaster's salary was barely a living, and his widow mother was getting old and too feeble to do the cook's work she'd done to raise him. He'd been shy and nervous while he talked, never meeting Prem's eye, picking up and putting down books lying already crestfallen on his rickety master's table. He'd been standing. Prem had been sitting on her special chair. As should be. She couldn't sit on the dirt floor like the other girls.

And that if he didn't come back . . . if that were to be the case, then he . . . well . . . he wanted Prem to be very, very happy, always.

Prem had felt very puzzled. Why wouldn't she be very happy, always? Once with Kanan—both of them magically married to faceless, docile, and generous husbands—and away from Mai-ji, what stood in the way of her happiness? Then, to her astonishment he'd quavered, "For she's a jolly good fellow, for she's a jolly good fellow . . ." Et cetera.

He'd probably never even seen a belt, a buckle, or boots, leave alone a rifle. To school he would always wear the same pair of creaking, dusty rubber pumps over threadbare cotton socks showing under his frayed, folded *dhoti*—folded by his mother, probably. At tiffin break all the girls would unsubtly make fun of him as he sat under a tree a little away from the one-room schoolhouse, eating his lunch. Coarse *rotis*, fried potatoes, a green chili pepper, and maybe a small onion and a bit of pickle, wrapped in a piece of cloth.

Yet, he was going to war. That night he lowered his eyes before her disoriented, empty gaze. Not because he would deny her anything, but because he knew that her audacity was not for him. And, of course, he needn't answer her question. She had to see his bursting, thrill-damaged heart clearly through his frayed vest and poking ribs. How could he hide it?

Prem didn't go home until daybreak, somberly refusing Jagat's attempts to walk her back then.

That daybreak, he stood—speared by painful longing and rigid with anguish—at the door of the shack, bathed as on rare mornings in tender, unfamiliar daylight, while she grew distant on her path homeward. He was able to see that she was off balance sometimes, slipping and sliding on the faint mud-slicked ridge winding between drowned rice fields. He wanted to rush to her side every time he saw her teeter. He feared she might step on a snake or a scorpion vicious and stupid with fright from the waterlogging. But she'd strictly forbidden him to follow. And made him promise he'd never tell anyone what she told him the night before.

CHAPTER 5

Prem couldn't forget and didn't want to. However, she had actually seen Jagat close up only once. Before that he'd only been the poor, bumbling schoolmaster, not a real person. Then came typhoons of need, and desire and passion, and . . . war. Stormy weather everywhere. Didn't make for clear-sightedness. Whenever Prem tried to fix Jagat, his shape, his features, in her memory through a vision astigmatic since Kanan's wedding, she still saw Kanan clearly, but she could only remember slants and corners of Jagat. His elbows jutting and angular. His ankles ashen and bony. A small bleached scar across his left eyebrow. Ribs sticking out painfully. One curl venturing forth and tumbling over his forehead when he was animated . . . he had thick, shiny black hair. Quite beautiful. She remembered these things as if she'd only ever seen him through a piece of cloth with holes punched in it.

How changed everything was. Kanan had been gone a few months. Prem's wedding had been fixed with Sir Naren Mitter. It would take place in six months. For some days Prem had felt restless, warm, apathetic. She'd been sick several times. Her appetite was practically gone. So this was love? Like a sickness?

That Friday afternoon in school when Jagat Pandey made his earnest, trembling declaration of eternal love—it seemed thousands of years ago now—the fleeing sun casting back one last spear of anemic light into the shadow engulfing the land, the land already dreaming fitfully of the mesmerizing night to come, Prem had sensed that she had power over men. That day, in that forlorn school-room with a goat tied to a stake outside bleating incessantly, she, the village princess, with her queenly future, had looked at that *sepoy* to be—while he, rail thin and pale, had stood before her splotched with blushes—and laughed out unwittingly loud. She'd seen pain slashing his face and felt sorry for several moments, but then comedy had again overpowered compassion, and she'd laughed some more. She'd tried to summon up grim visions of stern men fighting wars, soldiers saving hapless women, but his singing "For she's a jolly good fellow . . ." had undone her. And he'd simply stood there, before her—poor Jagat Pandey the village schoolmaster—a forlorn figure, her skinny adorer, soon to be Havildar Pandey of some Rifles of the British Army in the Great War. He was a darling, funny moth that had hurtled into her flame and burned down to ashes. It had been gratifying. Though also shocking. He was the village schoolmaster. She was the village princess.

She'd tried to stop laughing, seeing her poor schoolmaster's face twist as it burned up, but she hadn't known how to bridle her hilarity near allied to pique. Pique, because deep within she too was always burning, her mother's unnatural neglect like hot oil rubbed on torn flesh. Sometimes, sadly, it made her want, just a little, to know that others could burn too. A little. Sometimes.

She couldn't remember just how it had all that ended that afternoon. Maybe the carriage had been late, and she'd laughed too much. Maybe it was timely and Jagat Pandey had been spared some of the anguish of loving ridiculously, hopelessly. But she wished she could go back there, then. She remembered how, at Kanan's wedding, she'd begun to be full of something more than triumph. Though she hadn't exactly felt a great upheaval when she'd thought of her schoolmaster, she'd known intuitively he was something beyond a first conquest. He'd swept her off the ground not with joy or desire or passion—she was fourteen and had great prospects—but with exultation.

But this morning, months after he'd left, her hands lay still on her opened Tennyson. His Tennyson; a parting present from him. The poems made her ache, again—besides the dull, steady back pain she had these days—with their intentional freight of impossible ardor and languor. She cast a panicked inner eye over the worlds inside and outside her for some flash flood to fill an abysmal loss. Maybe even another person, maybe gilded over. Because, after all, Jagat Pandey had only been the schoolmaster, and she was the princess. Maybe that was why things had ended as they did. That sort of distance makes only for difficulties. She was no naïf; she understood. Especially after Kanan's wedding. But she didn't understand all the way.

Was Prem's heart hardened enough that she didn't remember a thudding heart under poking ribs under a frayed vest in a poor shanty in a village where a landlord's auburn-eyed daughter had a great fortune planned for her? A plan quite un-Tennysonian. Was she just plain callous?

She wasn't.

Did Prem's heart not twist remembering a night in a hut?

It did twist.

Did Prem dream, waking or sleeping, of what had passed between her and her schoolmaster? Would she remember?

Yes, to both questions.

Would she run away from her marriage to Sir Brown Baron Frog Prince because she had loved—alright, loved—Havildar Jagat Pandey?

No, she wouldn't. That would be silly.

It was the second year of the war to end all wars. Mist ambled on Prem's father's fields as she squinted intently and tried to imagine the scene as mist rolling up and down English hills. Her eyes blurred from involuntary, disobedient tears. Still, out of the formless, steamy gray before her she tried to force into being the turquoises, emeralds, and sapphires she conjured up when she read Alfred Lord Tennyson's poems. In Jagat's book.

Jagat, who'd made her feel so ethereal, so fabulous, so desired and . . . so jolly . . . at Kanan's wedding. Even as the incessant motion of people, things, and words had engulfed and, in the end, frightened her at the wedding, she'd pushed the sour mix of dread and longing some distance away by muttering again and again, "Soon I'll be gone too; soon." Somehow, Jagat Pandey had got mistily mixed up in that, quite unreasonably.

And then he was a soldier. Or dead. A dead soldier. Could a man be dead and still a soldier?

That evening Prem was very sick again, and Shyampiyari froze in fear, wondering what to do. She had a suspicion that was fossilizing into terror. She wanted to protect her Bitiya from that witch of a mother, and of course also from the rest of the world. Bitiya had to be married, her life must not stop here. Prem lay on her bed, ashen and sunken, and shook her head at whatever Shyampiyari said. Shyampiyari held Prem's hand as the girl cried into her pillow, her body rigid. "It will be alright, my baby girl," Shyampiyari whispered, though she didn't know if it would.

When the country doctor came secretly—in the dark of night—only Shyampiyari and The Dusty One received and brought him inside the house. Shyampiyari had chosen The Dusty One because she would not talk. Or at least she was less likely to than any other person in the household. She'd gone to fetch the doctor without asking questions.

When the elderly, troubled doctor snapped his medical bag shut with a click that sounded like a shot in the silence, Prem turned to Shyampiyari and began to weep.

"Please don't tell her. Please don't let her know. Please don't bring her in, Dhai . . ."

Prem didn't have to say who she wanted kept in the dark.

"There, there, there," Shyampiyari mumbled. Tears, long absent, had filled her own ancient, dim eyes. She patted her girl on the head, the back. She pressed down Prem's arms with firm strokes to her side, as if to restrict her and keep her safe. Now that it was too late, she knew she had to betray her.

The doctor had said there was only thing to be done now. So Shyampiyari had to tell Saroj. "The real mother," she spat out into the dark.

She wobbled to Saroj's room like a broken thing, looking so unlike herself that despite her indifference Saroj, long in bed but sleepless as usual, shot up straight. It was already past nine o'clock, it was velvety dark outside, and a solitary storm lantern glowed in a corner of the room. "What is it?" she said. "Why are you here?" Where's . . . ?" Before that sentence could end Shyampiyari had broken down in harsh, noisy sobs.

"Then you are the reason this happened." Saroj had heard her out, not moving, her face without expression. When she said that, Shyampiyari yelped again and slid down to her haunches on the floor, her ragged, violent sobs turning into a drawn-out whimper. She had no defense, no excuse. It was under her watch that the thing had happened. Shyampiyari hadn't been watchful enough. Shyampiyari hadn't spent nights awake looking out windows at the fields and the fog. Finally, as her moans died, Shyampiyari struck her head with the flat of her hand.

"Kill me, *einh?*" she said. "Just kill me. I'd rather die than watch you make Bitiya suffer more." She wanted to curse Saroj, to remind her that she herself was a monster, not a mother, but she was afraid and she was weakened.

CHAPTER 6

Prem's labor pains began one chilly evening. It was March, and evening had come early, falling like a soft gray blanket over the village and its sleepy inhabitants. After eight hours, during which Prem made hardly a sound except for the few moans that slipped through her clamped lips and clenched teeth, she was exhausted. Shyampiyari hobbled back and forth, bringing in boiling water, clean rags, and cloth strips soaked in the coolest water there was in clay pots around the house for Prem's face and forehead. Prem's face was purplish, bloated with anguish and fear. Her head kept turning from side to side; her eyes were half rolled up in her head. Saroj sat still in one dark corner, motionless, wordless. Offering no help. Showing no emotion. Prem sensed her even in this agony, sensed that she would not come near, would not reach out. The way these two sensed each other had always been wordless, like hair standing on the skin of one when the other was near. She was grateful Saroj didn't approach her. She didn't want her mother to see her when she was twisted and breaking; she wanted her mother gone. It was the one thing, the only thing, her mother had ever done for her: staying away.

At one point the midwife brought in secretly pumped Prem's stomach, then made her walk around a few times till Prem's legs gave way. Then the midwife and Shyampiyari brought her back to bed and she sank into the sheets like a stone in water. The midwife pushed Prem's knees as far apart as possible and peered into the space between. She crooned and keened softly. She was enticing the baby to emerge. At times she went to the window and looked for the moon which hid and peeked behind clouds. The midwife made soft, encouraging predictions. The moon was easily escaping the clouds; this presaged good things, she murmured. She poured doses of a liquid from a vial and made Prem drink the dark, thick liquid. Prem gagged, drank, retched.

There was some tenderness in the midwife's touch, though hired. How relieved Saroj was that the woman was here. It made Saroj herself superfluous, almost invisible. She was going to make herself watch every single thing happening, but she couldn't do more. She couldn't come near more quivering, palpitation pain, more suffering, more repentance, more despair. She'd had enough. Her sixth sense also said her daughter didn't want her near, didn't want to be touched or held by her.

Why didn't I die that night on the train? Why, if I couldn't do it before, did I not end it that night? Did Shaitan keep me alive so that sin would live on through me? Did I feel hope only so that it would become the noose around my neck? Is this my sin? Did I do this?

But she said nothing; she remained a motionless spectator. When finally Prem—fifteen—couldn't push anymore, when she sank back on the hot, damp pillow and wept soundlessly, tears dribbling down the creases around her tightly squeezed eyes, Saroj closed hers too. Then she said a little prayer.

Let her die now. Let it end now.

Then an animal began screaming at being ripped apart alive and Saroj had to open her eyes. She saw the midwife and Shyampiyari doing something between Prem's legs. As Prem howled, the baby emerged. It didn't cry. Prem was still heaving, mouthing and clawing the air silently, but she knew the baby had come out. Her eyes roved, stopped on Saroj for a second, then swung to where Shyampiyari and the midwife were bending over something a little away from the bed.

Because what will happen next might kill her, unless . . .

"Let . . . me see . . ." Words came as if from a slit windpipe clotted with phlegm and blood.

"Wait a little . . . ," either Shyampiyari or the midwife said.

"Please, please . . . Dhai . . ." Holding the baby close would help, would smack back the circling, crashing waves of pain. Shyampiyari came to the bedside and gently touched Prem's forehead. "In a bit," she said in a soft croak, "after the baby's been cleaned up."

"Boy or girl, Dhai?" Prem asked.

After a second Shyampiyari said, "Boy."

And Saroj couldn't stay any longer, it would only be worse the longer she stayed, and she left the room. If Prem saw her leave, she said nothing. Shyampiyari asked Prem if she wanted more water, and when Prem nodded slightly she poured water from a clay pot directly into Prem's sunken mouth and also dropped in something else. In seconds Prem's eyes closed and she slept.

She was told later that the baby had died. Stillborn—the midwife and Dhai couldn't resuscitate it. For the next few weeks she was barely awake, and when awake she was confused, sore and tired. Dhai Shyampiyari went on giving her the small pills, saying they would help the healing. In a sense, Shyampiyari believed this.

What color were the baby's eyes? Prem asked this again and again when she started out of her bouts of surrender to sleep and the pills, and Shyampiyari explained again and again that the stillborn baby's eyes never opened. And Prem sobbed each time at this answer—weakly, helplessly, hopelessly. Why she especially wanted to know the color of the baby's eyes she could not say.

Soon after Saroj left the room that night, and as soon as Prem was deep in sleep, Shyampiyari and the midwife had left the room, clutching a small bundle. That night Saroj did two things she'd sworn off forever: make a decision, and take needed action. She had to do those things without, again, knowing their exact consequences. There was no choice—again. Stony-faced, dry-eyed, she gave an order. And immediately turned away, closing her door on Shyampiyari's anguished, disbelieving face.

Behind the closed doors she prayed—ineptly, long out of the habit of praying—to be forgiven, again, for another great sin. She prayed to be forgiven for having prayed—for a few moments—that her daughter die before grief without end became her trousseau, and her feelings for her mother ripened into pure hatred. Then, more composed, she prayed that Prem would soon feel the shock of some modern city's raucous, luminous civilization as protection against the waving cornfields and thin winter sun of these provinces; against sudden, ridiculously primitive death from ancient maladies; against ruins men made. In spite of what has happened, please let my daughter have—Saroj mouthed silently to some unseen arbitrator—one husband, one life, and her children about her. *I've paid my dues. I've burned all my life. I am my funeral fire, my own ashes. Now, let me go.* This time she'd done what had to be done. Prem would never live in dread, never have to fear any man. That's how it should always be . . . *that's how it should have been for me when I was a widow at nineteen. . . .*

Girls and young women in sentimental romances are expected to throw themselves off a cliff, or pine away to death, or go mad, or become saints when they are "ruined." But real girls and women seldom do these things. A month later Prem got out of the bed where her unmet newborn had been born and taken away, took in both hands the gilded noose offered, and put it around her soft neck. What must be, would be. She didn't care anymore. No letter had ever come from the front. Some ageless pain did still well up every time she remembered a thin, young face incandescent with ardor, already transcendent with loss. Or the night rain that had fallen like silver on a thatch roof, washing away unspoken, incalculable, even unforgettable grief and unbridgeable distance. But then,

Nothing.

She never would find out what color her baby's eyes had been.

CHAPTER 7

So one bright, auspicious day in 1915 a cluster of men who look like carved ebony figures clothed in startling crimson and white sit under a festooned canopy at the entrance to Manohar Mishra's great farmhouse. They blow strenuously into their shehnai horns, deftly finger their flutes, make love to their mandolins. These men always come to weddings. There, for three days of pomp and ceremony, these solemn, impassive men make music of such sadness and passion that when bride, mother, and father have to say their final farewells, have to be gently separated from one another by friends and relatives, the tears of all three have, thankfully, almost all flowed.

And the dry, dusty road winding through hillocks and slopes in the distance brings a shiny Model T and from it steps a gleaming Rai Bahadur Naren Mitter, all monocles and suspenders and patent leather twinkles. Behind the Model T, bullock carts bump down from the train station with the Rai Bahadur's retinue in them. An army really: pasty-faced city men—their brilliantined hair banished from foreheads or sitting like low, snug bowls on heads; their elegant linen shirts, coats, and trousers protecting soft, rubbery limbs from country dust and pollen; their cigarettes in holders and their Three Nuns tobacco in old briars burning maniacally in this rich, earthy air, bracketed in adventurous smirks or mortified grimaces—jostle and jigger over stones and potholes shoulder to shoulder with stoic servants holding stuff.

For a day they are stupendously fed and entertained. Village style.

Manohar Mishra has provided *nautankis, shikar,* and *kusti* tournaments. The city boys seem not to like the country liquor and the tawny, tangy dancing women. They can't hold shooting rifles, and fall asleep at the watering hole watch. As for the glistening, thudding thrills of kusti, it's an absurd idea. They lift their white trousers gingerly off the ground on seeing the smallest clod of earth, and oil isn't going to touch an inch of them. Shyampiyari grunts copiously and spits ebulliently on patent-leather shoeprints.

Corpulent and confused, Manohar Mishra sweats in the cool air. Who knows what he thinks of his daughter's coming elegance, her grand marriage, his serious, older Brown Baron son-in-law, his possible future city grandchildren. The world, absorbed in the drama of his wife and daughter, has stopped wondering about his state of mind long ago.

The Kolikata Babus' sophisticated tastes stump Mishra Babu-ji entirely, but even from behind closed doors Saroj sees that *Jamai Raja* will shrug off if not like his wife's people's bucolic ways.

Always, always, silhouettes at the back of Saroj's mind. One, the man who tried to take whatever he wanted by force. Others—small yet abysmal—appeared later, but she will not name them. This Bengali Baron Babu, on the other hand, is a civilized man. A man the *gora* devils have knighted, true, but a Bengali Babu nevertheless.

Sir Naren Mitter had been born Narendranath Mittir, alias Naru. Short, podgy, nearsighted; a shopkeeper prince. No mystery, no terror, no drama; Saroj herself would have chosen him for her daughter if she could remember what it meant to choose anything, least of all someone's fate. So Saroj—unknown to everyone—watches from a window and silently approves, her heart thudding all the while with feelings so jumbled they can't be named.

Prem is nervous. She feels a niggling, ageless pain push up every time she remembers the past year. One night in particular when the rain had fallen like a silver shower on a flimsy thatched roof, trying to wash away eons of incalculable grief and unbridgeable distance. That night even more than the night later of animal suffering. But she knows what can be and what cannot.

"Not this one, Oldie! Go bring me the sari with the crystal-rimmed roses on the green silk ground. Go! Go quick, Dhai!"

She's beginning to experiment, falteringly, with the language of command, even with her beloved old nanny now bent into a permanent horseshoe. She isn't naive. She knows what is happening has to happen; some things can be and some things can't. She sees that a moment of decision has come. On a screw turning inside where her heart is, grief for a girlhood ended in a waste of loss never stops drilling upward and scattering shavings of unpredictable tears. But she accepts reality as she finds it, a talent she will polish and that will serve her well. Though she doesn't embrace her fate of a magnificent marriage to this stranger from Kolikata, the new Bengali Babu whom the British love, despise, and rely on, this whitey-brown dignitary of Empire, she nurses a forlorn hope of finding love, a second chance.

Shyampiyari is secretly proud of the girl she has created: a perfect votive, flame tempered by grace. Admiration breeds capitulation—Shyampiyari is a slave, all over again, of this girl who once fell asleep with her face buried deep in Shyampiyari's rank-smelling rough wrapper, a thumb thrust up to the hilt between plump, moist lips.

And she's grateful. She made terrible mistakes, and has been forgiven.

Prem readies herself for battle. She is scrubbed and polished to a sparkle by maids and female relatives dragging her from one urn of unguents to another mellifluent bath to another airing in sandalwood smoke to another cleansing: turmeric, yogurt, gooseberry, milk, honey, lemon juice, spice pastes, and aromatic oils in proper order. Saroj only peeks occasionally from behind a tall door or a thick pillar because some enthusiastic beautician has been emboldened by the merriment and festivity of the hour and urged her to come see her daughter transforming into a splendid galleon to join, or rather head, the lord's Armada. But Saroj's vacant face, bleached eyes, and hair, fast turning salt and pepper contrast sharply with the colors billowing around the lovely bride-in-making. Whom she barely knows. Whom she can't quite look in the face, quite lock eyes with, as if invisible hands turn her face away, tilt her head toward something else, also invisible, smaller, and more powerful, if she tries.

Please. I tried. She did what she had to. Without looking she thinks again or at least hopes again that Prem is entering a new world, a far better world than her own, the world in which Saroj—it so happened—began hating her husband and the household with a deadly rage when Prem was born.

Was it the child's fault? No. A voice screams inside her head: Then whose fault was it? That night almost decades ago, as the bullocks had lurched forward, she'd been sure Munia would be at the next station, as she'd promised. But Munia did not come, the clocktower was deserted, though the train left only ten minutes late that night. Why didn't Munia come? Saroj cried every night for years after she came here. Saroj herself doesn't know when, how slowly and slyly, loving— no, enduring—her second family proved beyond her powers. When melancholy, quickly turning into a bottomless darkness, swallowed her whole. Like the fresh livid stamp of a branding iron, rage swelled, hissed, and smoked. It would for the rest of her life. Her body tired but the rage didn't. After giving birth she tried to hold her daughter, to feed her. She couldn't stand it. And she had no milk.

When did she start to recoil at the thought of her new husband touching her, when did she begin to stiffen at his very approach, to radiate a scorching freeze incomprehensible to him and to everyone else? He would sweat copiously every time he came near her. *Why do you avert your eyes and your path from mine, my beloved Saroj, my lotus flower? What did I do wrong?* His eyes would beg. A part of her would pity the good, kind man till her fury returned at the sight of a man asking for something, again. Saroj could not answer, even if she tried. No words came out, and she would have even been glad to tear her chest open and show him the laboring smithy called her heart. Instead of having to speak. Just show him.

So she has had to make her days out of the bits and pieces of living she can still find on her own. She will not trust again someone else's carpetbag. She has eyed her second and freely chosen husband's entire household—his servants, his land, the child—masked, askance. As if they were to blame. Because Saroj needed someone to blame, and they were all she had.

Now, though, she's almost salt and stone. This is practically freedom for her, the drying up of tears. And also the reward. And the punishment for any woman who dares once stand up straight and tall in the eternal war between men and women. No, not the child's fault, but the child was the reminder of the intolerable truth.

When her eyes do meet Prem's, she hears her daughter saying silently, "Why have you done this to me?"

Silently, she replies, "You don't know how lucky you are."

This last year she has begun to see Prem a little differently—to see the endurance, the steel, inside that plump girlish body—but it's too late now. All that remains, all Saroj has, is the satisfaction of having once thwarted a very evil man who took things by force. At least she didn't give that evil man the satisfaction of complete victory, utter violation. Not complete.

Prem is married with great pomp and show and goes away to Kolikata. In a Rolls Royce, not a tonga. At departure she clings to Shyampiyari and cries audibly. The village is relieved, satisfied with this appropriate display of grief from a departing bride. They are used to strange behavior from the people of the big farmhouse; they don't bat an eye at Saroj's absence.

Part 2:

Kolikata/Calcutta, 1916–

Part 2: Kolikata/Calcutta, 1916–

CHAPTER 8

It's almost the end of 1916. The Great War blazes fiercer than ever. Indian soldiers conduct themselves heroically, fighting and dying prodigiously for the Empire. Prem has been married for over a year.

Prem knows fairly well now that she doesn't love her husband. She frets and indeed mourns that she probably won't wake up one day loving him. Or even liking him. But what's hardening now like the sunbaked clay of village summers is a faint, clotting insight. It seems love can't be automatically grown and harvested from any soil and any seed. Prem had guessed; now she is positive. Again and again, she remembers her parents: Babu-ji's joylessness; Mai-ji's lovelessness. But she'd always pulled in the opposite direction from Mai-ji. She wants to, needs to—love. She doesn't want to live like a wraith, as her mother does. She wants to live all the seasons of her life in their prime. That's why she made up her mind to bury every last thing of the past in the crypt of stolen time. And try again.

And so it almost broke her spirit, and did break her heart, when she discovered after marriage that she didn't understand her husband, didn't know how or if she could love him.

It isn't an entire surprise. Some part of her is dead already; she's already betrayed herself. And yet, the failure of a second affection—or at least a convergence of inclinations—to arise in her marriage to Sir Naren Mitter is a dizzying blow. She does not think it's better this way, unlike her mother.

As to Little Naru, as Sir Naren was once known in his family, he knew early on that since they had no land—the 1905 Partition of Bengal uprooted his family and brought them to Kolikata from Pabna in what later become Bangladesh—he had nothing solid to hold on to and grow upon. That his fortune would have to come from thin air. It did. Rumors, promissory notes insufficiently shredded, a drunken Englishman's delirious ravings about bribable factory managers, a jute mill deliberately burned down by the owner for insurance compensation—of such gold chips of information Little Naru made the foundations of his fortune.

He's poured it all into solid things that don't melt into thin air. He supplies materials for the British empire's barracks, railroad tracks, bridges, and new hotels. Especially hotels, in only a few of which brown sahibs like him are allowed, yet. Partly as a result of dizzying commercial pirouettes by him and his sort of men, a few million people have died in small and big famines, but this son of former refugees, unlike village wags, has no patience with beggars and losers. "Indians!" He says frequently. "Scampering and squealing rascals, piling together like rats, like they say the Jews do in Europe."

Sir Naren isn't one of those Jew-like "Indians." After all, though he can't enter its social clubs and hotels, the Empire has knighted him for his ample services and keen loyalty to the master race. What more? Sir Naren Mitter is a pragmatic man who holds steady. He neither sides with the anticolonial nationalists whom he personally considers maniacs, nor does he openly abase himself before his white masters too much. Very few self-made men of Empire have pulled this off, but Sir Naren's impenetrable *blandeur* has preserved him.

Of course, one day this great man needed a wife, and he found one in the provinces. Now that he has married, his wife's expected and indeed required immaculate social *eclat* will also be requisitioned to keep the family in the foothills of the British empire. Of this Prem, now Lady Mitter, has been made aware.

Very, very privately, and very, very infrequently, perhaps under the influence of an overgenerous decanter of brandy—and among men whom he considers tied to him by a dense web of mutual self-interest and inconvenient information—Sir Naren agrees that the devil helps him, for all white men are devils, more or less. In public, he enacts a solicitous admiration for the British already looking anxiously back at past imperial glory and gloomily onward to rain-splashed London and mud-spattered English countryside. But of his own kind, the "*bheto Bangali*," he has the lowest opinion. He despises the soft Bengali mother's boy made, they say, of equal parts water and oil, as much as he hates the muscular Indian nationalist.

So whom or what does Sir Naren love? Has he ever loved?

When she first arrives in Kolikata, for days, for weeks, Prem, now Lady Mitter, drifts in a fog; she doesn't know what's happening around her. On the first night alone with her husband she sees behind closed eyes a moon breaking through a small open square of a hut in a village. She opens her eager, liquid eyes wide in panicked need to see her husband's face—if this is how it's meant to be, this is how it must be—but sees a balding head bobbing rhythmically near where her heart must be, hiding the rest of herself from her; feels her body halving and the lower half decoupling from her, guessing this is how some eternities are. Tears glide out of her eyes as her husband finishes up.

Soon, she will turn a corner she will never retrace. But for now, she scolds herself that she feels revolted by the lordly lord's orotund, sleeked-down looks. *How do men's looks matter?* She asks herself as she's been taught to. He's wealthy, stable, and not cruel. On the first night he even made fumbling attempts to "woo" her, fastening a rope of fine gold chain blistered by diamonds around her neck before claiming his conjugal rights. He hasn't yet denied her—in her imagination—any of the things she hasn't yet asked for. She shouldn't be disappointed in his beaver-like body and his beady eyes. She grapples with her wayward self and reproaches herself sternly. Dhai told her many times that rich men's looks don't matter. Only someone like Mai-ji would refuse to love an older husband who was rounded and waddled. That wasn't right, and it wasn't going to become right any time soon, Dhai had asserted with confidence. Then what is this madness in Prem?

Her husband doesn't speak often, and at dinner they sit facing each other across a polished table so long that the gas lamps burning in sconces around the room seem to bend sideways and whisper among themselves about this odd couple and their strange, silent union.

Prem never mentions any of this to her father when he writes her, asking for her "good news." She returns Babu-ji good news: she's happy, excited, seeing the most brilliant facet of the jewel in the crown—Kolikata—from a superb perch in the heart of the prosperous and posh Alipore area. Yes, she misses the village. Yes, she thinks of him often. (Every day she thinks of him, of him and Mai-ji, wonders if it had been like this between them, if this was why . . . but no, it couldn't have been, her husband and Babu-ji are very different men . . . and Mai-ji didn't . . .) She's very well, but she thinks of him, yes. She sends Babu-ji her everlasting respect and affection as his dutiful daughter. She hopes Mai-ji fares well.

As to what Sir Naren might love, she knows she mustn't insist on being among such things. Sir Naren is a connoisseur of things besides white skin. Like buttery continental food at the Great Eastern Hotel, mouth-watering Chinese at the New American Kitchen and Chung Wah, imported clothes, unimaginably expensive cheroots, the best single malt money can buy in India, supposedly genuine European masters bought at art auctions where his bidding is done through an Englishman who acts as proxy bidder and agent for brown sahibs like him, and so on. He's immensely proud of his newly built mansion in Alipore, rivaling other upstart classical structures flaunted by British Mammon types. He's fanatical about of his collection of antique walking sticks fitted with secret rapiers, each one a masterpiece of craftsmen now rotting alongside their kings and princes in soil slowly surrendered to Englishmen who came as merchants and stayed as tyrants. And last but not least, he's immensely, tumescently proud of his wife. She's half his age and dazzlingly fair, that white skin the only thing the once-upon-a-time refugee boy insisted upon in his choice of bride. As his family and fortunes expand, Sir Naren Mitter dredges the fair wartime city's golden veins unimpeded, rampant, by day, and his wife's golden body by night. But pride and love are different things.

Prem makes herself say that every morning. *Accept, accept. Let go.* Will it work?

CHAPTER 9

Sometimes in the pigeon-cooing, raven-crowing, sparrow-chirping afternoons, quite alone, absolutely lonely, Prem thinks of her mother. When she was growing up she'd always known the village folk whispered bad things about Mai-ji. Her own beloved Dhai Shyampiyari probably fanned the fire of slander and scandal assiduously. There's talk everywhere in villages like that. About two hundred people at most lived in Prem's village. Most of them were tenant farmers. A few were small independent farmers. There was one country allopathic doctor, one or two ayurvedic healers, two homeopaths, one shoemaker, three tailors, and umpteen hostlers. Several grocers and shopkeepers. There was a priest. There were monkeys ruling the temple grounds. There were servants of the big landowners' households like her father's. Rumor, therefore, was the necessary equalizer.

Prem too had grown up feeling very deep inside her body her mother's untold, unnatural collapse, like red chili paste rubbed on broken skin. Mai-ji didn't love her. Why? She didn't know. Must be that there was something about her, something wrong. And this had to be Mai-ji's great misery and mystery. Prisoner of one's own unlovable, not-right child. Prem didn't know as a girl if she loved Mai-ji either. She'd never been much around her mother. For a long time it had scalded her that her mother didn't love her. That she was her mother's prison. So, sometimes, when the need to know, to touch, to hold a thing that was rightfully, undeniably hers overpowered Prem, she scratched the itch by groping and clawing through an old trunk Mai-ji had brought to the farmhouse as a bride.

She specifically remembers, as if it were yesterday, what trouble that led to one afternoon ten years ago. . . That old iron trunk was kept under Saroj's bed, in her own bedroom where she slept alone. No one was supposed to touch it. No explanation given. One grumpy day, Prem had tiptoed into that practically forbidden bedroom. Opened the trunk. Begun ransacking, picking and moving, this and that. She had hands that itched to hold, to take and keep. She picked up a photograph. It was Mai-ji with a baby. Of course the baby was Prem. And this was the first picture she'd seen of herself. She scrutinized it closely.

What a sweet, sweet little baby she'd been! Such nice curly hair gathered up with a bow on one side, eyes bold with kohl, kohl smudge on left temple to ward off the evil eye. In the picture Mai-ji was even smiling.

So, that was possible.

Prem peered more closely. Indeed. Looking sideways at baby, not at the world, Mai-ji was actually beaming. The world was shrunk into mother, baby, photo. The kind of world Prem had given up wishing for.

But this meant that Mai-ji had loved her once. Very much. But then something bad had happened. And Mai-ji stopped loving her. Things can change very quickly.

What kind of mother—Prem heard Dhai's voice—*doesn't love her own child?* She replied to Dhai: *A mother who . . .* But she wouldn't remember her own formulation. There were footsteps right behind her. Light-footed, quick-quick footsteps.

Mai-ji was right behind her. She never wore, unlike other women, *payals* around her ankles to announce arrival and departure, fade-in, fade-out. And Mai-ji snatched the photo out of her hands. And the photo tore. Diagonally. Into halves. Prem kept most of Mai-ji.

But Mai-ji wasn't even looking at her. She was only looking at the picture. At the baby. The baby who hadn't infuriated, disappointed. The baby version of daughter who now infuriated and disappointed. Mai-ji was bent slightly over the trunk, over Prem, forearm and hand foisting the silver baby right at Prem's face. Through vision blurred by fear, Prem noticed a series of dark reddish-brownish cuts on Mai-ji's fish-belly-pale inner forearm. They looked a bit like gills, crowded closer near her wrist. Some of them were like tiny mouths partly ajar, small lips stained dark brown. A little bit of pink jelly peeping through those. Like a naughty pink tongue tip. Others were nearly sealed by braided scar tissue like centipedes.

Cuts of different lengths. Prem's head swam. Nameless, shapeless dread brought on stabbing hiccups. Then, Mai-ji turned away from baby Prem and looked at girl Prem. The girl who would always be out of the picture.

Prem did her best to look back at Mai-ji who'd once loved her. Identical eyes, dilated in unidentical fear and rage, looked at each other. Centuries passed. The eyes, once one, had had time to separate, individuate, become windows to two different souls.

Finally, Mai-ji said, "Why? Who said you could?"

Prem dry swallowed. She tried to force back painful, pricking tears. She wanted to tell Mai-ji the trunk was already unlocked. That her throat really hurt, like a fattening worm inside it was growing more ridges and rings. *Oh. Ohohohohoh.*

"Give me that," Mai-ji said pointing at herself in Prem's stiff fingers. "And get out. Right now!" Mai-ji was still speaking as she reeled back and raised her free arm in a gesture as unfamiliar as bone-chilling.

Something warm and wet trickled down the inside of Prem's legs. She wanted to die. She wanted to tell Mai-ji that she wished she could die. Or that she wished that at least one of them would die. That she wished Mai-ji no harm, but she wished that . . . She wouldn't remember later what happened after that.

And a few years later Mai-ji had walked into the pond. As if she owed no one anything.

Sometimes in the dog-day afternoons, in a castle in Kolikata with rooms she hasn't even seen yet, and not one person to talk to, Prem replays repeatedly, unwillingly, that day Mai-ji caught her opening the trunk. Actually, her most vivid memory of the day—she knows she urinated but she doesn't quite remember the moment or sensation—is of the cuts she saw on Mai-ji's arm. Did they ever heal?

CHAPTER 10

Prem also remembers how, when they were girls, she and Kanan would compare mothers. They generally agreed that if Mai-ji was mad, Kanan's mother—The Dusty One—was eerie. Like Mai-ji, she too had come from some unknown place. That was quite a tale.

One foggy dawn—Shyampiyari loved to paint this story with dramatic gasps, flourishes, enhancements, and shudders for Prem and Kanan as if it was a fairy tale—a woman had stood at the edge of the orchards closest to the great house, overlooking the back pond. A starved-looking girl clung to her side. The servant who'd first glimpsed them in the swirling, beckoning mist ran back to the house babbling about ghosts. In time, the woman and the girl were discovered not only to not be ghosts, but to have hearty appetites.

Then the woman wouldn't speak when spoken to, only her veil nodding at the more lionhearted lady's maid sent to question her when she meant to answer yes to a question.

Only one thing the woman insisted on. Insisted in her cracked, coated voice. She had to see the lady of the house.

The maids exclaimed, then tittered, then shook their heads in outrage, then scolded. "What? You want to see the goddess?" They asked in astonishment when the woman wouldn't give up. "Hai, even seeing God is probably likelier than meeting the lady of this house!" But The Dusty One didn't budge, didn't humbly bow her head in servile acquiescence and resignation. So Shyampiyari found herself—she was the only one who'd dare, in the end—leading The Dusty One to Saroj's fortressed bedroom. She flapped, clacked, and squawked forcibly at the woman's foolhardy audacity, but was secretly in awe.

She knocked on the door of Saroj's deathly still room. After several minutes, during which Shyampiyari mostly glared at the woman's thick veil and spat into a corner, the door opened.

Saroj stood at the door, blocking any view of her room. She was always simply dressed, and that day she wore a plain white sari with a thin, dark-green border. Almost widow's weeds, Shyampiyari groused violently, silently. Saroj's eyes looked through Shyampiyari and straight at the woman behind her. Shyampiyari thought they widened almost imperceptibly but didn't blink. Shyampiyari, too cowed after all to say anything, turned around to the veiled woman. The woman had lifted her veil. Shyampiyari almost reeled from shock. The woman's face was craggy and lined, poverty and a rough life written on it. But it wasn't the face that Shyampiyari gawked at.

It was that the woman was staring straight back at the mistress.

The door closed on Shyampiyari, who beat a flapping, furious retreat after a few stunned moments, vowing to make this second madwoman's life as unpleasant as possible if she should—god forbid but of course possibly by the whim of the other madwoman, the mistress—stay on. And it was as she'd feared. Saroj herself came out of her room with the woman after ten minutes or so. She summoned the servants and spoke to the household. This shocked them because such appearances were rare. Some of them had never witnessed the full stature and presence of that small, alien figure: the elusive mistress. Though her sari veil was pulled down low over Saroj's face as mandatory when men who weren't kin were present, no one dared to raise their eyes to her face, except Shyampiyari, and Mishra Babu-ji's old Munshi who'd grown old with the very estate that he managed.

Saroj made it clear: "This woman and her daughter are to stay and are not to be bothered. There's plenty to do around the house. The woman will be made useful. The girl too, in time. Munshi-ji, will you please see to including a portion for the expenses of these two to the household budget and accounts as needed?" The old Munshi nodded meekly. Then Saroj looked around the room, though still from under her veil, at the faces in a semicircle around her, as if waiting. No one said a word. Everyone bowed and nodded. For matters of servants and housekeeping, Mishra Babu-ji's consent was neither needed nor expected; everyone knew this. Then Saroj closed her door again.

No one knew or could guess what had passed between Saroj and the stranger. Everyone, eventually, would stop asking.

Over time Kanan drifted farther and farther apart from her mother. She became a lady's maid-in-waiting, sort of, a homebody, a civilized, dust-free be-ing. She grew sleeker, tidier, better smelling than her mother. She brushed her teeth with a neem twig instead of the oven ash that the servants used. Once or twice a week Prem forced Shyampiyari to oil and comb Kanan's hair along with Prem's own.

The Dusty One remained untamed, unchanged. She preferred the fields to the house. She was still dust caked. When her work was done for the evening, she usually sat alone under a spreading saal tree a little way from the main house and ground and rubbed her favorite coarse tobacco in her palm for a long time before popping it into her mouth. She sat quite still, quite alone, until the servants were called to dinner. Inside the house she silently kept to herself, her face hidden by her long, coarse veil. A few male upper servants of the house or farm attempted lewd or cloying overtures. They were quickly dissuaded. The flashing blade that peeped out from underneath that veil earned The Dusty One the name "*Sori Chhori.*" The weapon hid in the folds of her baggy skirts.

Of course, Kanan practiced avoiding her mother, day and night, at all costs. At night The Dusty One brayed, "Girl! Girl?" and gave up and went to sleep. Then Kanan crawled out from under Prem's bed and joined Prem and Shyampiyari in the bedtime story session before all three were at one point found fast asleep at angles to one another on Prem's wide bed.

Kanan learned early to read the language of wretchedness on Prem's body. Sometimes, she'd reach out to cover Prem's soft but clenched fist with her own bony, work-stiffened hand. Prem would sigh, grateful for this hand reaching for her, pulling her out of the dead, dark water she slipped into so often. She thanked God very, very much for Kanan, who was a delightful tomboy; she swam, stole from the orchards, set scrub on fire, pelted bullies, and held her breath under water better than the biggest lunk in the village. With Kanan's tough, warm hand over her own soft, cool fist, Prem could foresee how the future could be: their strange mothers vanished, she and Kanan—and possi-bly Shyampiyari—living together, always. They might all run away together, Shyampiyari too. Leave the village behind . . . Never return. Bliss. Without worry, without dread.

Especially that night after the trunk and the blacking out, Prem had longed for that future. All happiness was in that future alone; without worry, without dread. Darkness descended, as it always did, but that night like never before.

Prem woke up that night, Shyampiyari on one side, Kanan on the other. She awoke fighting the pungent air seasoned by tiny winged things rising in smoke from palm-shaped clay votives—to keep away evil spirits—flickering in each corner. Shyampiyari, up like a shot, tried to cradle her little girl in sleep-numbed arms. Prem fought her off but Shyampiyari—and now Kanan, also awake—held her close, shushing her patiently.

"What, little mother?" Shyampiyari asked.

"What, Premu?" Kanan asked, softly.

Amidst keening, wailing sobs Prem stuttered that she'd had a dream. "Tell Dhai, Bitiya, my little one, tell," Shyampiyari crooned and rocked, cupping Prem's agape mouth to muffle the noise of her wheedling. "There was a cobra-a-a-a-a . . . ," Prem started up again in a moaning, wailing cry that went right through the old woman's heart like an intent arrow. Prem wanted to recount the dream but the details and contours of it were gone from her. "There was a cobra . . . before me and I couldn't run away because it stood in the way and . . . and . . . it bit me! Again and again!" Prem looked around the room as if the snake might be lurking in a corner. Snake, or evil spirit. Kanan brought her a brass pitcher of water and made her drink. Shyampiyari and Kanan began rubbing her back: hard upward strokes to force the evil dream out of the little body. They made her drink more water.

Finally, Prem had to relieve herself. She urinated next to the tiny puncture near the floor on one of the walls. Most rooms in the inner quarters of the house had these punctures. At night women of the house, especially young ones, "went" in this way rather than die of snakebite—or worse—in the bushes outside. When Prem finished, Kanan splashed Prem clean—she was used to doing this—then poured water over her feet and washed away the urine. They heard the water run out, a low, thin gargle.

The snake in Prem's dream was a cobra with a raised, fluted hood. A king cobra swaying mesmerizingly and then whipping its head down to hook its fangs into her repeatedly, everywhere. "No snake, Bitiya," Shyampiyari said, again and again, "no snake. No snake can come near my Bitiya because Shyampiyari is here, no? Dhai is here?" It sounded like a question and it was. "Dhai never lets any snake come in, no? No, no—she'll never let a snake come in."

Shyampiyari was feeling more than a little nervous remorse. She'd started that evening the famous tale of Behula and Lakhinder. So young, so well matched, parents rich and simpatico. A marriage story better than any love story. The gods willing, man and wife were meant for each other, meant to live a hundred years each. Have at least a hundred children. Both Behula and Lakhinder were "raised in the palms" of many devoted hands like Shyampiyari's own, as the expression goes. Children of merchants rich beyond belief. Their only children. And only children: seventeen and fifteen at most.

The gods were not willing. Prophecy loomed: Lakhinder was to die of snakebite the night he married.

The dice had been cast: the armies of grotesque bad luck had started marching from the moment Lakhinder and Behula were born. They were cannon fodder in the gods' absentee landlord tricks. The match was tied. The game was rigged.

Lakhinder's father built the nuptial chamber of solid iron. No snake, not a thing, could penetrate iron. But how was it that by oversight—or was it malice for unpaid wages?—the workman left a little hole near the floor? Of course, the creeping venomous thing pushes itself through and bites Lakhinder quite dead.

Shyampiyari had stopped there, telling the girls there was a happy ending, but they'd have to wait for it till the next evening. Prem had kicked and punched her but Shyampiyari, already yawning, was inured to that. The story would go on. People were always building bunkers waiting to be stormed laughably. Every day the sun rose after countless worlds had burned down unimaginably. Women who frightened their children into fainting would meet their just ends. Such things Shyampiyari had said to herself, incoherent with sleep.

She tried forgiving herself now—she had only saved the best for the last. Wasn't that how all good stories were told? It turns out that Behula sailed in a boat of heartbreak on a river of black, moon-whipped water, reaching heaven with Lakhinder. Lakhinder's body was inert, beginning to rot. Behula beseeched the gods to revive her young husband of a night, consummated or not. The gods—tiny or towering—forced her to dance the broken-bird dance before them in their godly way, in their golden, pearly hall. Only then they brought Lakhinder back to life, and everyone was happy ever after. Behula's fame as the good wife spread across the land and from sea to sea. Wasn't that a wonderful tale of good wives devoted to husbands—not much seen now, Shyampiyari would have snuck in somewhere—and of the horror of being a widow? Yes, of course she'd been saving the best for last, she tried telling herself.

Luckily, Kanan had a brainwave as Prem huddled against her, her little body still fluttering with long, perforated sighs. "Tell us the rest of the Behula-Lakhinder story, Dhai," Kanan said. "Please Dhai, please!" Prem was staring into the opioid darkness of the room. Her thumb was shoved well up into her still trembling mouth and her eyes dark, still, wordless. Shyampiyari resumed the story after glancing from Kanan to her. Before she could say much, Prem took out her thumb. Her arm shot out toward the corner where she'd urinated. Shyampiyari peered into her face, and then together nanny and princess looked at beggar maid. Kanan knew what was wanted. She went to the spot. She squatted over the still wet spot where Prem had peed and washed. Then she stuck an index finger into the hole through which urine and water had passed outside. And she didn't mind. Snake-proof now, the room was . . . From there, she listened to the happy ending as Shyampiyari trotted it out. In the murky light and muggy heat, the two girls' torturously tight braids curved upward as if fire smoked.

But then Shyampiyari—foolish old woman with one thought always in her head—muttered again, jumbled but still audible. Prem still heard, sat straight up instantly, thumb still in her mouth. Shyampiyari, afflicted by an unusual tongue-tiedness, refused to repeat. She knew she'd gone too far again. But Kanan had heard too. She'd withdrawn the finger and returned to the bed. Kanan's fingers laced into Prem's beseechingly with a small nervous pressure. Prem, in the grip of a dark mood that heeded no consolation or conciliation, pulled Kanan's head closer by one unruly braid and slapped her hard. A red welt spread across Kanan's cheek. Prem hit Kanan again and again. Then she hit Shyampiyari too. "What? What did you say, Dhai? Tell me again or I'll beat you all night!"

Shyampiyari would say nothing. Shyampiyari had clamped her toothless mouth firmly shut. And as Prem beat her and cried, she sputtered: "Dhai, when will my mother die? I want her to die!"

Kanan looked on, eyes reddened. Prem knew the stinging slap wasn't why Kanan was crying. She was crying for Prem, her young life's treasure and burden. For Prem's pain, for her haunting dream. Prem hit her again and again, just to rub in what pain felt like, though still crying. Then she began sobbing and retching and hiccupping again. "Why won't Mai-ji be . . . like Behula? Why is she so . . . so bad? What did I do to have this bad luck for a mother?"

In the smoky air and palsied light three odd shapes huddled together, all resonating with a child's suffering.

That night was the first time that Shyampiyari dug out of her own small dented tin box in a corner of the room something which she popped into Prem's mouth. The girl became motionless within seconds. Kanan didn't sleep that night.

Prem never went near her mother's old trunk again.

Far away, elsewhere, cannons went on booming, and young men sowed the earth with themselves, as always. There were so many wars going on everywhere: in Russia, in Poland, Africa, Tibet, the Ottoman Empire. Young men everywhere marched, straggled, crawled, sobbed, and crept toward Elysian fields, to the afterlife of heroes, as they've done since the beginning of recorded time. Oblivious to all this, in this also savage georgic backwater called Bihar-Bengal—once the seat of great Indian kings and prophets, now known for grueling poverty, unjust land tenures, droughts and famines, and the tyranny of naked might—Prem and Kanan, both feeling unlucky in their mothers, planned and waited for confusion to their own intimate enemies.

How could they have known that as girls, their future could only be separation from each other? Hadn't the sentimental novels predicted eternal bonds and docile husbands?

CHAPTER II

One day Prem, now Lady Mitter, slowly, heavily arrays herself, as she does every day, in the grand drawing room where her husband has definitively said she should now hold court in the afternoons—not specifying the courtiers but leaving them to her hopefully budding imagination of greatness. Every day she faithfully obeys—immensely graceful and terminally wretched—until she can flee at the sound of the high tea bell.

That afternoon, unlike the other absolutely unrippled ones, the butler brings in a card. It's a simple white card made of thick velvety paper bordered by a slender golden vine. Inside, it reads, *Madam Lilian Hartfield requests the pleasure of a meeting with Lady Mitter.*

Who's this Lilian Hartfield? Prem wonders. Then infers that it's the English lady etiquette teacher Sir Naren has hired to teach her how to become Lady Mitter. Her recitation of Tennyson before him, poised and assured of thundering applause as the prima donna she used to be in the village schoolroom, had made him cringe visibly, exaggeratedly. "Enough! Enough!" he had said, even before she had fairly warmed up to the searing crises of Lancelot and Guinevere in that other sad lord's *Le Morte d'Arthur*. Barely masking his irritation he had said, "You will need a teacher."

So. A teacher has been hired to teach her how to speak proper English, play the piano, dress for Calcutta high society, be the great lady that she must become—and fast. She'd almost forgotten about the decision—"You will need a teacher"—which she'd understood, of course, as command, as Sir Naren's plump index finger had wagged disapproval of her *manège*. She hadn't said yes or no. It didn't matter. She well recognizes that she is here to follow her husband's orders. The sentimental romances had been dead, dead wrong.

She shames her husband by being such a clodhopper. He said the other day that even her vernacular accent and pronunciation are—"I'm sorry to say"—unacceptably bumpkinish. Prem smiles a little wan smile afterwards, remembering how she thought Kanan was a bumpkin, in that other world and life called the village.

So, the teacher is a good start. Why not? She's started over in so many ways. She should continue her ascent to greatness. If it's lonely in high places, it's lonely everywhere else too.

She asks the butler to show in this Madam Hartfield, assuming the "Madam" is just a fancy golden feather to ease passage. Bumpkin she may be, but this card seems pretentious. The paper looks thick and expensive, though.

And then Lilian Hartfield comes into Prem's great drawing room ablaze in broad daylight with crystal and gold chandeliers, Persian carpets with dense, throbbing hunt scenes, gleaming Italian wood and English veined marble furniture, and precious *objets d'art* from the world over including, it's said, an original by Sir Joshua Reynolds himself. Prem has been installed among these splendors, but Lilian Hartfield walks in as though born to the manor.

Lilian Hartfield is holding a little boy by the hand. The boy seems about three, barely reaching up to her knees. Who is this boy? Must be her son. And does he always go on visits with his mother? What about school? Prem is mildly miffed. She doesn't want to deal with children. She doesn't want to see or think about children. Little boys, especially. But this boy is right here, right before her, unmistakably present.

She thinks in a flash: this is how a boy who wasn't found and lost or sent off to fight and die looks. This boy wears knee-length trousers of some dark feltlike material, a navy sailor jacket with an embroidered anchor prominent on the left breast flap—heart beating for England, surely—dark long socks or leggings, and shined leather boots. It's a tiny Englishman, sailing the far seas already. No doubt his parents love him, will die for him. Prem has to pull back from checking the color of his eyes. This boy won't have to sail away to feed his old mother. He belongs to the race that writes and rules the destiny of others. He plays now with a toy soldier his mother has evidently wisely supplied him with for the visit.

Greeting the guests haltingly in broken, childish English, Prem calls for tea. Tea is brought in on a gleaming silver tray; the servant leaves. Prem stares at Lilian Hartfield. Lilian Hartfield stares back. Prem grows warm around the ears under that frank, cool scrutiny. Lilian Hartfield seems steady, unflapped. Sailor boy, Prem is able to see now, has his mother's blue eyes and keeps playing with his toy soldier. Hasn't said a word to his lady host. These are the famed English manners?

Prem needs a fan to cool down but she isn't used to carrying around the ivory hand fans in style among society ladies these days. So, nervously, she pats her upper lip with the silk handkerchief pulled out of her bosom. Still, no one has spoken. Then Prem resolves to live up to her role as a great lady. She can barely summon up that avatar, but that is who she must be now.

She tries to toss her head back a little and thanks Lilian Hartfield for coming to teach her.

Haltingly; beg excuse her English.

Lilian Hartfield smiles at that. Briefly. It's a smile Prem can't understand. She also sees in that moment—English beauty is not like Indian beauty, and it's as if the sun just broke through clouds—that Lilian Hartfied is, or at least was, beautiful. At first she'd seemed pinched and drab, the usual withered English-woman-in-India look. But now, in the light of the smile, Prem takes in Lilian Hartfield's red-gold hair—tied up in a soft, loose pile—the elegant line of her neck, her wide-set soft blue eyes. She's wearing a simple gray wool cardigan over a long skirt, ribbed stockings, and medium-heeled pumps. Classic. Even Prem the bumpkin knows that.

Lilian Hartfield—Prem wonders why she keeps saying both names inside her head—also wears an immense, eye-catching ruby circled by diamonds on one of her long, slender fingers. Prem always notices jewelry. This ring can't be missed anyway. Some poor man must love her a lot.

"Well Lady Mitter, I'm not here to teach you, though I suppose I could," Lilian Hartfield says. Her voice is elegant, almost musical, as if she may be a singer or reciter of poetry as well as an English teacher.

Prem is taken aback. Who is this woman then? Come to think of it, the child, the clothing, the ring, don't really fit someone who lives by house calls for English and piano lessons. Prem has only been in Calcutta—the anglicized name she's been required to swap for the traditional "Kolikata"—a year or so, but she knows this much. It's embarrassing, this mistake of hers. Falling further into shameful habits out of shame, ashamed of the shamed act and the shame even as she does, she gives in to a new nervous, fear-induced tic of wrapping her silk brocade sari's loose end around and around her index finger. She must become better at learning the sharp parings to the bone where the classes and races separate from each other—it's different here, stricter and trickier than the caste-warped village actually—like better and worse cuts of meat.

"You must wonder why I'm here . . . who I am . . . ," Lilian continues in that gentle, steady, musical voice. It's a question with the cadence of an incantation. She pauses, takes a sip of tea from the priceless Sevres porcelain cup reserved in Mitter Mansion for European guests, her eyes never leaving Prem's face. "Actually, our connection is through Sir Mitter."

Now Prem is abashed. This is the wife of some business partner of her husband, come to pay her a polite social visit. And she imagined her to be a lowly paid teacher. She nervously grips harder one armrest of her chintz lounge with the same hand that she's bandaged hard with her gilt brocade sari border.

The clothes are a little too drab, though. She might be forgiven for her mistake.

"Roderick dear, say hello to Lady Mitter, my dear," Lilian says.

Something unexpected unrolls, fills Prem. She can only call it a sense of power. Shot through and through with pity. She's intuited instantly, without doubt, what connection Lilian Hartfield has with her through Sir Naren. Village bumpkin, but all the same. Then, for just one second, she wants to fling away her teacup and run to her bedroom upstairs. Maybe all this is too big for her. She's only seventeen. Some kind of test? What kind of test? A test of her limits? Loyalty? (To whom?) Generosity? Charity? Cunning? Wifeliness? Modern outlook? Worldliness? She understands nothing about what's crashing around inside her ribcage right now.

"Please tell how much you need," Prem says calmly. A few moments have passed. Somehow stuttering English sufficient for the need of the moment is coming to her after all. . . . Can women only have power when they don't love, or when they're wealthy?

But Lilian shakes her head. There, that hint of a smile again. And sailor boy is now suddenly looking at Prem square and clear. An obnoxiously self-possessed boy, this!

"I don't want money," Lilian says.

Do all castoff mistresses say that? Prem wonders. Probably. But some arrant flash of boldness, even daring, shoots out the words: "Well, you cannot have my husband back, you know."

She can't help glancing again at sailor boy as she says these words. Did he hear and understand? He's bending over his dead soldier again, but she sees a wide forehead and long, winged eyebrows. A single forelock has escaped from the damp-looking, fiercely slicked-back light-brown hair. She's also extremely surprised that she has been able to say that much. In English. Maybe her new hunch that there's power even in powerlessness has made the words form.

Maybe Lilian Hartfield senses some of Prem's council of war with herself. It's hard to tell with her. That English impassivity, that stiff upper lip thing. Just as it's hard to tell if she's surprised by a diminutive but upright Prem, or by her lack of instant outrage.

The next surprise is greater. Lilian Hartfield, instead of taking offence, only laughs a clear, crystalline laughter that will come to be both irritating and fascinating to Prem.

"I don't want your husband back, Lady Mitter," Lilian Hartfield says. "No," she shakes her head almost reassuringly, maybe taking note of Prem's deepening flush. Again she says, "No."

Prem feels another new, sharp, almost zingy sensation. Could it even be grudging, treacherous admiration swirled with resentment? Is Lilian Hartfield suggesting that Sir Naren isn't worth having? Is Lilian Hartfield . . . ! Is she?

So her husband once loved this woman? Between them, love seems neither her forte nor his, but she assumes that given that, he may have loved this Lilian Hartfield. She has come here without fear, Prem senses. Otherwise she wouldn't be here. Prem marvels—this more than anything—at a woman who doesn't live in fear.

And the woman's fearless because? She must hold Sir Naren in her power still. Otherwise . . . Now she doesn't have to guess who gave Lilian Hartfield that immense ruby ring, almost a collectible. The ring has to be of sobering value. A sort of heirloom.

Rubies are louder than diamonds, but this one's like blood on fire.

Gora *mem*! Everyone talks about how fiercely free-spirited they are. Seems true enough. Unwittingly a popular doggerel pops up in Prem's head: "Alright, very good, mem eats biskut, *kut kut kut kut.*" This is a vernacular version of the widely acknowledged stiff upper lip, sangfroid, etc., attributed to the English. The Englishwoman eating biscuits daintily no matter what else is burning down. Prem almost grins. Lilian has her plate balanced on her knee as she drinks tea and takes an occasional nibble from the chocolate wafers on the plate. Yes. *Kut kut. Kut kut.*

Monster. Witch. Is she even a little ashamed of using her son to come here and blackmail his father?

Maybe Sir Naren loved this Lilian Hartfield because she's British. It's possible. Sir Naren adores the English in a special way, like a cat hews to a master though ready to scamper at any sharp, sudden move. Sir Naren loves white skin; she knows this intimately. He insisted on white skin in a wife. If Prem hadn't been wearing a sari and diamonds and pearls, and if her hair hadn't been dressed in a classic matronly bun strung with jeweled brocade ribbons, she might have passed for English.

Well, maybe. Englishness is more than skin. It's a toughness. Underneath the skin.

Does Sir Naren still love this Lilian Hartfield? Did he buy that ridiculous miniature sailor suit for her—his—son? Maybe. But there! These thoughts rampage and drag behind them the word "love" like an enemy carcass. What is love now? A dead soldier. A toy soldier. Marriage explains itself, producing heirs and capturing the world's serious attention. What's love? A bastard. Stillborn. She can't say for sure but she thinks Mai-ji once said something like that to Babu-ji when she thought no one was around. What does it matter, what her husband and this woman may have had?

For example, did he write her love letters? As men say they will when they leave?

Well? Did he?

Because, with all her poise, elegance, and ineffable English beauty, her gleaming hair and long English neck, her ruby and diamond ring—especially the ring—and sailor boy, this Lilian doesn't have and will never have what Prem, Lady Mitter of Alipore, has, and will always have. And so in an instant, without knowing, without thinking, Prem actually clicks into place in the till-now-lifeless mold called Lady Mitter.

And how does English toughness go about the day? As assumed power, entitlement, and certitude. Prem gropes its shape. A mixed-up kind of Englishness of a tropical sort starts pushing its way under Prem's skin. The Englishness tingles, not like Mai-ji's red-hot-chili-paste indifference but maybe like a nice mulligatawny paste adding that special English flush to skin already white. Skin like peaches and cream, but beneath the soft skin, there where it really matters, a heat, a tough Englishness, an English kind of toughness—lacking so far—settles. Flares. Inflames.

Toughness—if one is not born with it—can in fact be achieved, Prem sees; can even be thrust upon one like a dubious British baronetcy and its consort. If she hadn't considered her situation fortunate or elevated till now, not felt especially proud of having a rich Brown Baron husband, the truth of her luck floats down and settles on her like gold-dusted pashmina. It's not who you love that matters. It's who loves you. Or has to. Dhai pops up in her head: "A man who covers his woman in gold truly loves her." This house, the position, the wealth, came to her as a matter of course; she'd looked around and registered. And felt contrarily wretched. But now her dazed, wrangled heart feels some distant magic as she glances down at her thick brocaded silk sari (even though part of it bandages her right hand), at her heavy nine-stringed pearl necklace—pearls as big as parrots' eggs—and at her massive, solitary diamond. Not a ruby. A diamond—like a harsh, tough sun. Only a diamond can be good enough for the first Lady Mitter.

But what about the child? What mother comes to bargain for money using her child as a shield? How's that any different from a woman having her baby taken away because she had nothing to fight with? Poor child! Poor boy! What has he done to deserve a mother like this? A life like this? Unexpectedly a tenderness for the boy flickers in Lady Premlata Mitter.

Kanan had once said something about living and let live. When a line of enterprising ants was about to pounce on an overturned baby grasshopper at the pond, Kanan had flicked away the self-assured ants, cupped up the kicking baby grasshopper in her palm, and set it gently on a tree about three feet off ground.

"Why do you do that?" Prem had asked. "Ants have to eat too."

"Yes, but fair fight, no? Poor thing is already wounded. Can't get up."

"Hmm," Prem had said. "All is fair in love and war." She'd picked that up in school and trotted it out without knowing if she believed it because Kanan had stopped going to school after a few months of trying—she was a hopeless case—and Prem lavished all these English type nuggets of wisdom on her. But Kanan had only smiled and nodded. She did that more than usual when she didn't want to disappoint by disagreeing.

"Live and let live, no?" she'd said.

Quite funny that thing pops up now before this elegant, long-necked creature and the boy.

The creature may not deserve being saved, but what about the innocent boy?

"May I?" Lilian asks, having already fished out a packet of Birdseye cigarettes from her prim gray purse. Prem isn't shocked. In Kolikata many women smoke openly, mem or not.

"Of course."

Then Lilian Hartfield says what she wants.

And Prem is flabbergasted.

Just like that. Are there no limits to the audacity of Englishwomen? What kind of cheek is this? And what kind of selfishness? With barely a pause between sentences? Sailor boy seems still intent on dead soldier. Even at the mention of his own name just now by his mother he hasn't looked up or stopped for a moment, so intent is he. Does he know that his mother just offered to give him up? That she just wants to be done with him, to be free? That he's another boy about to be thrown away, sent away, never to be seen again?

Even Mai-ji wouldn't have dared go this far. Again, Prem is overwhelmed by close contact with English toughness though she's beginning to get the hang of it. Again, angry disbelief forks its way down her head into her neck, to her chest, then stomach, then lower, making her feet grow leaden. Why do women who don't want children have them while . . . ?

"Please, you leave . . . my husband . . . ," Prem stammers. But she can't help glancing at the boy again. How's he taking this? He's small, delicate-looking. He's still looking down at his soldier, the hair on the top of his head like bleached straw. He has tiny, soft fingers.

"Yes, I know," Lilian says. "But please, listen. I can do something for you too. If there's any way that we can make this happen . . . that you can . . . in return for this I will teach you everything you need to learn, and better than anyone you can pay. There's a lot to learn, I can see, and I think you'll be happy with the results. Things are not as they seem, you see. As Naren's wife"—*Ouff! What derring-do! Calls him "Naren," which even his wife doesn't!*—"you have a place in society and an image to maintain. I can teach you how to speak English like the English, how to dress, what and how to eat, throw parties, play the piano, decorate your house, travel in style, draw . . ."

Stop stop stop stop stop stop. He won't let me do things, choose things without his approval.

She must have said something aloud. Or, Lilian is a keen face reader. Lilian says, "Not only will he let you—when he knows who Roderick is . . . men are such vain fools—he won't be able to say no to you when you ask him for something someday."

"What?" Prem's thoughts are scrambled, her eye keeps wandering to the great mahogany grandfather clock.

"Anything. After this you can ask him for anything."

Why? "How you know?" She's been stunned back into childish English again.

"You are giving him the choice to have his cake and eat it too." Lilian is confident, precise, cool, and magisterial.

Prem puts up her bandaged hand, vaguely, involuntarily. Trying to impose a few moments of silence on this rising drumbeat, this twirling carousel of mysteries and marvels. On this Englishwoman who talks, talks, talks endlessly, with utter self-possession. Take in Sir Naren's son whose mother doesn't want him—strangely, newly achieved stepson—and so live and not let die? Remember the grasshopper? It kicked and kicked while on its back. Sheer, unstoppable instinct. Wounded things kick their limbs in the air. They want to be lifted, to find ground beneath their feet.

Do this for Babu-ji's sake? Flung away, in pain, he kicked only as much as nature absolutely decreed, afraid of accidentally hitting and hurting Mai-ji. Maybe for Jagat's sake? Had he fallen in battle? Had someone saved or spared him, lifted him as gently as possible and put him away somewhere safe, even temporarily safe?

Or for the sake of the baby of colorless eyes whom she never held?

The seconds loudly tick past; Lilian watches her and smokes, her eyes blanketed. Prem's thoughts are stormed by memories, faces, eyes. A voice in Prem's head whispers: *Sometimes you are saved by being allowed to save your saving for the next time. If you weren't able to save that first time, sometimes you get a second chance. This is your second chance,* the voice murmurs, tentative but tireless, like Kanan's. A child doesn't come into this world a sinner, a liar, a robber. A child comes, invited. It waits at the gate to life for hands that will gather it up, hold it close, keep it safe and warm. If it isn't held, loved, protected, and dies, it's because the hands shook, missed, killed.

That afternoon, had she had time to think longer, Prem might have turned Lilian and Roderick away. Had she thought of how much she feared her husband, maybe she would have done it also. But in that moment, in that hour, something happens: Prem understands that because she doesn't, can't love her husband, she doesn't have to fear him either. She doesn't have to be afraid of him! The message rings like temple bells inside her head. Not afraid! She thought she was; she thought of herself as small, powerless, and beholden. But in choosing between appeasing Sir Naren and a helpless child's need there is only one thing she can do. She'll do it because she was once that helpless child. If Shyampiyari hadn't picked her up when her mother didn't, she would have died.

Still, the shell of habit doesn't shatter all at once. Prem feels half in, half out of it. And struggles. It's almost time for Sir Naren to be home. The minutes flock away like swallows in flight. When Sir Naren returns the whole household will be on high alert. Every need of the great man must be anticipated and met. Every mood of his must be surmised and humored. And she is part of that retinue and routine, Lady Mitter though she is. Only she can fulfill certain needs. She does her duty; she does as she's told. But she wasn't always like this! What does her husband know about what she has done? If he knows, he hasn't said a word. And why did he never tell her about Lilian? So who says a marriage can't be based on mutual assumptions of deceit and transgression? Of course it can. That may be what marriage is.

"Yes," she says. The word strikes her own ears with the headiness of insanity, intrigue, intoxication, insight. Yes. She too can say yes to something.

Lilian doesn't show surprise or joy or relief. She looks down at Roderick and gestures to him to come to her. When he does, she lifts him up and places him on her lap. The boy is now clearly tired, maybe impatient, but he doesn't make a single childish, petulant movement. Then they look at Prem like two noble cats with duplicate soft agate eyes.

It's hard to say whether Roderick at all resembles her husband. Clearly a mix, people will say, but his skin is wheaten, his hair a reddish brown, and his still rosebud lips a pretty pink. His face is thin, though. Thin, calm, and gentle.

But the afternoon is waning. Sir Mitter will come home. He'll find this strange trinity in his drawing room. The matter will go out of Prem's hand. Sir Naren is neither forgiving nor forbearing. He thinks there isn't anyone—except Englishmen—he can't buy in one market and sell in another.

She smiles at the boy.

"Come here, Roderick," she says to the boy. He comes up to her dutifully, his thin face unreadable. She looks at him, unsure how to reassure him. Shyly the boy turns away from her and looks at his mother. Then he walks back and puts his thin arms around Lilian, who picks him up and seats him on her lap again.

They remain seated. "Please, Lady Mitter, take this," Lilian Hartfield says leaning toward Prem. She's offering Prem a handkerchief, white as sculpted milk. A perfect tea-party tableau. Civil and dainty. Prem has no idea how long she's been crying. She wipes her face, her nose, even her neck with that soft, milk-white handkerchief and surprises herself with the snagging of a last moan in her throat as an *unh-unh-unh* that sounds uncouth even to herself. Grief shouldn't debase the mourner into such ugly noises. Into becoming a snuffling, grunting animal. The handkerchief is returned crumpled, fallen from grace. She's worried that the child has seen this, because after this how will the child ever be able to entrust himself to her, to this weeping, sobbing, molten muck? But the child's eyes are patient, compassionate. They don't reproach her. And then they close—he's only three or so—and he slumps, nestles into his mother as if he wants to sleep. And Prem knows he knows.

"Thank you," Lilian says. "He's a good boy. You will see."

CHAPTER 12

There are six things Prem won't do: Prem won't become Mai-ji; she won't become a ghost; she won't vanish; she won't wall herself up; she won't fret; or carry on.

She will take charge.

"You come every day. You see him every day." She tells Lilian in her not-yet-so-good English that afternoon at parting. She feels a surge. Is this power? A flutter in her stomach. Intense compassion, not pity. Children are innocent.

Roderick is innocent. He's three, and already he's losing almost everything he knows; his world is ending. She knows how that is. And about surviving beyond. A child must be given a fair chance at survival. If Lady Mitter has anything to say about it.

When Sir Naren comes home that evening, he finds on his writing desk in the library a perfectly simple, perfectly elegant white visiting card with a gold vine border. He comes to the bedroom. His lovely, succulent wife is dressing for dinner, still in her village finery but a lot more artfully than six months before. Normally he would exercise his conjugal rights at this moment: an especially, inexplicably delectable, arousing moment. Something has already shifted. Sir Naren is a throbbing boil of rage. Out of the corner of her eye, sweat beginning to dew her forehead and armpits, Prem notices his soft, fat hand trembling.

Sir Naren holds out the card to her. His expression is unidentifiable. His sparking lunettes mask his eyes and the rest of his face remains frozen as it always is. Prem feels sweat roll down her temples. She delays meeting his eyes in the mirror. She keeps rouge-ing.

"When?" he asks.

"This afternoon," Prem says.

The Brown Baron passes one hand over his face, wiping his forehead. For once words fail him, as does his imitation *sang froid*. He stares dumbly at her for a few moments, then his eyes wander to the windows flung open to let in evening air.

What does he see there? Does a spasm of some true feeling irradiate and undo him? The face of true love? A firstborn? Did he know about the boy? Did he willingly let the boy go? He had a choice, without doubt. What is the old goat looking at?

Maybe he sees an old scene.

Or maybe he's raging silently at this humiliating exposure.

Maybe he looks away from the lovely side of Prem's plump neck as she tilts her head to fasten an earring, overwhelmed by something he cannot name. Or maybe he sniffs the evening air for needed droplets of mind-numbing, gritty air sprinkled with effluvia from his factories, where boys like the one he once was slither like iron filings hurrying toward the magnet called absolute authority.

And Prem too is prepared to slither and hiss as pretense is ripped away like a skirt snatched from a girl surrounded. Something is swelling in her too. She sees—looking straight ahead at the mirror—how her large diamond drops have caught fire from the sunset tormented between light and darkness.

He asks coldly, "Who gave you permission to receive her?"

One heavy diamond earring yet unfastened clatters from Prem's trembling fingers to the cold marble floor. Every inch of her body closes in upon itself. Maybe the shell of habit is putting itself back together. But memory, eyes, faces reappear. Men say they go to war for women. Jagat had said so the night she asked him why he had to go: "For my mother, for you, for the honor of all women." She'd stared at him then, unable to put the ideas in place, in order. Jagat vanished. Are all men liars? Why do they really fight their little and big wars? Do they really do it for women? Or do they put women inside the ring as prizes to win and trade?

And she says, her voice cool and calm, "Roderick will stay downstairs with one of the ayahs, I think. He'll sleep there until there can be another arrangement. I think the room on the second floor, next to the guest bathroom there, would do very well. Don't you think so, Sir Naren? The boy can use that bathroom without having to go too far in the night." There is exultation in calling her husband by his name, albeit following the hardtack title. . . She still can't quite summon up "Naren," unlike Lilian. . . .

He turns to look out the window again. He's a blur in the mirror. She can't guess what he's thinking or about to do. She admits to herself that she's petrified, wondering how long she'll have to keep her boxing gloves on. But she doesn't retract. She looks straight at him. She even has to admire him a little at that moment for the way he's pulled back, cooled down, regained his frost. He certainly knows how to deploy the stiff upper lip whipped into him by his masters. Prem feels grateful that he's a quick study, in this instance.

"Do you understand what you're doing? What you're getting into? Dragging me into?"

"Miss Hartfield will be coming to teach me English."

"No! Absolutely not! I shall have none of it. None of this will be."

Monster. The real monster. Indurating, coarsening shame. Prem steps closer toward the husband more than twenty years older than her. This small man in lunettes and big clothes. Big English clothes. A clown in motley. A clothes-peg for mantles too grand for him. She sees this. Now. Unexpectedly feels a little sorry for him. And freer than him. Good. After all, she married him to become free. It took a little time. But. She, Lilian, both are freer than this poor Brown Baron. This is a gift from Lilian. Lilian did make her see this. Use your power. Use power when you can get it.

"If the boy leaves, I leave," she says flatly, simply.

Enough. No more children sent away, taken away without her consent.

Sir Naren has to grope for one of the chaises in the room. He sits, breathing harshly, his head disappearing into his jowl, his jowl into his dewlap, his dewlap into his flabby neck, his neck into his soft shoulders. His belly hangs out between them; his short, fat legs are inadequate crutches for his falling glory. His mouth is half-open. Prem, again, feels a little sorry for him. Such a small man. Maybe a boy himself. Not much more than that. A boy eager to please a master.

She walks downstairs to the vast dining room. She doesn't pick up the diamond earring. She knows he will. She knows this now.

He follows after a few moments. He stoops—with difficulty, almost squatting—to scoop up the earring. He regards the petite, straight back before him as he follows and wonders how he could have missed all that steel till now.

So Roderick stays.

CHAPTER 13

R oderick—strange, solemn child—wordlessly kissed his mother, unclasped his arms, and stood by Prem's side as his mother turned and walked away. Her parting words were, "Now Lady Mitter will look after you. But I will visit. Almost every day. You are my good boy. Mommy loves you." At this, finally, Prem's stomach lurched painfully. Stealing a look at Roderick, she saw only the sleek top of his auburn head. His small cardboard suitcase stood beside him, like a faithful dog. Lilian's eyes telegraph something fleetingly. It doesn't look quite like gratitude, but it might be. Or it might be a reminder of gifting one precious, new knowledge: a day might—will—come when Lady Premlata Mitter will have bargaining power because of a little debt Sir Naren owes her. Known only to Lord and Lady Mitter and Lilian Hartfield, that debt will be payable in some other act of salvage. Prem welcomes, anticipates that day— she knows how fickle fate is—and she wants to stay ready. If her bounty costs her anything at all—and how much costlier can anything be than the already almost daily tax—Sir Naren will certainly owe her for the rest of his life.

Roderick lives with her and Sir Naren in the great house empty of children on the family floor, all three of them together. Looking at him, Prem's heart still does the somersault now becoming familiar: from compassion to dread, and back. She mustn't let him become another fawning dependent in Sir Naren's house, in her home. In his father's home. Why Lilian did this doesn't matter. Roderick is Prem's now. She stood up to her husband for him.

Lilian comes six days a week and takes Prem by hand into the wonder world of Englishness. Besides the invigorating, enhancing basting of toughness under already fair skin, Englishness is now drizzled or even poured over that skin to give it requisite gloss and crackle, the sort of finish Sir Naren would have been agog to pay for had Lilian taken his money.

But it's not easy. Even now, between these two women there are snares everywhere. Hopping and skipping together through enchanted minefields of anger, frustration, and pity. Another deadly tango of conqueror and conquered . . . who can say what is what and who is who. It's a school of hard knocks for Roderick too despite best intentions. Mother and son meet every day. Prem has set no term or limit on the meetings, but they always last only a few minutes. Then they separate. Every day. Except Sundays. Lilian doesn't come on Sundays. And Roderick too seems to take a deep dive on Sundays; Prem doesn't see him at all except at dinner. After a while Sir Naren gets used to Roderick being present. Begins talking to Roderick at dinner. Roderick returns short, sufficient answers. Some would call this a strange arrangement.

And then Prem finds herself with child. Now she's finally doing her true work, extending the Mitter lineage. Sir Naren begins to smile now and then, though with considerable hardship at doing something so unfamiliar. Prem is excited and yes, terrified. She begins to have a new recurring dream. Night after night she wakes from it with a feeling of being strangled, a loss of air, a tremendous, drawn-out gasp. Sir Naren sleeps soundly through all this. He's a hardworking man.

In Prem's dream, she and Kanan run through trees dripping with a vile damp, the narrow openings between them webbed with creepers. They lose their breath, give up. Expecting to be found, taken back to stand before their mothers. Starting out of the dream Prem is actually rather reassured by Sir Naren's substantial, round back beside her, snores rattling his torso like tin soldiers dueling inside. No forest. No Kanan. No one at all. She lies down again, trying to sleep, and in the fitful sleep of pale dawn she sees only herself standing in a vast hollow, the night sky like a spider over her, her hand clamped around her sari border. There is a hibiscus flower knotted in the sari's border. She's twirling that border around and around her index finger.

She has no one to talk to about this. She desperately wants to invite Lilian into her loneliness, but Lilian hews strictly to their terms and only appears at her scheduled time, goes through Prem's many lessons, stops awhile with Roderick, and leaves.

Another girl, another mother, another time, another death. Does a shadow stand in a corner of Prem's immense, magnificent bedroom until it blurs at daylight into a panel of dark velvet drapery? She scolds herself: don't act like a fool even if you feel like one. In the morning she drinks her coffee in bed, not relishing it—her morning sickness is exhausting and her palate tasteless these days—and realizes she has a splitting headache. Every morning. In broad daylight she glances toward the corner window. Nothing there. Just that something shadowy floats over her again for a moment. A heavy shadow. Stays on her heart. Only when the unborn baby kicks and leaps, her breath eases a little. Her heart is shaken a little loose, softened a little, by the baby.

She's been informed by her husband that the children who come into the world through her body must be quickly sent to regraft on the breasts and hips of ayahs, maids, and distant spinster cousins who throng the house with their unspoken longings and regrets. Sir Naren wants to be regarded as a generous, magnanimous as well as modern man. He doesn't know most of these people who live in his house but neither does he care. Sometimes Prem thinks: so many servants, so many dependents, so many lackeys and toadies. Prem tries to blot out a too-swift whirl of faces and names and the rogue air raids of memory. Sometimes an odd worry crosses her mind: what will all these people do if some day Sir Naren can no longer board and feed them? For herself though— she who grew up in a rambling, bustling village farmhouse—this abundance helps to forget other things that come in her dreams, things she needs to re-member to forget if she wants to live.

Her father has written to her faithfully, regularly, but she's heard nothing from her mother. She wonders if, as is tradition, her mother will be expected to be with her during the pregnancy and birth. The thought petrifies her. She pushes it away. Mai-ji hasn't even added a line in the letter from home. Home is not Mai-ji. Poor Shyampiyari would write if she could. Babu-ji says that she danced a jig of joy, practically, when she heard of Bitiya's coming baby. Prem wonders if Shyampiyari traveled back at least for a moment to a night two years ago when there was no rejoicing, no welcome, for another child. *If only Dhai could be here.* It's out of the question. People will talk if despite Mai-ji being alive Shyampiyari comes to tend to her. Villagers! They will say.

Lavish gifts arrive from the village, of course. And still no word from Saroj. After going through the ceremonial woven bamboo trays heaped with saris and sweets and gold and silver jewelry and coins—some for the expectant mother, some for the expected baby—Prem pushes her middle and index fingers into her temples and closes her eyes. Nothing. Not a word. Mai-ji remains Mai-ji. Not a monster, as Shyampiyari would have it, just stone.

She hasn't mentioned Roderick to Babu-ji, of course. With her eyes closed again she sees Lilian with Roderick, the first time. She remembers Lilian's stillness—maybe not the stillness of stone, maybe that of a deep pool. She sees in her mind Roderick's small face barely making it in the evening above the massive dinner table where Lord and Lady Mitter sit at opposite distant, dim ends. Can the coming child change any of this? Is that too much to ask of a child? Can there still be hope that life will win over death and deception? Distractedly, she flicks this thing and pushes that on the gift trays—she has too much of everything to care for more things, and the motley parterre of sweets on tinsel-and-gold foil nauseate her right now—and touches something hard and cold.

She digs in below a fold of velvet cloth and brings out two thick golden coils meant to go around small, pudgy ankles, at their ends little elephant heads saluting one another. They are beautiful baby anklets. They make her think of pudgy ankles growing inside her and she can't help smiling, a rare thing for her these days.

One of the women in the long line of those who had come and gone before her left this behind for Prem so that Prem, their miracle, a survivor, would smile today. Babu-ji knew what this would mean to her. He sent it on. Now, when she needs it very badly. The smooth, hard shiny circles rotate in her reverent fingers as Prem laughs out in delight. The gold, obviously old, is reddish. Solid. Like the miracle of love that comes down through women and lasts centuries. An unknown foremother's love. Prem's heart shrugs off a little of the dread and melancholy always tentacled around it. She is able to say a silent prayer, to feel gratitude. Holding an anklet in each hand Prem, for the first time, celebrates her coming baby. She has wanted the baby, of course, but now there is a delightful confidence, thankfulness in her heart that wasn't there before. In one instant, these anklets, these ambassadors of tribal love and blessings for her unborn child, have made her fall in love with the child, a child of the whole tribe. She will love this child very much. She will be a good mother. She holds the circles to her heart, then to her forehead, the gold warming up from her touch and breath, and murmurs and cries.

CHAPTER 14

H er son is born. During labor Prem feels several times that death is by her. Standing like a small shadow in a corner, fading in and out of the darkness of the birthing chamber. She blinks rapidly through tears in nearly glued eyes each time she thinks she sees the shadow. She wonders if Jagat died in the war. Is it him, then? No, the shadow is small. She wonders if it was like this for Kanan. She thinks it probably was worse. It was Kanan's first time. Kanan died. Prem is not ready to die. Prem can't die. She's got responsibilities.

She's perplexed but euphoric to meet the baby; after a while she hands him over to the ayah and nurse reluctantly. She's exhausted, and she wants to sleep. The baby is brought in again to suckle. He grips her breasts like a hawk. She lies back, eyes squeezed shut, waiting for the agony to end. It gets easier in a while. She looks at the baby in her arms. She promises him that she will flood his world with love. When he's taken away again his cries do not fill the house, because Mitter House is vast and the ayah has been told to dandle the baby in its crannies. He has been named Harish.

A telegraph comes for Manohar Mishra. Special evening posthaste delivery. It comes to the old Munshi. Munshi rubs his unsalvageable, soda bottle eyeglasses—finely veined by age and scratches—with his damp neckcloth and reads, then hotfoots over to the master's inner living quarters. Mishra-ji has just started on his special evening hookah—lukewarm substitute for a loving wife's plump raised arm offering paan, but welcome as such—but receives the telegraph with alacrity. Telegraphs are no mean matter. Usually they mean life or death.

Thank Heaven, this is a matter of life. A new life in Kolikata.

He sends word to his invisible, unreachable wife. Then he and the Munshi contentedly gurgle on separate hookahs for a half hour. In celebration, old half-sighted Munshi has been invited to smoke with Mishra Babu. It's an immense honor. Separate hookahs, but still.

Saroj gets the news, and the telegraph, which she can't read because it's in English.

And almost immediately stares down a dark, airless chute toward an inferno called the past.

This is not the feeling expected of her. She should be elated that she has a grandson, that her daughter is well. But even right now, when she stands at the window—thick fog rolling and parting over fields stretching before her, with shimmering, scaly monsters coming to drag her down where she doesn't want to go—she senses sin and shame standing sentry. And, as usual, a face with piercing green eyes comes into focus, brighter in swirling darkness, demanding answers, asking why.

Saroj has no answers. Only questions. Again, this day in 1916 Saroj asks herself if eighteen years ago she should have gone to the room of the evil man. Not man, but evil spirit. Should she have gone to him to save what mattered most to her? Done so and in the process stained the book of her life's only golden hours, the purest love story? But maybe saved everything else . . . ?

Yes, she had left voluntarily. But the empty place inside her doesn't know that. Till this day it knows nothing, listens to nothing. Not even to good news that her life has now created another new life, a baby boy in distant Kolikata. She will not make plans. She will not make preparations for a journey to see the baby. She knows where plans lead.

She'd left home almost a year to the day after a young man with sun-splashed green eyes died. His Name was Naveen Chand. She had loved him. The night train to Patna from her village had snaked through a vast plain, checkered bronze, green, and ochre in daytime with wheat, corn, and millet crops. She had tried hard to stop the train, to get off and go back for her soul, her life itself. She would have jumped off the train. But her legs had given way. The spirit had billowed out of her like smoke from a dead fire mingling with gray gauzy moonlight spread on sleeping bodies like a shroud on corpses. The emergency chain had been too high for her to reach. She'd begged and tried to wake someone up; no one heard or stirred, no one pulled the chain for her.

When Naveen Chand died some said she should burn with him. They said it was her fate and her duty. To live on after her husband's death was sin. But she hadn't been able to do it. As a girl she'd once heard the sounds of a woman burning as a "*Sati*," a so-called willing, faithful Hindu wife accompanying her earthly lord on his final journey. The beating of drums, the crackling of fire consuming flesh, bone and wood with an occasional great snapping crunch, the stench of burning meat, and the constant, deliberate staccato of massive bamboo poles hadn't been able to drown out the terrible sound of agonized begging for life.

Terrible sin. Or terrible pain. Or both, for a woman who doesn't obey.

And how could she have chosen the fire when she had so much to live for? What would Naveen Chand's spirit have said if she'd mounted the pyre with him?

So she had chosen to live. And she'd been allowed to choose that. Widow-burning was less and less common. The days of the "Sati" begging for life were almost at an end. The British Maibap frowned upon the practice; they said it was barbaric. People were jailed for burning their womenfolk alive for their share of the dead husband's property. But Naveen Chand couldn't have imagined what her choosing life for his sake, for his legacy, came to mean for a very evil man, his older brother. Choosing life must have been a sin, because after that her choices shrank to that man's will or mercy.

And then, and because of it, the second, greater sin was committed. And the fire of that sin never went out.

She had loved Naveen Chand with every part of herself. A young god with piercing green eyes and a heart full of kindness and love. All the women used to say how lucky she was in her husband. What a handsome man! And a good man, a kind man, who'd loved her as she'd loved him—tenderly. She'd never been happier than in her married home, a modest petty landowner's brick house. A joint family of two brothers and their families. Naveen Chand was the younger brother.

Whose fault was it, the things that happened?

The sun had not quite set the day the young husband of her heart walked across a waterlogged field munching roasted, parched grain. This you may not do because it is like insulting the earth that bore you and gave you grain. The earth should not be spurned when she is lying choking, drowning, by your feet made of her own salt walking over her agony. Smallpox. Melting the toes, the feet, the nose, and the eyes into each other, making everyone wish Naveen Chand's death would come sooner.

Now she's almost forty. Practically an old woman. Then she was eighteen, Naveen Chand twenty-one. When Naveen Chand's young, defeated body burned to ash and sticky soot and the mourners returned from the burning grounds, the men as usual huddled in the fields outside over steaming milky tea and piping-hot corncobs rubbed with salt and lime. Older Brother-in-Law must have left them making some excuse, pleading his grief. Saroj was sitting on her bed, her knees drawn up to her face. As she'd sat all day after touching Naveen Chand's feet before the funeral procession set off. She wasn't able to see his face. Perhaps she could have if she'd asked. She had not asked. She wanted to remember him as he'd been before the sickness. The procession, all men, chanting "Lord Ram is the truth"—had borne Naveen Chand's corpse on a narrow plank past her little square of a window. She hadn't glanced that way. When she saw a tall silhouette against her low bedroom door—this room she had once entered as a bride, decorated as a wife—her numb arms refused to lift her veil to cover her face, as customary, from any man but a husband.

"You. Come with me," the silhouette said in the deep, gruff voice of Older Brother-in-Law.

Saroj understood instantly what he was asking of her. She'd had a terrible suspicion. Older Brother-in-Law, whom she'd never looked in the face as a younger sister-in-law, had stared fixedly at her across Naveen Chand's shrouded, sandalwood-smoked, putrid corpse during the wake, the family sitting in a ring on the floor to detain the restless spirit until cremation by holding on to some part of the body. She'd been at the head and Older Brother-in-Law at the feet of what Naveen Chand had become. Somewhere near her a child fretted. Her veil was pulled over her face but veiled women learn how to look through and below veils at what they need to see, and the coarse cheesecloth-like fabric of her widow's garb didn't wipe out the middle distance. Now unveiled, every suspicion was confirmed at meeting his eyes.

"No." She said. Just that much. She didn't raise her voice. She didn't look toward him. Just stared straight ahead, adding, for clarity "I will not. Ever. Don't you ever come back."

He left, but he came back the next night and the next night and the next, pounding on her door now always locked after it got dark. "Let me in. It's my right."

Staring into the darkness this night of great good news, Saroj remembers how she would watch the flame of the clay lamp in the corner dance wildly each time, as if frantic at his command.

She'd merely grip the short blade under the pillow harder. "I will see you out of this world before you have your right," she'd mutter into the formless dark.

Sin leads to sin. What could she have done then but pledge herself to an elderly landed Bengali gentleman in Bengal-Bihar—willing to marry a distressed widow—so as to escape Older-Brother-in-Law and his demand of concubinage? Trapped in the family home where everyone spoke in low voices and kept heads bowed in fear of him, her only hope was to sell herself quietly and quickly. What other way had there been to escape? She could have thrown herself at the feet of some gora soldier, begged for shelter. They gladly accepted women in her situation, her maid Munia had breathed fiercely once. Her own sister, she'd said, took up with one when her husband died and . . . everyone had also heard stories of what happened to women who went to the gora barracks. Those white devils were flesh-eaters, after all.

The nineteen-year-old widow with a mind sharp as a blade had under-stood, immediately, the connivance of men with men, no matter the color. She wouldn't accept it, that was all. No, she would at least not give Older Broth-er-in-Law that satisfaction—if not of the violation then of the victory of slander—she'd thought with a slit of a smile cracking her hard, tired face. In those days her spirit was still strong. She'd fought off the mad dog at her heels for a whole year. Meanwhile, she'd been bold and lucky. She'd sent Munia with her eight-by-five-inches full-length picture—cutting away the half with young Naveen Chand standing flushed and erect, next to her, as she, the new bride, sat on the flowered studio throne—to the village matchmaker, wheeler-deal-er and general grocer. The loyal Munia had served faithfully as go-between all through the affair. She'd carried Saroj's notes stealthily to the grocer and brought back the grocer-matchmaker's answers.

"You will come with me Munia, won't you?"

Though in the daytime Saroj was stony, uncomplaining, every night she would cry, soundless and swollen with grief and rage. Munia had held her hand and nodded yes yes yes to that question in the darkness.

"You're doing the right thing, *Chhoti Bahu-rani*," Munia would say every night, stroking Saroj's burning forehead after Older Brother-in-Law had come, thundered and gone once more, before she lay down on her pallet near Saroj's bed. She would have died then without Munia. Munia was the only faint glow of kindness in those nights. And Munia too said she'd rather die than live without her.

Munia had actually balked at first at the age of the gentleman from Ben-gal-Bihar who wanted to marry Saroj. "What else can I do? Go to his bed?" Saroj had asked her, pointing a finger in a direction that needed no naming.

Pained, abashed, Munia had brushed away a tear and said nothing, merely shook her head. Of course not. So, there was no other way out. At least Saroj wasn't ending up in the gora barracks.

Where are you today, Munia? Saroj asks silently, even now. Why didn't you come? Where did you go, you devil? Did you sell me out to your master, the other devil?

This night, after many months, when all this has returned with news of Prem's son's birth, the sun-speckled green eyes are back staring at her. They look at her in reproach, desolation. They say to her, "After everything, what forgiveness?" Isn't she a baby-killer? She doesn't try to answer, to explain. Then, with the hobble and lurch of a sixty-year-old woman, she goes to her old trunk, pulls it out, sits on the floor by it and opens the top. Stares vacantly for a moment or two. Two little gold anklets aren't there anymore, of course. She had polished and wrapped them herself in a length of velvet, and asked her husband to pack them carefully with the other gifts headed to Prem in Kolikata. Manohar Mishra, a somewhat excessively curious man, may have wanted to know where the anklets had come from, but the look on his wife's face had, as always, dissuaded him.

The anklets were the only valuables she'd ever cared about. She didn't wear jewelry and didn't know where her own were; most likely in her husband's coffers, or gone with Prem as a bride. That was alright. Better that way, in fact. She didn't know and she didn't care. She deserved nothing; she should have nothing; she wanted nothing. So, of course it had been hard—terrifying, actually—to send the anklets to a grandchild she'd probably never meet. Giving away the last bit of the past, the last link to the little bit of remembered happiness. . . . But in the end she'd done it. No one would ever know why, or where they'd come from, of course. No one would know that she'd sent them. At least her daughter wouldn't. But she would know that she'd tried at last—to do the right thing. She had never given anything to her daughter—hadn't been able to. Maybe this would bring her a little peace . . . maybe.

It was all she could do now. Be a bit of the mother she never was. Maybe she'd be forgiven . . . a little. In God's eyes. She, no mother to her daughter, a monster, a witch, a damned soul, a woman with no milk for her own baby—she knew all the names she'd been called over the years in the house and in the village—was trying to atone by sending her daughter the last piece of her broken heart.

Part 3:
The Great War, Calcutta, 1917–

CHAPTER 15

A year has passed so quickly that Prem feels like she's in a different world. She is too. This war has to end. The world is gasping for the peace reborn from the earth well manured by those who haven't come back from the dying fields. A rather "small handful" of Indians, say the British, have lost sons, husbands, or brothers. So the survivors and relicts of that small handful then enter that leper colony whose members are shunned by the fortunate who didn't send any boys and men to the front. The fortunate always fear that bad luck might be catching. Prem walks the border between the blighted world of the lepers and the land of the fortunate, the spared. She has never heard from the front. That makes her a leper colony member of sorts. But everyone says there will never be another such war, thank God. She has—at the very least—two boys to keep away from war.

On lighter, brighter days Prem also thinks—while there's life, there's hope. Or, while there's silence, there's hope. Who can say?

The year 1917 is almost gone. Two weeks after Roderick's fifth birthday Prem receives a note from Lilian Hartfield on a Sunday evening. The same card paper, the same golden vine. Lilian writes:

Dear Lady Mitter,

I hereby give notice of my intention to discontinue my services as your teacher. It has been an honour.

Yours ever,

Lilian Hartfield

Prem cries out upon reading the note. Sir Naren, who's undressing for bed, whirls around. He tries to be careful with the mother of his son. Son, not daughter. A son. A woman whose firstborn is a son is an auspicious, valued spouse. Prem is deathly pale and waves the note at him. She can't speak. He reads it and tosses it into a wastebasket. His face is, surprisingly, working with emotion.

She asks: "What did you do?"

"Me? Are you out of your senses?"

"Why is she leaving?"

"How should I know, madam?"

Prem rocks back and forth in bed in her favorite self-comforting seated position: knees pulled up to her chin, arms wrapped around her knees. Why is

Lilian leaving? What's gone wrong? Why does this feel like another world's end? How many more worlds does she have left to lose?

"What is to be done?"

"Nothing," Sir Naren says. His fat jaw continues to tremble and his beady eyes are now narrow slits holding brimstone.

"Nothing?" Prem mouths weakly, not sure if she's making any sounds.

"Nothing," he repeats. "People like her deserve nothing. I owe her nothing."

"People like her?" Prem bursts out. "She's Roderick's mother, Sir Naren!"

"What do you want me to do?" Sir Naren asks, his voice high.

"Tell her Roderick needs her! She's the mother of your son!"

One day two years ago Prem had gathered up courage and asked Lilian the obvious, momentous question: What kind of mother willingly gives away her child?

"Why you want he stay here?"

Lilian had said, "Because he has a better chance here with you and his baronet father than as a half blood with a penniless English mother."

Hearing Lilian say those words had quickened an ardor in Prem—Prem, who still dreamed wide awake of justice, of redemption, most nights after her wifely duty was done—for some ineffable thing Lilian had. Dreams had thus far been the only antidote for her grand, arid marriage. Lilian had somehow learned to do without dreams like hers. Instead, Lilian had chosen what was best for her child rather than for herself. Lilian was brave; Lilian was noble. Lilian's renunciation was her battle axe. But how could Roderick know that? He'd only know that his mother had left him.

"You are the mother of my son!" Sir Naren's eyes seem about to leap out of their sockets. "Hear me? You are the mother of my son and that's that. That boy may be my responsibility, yes—now mind you, I'm not acknowledging anything by saying this—but you are my wife and your son is my son and this is my house and this is my family! I made all this. I! Me! Alone! When I say something, it stands. It happens. I've already indulged you enough about letting the boy stay here. It shouldn't have happened, but I see that it is better for him. Especially now . . . this disgraceful woman . . . yes, whoever he is, he needs a home, and so he shall have one. But no more! Nothing for his mother! She's a profligate, a bazaar woman!"

A bazaar woman? Well, that's a bit rich, the now fluent user of the Queen's English thinks.

She returns to the pitched battle.

"But how will she live? What will she do?"

"That's none of my concern, madam. She has been allowed plenty." Sir Naren has returned to frost, and lifts the eiderdown quilt and inserts himself below it. "None. Understand this clearly. That woman is nothing and no one to me. She's been allowed plenty through this . . . this . . . hook she has me on. Let her leave, and from today her name must not be said in my house. Understood?"

Prem is dumbstruck. She has started to learn to fight, but her tears puncture her eyes and dizzy her. She lies stiffly on her back, staring at the vaulted, gilded trompe l'oeil ceiling of the bedroom. She resents this man's presence in her bed. She's shaken by his treachery, his cowardice. She hopes he won't reach out and touch her. And she wonders what he means by "she has been allowed plenty." The ring? Very expensive, yes. But does he think that's payment? Enough? After she's come to this house and given finishing lessons to his wife, with whom she's had to leave her boy? Does he think his debt is crossed out?

Lying beside his young wife's corpse-like body Sir Naren remembers Lilian. She used to play the piano at the Grand Hotel, the toast of all Englishmen and Indians there. Her father had been a piano teacher of minor celebrity. Her mother had been a theatre actress, rumored to be half Armenian, slightly notorious rather than celebrated. How Lilian got all that grace, charm, and serenity, growing up like that in a family of eight children—two more had died—he couldn't understand. All he knew was that she never displayed a moment of crassness, crossness, or slovenliness in all the time he knew her. And that among the men who'd have laid down their homes and lives at her feet, she chose to be his awhile. Until she realized that he would never be bringing her home.

Because he wouldn't.

He couldn't. What did she think? Who did she think she was? He had a part to play in Calcutta's business world, its high society. He couldn't afford to make his English associates angry by marrying one of their women. He'd built his little empire within their big one. And she left him because he wouldn't. . . . Absurd! He asked her to keep the ring after she rejected his generous and sincere offer of her own lodgings with her own money, for life, guaranteed. And then four years later she brought a child here. Is that his child, really? How will he ever know? But the possibility does exist—Sir Naren isn't sure he doesn't see a resemblance—so how can he throw him out? His mother, yes, but him . . . ?

He'd come back early from his office at the beginning. He wanted to confront Lilian, to ask her questions. He never caught sight of her. She, moving like a ghost, yet ripping the fabric of his respectable domesticity, came and went, unannounced, invisible.

The woman is wise. Because instead of leaving Roderick with Prem off the bat, she stayed on a few years or so to watch Prem, to measure her, to be sure of her kindness. And once she feels sure of that, and once another child has come to this house, she's leaving. Again.

And what would have happened if he'd married Lilian? It was unthinkable. Both would have suffered, and the child especially. (Assuming the boy was his, which, frankly, he rather thinks is the case, given the boy's appearance and intelligence. . . .) The rules for affairs and mistresses are different; affairs are more flexible, tolerated. Society would explode at the outrage, the audacity of crossing impermeable race lines through marriage. Even if he'd converted to Christianity, which was unthinkable to begin with. His English patrons and associates would cold-shoulder him at clubs and hotels and torpedo his businesses.

He and Lilian would be eternally damned creatures, ostracized, left rotting and ungluing in their lonely, darkened world. Even Roderick was better off being a bastard than such a child.

The woman lying next to him—just a girl really—despises him. He knows. But he has to—has always had to—maintain a certain gravitas in his household, because once the ground shifts, foundations crack, buildings totter. Had it not been for Lilian he might yet have lived contentedly, unwavering, at ease with himself. As things stand, he's not allowed to crumple, admit weakness. Men like him hold up the world. And the British empire. Men like him must be exemplary.

As a boy he learned what hunger was. Just after that last brutal flooding of the river of his childhood that took his mother. Snakebite. Famine loomed; his family's farm failed. Everyone scattered to corners of the country he didn't even know about. And now look at him. And can such a man be expected to blow his life's work to the sky and follow his heart? How unfair! And he didn't even know about the boy till Lilian brought him here. She kept it a secret from him till then. Why did she? It wasn't fair to him, was it?

He would like to turn toward his wife now and seek some solace. He can't. She will respect him still less. He does fine without love, but respect is crucial. Dignity is paramount. He doesn't know when he falls asleep. He trembles with fatigue the next day.

And Prem, excruciatingly, woundingly disappointed in her husband again, decides to create a life of surrounding herself with the children.

Roderick now comes to her more readily, but she knows this is in part because he misses his mother terribly and he's curious about this new baby. He's still only about six. He probably doesn't yet understand exactly in what chain of relationships he's a supposed link. She almost hopes he doesn't. This can't be forever, but enough pain has been heaped on everyone's plate for now. She wishes Roderick would occasionally chat with her as she sometimes hears him chatter with maids or his own ayah. Near her he seems to become tongue-tied, tucks his chin into his chest, won't look up unless called several times. She sometimes looks up and catches him staring at her—baby Harish bottle-feeding like all newfangled babies of civilized and almost-civilized nations, making the Indian nanny's eyes nearly roll back in their sockets—and smiles, but instantly he looks away.

One day she can't help herself; she asks: "Do you think about Mommy?" To her great surprise Roderick actually nods slowly, but he doesn't look at her. Prem regrets the question. She remembers Mai-ji. And the loving crone. And the dead. Tears standing out in her eyes, she strokes Roderick's head softly and says a prayer.

CHAPTER 16

In very late 1917, one evening Jagat is hit in his trench. He's hit in the shoulder. A sharp whistling sound past his ear ends in him feeling his arm has been shoved into ice. No pain. Just a bloody, rotten numb cold. His arm has frozen, and he can't move it. The blood instantly turns a patch of liquid mud around him dense brown. The sight—seeing his blood outside his body, and not even red but rust-colored—unhinges him. His mates clamp their hands over his mouth as he screams in fear and furious revolt against being here, placed here in the mud with others like him, some dead, some dying, some gone every week. He has to be dragged away from the barricade, deep into the guts of the trench, and has his first taste of alcohol—brandy literally dumped into his open, screaming, then coughing mouth—as the surgeon begins work.

Jagat doesn't know if Prem ever got the many, many letters he wrote her. Before leaving for the "front"—he had no idea where that was—he'd pressed some of his very last coins into the hands of old Shyampiyari. Because Prem told him, in the velvety darkness of that one night together, that if she ever had a mother it was Shyampiyari. The old woman had looked at the coins, looked him up and down, muttered something, and slipped the coins into some fold of her clothing. He had no right to expect any more—he had no right to expect anything.

But Jagat . . . poor racked, heartbroken Jagat, who said he never expected anything back, couldn't quite rise above the generality of humans to really mean that. At the front he realized he'd entered living hell. As he shivered, flattened like a sprat gasping in shallow water behind the brief, pocked barricade of mud and stones, his rifle pointed toward an enemy he couldn't see but believed in—he saw his fellows in the trenches carried away every day—he told himself he never expected her to write back, that she would likely get married and sent off to some rich man's house soon. But when the sack of mail came even to these battered, bandaged, bleary, drenched, and maggoty men who crawled through swarming mud and blood to save civilization for their great white king George the Fifth who lived in London, he learned that hoping against hope places the last boulder against trapdoors. Remembering the mailbag as he lay in rain, sunk in churning mud behind the laughable melting barricade that was supposed to protect him, he prayed that the next bullet would take off the top of the next man's head, not his, and wanted to atone, to be penitent for that prayer, but couldn't.

Later, he shuffled back, crumpled, his eyes smoky and stinging. He returned from the brown mailbag spun from jute grown near that place he knew as home—where Prem might not be anymore—and reentered that zone where he was now, the zone between longing for life and wishing for swift death.

Still it helped him to write to her. He wanted her to remember him, to hear the echo of his voice, especially if he died, though he so wished to live, life was so beautiful, so precarious. . . .

Tomorrow, the 15ᵗʰ of September, I go on a cavalry attack on the enemy. It is not likely that I should return alive because a cavalry charge is a very terrible affair. Let me say, please, that you have never written back to me has not annoyed me. Don't grieve at my death either because I shall die arms in hand wearing the warrior's clothes. There is no happier death for a man, especially one such as me who has been fortunate enough to adore you and freedom above all else. Give my respects to your parents and tell them not to grieve as we must all die someday.

He would always remember the words of each letter he sent. How could he not? He'd written and rewritten them so many times to try to make them suitable for Prem as well as his state of mind. Later he would berate himself—how morbidly full of self-pity the letters must sound, and what made him think her father and mother would have the slightest interest in whether he lived or died—but still words would dance up like flares from that vast, dark plain, flickering and smoldering along the tunnels where men cowered and crawled like insects. Glimmering vividly before his closed eyes, nearly glued shut by smoke and flashing gunfire—every day, all night, and sleep never came—he saw the phrase, "adore you and freedom above all else." He was half-crazed—by fear, by starvation, by cold, and by longing for Prem and life.

Why had the British Maibap made recruits like him watch the bioscope *Britain Prepared* before ships and trains carried them away upon the *Kala Pani* whereby orthodox Hindus like him instantly lost caste? This war wasn't going well—not at all well—and Britain was hardly prepared. At least, if Jagat and his fellow soldiers were an index of that, it was not prepared at all. At least Jagat was not prepared. He dug out of his rotting army-issue boots the trench effluvia crawling with maggots that belonged to the dead and dying becoming living mud around him. He was not even twenty. He was dead before he'd lived.

Another damp-spotted letter went something like this:

We are in France, a very cold country. Pardon my delay. On the 19th of November I began writing a letter and found that the ink was frozen in the inkstand. I broke the inkpot, took out the ink, melted it over the fire, and wrote the letter to you with the melted ink. The fighting is going on with great vigor and thousands of mothers' sons perish daily. There does not seem to be any arrangement to bring the war to a decisive issue. The matter is in the hands of God.

One of the letters he sent was written in an agony of heart-juddering panic and fury.

This is not war. This is the ending of the world. This is just such a war as was related in the Mahabharata about our forefathers. We die protecting your honor, and the honor of all our cherished womenfolk. I will spare you the details of the trenches in which we lie like rabbits with feet tied, waiting for death. The shells pour in like monsoon rain. The corpses cover the country, like sheaves of harvested corn.

Even in his utter duress he was a poet. Keening bard of the fields of carnage, falling in love with the world, with life, as never before. Helpless. He came to see over time that like most of his fellow soldiers he was merely a pawn. A pawn of the Raj, of Europe, of poverty, of the powers that be who would always call the shots. And that among them was the girl he had loved . . . loved. Who'd come to him one night in grief and terror; whom he'd vowed again and again to love and protect. They both knew he was leaving for the front but they'd pretended. She'd said she believed him, trusted him. He'd said he would always be there for her. She, as one of the powerful and rich, might grow into a woman who would conquer and rule. Maybe she would master the crazy world and its ways. Maybe she would dazzle in that brave new world where entry was prohibited without permits like beauty, money, or servility. Maybe she would rule—no, not maybe, she certainly would—another man. And she'd have husband, life, and children.

Though he crawled like a drowning beetle through mud and blood, though his desire was that of the moth for the star, he was so glad that he had chosen so well, so high. Come what may, he was a poet, an artist of yearning.

CHAPTER 17

The Great War finally ends. Some months later, Prem acquires another child. A girl this time.

She will remember how old the girl was when she came to Mitter Mansion because she knows when the girl was born. The little girl won't remember; she was never told her date of birth unless it was the one day in the year of especial gloom and unusually excessive mistreatment of her. But the girl, though only six, will remember her arrival at Mitter Mansion. Among other reasons because after that the voice of her grandmother will cease to squawk, "You were born cursed! You'll swallow alive everyone wherever you go!" Her sixty-year-old grandmother has a broken heart that stalks around outside her ribcage in the shape of her only child, the girl's father.

The girl rarely sees her father except when he's drunk and beats her silly, or goes after his mother if the girl has scuttled deep enough away under the bed she shares with the old woman.

The girl will also remember her father peeking through the iron flourishes of the great, closed gate at the rearing colonnades of Mitter Mansion, gripping her hand as though she might escape. As he has raised her, so to speak: also by the hand.

He's a man in the shape of an inverted question mark: a concave bracket sprouting a horsey face on the thin stem of an unexpected turkey-gobble neck. He smokes cheap *beedis*. A ghostly pair they must seem to passersby. He doesn't talk. The girl has no words at all, only eyes. She is tiny—has a bushy head of hair almost half as big as the rest of her. Flame-colored bougainvillea, named after some French sailor (the girl will learn one day) looms over the wrought iron gate, dwarfing even that metal juggernaut. The towering creature makes her realize in a new way for the first time that she's very small.

The squat keeper who stopped them at the gate scurries back from the mansion. Permission has been given to enter.

That day by chance Prem and Sir Mitter are presiding together over the grand scene of their sumptuous union in the drawing room. It's a classic state appearance: the young woman untimely blasted by the early frost of joyless marriage, and the much older man preserved by self-important title to a young and beautiful woman, joyless or not. A painful thing to see; even the servants look coldly, eyes hooded, upon the couple. It's Sunday—one of the rare Sundays Sir Mitter has condescended not to go "to office," that masonry his lady has yet to see. He sometimes orders these tableaux, special audiences. Their two-year-old son Harish is being dandled, force-fed, and trilled over somewhere in an immense nursery that overlooks the manicured cricket fields at the back of the estate. Roderick is at afternoon lessons from some tutor.

When the girl and her father walk into that dizzyingly grand drawing room with two living deities in it, the girl feels wearily prescient. As if she has an ancient intuition. She keeps her eyes on the floor, knowing everything and everyone here will want to shame and mortify her. She sees an important-looking and unnaturally erect man and a beautiful expressionless woman sitting on separate golden armchairs with red velvet seats and backs. Her father tells her to bend low, to touch their feet. To show respect to "Lord and Lady Mitter." She creeps as close as she dares, shooting a glance up to see if the lord and lady are expressing outrage. They are not. About a foot away from their four feet, she touches the gleaming floor and brings her fingertips up to her head to receive the "dust" of those important feet. She goes through this terrifying ritual not because she wants to obey or please her father, but because she thinks it safer to stay on the good side of these two enthroned people who look like the tiny gods and goddesses on miniature gilt thrones in Hindu prayer rooms and alcoves, known for being both bored and turned on by human misery.

The deities are about the same height but the lord is twice as round as the lady. He's wearing English "suit-boot," as the girl's neighbors would say. She doesn't know the names of the pieces of "suit-boot," but she knows that his clothes are the true English prototype of her father's harlequin masquerade "pant-shirt." The lord's shoe-tips, moreover, gleam like the headlights of a truck that hurtles past riff raff, scattering them off the street, barely sparing lives. The lord also has a thin, black moustache and almost no hair on his head, which sinks a little sadly between his shoulders, like the moon dipping and peeping out between dark clouds, smoking a mahogany pipe.

The lady! Years later the girl will still struggle for words to describe her first sight of Lady Mitter.

Quite small and slender. But you can't miss her firm carriage. Or the tired, stony look. She wears an oxblood-crimson sari of some fabric softer and glossier than anything the girl could have imagined. Its border is a stiff, broad panel of gold drizzled with tiny crystals that change color on the slightest movement. The sari passes across the lady's chest diagonally from right to left climbing her bosom's swell, drapes around her, then cups her right side like a calyx before cascading along her right side almost to the floor. This is how great ladies wear saris. The girl doesn't know this, but it's because this is how the English say Indian women should wear saris, instead of unpleated, unswagged lengths of fabric like burlap wrapped around their bodies, leaving arms and shoulders uncouthly nude—whether mistress or maid—for graceless labor or shameless comfort.

The lady's dark, glossy hair is puffed artfully and fans into a luxurious terraced garden—or maybe an exotic bird—over her head. More tiny but blazing crystals, skillfully threaded through and woven in, glitter in that viscous sculpture. The centerpiece of all that magnificence is a huge rocklike gem set into the foothills of the bouffant hairdo: a brilliant moon on a dark, starry night.

The girl sees two very different moons side by side. Then the lord leaves. The girl doesn't hear that Lord Mitter tells his wife sotto voce that he's queasy—nothing, nothing, the usual recurring dyspepsia, for heaven's sake—and must leave her to deal with these people. The girl hears the polished, headlight-snouted shoes moosh-moosh as the lord walks away. Then she focuses on the lady's face.

Almond-shaped brown-gold eyes. Dark, winged eyebrows spanning an egg-shaped forehead.

Prem is glad, after all, that Sir Mitter left. She has recognized the concave man as the Kuleen Horse who once gave her a horse's egg to have access to Kanan.

Memories attack without warning.

Memories of the day when Prem's world began to fall apart, when Kanan vanished into the room where she was to spend her first night with the Kuleen

Horse—the bolt inside latching gratingly as Prem watched, mute, with other women ululating—and emerged the next morning wordless and confused.

It was her fault. She'd let Kanan get married, even celebrated with too many sweets during the marriage. Thought it was a great big game then. She'd even connived in the ravishing. Took one dirty coin to let the horse go to Kanan's room. From that room another stranger—not Kanan—had emerged. That stranger didn't want to steal pickles, swim back and forth across the weed-blanketed pond, sing, or laugh with her mouth wide open and her head thrown back. No long strides. Kanan was walking as if hobbled to a turning grindstone. Her once dancing eyes had changed into the dull, pain-inured look of a harnessed animal.

A small turn of the handle, a cracked door closing, had opened onto a great empty wilderness. First the place where Mai-ji should have been, never was. Now the place where Kanan wouldn't be either. Everyone was leaving; everyone had pushed her out of their way. No one would ever tell her why Mai-ji had stopped loving her. No one would tell her "It doesn't matter, I'm here." Prem's gaping wound hadn't allow her to think clearly about where things with Kanan went so wrong, how the best-laid afternoon plans at the pond ended up being such miserable folly.

She'd stared at the new Kanan, or at the closed door behind which that girl vanished again and again. She'd wanted to free herself from the noose of disappointed attachment—it's the rooted, deepest training of the child who feels unloved—but inchoate pain, rage, and fear had twisted up and choked her. She couldn't make a sound, didn't know how to be cured of this pain. She'd already intuited that maybe, like the carcass of an unintended slaughter, her first broken love might have to be buried deep.

The day after Kanan's nuptial Prem, having stripped herself of her finery and splendor, was sitting behind the closed doors of the cool, dark household storeroom, spine jammed against that durable wooden door as hard as possible, to hurt as much as possible, knees pulled up to her face, face hiding in the dark nautilus of her body.

Someone knocked. Kanan was asking for her.

Prem had bolted up, pricking up her ears better to receive, to savor, to absorb the words. Sweet words. Precious words. Kanan needed her. Kanan wanted to see her. She too had realized the utter foolishness of this marriage plan of escaping the village and farmhouse to be together. Kanan had concocted some other, better plan. No, wait. . . . Kanan needed Prem's counsel to make that other, better plan. Everything was going to be alright. Prem's eyes burned—she hadn't really slept since the wedding—though she shivered.

She'd had to stoop to enter through the low lintel of the door to the "nuptial" room. She found Kanan lying on the bed in an awkward sprawl, in the same threadbare wedding sari two nights old, the old silk scattered around her like dried petals. Kanan sat up when she saw Prem and held out her arms. Long, thin, convex-jointed arms. Bony arms. Warm arms. Known arms. Needed arms. The hard, painful lump in Prem's throat was just awful. But the Kuleen Horse was also there. Lying on the bed not far away from Kanan. He was smiling—grinning—as if he was happy. Prem had to look away.

As soon as she was close enough, though, Kanan had pulled her down onto the rumpled bed—Prem noticed a faint, sour smell from the bedclothes—and wrapped her arms around the younger girl. Then simply laid her forehead on Prem's shoulder. They'd sat silent—Prem rigid, Kanan limp—awhile, neither able to speak yet. Then Prem's shoulders, arms had relaxed, and she'd burrowed into Kanan's familiar frail shelter.

The familiar flow between them had started. The Kuleen Horse watched them. His jaw seemed to be working, rebel wrinkles and flaps of skin trembling on the visible bones. Prem tried not to think about him, her frightened heart slowing down in Kanan's familiar embrace. They half lay, half sat on that bed of the strange odors—together again, which was what mattered—and Prem almost fell asleep. She was so very tired.

But they were both crying.

"Prem."

"Tell me, Kanan."

"Don't forget me, dear."

"Don't be stupid."

"You will write often, won't you?"

Prem had nodded yes, unable to speak from the grief crushing her.

"*Chirobondhu.*"

"Chirobondhu."

Kanan had glanced at the Kuleen Horse. He was half sitting, propped on an elbow, beady eyes twinkling and dirty teeth on view as if he wanted to show the girls, but especially Prem, how happy he was. Prem followed Kanan's glance, frowning. She wanted the Kuleen Horse to know his place. He was a clerk in Kolikata. He was nothing here. Nothing at all. But the man hadn't stopped grinning. His eyes were boring into Prem. Prem scowled, her heart beating fast.

"Premu, my 'Him' . . . ," Kanan said. She wouldn't look at "Him" directly. Without looking at him, she jerked her head at the Kuleen Horse, directing Prem that way.

Irritated, Prem glanced again at the man. Shamelessly baring doglike yellow fangs and rotting *saal leaf* gums.

"What?" she'd moved closer to Kanan.

Again, Kanan had done an awkward seated twist. "Wants to . . . ."

Lost your tongue? Prem had queried angrily, silently, raising her eyebrows.

"Yes, yes, tell her, tell her . . ." The Kuleen Horse was still, unbelievably, grinning. He was massaging the ball of his left foot, sitting almost upright on the bed now. The massaging made a dry, scraping noise.

"He wants to know you really well."

Prem had looked the Kuleen Horse in the eye for as long as she could stand and then turned back to Kanan.

"Fine. Have you told him, then?"

Kanan gawked. Her eyes were empty.

"Have you?"

Again, Kanan moved like a puppet jerked on strings. Wordless.

"Yes, my dear." It was the Kuleen Horse talking. He'd said "my dear" in English. Who was he calling "my dear?"

"Yes, Miss Prem, your friend has told me all about you. Yes, that you will visit us. You girls want to keep house together. Yes, of course, why not, why not! It will be our great good luck. If you aren't welcome at our place, who is, Miss?"

From his side of the bed somehow the man had managed to sidle across so that he now half sat, half lolled only inches from the girls. *What was he doing?* Prem had grown angrier. *And what was Kanan doing?* And then that hand that had been rubbing the filthy sole and heel was on her thigh. Her right thigh. The Kuleen Horse was ever so surely massaging Prem's thigh. His scuffed, calloused, dark hand was printed on the sky-blue silk sari Prem had changed into before coming. The hand sank a little deeper into the silk with each stroke up and down: rhythmic, steady, almost jovial.

Prem sought Kanan's eyes. Kanan was looking down at the strip of dirty sheet between her and Prem.

Murmuring, the Kuleen Horse had said, "After all, you are like sister-in-law, and they do say sister-in-law half wife. Yes, yes, you will come, Miss, you of course come . . ."

"Ei Kanan!" Prem's yell had crashed into the emptiness surrounding the man's excited murmurs and the rustling silk. And Kanan had started as if she'd been asleep.

"Yes, Premu, you must come, he says he will let you come. Isn't that nice, Premu?" Kanan had, somehow, managed to keep her arms looped around Prem even as she sat in an untidy heap like a broken-jointed crawfish.

Prem felt a long, hot needle drilling into her as she looked at the Kuleen Horse's still moving hand. She could still feel Kanan's insecure arms looped unsteadily around her, but distantly, as if in a dream of drowning. The needle meanwhile kept pushing through Prem's eardrum—muffling the murmuring and rustling outside—and probed her chest cavity like a ruthless assassin looking for the softest, most sensitive part of her to plunge decisively into. Then it swelled into a huge flaming shaft, tearing her apart. Instantly, terrible pain.

She wasn't going to go live with Kanan in Kolikata. No, never. Nor ever see Kanan again after she left. Who was this crumpled creature, anyway? Where did her Love's Garden go? She felt the path of the arrow through her expanding. Before it could blow her up she tore Kanabala off her.

"Prem, please . . . please don't . . ."

"Why? Why do you let him?"

Kanan had faltered, looked down, then raised her face again to Prem, miserably.

"What else can I do? I'll take care of your children, right? Remember what we've decided to do?"

At the pond where Kanan had unveiled her Kuleen destiny, she and Prem had promised each other this: they would love each other forever; they would love each other's children forever; when one of them had a boy and the other a girl, they would marry the boy and girl forever; they would love their grandchildren forever; and, if time permitted, they would love their great-grandchildren forever.

In this way they would be together forever. No matter what else happened. The critical word was *forever*.

That afternoon they'd each folded a sprawling red hibiscus flower with its shamelessly flaunted pistil and stamen into a spongy roll. Then they'd gingerly and methodically placed their own upon the end of the other's sari, bunching and tying the cloth at the end into a loose knot over the rolled flower. Someday they would tell their grandchildren and great-grandchildren, show them the preserved flowers of love's garden laid side by side, just like she and Kanan would be in their last days.

"But what if the girl's older than the boy?" Prem had asked Kanan. It had always been left to Prem to think of problems, find solutions. . . . *Dear silly Kanan was all hahaheehee.*

Kanan widened her eyes, a sign that she had no idea what then.

"One of us has another girl then, and we marry that one to the boy."

This had seemed satisfactory, possible, and finally, wonderful. Kanan had smiled widely, showing almost all of her black-eyed pea teeth.

But when in the nuptial room Prem looked at Kanan, a cowed creature almost crawling on the bed, a strange rage clotted in her head and essentially stopped the flow of blood to her heart. Her heart instantly began to grow cold, of course. The cold circled inside and then outside and around her, slithering, coiling and swaying between her and Kanan like a cobra.

These people. These weak, wretched people. Deserve what they get. This slumped creature on the bed is weak. Weaker than I'd thought. Weaker than I'd imagined. Weaker than Mai-ji, who at least let you know she didn't love you, didn't care, didn't know how to. Weak like Babu-ji. Weaker.

This creature was not magnificent or fearless. She was afraid of the man, her husband. Of that horse-faced, gap-toothed, chinless wonder.

"This is why you called me here."

"Prem, my little, sweet Premu . . ." Kanan had held her thin arms out to her girl again, her fingers fluttering like the wingtips of a wounded bird.

Too late. As the monsoon of grief swept through her, Prem couldn't name the particular storm—it was betrayal, yet it was more, and less, and also another end of hope—she began to see a receding, blurring shape. Kanan fading. Kanan was becoming a separate person. Not part of her. A separate person who might detach from Prem at any time and attach to another thing, person, horse, monster, snake—who was afraid of a clerk from Kolikata. Worse . . . someone whose loyalty had already detached, turned away, reattached. Prem knew she could be wrong, but the hollering inner storm was too loud, the winds whipping inside too high. The screaming, high-pitched thing inside her was ravening for blood.

She'd clambered off the bed—frantically swatting away Kanan's fingers, hands, like the touch of a leper, a scorpion—and taken off her sandal. And found her ground. And then with her sandal she had hit the disgusting, greedy, clawlike hand—now retracted—again and again, as hard as she had the strength for. The claw had folded, the man had yelped. Kanan's broken, beseeching voice had begun to be a whisper from the past. Then she'd struck the man across his face with her sandal. Harder. Twice.

Then she'd left the pair spattered on the dirty bed in the dirty nuptial chamber and run out of the house and then the estate, and taken a narrow little-trodden path through the mango trees, past the pond's empty eye socket and fields of shush-shushing windswept rice. She was blind with intent. As she'd half walked, half run, a real storm had hurried up from the east; the kind of monster of a summer storm that scythes through palm fronds, flattens entire rice fields with one backslap, and rips off the rough thatches of huts like Jagat Pandey's in the distance.

CHAPTER 18

Prem grips the armrests of her chaise as she faces the girl and the Kuleen Horse. His face raises a storm of rage and dread in her even now. She also sees in the Kuleen Horse that petit bourgeois coxcomb mini version of the Babu, the kind of castrated Indian chattel of the ruling race that her husband points at and laughs; this once she faintly, unwittingly thinks she sees her pompous husband's point. Voices from childhood—demented, crackling with anger, cracked with pain—surface to sink and send ripples lapping at the edges of her self-control. She must remain calm and composed.

The girl looks nothing like Kanan, if she's in fact Kanan's daughter. But now that she has something of a guard herself—Harish and Roderick, if no one and nothing else—Prem finds she can very tentatively return to the closed, forbidding doors of a locked and shuttered girlhood. Temptation lurks everywhere, after all—the temptation to believe she can reopen the doors and find things as they used to be. Broken but reusable. Damaged but redeemable.

The girl is barefoot. Her bony toes—now those are indubitably Kanan's toes—are digging into cold marble. Not much to look at. A kind of pale darkness, but with a greenish tinge around the mouth. Malnutrition, Prem surmises. She feels her stomach churn. Is she seeing more Horse than Kanan? Apparently so. And an old, powerful rage begins to surge in her blood, shoring her up. She doesn't know what's happening, but she knows it's happening.

The man whinnies his story. His lament, really. This motherless girl. How to raise alone? On very small salary, Ma-daaam.

Prem sees that the girl can see many things.

The girl sees that the lovely, taut hawk on the throne knows that her father is garbage, a creepy-crawly: crushable, but willing to bite when he can. A liar. The girl wants to ask him to stop but she's too scared. Also, she wants to get away from here as soon as possible. She looks around the room for an escape in case either the beautiful hawk or the ugly creeping thing suddenly burst into a tearing, unto-the-death fight. She can't believe that she's hearing her father say he would have enlisted in the war but for her, the girl. *So* many brave men gave their lives for such a great cause, he says. "But for my daughter."

The girl sees another change in the lady's face. Coming into view of muscles and bones that were hitherto invisible. And that the lady doesn't believe her father, not at all. Conflict between adults will always skedaddle across her skin like hot oil splashes, she never will be able to stand it. She doesn't know why she wants—she doesn't especially believe in ghosts or anything—to conjure up that dead mother who links her, in her father's whine, to this lady, that mother whose face she can barely make out from her parents' one wedding photo. In her fright and unease she considers saying "Look! Ghost!" Create a diversion. Point to a corner where she wants to will into being a macabre shape, a drab sari border hooding her entire face, coming a long way down her front. . . . This is a periodic nightmare of hers, this faceless shape in a low veil; she thinks it must be her dead mother. It might be no bad thing, she thinks, if for once, right now, her mother wants to do some haunting. It might be a good thing if she now decides to referee nasally—the way ghosts are said to speak—the snake and hawk impasse, impending contest. But her mother remains unavailable for this as for many other things. Never been there for her.

The girl has seen the lady glance at her feet. She feels concerned about this. She tries retracting her toes the way cats retract their claws. Her toes are bony spindles; her toenails are jagged and dirty. The milky marble floor chills her feet. Her father—as much as he smartened up for this visit—was told to remove his shoes too before entering the lord and lady's drawing room. And she too, of course. That's what their maid does when she comes to work in their shanty for the daily hour or so her father can afford, to help her grandmother keep house. The maid's frayed makeshift slippers are of recycled rubber tires. Her father's shoes, she now understands, look like the same cheap stuff. It's hard to have the right shoes, she thinks. And to be in the right shoes. Between the lord's moosh-moosh shoes and her father's rubber tire recycled shoes, she sees an impossible distance.

Her head droops not only because she and her father are people who have to enter this house shoeless, but that even their feet are ugly. Her father's feet, she notices for the first time, are darker than hers and uglier. His pointed nails are a moribund brown, discolored grayish patches of something growing between his toes.

She comes back to the immediate scene. The lady says to her father that she can give him a little money. And her father says he doesn't want money. She's flummoxed. Generally, money is what her father wants. Leads to huge quarrels with her grandmother who often rages that he's stolen from her stash again and what a wretched son he is and how he will steal the very hair off her corpse before she's cremated to sell to wigmakers, etc. . . .

He doesn't want money?

Her father says he wants the lady to take the girl. And to keep her. To raise her.

Why would she do that?

"Why? Why can't you keep her with you? She's your daughter," the lady asks, her voice marrow-freezing.

Prem wishes she could throw her slipper at this worm again. She won't. Kanan's daughter is here. He's cunning—he's brought her along as a shield, no doubt. She wonders if she can have him shoved out of the house. She feels sick.

"Ma-daaam," the girl's father says with a deep makeshift bow, "I'm still a vigorous man and might marry again, and she—"

So. Her father wants to marry again. Though the girl is tiny and power-less and young, she sees that grown-ups are just puppets. Of each other, or of certain bigger, inexorable order forces. She knows one of those forces is money. Another must be her father's need to marry again. She knows he makes evening visits somewhere that her grandmother swears and scolds about.

"And what's that to me? Is my house a charitable institution, an orphanage?" The lady's voice has suddenly risen. The girl's toes and toenails dig harder into the marble. When there's shouting around her she wants to hide. But the lady's voice is also unsteady. The lady is acting a part too. She's a puppet of something too. She seems almost afraid. Angry, but also afraid. But not afraid like the girl, who just wants not to end up being beaten. Not afraid like her grandmother who's always afraid of starving. Some other kind of afraid.

What is it the lady wants? Or doesn't? She watches intently. The next few minutes of adult theatre will be her future. She senses that. The girl's father sneaks a scowl at the girl, as though it's all her fault, as though if only she . . .

He resumes. "Ma-daaam, as you know, her mother would talk about you all the time. Day and night. 'My Premu this and my Premu that.' All only Prem Prem. Only Prem Prem, all the time."

The lady raises one hand jerkily and seems to communicate to him something the girl can't understand.

"Ah yes, yes! Ma-daaam. Lady Mitter. All the things you did together as girls . . . all the time, Ma-daaam." Her father fishes something about a hand's length, wrapped in newspaper, out of a pocket. He holds it up to the lady. At first the lady refuses to acknowledge it. But her father compels this lady somehow, the girl sees. He goes on looking right at her, shockingly bold, oddly steady. The lady reaches out slowly for the thing—takes it. She unfolds the newspaper wrapper. Something long, brownish, obviously fragile lies in it. The girl peers, tiptoed. What the parched and crinkled thing the color of dried blood has to do with anything the girl can't guess. The lady slowly closes her fist over the thing still in the newspaper and looks back at her father. The girl sees flecks of brownish, powdery dust escape the lady's fist.

"Promises, Ma-daaam. Sacred promises of innocence."

The lady, oddly, hasn't returned the thing to her father, leave alone throw it back or down as the girl half expected. She's looking at it again. It's still lying on the palm of her upturned hand. She looks very different now—still beautiful, but almost bloodless. As if she has in fact seen a ghost.

What is it?

"Sacred promises, to the dear, innocent departed," her father says again.

It's so quiet. The girl imagines a fine, dark web being spun, in which the three of them are slowly being drawn closer, bound with each other. Who's the spider and who's the fly? The girl isn't sure. Her father is telling the lady something more than his words say. And the lady understands it. The girl knows and understands that much. She looks from one adult face to the other. Her eyes, of their own accord, begin to become hooded in anticipation of a great, ugly squabble which she must witness and escape.

Her father has never mentioned this lady or any other childhood friend of her dead mother. The lady's fingers—tipped with oval nails painted red—tap-tap on her throne's arm. She still hasn't looked at the girl directly except maybe when the girl was checking feet.

"Ma-daaam, she thought—"

"I know!"

The girl flinches. The lady is really angry. At last. Of course. A matter of time, with her father.

"If people like you don't care about people like us, Ma-daaam, where will we be?"

But now the lady says she needs some time to think.

What happened? Why?

The lady rises to leave. The audience has ended. The girl's father grabs the girl by her arm as if she were an unfairly heavy gunnysack. On the way back home the girl prays silently for one of the lighter beatings.

CHAPTER 19

After they leave, Prem doesn't move. A maid has to come and ask her to come have dinner.

Prem searches for a sign. Lord Mitter inquires distantly about the afternoon's proceedings, and snorts about riffraff.

News comes from the village.

Never mind if Prem tried to snip off the cords. Still the village has come to get her. Shyampiyari has died.

Her father writes sadly, ruefully, tuned to his daughter's heart in some disorganized way. Shyampiyari has left a bundle of things for Bitiya, requesting that Bitiya alone open it. Should he send Prem the bundle? Prem wipes tears. Poor Dhai, how she loved her Bitiya. What old flotsam could she possibly have left that Prem would want or need? Sir Naren shutters his face. He has no idea what to do when his wife cries.

Prem writes to her father the next day. The bundle can wait; hopefully, she can soon visit. Maybe with her little boy. Half of her mind is elsewhere. She makes half-baked plans. Her husband is not home; he sends word that he will be away for a few days. She rejoices. Outside the window of the little forgotten room that she has recently reconnoitered into a private parlor, the young moon darts in and out of massing rain clouds gathering on a sky like molten lead.

The Kanan dream skips that night. Instead, Prem dreams of Dhai. Dhai lifting her off the ground when she tumbles, her stooping shape almost cracking with the effort. Dhai telling her outrageously scary stories as she ruthlessly scrapes her hair back into agonizing, springy plaits at night, her voice that of a saw if a saw could chortle. Dhai scolding; Dhai insisting on first dibs and the best bits for Bitiya of any savories or delicacies the kitchen makes; Dhai chewing paan; Dhai talking once in a blue moon about her own village as if it were a lost continent.

Prem awakens with a start. How did she not think much about Dhai all these days? How did she neglect her so? Never visit her? Never bring her up to Calcutta, a place the old loving heart would have felt flattered to be asked to visit?

Which is why she returns to the same old question. The question always is *Who is to blame?* Even five years ago, did she abandon Kanan, or did Kanan . . . ? Did Jagat never write because he died, or . . . ?

Always, it's the weak who are to blame. So far, she has been the strongest of them all. Yes, even stronger than Mai-ji. She's had to be, for all the weak people: Babu-ji, Sir Naren, Kanan, Jagat, all those weak. . . .

One dried flower. Everything has returned in its wake: everything buried deep and meant to stay buried.

Four months after her marriage Kanan had written a letter to Prem:

My dearest friend,

How are you? I am well. "He" is well. The first is on the way. It feels so heavy at times that I think it must be twins. I try to eat some barley soup every day. Our place has two rooms, and faces the big market off College Street. One of the rooms is the kitchen and my mother-in-law's bedroom. "He" and I sleep in the other room. Sometimes at night it is inconvenient because mother-in-law has to go, and then I am always ashamed, because you can hear everything everywhere. I miss the village; the sky gets smoky here from about six in the morning, because all the women are firing their ovens, and the smoke gets about so! Kolikata is a very great city, but it is full of smoke, and a peculiar sadness comes over me every afternoon. "He" leaves at about nine for work, and from then on I cook and wash. Mother-in-law does the shopping. Says she does not think I can handle the shopkeepers here, being a country girl.

In other news, I haven't gone out yet since the day I came in. I asked him the other day if we could see the bioscope some time, and he seemed angry. It is a hard life for him, after all. Some nights he doesn't come home till midnight, and then he is falling down. Yes, he drinks, it seems. I am somewhat used to the smell now. I wash his clothes as best as I can for him, but the water is not very good and now in my condition, the common pump-yard can be slippery and hard to work in. My favorite wall-spot is just above my head; it looks like Shyampiyari's head in profile. How is she? Very well, I hope. I find myself sad sometimes to look at it. Wish me well with this child. I am going to be a good mother, but I don't know if I can have as many as I wanted, because there is no room.

Your loving friend,

Kanan Debi

Three months later, she'd died in childbirth.

At daybreak Prem wakes up Sir Naren. He scrambles awake at her insistent poking with her index finger, a bumpkinish way of waking him he as frequently forbids as his wife persists in it.

"Wha . . . ?!" He ejaculates. "What is it?!" Has one of mills burnt down? Maybe a bridge he built has collapsed. Maybe there's been an earthquake. People are buried under debris. Maybe the British have given India independence. Maybe Mahatma Gandhi, the father of the people of India, has instigated another peasant resistance movement. (In this he is impressively oracular.) All sorts of things do bide their time to shred the slumber of the industrious rich.

"I must bring back the girl I sent away yesterday," Prem says, sitting on the bed with her knees folded almost up to her chest, arms pythoned around them.

"Why on earth? Madam, I forbid it!" Sir Naren rumbles but it sounds like a wail. It's still early.

"I'm going to keep her."

"Why?! Are you out of your mind?"

"She needs me. I mean, she needs someone to raise her, to take care of her. You saw her father."

The half hour after that is thunder and storm, and Prem remains hugging herself tightly while Sir Naren rains down his fury. But after much furor, flutter, and fuming he agrees to a second interview. "That's all," he says, glaring at his wife. She nods, poker-faced, leaves the bed and commences her day. Sir Naren watches her leave the room. The day bathing in milky dawn outside dances its eyebrows at him through the opening between the heavy velvet drapes. He feels nervous. He hasn't forgotten the steel spine. He wishes he could.

The girl hasn't felt happy, of course. Her father is trying to get rid of her. On the way home he said to her, "And you had to be not just a *kahlo bhoot*, but a girl too." She hates that expression "kahlo bhoot" though she hears it often, being dark skinned. She's not at all sure how she feels about the lady, but that is par for the course. She's sure about her father, though. This to-do makes her ask, one more painful time, why she was brought into the world if no one wanted her. Makes her ask if anyone will ever love her. If, because of her plainness and being "kahlo," she can ever be loved.

Plain, dark-skinned girls can be secretly obstinate. Secretly, the girl demands even without the vocabulary for it to not just be loved, but to be treated like a poem—like a dream come true. From where she gets such fancy ideas is a mystery. This is not how she hears grown-ups discussing her. They speak of her as if she were unclaimed baggage. They play with her whole life as if it—she—were a toy. And still she has fantasies of improbable futures, terrific adventures, tremendous opportunities, great loves.

If she has to live in the mansion with the lady and lord, because no one else wants her, she fears she'll be a thorn in their side too. But if she lives with her father's new wife whenever that one comes—because the lady will not have her—it might be even worse. She's talked to a few shanty kids who've acquired stepmothers. Her consternation has slowly spread into helpless fury. No, there's nothing to be happy about at all. Her father flogged her mercilessly the night before, after the visit to Mitter Mansion. Her jaw and back ache. But since children often joust with equal gravity against unalike phantoms called hope and despair, she's a little pleased if tremendously surprised when a few days later—it's a Sunday—a package comes with a man who arrives to tell her father that Lady Mitter has decided to take his daughter in, and keep her, after all.

In the package there's even a dress for the girl. It's a very fine dress, obviously, but did it have to be a blue-black velvet frock with a tarnished gold lace running along the neck and hem of the dress? It looks old, it's discolored in spots, and who ever chooses a blue-black fabric for a "kahlo bhoot"? It also makes the girl sweat copiously as soon as she puts it on; in their shack the air doesn't move as it probably does under the long, rapid ceiling fans in the mansion. She looks at herself in her grandmother's one cracked hand-mirror. Piece by piece by piece she examines neck, shoulder, chest, behind the knees and shins. The sleeves of the dress droop well below the middle digits of her fingers, and the waist of the dress comes almost halfway down her thigh. The girl thinks it's too big and looks ugly on her, and frowns horridly. She brings the mirror to her face and also makes a dreadful, ugly face at it, drawing back her lips and flaring her nostrils. *You really are ugly.*

She whips herself up into a grouse that the dress is an insult. "I'd rather not wear it," the girl says to her grandmother who is visibly, oddly overcome by the situation. Of course, she knows she has to. Looking up from the communally circulated newspaper of the tottering tenement building, her father frowns, then spits sideways into the corner of their single room. His spit is orange and frothy from the paan and tobacco churning inside his cheeks. The girl sees this as a further insult. As young as she is, she has some pride. Grandmother, however, for once looks other than irritated or outraged. "*Bah bah*, it looks quite nice," she says. The girl could have been knocked down with a feather. "O our

Tutu! Come back and see us again, won't you dear?" her grandmother croaks. The name Tutu was her endowment upon her motherless granddaughter. She seems sad. The girl thinks wonders will never cease.

Soon, her father grunts and grabs her again by one forearm, and off she goes flapping after him like an empty sack into a shiny black car around which neighbors are buzzing like hungry flies. The girl has one moment of looking at her feet and realizing that she still has ugly, cheap shoes. She'd rather have been sent nicer shoes than this stupid, too-big, too-hot velvet dress.

"O Tutu, where are you going all decked up, riding in a Baby Austin?" a mocking voice calls out. Tutu ignores it. It continues to carol:

Kolikattiya gori! Baby Austin-e chori!
Dhakuria-r Lake-e, Piya ko saath leke!
Chole she enke benke . . . !

They're singing the popular woman-hating ditty that cruelly misapplies to her:

Calcutta Babe! Riding in a Baby Austin!
Going to Dhakuria Lake with the lover who's a cousin!
Ooh she's on a r-r-roll . . . !

CHAPTER 20

The girl and her father arrive at the mansion; it's still midmorning. A light fog sits over the city, the air is still cool, and invisible birds chirp. The mansion looks like a storybook castle.

"You may call me *Mashimoni,*" Prem tells the girl that day.

"And we will call you Roma."

The girl doesn't think about refusing. Roma is a grand, modern name. This the girl likes. She has no truck with her old name, Tutu. All her life though she has called women who are—who look—nothing like this lady, "Mashimoni," and she has trouble mixing those "Mashimonis," crumpled wives of adjoining shanties—with this one. She dry swallows before she says it. "Yes, Mashimoni."

Mostly, she feels scared; mostly, she feels utterly bewildered. Her father's gone. Suddenly everything blurs and darkens, and the next thing she knows is that she's lying on a grand couch; this new Mashimoni is fanning her gently and calling for barley tea. She's sort of glad she fainted because she's never had so much fuss made over her, and if fainting does it then so be it. But she's so scared still that she pretends to be more knocked out than she is.

Later this Mashimoni will tell her that she'd also renamed her mother once. Roma will then think, part angry, part sad, that this sort of thing is a habit with Mashimoni. People like her and Sir Naren have appropriated the power to name, practically power of life and death, over people of her sort, her father's sort. Like a cat or a dog that needs a name—all cats are Meni, all dogs are Neri—in lieu of a rope to yank them by. Maybe they've always had this power and they always will. Roma's own father, after all, didn't even trouble himself to give his daughter a proper, formal name. She was carelessly named Tutu. A ridiculous, poor people's name, as Mashimoni says, not without kindness, but without care.

But this new Roma feels that though this Lady Mashimoni has given her a new, grand name, the other things she gets seem older or used. In this she's right, because this is not Mashimoni's doing; the naughty maid who's been delegated to find Roma a wardrobe appropriates some of the allowance and buys old clothes, shoes, and dolls at *Chor Bazaar*, where they say you can buy anything you can name or imagine. But Roma doesn't know this, Prem doesn't have enough time for such piddling details, and no one else cares. More shapeless, ill-fitting dresses, plastic fakes of dainty slippers with hard edges that cut into her feet, a ragamuffin doll with one button eye, a cracked glass globe with two dancers in an embrace unto death. More than she had before, yes. But not enough.

Prem worries—sincerely—that the girl is just too plain or too slovenly for anything to look really good on her.

Things slowly settle down. Tutu aka Roma is enrolled in the prestigious Loreto Girls' Convent—another bruising encounter of Lady Mitter with Sir Naren resulting in this—where for the first month or so her primary instinct, dearest wish, is to hide under her desk. Every late afternoon after school, Prem sees the three children in the house—or the three she knows and can call by name—and the meetings usually follow a pattern. Roderick, wearing the uniform of the equally hoity-toity La Martiniere School for Boys where mostly English boys go—where his unshared travails as *"Kutcha Bachcha,"* or Eurasian, mongrel, mixed-race, would fill an entire saga—sits stiffly and politely at the edge of his chair, his fingers interlaced and hands crossed on his lap, facing Prem. Harish sits on his mother's lap, sucking his thumb—Prem still allows this because she remembers blissfully scrutinizing dear, dear Shyampiyari's face while sucking her own reddened thumb till quite grown—taking it out only to announce his need and preference for this or the other savory, delicacy, or extravagance on the tea table. Lastly, Roma sits across the corner from Roderick, looking blankly at the pages of a book she pretends to be reading intently, ears pricked for every word spoken around her. Prem says she's tremendously impressed by Roma's love of books, and tells the other two that boys should read as well as girls. Roderick nods politely while Harish ignores everything, his gob stuffed with food.

But that Roma! Somehow she just won't . . . ! Won't what? Prem can't say exactly. . . . She does as she's told and goes to Loreto Convent school, wears what she's given, puts up ribbons in her sleekly brushed hair as Prem requires, and has quite a few dollies by now. But Prem has never seen her play with one.

Prem didn't, doesn't want gratitude or servility. She wants affection. Girl time, one might say. Lilian Hartfield disappeared entirely years ago, and since then Prem hasn't really had a girl or woman to talk to, to connect with. The

women of high society whom she meets at parties and balls and official cere-
monies that His Lordship attends do not warm to her. Yet. She wants to make
friends but has sensed with acute intuition that wanting warmth and genuine
friendship is weak, laughable, in this society. Women befriend each other out
of self-interest, or their husbands' interests, or dynastic and matchmaking pur-
poses. Moreover, Sir Naren neither affirms nor denies whispers and mutterings
that he's the father of the obviously mixed-blood, almost English-looking boy
who lives in his house. At the chief justice's annual grand fete a knot of society
ladies—spluttering and bubbling like cooking pots wrapped in brocade and
gilt—whip their heads around all together as Prem passes them on her way to
the long table groaning with desserts and sherry (she has a sweet tooth), and
immediately fall mum. And immediately start up again when they know she
isn't quite out of earshot—but having waited the requisite seconds in pretend
politeness—and resume their lively bubbling and spluttering, out of which
the single phrase that reaches Prem is "poor thing." She knows instantly that
she is the poor thing, and tosses her head robustly to convey that she doesn't
give a "bloody damn"—a phrase she has picked up from her husband—but her
cheeks are scorched by the heat of the cauldron of shameless, dastardly slander.

She says to herself, "I'm a poor, ignorant village girl who keeps her husband's bastard in her house, is that what you're saying? Yes, so I act like a
villager, ladies; villagers at least care for one another, and come to stand by
you in your time of trouble." (This is not strictly true, and a time is coming
when such faith in neighborliness will suffer a terrible shock, but Prem is just
starting on a long course of self-fashioning necessitated by her grand match
and destiny. And because she has no real friends among the society ladies.)
With these society ladies she maintains a slugger's pose, fists corded and cocked.
Tough. As learned from Lilian.

So she is lonely.

She asks Roderick what he wants to do.

"Play cricket," he solemnly and instantly responds. This isn't helpful. Lady
Premlata Mitter can't very well run around a cricket field and hit, throw, or
chase a hardball. Though she's only twenty or so, and though sometimes she
wishes she could. In the village she sometimes played Kabaddi with other girls.
Kabaddi is hard. You have to repeat the word "kabaddi" without pause while
breaching the opponents' court, touching and failing out as many players as
you can, not getting caught, and returning to your team court without running
out of breath. She once asks Roma, in something like sheer desperation, if she's
ever played the game of Kabaddi. She isn't going to reveal her own immense
facility at the game till she has a cue of some kind.

Roma looks up from the book she's not reading and shakes her head and
goes back to staring at the pages. This is in fact true. Roma too has never had
many real friends. And little does Mashimoni know the extent to which she's
ostracized at her school full of pretty, fair-skinned, upper-class girls from notable families, and British girls.

Prem begins, unwittingly, inexorably, to think of Roma as a difficult,
strange, stubborn thing. Her blank silences sometimes make Prem feel accused

of having orphaned her twice. Prem even dreams sometimes that she somehow caused Kanan's death.

Did she somehow?

Of course not.

But what about her failure to stop Kanan's marriage? To stop Kanan from going into the Kuleen Horse's room? Why didn't she interfere boldly as she had with the starving, dusty girl who'd come to her house one day? But what would have been the use? After all, she herself had had to marry the Brown Baron and leave the village. All around her, around almost every woman she knew, there were only obstacles, terrible denials, stony prohibitions.

Except for Lilian.

Besides, if Kanan's death is anyone's fault, isn't it Roma's? Kanan died giving birth to her.

Of course she doesn't really mean it's Roma's fault. It's really the Kuleen Horse's fault. Remembering him, blaming him, hating him, gives Prem's frustration another vent. But there is another problem. Unhappily, Roma looks a bit like her father. The same wide mouth, narrow forehead, angular face, wide jaw, dark skin. Kahlo. It's so important for girls to be fair. A good match is hard to find otherwise. In fact, with a fair skin all of Roma's broad-boned, horsey look might have been allowed, even gone unnoticed. And so she returns repeatedly to a difficult tussle with herself when she tries to find Roma understandable, normal. She even asks her husband.

"Do you think Roma is quite normal?"

Sir Naren knits his brow and considers, silent.

"No," he says at last. "I'd say you've got yourself a real oddity there."

"There's nothing wrong with having a personality," Prem retorts, stung.

"No, but a girl should neither have too much personality, nor too much jaw. She seems to have both. And be a darkie."

So this process of borrowing love limps along. Roma's father only comes to see her two or three times, that too early on. Limp, shabby, clerical; a disgrace. Quite a low mentality, obviously, Prem has to concede reluctantly. Maybe, unfortunately, he personifies that "peon" thing that Sir Naren talks about endlessly. Sir Naren uses the word to denote those Indians (he says) who are "nobodies," abject lackeys of lackeys. It's because of them the British say that Indians are children, unfit to rule, he says, privately and not so privately. At the same time as she bristles—wants to shove his teeth back into his halitosis-ridden mouth, actually—she gets it, faintly. Her husband is at least a baron. Whether the British mean it or not, they've knighted him willy-nilly.

The few times he visits, the Kuleen but Peon Horse stays a half hour or so in a smaller sitting room with his daughter, the door never closed. They don't say much. When he leaves, Roma is clutching a bar of cheap candy or a bag of sugar-coated fennel seeds in her hands. Her eyes, usually blank, gaze hotly at her bribe. Then he stops coming altogether.

Part 4:
After the Great War,
Calcutta, 1919–

CHAPTER 21

Prem does find another occupation—some would call it recreation—though, which feeds some of her restless longing for romance, charm, and beauty in life. She loves this new thing called the bioscope. It's been around for over twenty years, of course, but in the village Prem hadn't even heard of it, or just vaguely. The first time she heard of it was actually in the letter from Kanan that she—stupid with revenge that day—tore up and scattered into her childhood's grave: the dratted, discolored pond.

Every time a new film is publicized, a servant queues up at the box office to buy tickets for Lady Mitter and the four or five upper maids or distant relations who will accompany her. Then comes the day, and led by Prem herself, the lesser ladies troop into the Rolls Royce and—with their sari veils carefully pulled low over their faces—troop out to the ladies' lounge of the great theatres newly built for audiences that can't get enough of this new delight.

Prem notes with care and detail how the actresses walk, talk, and sing. How they fan themselves in "distress," and faint easily and all the time, and must be revived by cordials. It fills her with admiration and aching longing. Some of the actresses remind her of Lilian. How fair they are, and how their hair is always so carefully layered, scalloped, and crimped across their forehead and temples, a style she immediately adopts instead of that huge bouffant style she once thought the height of fashion. She never sees, though, a female character like Mai-ji in the films. All the girls' mothers are loving and devoted, though some of the girls' mothers-in-law are termagants.

Sir Naren harangues. On his cheerier days he snorts. Prem doesn't heed him. She's begun to learn how to wipe her husband out of scenes he makes unbearably distasteful. That would be most scenes of daily life. In revenge she pastes him into bioscope scenarios where he fares badly. In one, the film called *Bilet Pherat*, Prem silently but ecstatically identifies him as the hand-fed cur of the master race who believes his frantic tail-wagging has transported him to a certain heaven called Anglo-Saxonness. There he coos and smokes his cheroot in pucca English "suit-boot," peering down from his lofty perch through the obligatory pince-nez on fellow Indians, speaking to them when absolutely unavoidable in a high-pitched, precious drone.

She begins to see the times she's living in. The country is swinging between the traditional and the modern. The mercilessly reamed "foreign-returned" Bengali fop rejecting all things traditional gives her the clearest view of who her husband is or would like to be considered. A modern Indian, a westernized Indian, with no patience or tolerance for old ways, old values. Still a domestic tyrant as many of his forefathers have been, but a votary of all things English in name. She doesn't at all chide her women for falling off the ladies' lounge seats, laughing, during *Bilet Pherat.* The bioscope theatre is, paradoxically, one of the very few places where Prem can be with any female tribe, unafraid, nearly public, almost free of men. Being a great lady helps clear her path when she walks into the theatre, but inside it she might almost be acting herself. All the world may be a stage, but the stage is also all that the world isn't. In the bioscope, you can be, meet so many strangers.

"Will you come with me to the bioscope?" she asked her husband once. Constantly living through other lives sometimes makes the harshest reality flicker.

He raised his eyebrows, so high they might disappear altogether, saying no more.

"Why not?" Prem insisted. She didn't know why that day she was especially reckless.

"To see prostitutes perform their tricks in front of a hundred people rather than one?"

Of course, all actresses are supposed to be prostitutes themselves, as well as daughters of prostitutes. Like Sushilabala who acted in *Bilet Pherat,* simultaneously swooned over as a "star" and derided as a 'whore." Young men of rich families are known to squander their youth in the honeycombs of such queen bees, then grow into irate ranters and damn them as the very gates to hell. Prem leaves the room. All those beautiful, stylish, poised women in the films—nothing but prostitutes? Maybe, but who made them so?

In her heart of hearts, she doesn't give a "bloody damn," as long as the women act, look, and sing beautifully. After all, she sputters mutely, what are you, old sinner, but a prostitute of the English? Who was Lilian Hartfield? What did you make her? She's not shocked at her inner diatribe, and goes to the bioscope as before. And thoroughly enjoys herself, and sheds tears when poor distressed beauties weep, and laughs when the effete Bengali "Sahib" trips over his arrogance and folly, and claps mightily when the nice young man true to his Indian roots—indeed, proud of them—rescues the beauty and crushes his vile, slavish adversary.

It's beautiful. The stories. The loves. The laughs. The trouncing of the enemies of love. The certainty that good will win over evil. That true love will never run smooth but will win the day in the end. The bioscope is beautiful. Real life is alright—especially since as time goes by she minds Sir Naren's violent antics less and less—but nothing like the bioscope. Real life should be more like the bioscope. Everyone would be much happier then. Everyone except the wicked and the heartless. Prem thinks sometimes, driven restive by her station in life, that happiness must be nice.

Finally, Roma begins going with Prem and the ladies to the bioscope. It is clear that she prefers the Indian films to the western ones. At the Empress Theater she soaks up the Eurasian Jewish actress Prudence Cooper playing the mythical King Nala's devoted wife Damayanti in *Nala Damayanti,* "The Love Story of the Ages" as per newspaper advertisements. About King Nala she doesn't care a "bloody damn," an expression she too has picked up in Mitter Mansion. But Damayanti aka Prudence Cooper's smoky, love-drenched eyes as she looks into the middle distance—her rounded, fair arm thrown back over her head in melancholy ennui—seeking only her star-crossed husband's long life and well-being, move her immensely. Her own eyes redden and fill. She doesn't usually cry. But here she has no doubt that her dead mother had been just like Damayanti, the ideal woman, and her hatred of her father redoubles.

She also steals glances at the dazzling woman sitting a few seats away from her, wiping tears and eating bonbons as she watches suffering Roma, thoughts unknown to her, and sweeps her up too in her storm of fury. Rage is light-winged, hops easily from perch to perch. Roma almost hates her Mashimoni, though she feels bad about almost hating her. Even when Mashimoni talks about the Behula and Lakhinder story she heard long ago in the automobile on the way home, and how deeply she'd once loved that story—and the nurse from whom she and Roma's mother heard it—Roma finds it difficult to cool down, be reasonable. She has observed the details of conjugal life in Mitter Mansion. And she knows her father used to beat her mother. Grandmother said so.

Not knowing her mother, not knowing a thing about her mother's married life, not knowing one thing about her life, really, Roma sometimes finds comfort in hauling Lady Mitter up to the witness stand fairly frequently for any crime that needs a malefactor. She finds comfort in mutely communing with the Eurasian Jewish Damayanti who—of course Roma doesn't know this—once danced for the Bandmann Troupe at the Gaiety Theatre, before she became a "star" in the great Heeravala Film Studios. Unencumbered by the inconvenience of knowing anything, least of all the truth, Roma watches her mother's untold myth unreel in Prudence Cooper's sweet, melancholy patience.

Prem, again unaware, is enthralled by all films, all of the bioscope, and goes as frequently as she can. One day there's a bit of commotion at the foot of the grand staircase of Cornwallis Theatre that leads up to the private boxes and ladies' lounges. Prem hears people say, "Make way, make way now! Heeravala Sahib and Pandey Sahib are here!" She knows that Mr. Heeravala is the great entrepreneur and film producer who's made the film she's walking into and the theater she is in, but she doesn't wish to be seeing peeking and prying like the other gigglers and gapers who instantly rush and hang out over the circular frames of the stairwell and landing. She walks straight on and into the viewing area, and commands her retinue to follow.

The film they see is *Pati Bhakti,* and its not-novel theme is the appropriate devotion of wives to husbands. Prem hasn't chosen the film for its theme or title, but really to please Roma, who has developed quite an ardor for Prudence Cooper and whose Leelavati in *Pati Bhakti* doesn't fail to give satisfaction. All the way home, Roma uncharacteristically chatters about the greatness of the film—its message being the sanctity of marriage—and the star, while periodically glancing sidelong at Prem. At first Prem doesn't notice the sidelong looks, slightly bemused as she is by Roma's saints' lives of good wives, but when she does the looks make her uneasy and irritable. Roma can hardly be preaching at her Mashimoni, Lady Mitter—the girl is barely six!—but her righteous prattle is certainly annoying.

CHAPTER 22

Jagat Pandey didn't die in the war, unlike sixty thousand of his countrymen who did.

He was discharged with an arm that no longer rotated, awkwardly pinned as it was to his permanently splintered right shoulder.

Once he was able to breathe normally, sleep straight through a few merciful hours of the night, sit in a coffeehouse somewhere, read a newspaper like a human being, smoke a cigarette without worrying about whether his head or something more disgracefully minor would be blown off next, he realized he didn't know who and where he was. So maybe he did in fact die in the war? Who was this man who'd come back across the black water? He wasn't sure.

His mother died when he was fighting in deserts and tundra. So he couldn't cremate her. He never got to make her life easier. Coming home he was given a tiny urn with ashes that, as her son, he had to scatter into the Ganges where the river was holiest. He went to the holy city of Gaya and did the rites. The river flowed before him, broad, shimmering, speckled by odd shapes and colors. Half-burned corpses, and also flowers. They say the dead come to Gaya to find peace, transcendence, the way to heaven. Why should the dead not want beauty as well as peace? Why not a few flowers—more than a few even—for the charred meat falling off charred bones?

He sat on the steps leading to the river after the rites. He had nothing, no one. He knew that Prem must be somewhere in a big city, but he also knew he'd never see her again. The setting sun turned the water into a rippling sheet of bronze.

He'd have to walk away or he'd step into that leering, winking bridge to heaven working so hard on not being a trench flowing with carnage, flowers and all.

Did he want to end it all then? Yes. But he walked away and didn't glance back. Suppose he wasn't quite done dreaming life's fitful dream.

No one cared about Indian soldiers in the greatest war in history (until the next greatest war). They'd risked their lives as all soldiers do, and also lost their religion by crossing the Kala Pani. For what? Nothing really. They'd come home to an indifference that paralyzed limbs and spirits already broken. They'd left poor and hopeless; they returned poor and hopeless. They weren't heroes, just pawns. Jagat asked himself many times why he'd made such terrible choices. But really, what choices had he had?

There are many things people crave, but during wars they crave nothing more than illusion and romance. They need reasons to keep going. Some find them in the bioscope. When Jagat saw his first bioscope after the war, he felt . . . he didn't know what to call it. The closest name for it might be reverence or submission. The movie was Cecil de Mille's *Male and Female*. Jagat began to dream feverishly as he watched, nearly breathless, mouth half-open. Gloria Swanson reminded him of Prem, directly and completely. Including her sulky pout. When he saw *Male and Female,* the story burrowed into his need for dreams. A rich maiden rejects a poor man until terrible reversals of fortune make her turn to him for rescue. It wasn't his story—never could be—but it was a great story to tell. Maybe in the bioscope of the coming years there would be such stories: poor boy meets and marries rich girl against her family's wishes and machinations, after many trials. Happily ever after.

Then one summer morning he stood outside Jamshedji Framji Heerevala's studio in Calcutta until the gates opened. When they did, he pushed past the gateman and ran toward the studio buildings inside. Behind him rose a coarse hub-bub, curses and oaths. He paid no mind. He was a strong runner since the war. But he was, in truth, a little crestfallen to see how tiny and sparse the studio buildings were. Not at all like the magical world he'd hoped for. Nothing befitting a man with Heerevala-ji's aura. He slowed down, almost turned back, and as his steps slowed, a man in a long black tunic, black trousers, and shiny black pumps stepped out of one of the buildings.

"What's the commotion?" he asked no one in particular.

The gateman had caught up with Jagat. Panting, he said, "*Gustakhi maaf, huzoor,* this bumpkin just pushed me aside and ran into the studio!"

And then a full, somewhat voluptuous face, with a graying handlebar moustache and unreadable eyes turned full on Jagat, who gasped in instinctive awe.

"How dare you?" the man said. "How dare you break into my property and injure my guard?"

The gateman's pride was bruised at the insinuation of injury by Jagat. He weighed at least twice as much as Jagat did. No surprise, given that Jagat's empty pocket went with him wherever he did and kept him on a strict diet. "*Nahi huzoor,*" I'm not injured. This thief must be oiled all over because he just slipped out of my grip, where I had him just"—he made fierce double fists and a face.

"Mollaem," the man in black called. "*Ji huzoor,*" said a bullethead that appeared from behind the tin door of one of the ramshackle buildings. As the whole man emerged and approached, Jagat saw that the owner of the bullet-head had a soldier's build and gait.

"Take this scoundrel and throw him outside the gate," the man in black said sternly.

Immediately Mollaem fell upon Jagat, his corded muscles and steel grip doing most of the work that the gateman's huffing-puffing suggested was happening. Semistarved and rail thin, Jagat was hardly a match for two adversaries.

But as Jagat was being dragged back to the gate, his cracked rubber shoes tracing a line of rout, he nearly turned his head toward the man in black—though his neck was in a headlock and his bad shoulder in agony—and shouted.

"Sahib! I'm a soldier! I fought for the empire, for this country! I suffered for this country, Sahib! I shed blood . . . I rotted in trenches for the same war that has made you a great man, Huzoor!" He'd guessed that this was Heeravala-ji himself: the great Parsi entrepreneur who'd been honored by the Raj for his wartime supplies of liquor with the title of OBE, Officer of the Most Excellent Order of the British Empire. His name was legend in India's film world. He owned half the theatres in the country.

"From one loyal subject of empire to another, Huzoor, give me a chance! Give me a chance Huzoor, and I'll be your slave—"

That was his final gamble, his one last ace.

"Stop!"

The two men paused, the gateman glaring at Jagat with hatred and contempt, but the other man quickly, impassively, letting go of his neck.

Later, Heeravala-ji told Jagat that he'd allowed him to stay that day because he knew what destitution and broken dreams were. When he was twelve, his father's banking empire plunged into disaster. He had to leave his fancy boys' school in Bombay and join the Parsi Theatre as a prop boy. From there, he worked his way up to being chief wine merchant for the British Empire, and then grew his own movie empire. And that was why he gave Jagat a chance. That, and Jagat's gumption.

Jagat became an employee of the Great Heeravala Theatres and did everything from sweeping floors to being spot boy, lighting assistant, grip, star actress Madam Prudence Cooper's hairdresser when the regular stylist couldn't return from an evening tryst with moonshine, cook, messenger, camera man, lighting assistant, and Heeravala-ji's scribe. His schoolmaster years came into good stead for some things, and his army discipline for others.

CHAPTER 23

Since Dhai's death the village comes back more and more to Prem. Sometimes she even allows Kanan to drift into focus momentarily. Dares to. For a moment. Her hands twitch then on her satiny lap, needing something to do. And she goes to the bioscope. One new bioscope company is coming into great prominence: the J.F. Heeravala Theatre Company which makes superb "mythologicals"—with astoundingly all-enduring heroines—that make Prem cry almost as much as she wept at Dhai's Behula-Lakhinder story when she was a girl.

Unfortunately, Roma has now taken to skulking in shadows and corners. Hiding behind maids and servants. She eats like a bird and hardly speaks. She is thin and looks peaked. The greenish hue around her mouth that she came with is still there, Prem notices, and she feels both panic and despair. Kanan's daughter has shown nothing of Kanan's obliging nature.

Prem doesn't even realize that sometimes Roma stands right outside the door of the blindingly lit drawing room where Sir and Lady Naren Mitter are giving a grand party. Pressing her face against the figured glass doors, imagining the horror her crushed nose and bulging eyes might create in there if someone sees her, Roma watches her exhalations turn people into ghostly blurs. Or, she stands silently in a corner of the great room, forced to be fashionably frocked and be-ribboned, her unwilling shape a familiar heavy shadow on Prem's heart straining to be light on these occasions of gaiety. Of course, in public Prem's poise and panache don't skip a beat. Alone, though, some days she asks herself, "Why? Why doesn't she love me? What am I doing wrong?"

A child. Someone's child. A lost child. A found child. Doesn't matter. All who have, keep, or lose children make themselves hostages to fortune. Surely Mai-ji has no idea what a blessing she had and threw away: a child's love. And here's that child still fighting to find love, keep love.

Roderick seems to like her far more than Roma does.

These days, if summoned, Roma appears dragging each limb as though it's about to fly away. Her very knock-kneed, cubist form in appearing upon summons seems to be her refusal—or is it mockery?—of Prem's ambition to love her.

It just stuns Prem. Why? Why can't love be grown? She survived counting on love blossoming like a tiny field flower on ample or withered bosoms, picking fertile ground wherever it might, shooting up through cracks in hearts like a weed. Confidently waiting for the pats on the head of Babu-ji or the old Munshi walking past even if they were absentminded. She remembers her mother's refusal—to even pat her head—and Shyampiyari's devotion that made up for it. A lot of Shyampiyari, and a lot of Kanan. And this girl gives the lie to all that bounty, making her think the past is as contingent as Behula-Lakhinder, or Nala-Damayanti. This girl makes the past's gold look like gilt.

This one demands more than fertile ground. She wants a great big reservoir of love where she's the only lotus. How is that possible? Prem has two other children. (Maybe three, if you count Sir Naren who is much closer to dotage than she is.) Roderick and even Harish, the heir-elect, have sometimes been launched from lap to lap, from heart to heart. They don't blame her for that! That's how children are raised—children belong to the tribe. But this girl wants to reign, dominate, spread roots—if a weed by birth, a proud weed among overfed roses. This is a strange newfangled idea, Prem thinks. How can a person give all their attention to one child? How does Roma get this idea? From whom? Is this what things are coming to in this "modern" age?

But Prem also sees things a little differently from five years ago. Though she knows every meanness of his nature and every cunning gleam in his eyes, she thinks her husband has opened her eyes to something: power is important, and it's not easy. Neither to get, nor to have, nor to keep. And that there are those who have power and those who don't, and there will always be worlds between them. Hence the difference between the Mitters and other Indians, the non-*Bilet Pherat*. Also, it is having exactly this kind of power that allows the British to go around lamenting that they themselves are hostages to fortune, Indians being children and their responsibility: the "White Man's Burden." One of the best forms of power—a very special privilege, actually—is becoming self-appointed guardians of folks whom one starts calling children who keep having more children, and then calling them one's burden or curse.

And then some have the power of denying oneself to such burdensome children. The British have both and exercise one or the other at will. And Maiji and Lilian had, or acted like they had, at least the second. Giving away children as if they rained down from the sky every day. And Sir Naren? Looking for only the purebred, pureblood child? And Prem herself? She's had the power to rename Kanan, and then her daughter. They've been her very own almost-white-but-not-quite lady's burden, haven't they? Kanan left her for the peon, and Kanan's daughter has the peon's look writ large upon her. And still Prem is trying with the peon's daughter. Prem hasn't abandoned the children billeted on her, hasn't denied herself to the most unreasonable, burdensome ones.

And the peon simply got away. Could it be that the age of peons is around the bend? That soon, peons will have the real power?

Sir Naren scoffs. "These people are like chameleons. Clinging to something bigger and just hoping not to get noticed. Survival of the sods. They never change but they can change color on demand."

But then Sir Naren married her, Prem, didn't he? She was a village girl and her father is nothing compared to wealthy Calcuttans; her pride in her father's status was replaced long ago by a clear awareness of this. During the early days of her marriage, once or twice she'd gushed to Lilian about what an important family she came from and how her father's fields, dairies, and pantries fed a hundred people a day. Lilian had shortly and sternly told her to never, ever, speak this way before any of the ladies of her husband's set. "They'll laugh at you," she'd said, "and you don't want to give them that satisfaction." Prem had been crestfallen, but also stung by the curious pain she'd instantly, oddly, felt for Lilian's own unspoken life. Her husband's ex-mistress had herself probably learned how to walk through and away from ringing peals of mocking laughter. Many times, she'd assumed. She'd promised Lillian she wouldn't make such a *faux pas* again, and she never has. So a peon can learn if she wants to.

Or maybe she has only changed color after all, becoming a bit more roughly English under the skin on the day she first saw Lilian and Roderick.

Alone in her perplexity, Prem mourns in the house full of broken, burdensome peons that her expected, planned love for Roma was to have helped brighten. There are many dependents in the house already, with the forced joy of peons glittering in many eyes. As Lady Mitter, Prem sometimes buries her moments of lonely panic in the ready-on-call homage of these lost people who make the warrens and burrows of her palatial house their refuge for days, months, decades. Them, but not Roma? This deepened frustration in her longing for wholeness, these multiple contradictions, are cracking her reality down the middle. How the poor become ghosts haunting the lives of the rich!

Sometimes she feels immensely tired. Astounded by this unnatural non-reciprocity. And then she feels unappreciated. Is it for children to require a particular map of love? Maybe this is what peons, with their tiny worlds, are like? Maybe this is the world to come?

CHAPTER 24

A Miss Sotheby has been hired to give Roma piano lessons. Roma doesn't want to take piano lessons. Prem insists on them. She is delegated by Sir Naren to insist. "The girl has to have one marketable skill, with those features."
Like your ex-mistress, mother of your firstborn?

One night, Prem hears a loud shattering sound and fumbles out of bed. In the hallway there was a large Chinese vase on a console. Priceless, probably, if her husband is right. It's in tiny pieces on the floor. No one around.

Sir Naren is furious. "You have to do something about this," he says, "if you want to keep around this pest. That girl's no one to us. Who is she? Why is she here?"

Prem tries to placate him meekly. "It might have been anyone," she essays.

"No, it isn't! Only one person could have done it. You know it's your precious charge. Have you any idea how much that piece cost? A Ming dynasty vase! Broken to smithereens! For what? Tell me, for what? Doesn't she know she's lucky? I'll send her back to her father if this doesn't stop, you tell her that!"

He storms away and out of the house. Prem is silenced because she knows Roderick would never do such a thing. He's lived here for a long time and his nature is careful, conservative. And Harish, only six or so, can hardly be imagined as the perpetrator. The vase itself is—was—three times his weight. If it is one of the children, it's very likely Roma.

Because she loves things of beauty, knowing or not knowing who did it Prem mourns the vase. And also thinks rebelliously that if it was that valuable Sir Naren should never have left it sitting on a small table in the family bedroom floor hallway. The family has grown, the hallways are often busy with people coming and going; children use bathrooms at night. They don't get to go to an en suite bathroom after nightly funny business. This is no longer just your house anymore, old goat, she wants to say. But faced with the ruin of venerable ceramic beauty she doesn't have enough brass or face to say it, and she stoops and slowly picks up the larger pieces of that blue-veined, green-glossed porcelain creamy with age. She asks a maid to pick up the rest. Then she drops the bigger pieces too into a wastebasket. It was a beautiful vase.

More things break. Walls are scratched, scored, damaged. A damask chaise at the bottom of the stairs down to the great hall and drawing room is ripped open, its stuffing all over the floor. Roma always denies everything. And no one ever catches the culprit. Prem feels helpless, afraid to go to sleep. She's used to waiting, it is true; all of girlhood before marriage was waiting. But this is different. Sir Naren hits the ceiling each time something is broken or damaged, repeating his threats. Prem points out the lack of concrete evidence. "Innocent until proven guilty," she says, quaking inside.

And then the worst happens. One of Sir Naren's parker fountain pens with a gold nib and cap is found crushed and shoved behind a library shelf. Who would do such a stupid, flagrant thing? Sir Naren doesn't plan to wait longer for—as he says—his house to come down around his ears in fire one night. He orders Roma confined in a dark closet for a day, only bread and water passed in.

Prem fights. "That is barbarity! That is like bricking up someone alive. The Mughals used to do that sort of thing! You can't do that to a nine-year-old girl!"

"Yes I can, when the girl has the Mongol inside her," Sir Naren tosses back as he, once again, leaves the house and takes his Aston Martin to . . . who knows where.

Roma is brought in resisting by two maids, and Prem can barely look her in the eye. She's so tired, so disappointed, with all of this. The more she wants to surround herself with beauty, the uglier the world gets. The time of the peons is at hand, she frets. They're bent on proving her husband right.

Roma's interrogation is, as expected, futile. Prem waves at the maids; she can't bring herself to repeat Sir Naren's order, and anyhow it's already widely known through the household that Lord Mitter himself has ordered the not-very-prepossessing or popular girl locked in a closet with a bread and water allowance. Roma leaves Prem looking back and screaming at the top of her lungs: "I didn't do it! Mashimoni, I didn't do it! Believe me, please! I don't know anything . . ." Her voice suddenly dies as if switched off. Prem fans herself, looking out the window, wiping angry, uncontrollable tears with her free hand.

She tiptoes past the closet where Roma is a half hour later. No sound at all from it. Her heart jumps and trips. Did the girl faint? Or maybe even die? She rushes to the door and finds a burly lock on the handle. Almost like overkill. She brings the house down calling for the servant who has the key. It turns out he's a young village boy recently arrived who was supposed to give the key to the cook. He got leave, though, to attend a night fair and carnival, and he can't be found anywhere. Just as Prem is about to have the lock hammered, Sir Naren returns and forbids anyone to touch the door or the lock, on pain of unspeakable punishment.

Prem doesn't come to dinner that evening, and Sir Naren dines with the two boys, speechless and grim. The boys are quiet as well. Roderick knows what's happened; Harish knows that his mother is sick and that Roma, whom he calls Didi or older sister, is being punished.

That night Roderick pads up to the closet, stolen food from the kitchen pantry stuffed into his pajama pockets. He's been making these night raids on the pantry for some time. He's about thirteen, and he's always hungry. He's fed generously, but almost every night a wayward craving swishes up before him like a tadpole, ending in a tingling sensation inside his stomach. His stomach grumbles and wrestles with the craving, but usually gives in. Raids are made.

This night he doesn't return to his bedroom directly. Nearing the closet, he steps into something warm and sticky. He draws his foot back hastily. A clear liquid has pooled out from the closet. And the sound inside is of a crying that's been going on for a long, slow time. He knocks very softly.

Roma's wet herself. She called earlier to have someone come help her. But then she heard Sir Naren's voice downstairs and froze. Since then she's been sitting in her own urine.

"Can you hear me?" Roderick asks.

Then he says, "It's Roderick. Roddy. Hear me?"

Roma knows his voice very well.

"Yes."

She hears him breathing just outside the door. A tsunami of self-pity brings tears shooting out of her eyes again.

"D'you have any food?"

"No."

"I can get you some."

"How?"

"I can slide it in under the door."

"Yes."

He's come prepared so something shoots in under the door. Roma hisses, "Don't let it get in the—"

"I say, what cheek!" Roderick gets up to leave at such rank ingratitude.

"Sorry," Roma whispers, her voice now sounding clogged, "but now this toast has . . . is . . . all wet. Can you try to slide it in more near the left end?"

Which Roderick does. And hears a hoarse, muffled "thank you." His soft heart swells with what he would like to call manly pity. His manliness fails him when he hears inchoate sounds at the end of the long hallway. Someone is about, maybe going to a bathroom. He hotfoots it back to his bed.

Roma is brought out the next day. She's running a fever. The family doctor comes. Gravely he proclaims that it's typhoid, and a pretty bad case. Prem doesn't come to dinner again, and Sir Naren foresees a long scorched-earth exercise and eats with unusual noisy relish. For the next fortnight not a word passes between husband and wife who sleep in the same bed every night.

Roma is put in a room with windows and door always closed. The typhus miasma might escape; the doctor has given strict orders about quarantine. The day and night nurses come and go, taking her temperature, force-feeding her medicine and the prescribed atrocious gruel. She doesn't speak much; she's knocked fairly unconscious by the fever. Only once, when the kindly elderly day nurse places a cool palm on her forehead and strokes it for a while, and then leans over and plants a light kiss on her forehead—she's lost her family to cholera and doesn't fear death—Roma turns her face away. The nurse says, "Now, there you go again. Can't you just be nice?"

Roma remains silent, so she says again, "You know my lady has a big heart—she only tried to teach you to be good for your own good." The nurse isn't about to touch the topic of Sir Naren's conduct with a twenty-foot pole. "Now be a good girl and try to rest." The nurse grumbles awhile, knitting in her chair—this difficult but also oh-this-poor motherless girl—and falls asleep. Her piece of knitting slides to the floor, unheeded. From Roma's eye, still turned away toward the shuttered window, a single tear rolls onto her sickbed pillow.

She has dreams that come and go like torn paper tossed into wind. She dreams that Mashimoni and her mother—young girls in the dream—are running through trees dripping with a slimy damp, having a hard time push-ing through narrow openings between trees webbed with creepers. They lose their breath, clutch their thighs, pant. Then they run again.

She loses all count of time. Time is just the flow of medicine, tut-tuts, mutterings, high and low fever, and gruel. More gruel. More fever. Less fever. Sometimes she knows it's night because the gruel stops for a while, and there are fewer noises.

Then, in that whirling, timeless time, one night her door opens slowly.

Roderick stands in the doorway.

He closes the door quietly behind him.

"Roma," he says. She hears the catch in his voice even though her senses are dim.

"You shouldn't be here," she mutters.

"I'm here, though. How're you? Are you getting better?"

She doesn't want him to see her cry. Before she knows it Roderick is at her bedside and then he's sitting on it. He takes her hand tentatively, very gently.

Roderick says, "Never fear. You'll be all hale and hearty soon."

"How long have I been here?"

"Um . . . about ten days. I think . . ."

She tries to pull her hand away. "You shouldn't be here, Roddy." Her voice barely rises above a croak, but there's panic at the end. "Go. Please, please go away."

"It's quite alright, it is," he says trying to sound as manly as possible. He passes his hand over her throbbing forehead once, awkwardly. "It's alright, old girl. Nothing will happen to me. I'm strong because I'm a boy. You'll see."

Roma can't remember more of that night either from fever or happiness.

CHAPTER 25

Children's bodies mend fast. Roma leaves her bed in a week more. In another week she returns to school. She generally stays away from Sir Naren now at all costs, but dinner always has to be together. The first night Prem, her face unreadable, asks Roma to "tell Uncle how sorry she is." Roma says she's very sorry.

Sir Naren makes a choking, harrumphing sound; then soup arrives.

From that time, Roderick and Roma sometimes play together in the back lawn, hitting a shuttlecock back and forth across a net, competing at hopscotch, or just sitting side by side talking or staring aimlessly into the distance.

"So where do you want to live when you grow up?" Roma asks. Roderick is chewing a grass stalk and takes some time to answer.

"England."

"Really?" They speak in English of course.

"And you?"

Roma shakes her head. She has no idea. Or much ambition. Or plans. She has thought once or twice about becoming a nun. She begins chewing on a grass stalk too. Roderick's face in silhouette, a young serious boy's face, looks adorable to her. She admires it covertly. Roderick stares straight ahead as if his job is to look at that far horizon, planning the future.

"What?" he asks after a bit.

"Nothing. I'm just thinking we could get married."

Roderick says nothing.

"But I don't know what I'll wear in England."

Roderick half turns and says, "In England they'll call you darkie, you know that, right?"

Roma is offended beyond measure. She hits back.

"And you know what they'll call you there, no? Kutcha Bachcha!"

Roderick, dancing his eyebrows, says, "No, ignoramus, in England they don't speak Hindi and Bengali, see. That's just darkies like you, yeah?"

Roma runs off and back to the house, unable to speak because of the scream formed at the base of her throat.

A few days later Roderick apologizes. "I'm sorry about what I said that day."

Roma sniffs and tosses her head. They're waiting for the car to take them to their schools. The last few rides have been hell. Poor Harish hasn't been able to get a sound out of either, leaving him perplexed and out of sorts.

"Really. I'm very sorry. I shouldn't have."

"Promise?"

"Promise."

"Cross my heart and hope to die?"

"Cross my heart and hope to die."

"Pinky Promise?"

Roderick's precariously balanced manhood—he's not yet fifteen—has a terrible struggle with this girls' school lingo. His own pals ridicule such language endlessly and always make closing statements that girls are "pansy." But honor and chivalry make him swallow his distaste and say in a small near-falsetto, "Pinky Promise."

Roma knows full well what this has cost him, and so she shakes his hand solemnly, forgiving him almost completely.

The subject of marriage comes up again, later, when the conversation is about adults.

Once he describes his mother to Roma as the most beautiful and tallest woman in the world who played the piano like an angel. She's for him a slim silhouette disappearing into a shadow with each day, month, year. Disappearing partly because he wants her to. Because she left him. Then vanished. But when he chooses he wants to be able to import her for whatever purpose he has. Like when the conversation is about how adults seldom tell the truth.

"I know," Roma says mournfully, "that Uncle always lies to Mashimoni about how many drinks he has before dinner. I've seen it myself."

"Peeping Tom."

"Yes, so? Don't they peep on us?"

"When I'm older I'll join the navy and leave Calcutta. I'll probably only visit once or twice."

"And we can get married before you leave."

Roderick glances at Roma with exasperation mixed with admiration for her tenacity. He's not sure if he can marry a girl with skin as dark as hers and a face sort of flat and broad, but you've got to give it, the girl's a good sport. Nothing in his world is as calamitous as being a bad sport, or being with one.

"I'm thinking what will I wear in England," Roma says with a bouncy Indian-English accent, a heavy sigh, and an undulating motion of the head.

"Balderdash," Roderick says, proud of knowing this word that he considers very toff. "You'll just wear saris like you would do here."

Roma refrains from answering, as her newfound womanly composure allows her man some leash. Boys will be boys. Now she always calls him Roderick, never Roddy like others sometimes do. He hates being called Roddy, and her decision is one part of her cunning plan to gain his trust forever. His "balderdash" and swagger make her happy. She wants a husband who can stand tall and say "balderdash" and "ballyhoo" and "Gone doolally, have you?" His face, even in shadow, is visibly stony, serious. A warmth spreads from the back of her neck into her face.

Thus these two, these hopeful, helpless two—half orphans, homeless really—plot a future where adults will need a pass to get in. Do all children do this? In one another these two find this achingly sweet, unlikely friendship. They make plans to set sail one day, soon, and only come back if absolutely begged to do so, and are confident of world and time on their side.

Servants, coming and going, sometimes see them. They wag their heads, titter.

"Do you know where your mother is?"

Roderick shakes his head. They're looking down at the grass where a hell-bent ant carrying a speck is weaving like a staggering drunk. Roderick proceeds to squish it—naturally, he's a La Marts boy—but Roma stops him.

"That ant is someone's child, you know. The mother will cry."

They both acknowledge Lady Mitter's kindness and care—Roderick a little more, maybe—but the conversation often returns to "real" mothers. Roderick tells Roma he can't hate his real mother, whatever made her do it. He says he remembers her smothering him with love every day of his life till she left him here. He says it's sad that Roma remembers nothing at all, has nothing to remember. That's worse. Roma isn't so sure.

"But if I remembered her I'd miss her more."

Roderick looks down and gravely nods. The fact is indisputable. Mothers known and unknown are both problems if absent. Why did she really leave, he wonders about his mother. Sometimes at night he imagines a stir near him, the faint scent of a woman once so deeply known, loved. He tells Roma this once, a little emotion breaking through his manly, downy stiff upper lip.

Roma nods gravely too. "My mother most definitely comes at night. It's easier for ghosts, you see. They can go anywhere, any time." Roderick is slightly miffed. Roma has this knack for taking other people's special powers and experiences and squaring them with her own exploits and so diminishing them.

Roma can sense Roderick is becoming aloof. She changes the conversation. "So what will I do when you are sailing in ships?"

Roderick decides to forgive her; she's more stranded than he is. He also knows that of the two of them, he's Lady Mitter's favorite.

"*Arrey*, you'll be there too, *naa*!" Roderick says grandly, having temporarily, for argument's sake at least, accepted his fate as Roma's intended, and his confidence fills the sails of their imaginary boat. It's a notable act of kindness for him to be more Indian than English in that moment with that pidgin duo: arrey and naa.

Nowadays, if he steals something particularly nice from the kitchen, he keeps some of it for Roma. If he finds a curious pebble or piece of broken glass, he offers it to her. They're setting up a little household, a treasury, an armory—things lost and found—on their pirate vessel.

Part 5:
India Roars, 1919–

CHAPTER 26

In April 1919 children and peons face a reckoning. The British haven't kept their word about giving Indians home rule status after the first great war. Next day Sir Naren froths at the furious reports in *Amritabazar Patrika*.

"Indians who died fighting for the Raj in the Great War? Riffraff! Village idiots and gadabouts! What if a million of them died?" Sir Naren rails. Everybody knows that the Indian veterans of the war were hardly given a welcome, leave alone a hero's welcome. But that's the fault of the nationalists too. Their antics have drawn people's attention away from the godforsaken soldiers.

"There are millions and millions more to take their place. This is a country of peons and children, and since when have peons and children acquired the right to rule?" Gandhi with his mad ideas about noncooperation and civil disobedience—*Satyagraha*, the madman calls it—is just creating cannon fodder and only one thing can come of it, etc., etc. . . .

Perhaps the empire is in accord with Sir Naren's population control theories. News spreads that the English Colonel Reginald Dyer ordered firing on thousands of peaceful protesters in Jalianwalla Bagh, Amritsar, the Punjab, a day ago. Hundreds of men, women and children tried their desperate, screaming best to crash past the gates and claw up the walls surrounding the garden. How could they? Dyer ordered the gates closed before ordering the firing. His aim, he would later declare stiffly and stolidly, was not to stop the assembly but to punish the dratted Indians. Stampeding crowds were surely and swiftly brought down by fusillade like partridges in flight. The fusillade didn't stop until the ammunition ran out.

Women tried to save themselves by jumping into wells with their children. They couldn't. Death's angel in the form of a zealous English officer picked off each soul thrashing toward life. It was a massacre.

But this kind of thing is never good for business. Sir Naren harrumphs and wonders aloud what new brew of propaganda the imbecile nationalists will concoct now. In the end this is how Gandhi is becoming such a big man, a saint, he avers. Because of nationalists blowing up bombs everywhere they can squeeze in. "Dreadful scoundrels, both sorts," Sir Naren says. "Everywhere you look, marching and shouting about home rule, rights for Indians. Balderdash and poppycock!"

"Indians!" He says to his wife as she sits at her toilet before that evening's soiree at some British official's house, she frankly cannot remember which. Prem's hands have been trembling all day. A dense, burgeoning mass seems lodged in her chest. She would like to cry but she can't.

"They pile together and squeal like rats, like they say the Jews do in Europe."

Prem says nothing, but Sir Naren catches her looking at him with an oblong glance full of . . . what? He doesn't know, can't say; it does give him a short pause. But now he can't resist prodding her a little further, deeper.

"Now probably some rascals somewhere, egged on by that disgraceful Gandhi, will make spectacular fools of themselves by blowing themselves up in a damn fool attempt to kill some English judge. They'll immediately become martyrs and heroes. And then there'll be police reprisals, and a few more fellows will hang. And Gandhi will start another fast, or go to jail. And then it will be back to business as usual."

"Why do you say such things?" Prem turns and asks her husband. "Are you not an Indian?" Her steady gaze burns holes in his bravado. "Or is it because you want to see how far you can provoke me?" Muttering but discomfited, Sir Naren leaves the bedroom to wait in the car for his lady.

Born in Murree, Punjab, in the foothills of the heavenly Himalayas, Colonel Reginald Edward Harry Dyer ordered repeat firing on the folks he grew up among but clearly considers dangerous. At his court martial he says he ordered the firing because conditions in Punjab are incendiary. People don't understand, he says, how bad things are. "India does not want self-government," he will write soon afterwards. "She doesn't understand it," he will assert, stiff-necked.

He will be relieved of his duties and his post, but he will become a hero for some people in England. The man of the hour who knew what to do. Dying in Longford Ashton a decade later—a venerable burger padded up by the twenty-six-thousand-British-pounds-sterling sympathizers and subscribers raised for him after his disgraceful dismissal from service—he will admit he still doesn't understand what he did wrong, and will rest his appeal in the court of his maker.

They say people saw Dyer's troops reloading and shooting at peacefully gathered civilians as Dyer repeatedly, imperturbably said, "Fire!"

So? Don't people understand the nature of power?

Sir Naren cannot retreat entirely at his wife's aggression, or his authority and all-knowingness would lie in pieces. During the car ride towards profit and pleasure, he resumes chuckling about the idiocy of grown men who pretend they aren't so and go around acting like schoolboys: chanting slogans, lighting firecrackers, sulking in corners, refusing food. Satyagraha, indeed.

"Hogwash and populism." Indians, all squealers and con artists.

"Maybe you don't understand the people," Prem counters. Coldly.

"The people don't matter!" Sir Naren retorts. "The people are a bunch of sheep. If you had had any real education you would have known about Thomas Malthus, who thought population control was a great idea. And what better way is there to achieve that but to mow down a few thousand heads that deserve it?"

Though she is stunned, though she feels that her heart will one day hammer out of her trembling, small frame, Prem says, "Well, you see, you married me and brought me here to your dollhouse, so I really didn't have a chance to get a real education. And by mowing down a few thousand heads presumably you mean shooting hundreds of defenseless men, women, and children in the back."

When the car arrives at the arched portico of the grand home of the host whose name she can't recall through the fog of her fury, Prem breezes right past her husband and into the brilliantly lit drawing room where people are mingling, muzzling, and mouthing mutual admiration and adoration. And suddenly her tears overflow and she has to hurry past the guests to have her cry and powder her face in the toilet room.

Chapter 27

Time, as it flows through these days, months, and years, is a dreamy schizophrenic. India has been a land of a thousand mutinies, and sometimes it feels like there will always be another one around the bend. And another, and another. And where will all these mutinies lead? Will freedom from the British really come one day? What color will be the light of that day? Shine on what? Light up the ancient, unruly land how? Will the butchery and sacrifice of the young and the old and resisters of all stripes—maybe Sir Naren is right that the bombs of terrorists shake the empire to its core and make Gandhi's peace work possible—add up to independence?

Independence on the minds of Indians. One day, someday, independence for India, India for Indians. People in the streets go around singing again the elegy of that eighteen-year-old boy from 1909: "*Ekbar Biday dao Ma, ghurey ashi.*"

His name was Khudiram Bose. Eighteen-year-old Khudiram joined the nationalist terrorists, the Anushilan Samiti, killed two Englishwomen (unintentionally), was tried, and convicted. Went to his death erect and smiling, never quailed during his trial, or his execution. In his memory the song:

> "*Ekbar Biday dao Ma, ghurey ashi.*
> *Hanshi hanshi porbo phanshi dekhbe bharotbashi. . . ."*

> "Mother, give me leave now so I may get on my way.
> I'll hang with a smile on my face, so my people can see the way. . . ."

His associate Prafulla Chaki remained less erect. He was captured and beheaded, his head sent as assurance to the authorities of the proper execution of the rule of law in British India.

Prem secretly subscribes to the nationalist organ *Amritabazar Patrika* while Sir Naren believes only the pro-British *Statesman* enters the house. Prem was nine in 1909 when Khudiram Bose, orphan schoolboy, was executed for planting a bomb intended for a British magistrate that mistakenly ended up killing two Englishwomen. But what a bomb it was! Now she understands. That bomb snapped in half the course of revolutionary struggle between those who, led by Gandhi, wanted peaceful noncooperation as the means to achieve freedom, and those who like Khudiram in Bengal, and later Bhagat Singh in Punjab—and yet to come, decades later, Bengal's own Subhash Chandra Bose—took up arms to force the British to 'Quit India.'

Prem isn't sure who's right. As she reads *Amritabazar*, her cheeks burn, her throat tightens. There's an exhilaration in imagining the bloodcurdling sounds that bring death and terror to usurpers and despots; that deafen English eardrums, rattle the windows of the Governor General's office; shake a throne very far away, illuminated, it is said, by the world's greatest diamond Kohinoor, stolen from India.

There's mourning in imagining a boy whose shoeless feet hung in the wind, his mother—the whole country, since that poor woman herself died of cholera years ago—crying. In thinking of other stubborn, fierce young men in secret cells, abandoned warehouses, and jungle caves—dedicating their short lives to Mother India and freedom, dying in notorious British jails and torture chambers, or with a bullet in the back—there's pride. Prem finds herself humming Khudiram's dirge when she's alone sometimes.

Battle comes home, of course. One day as Prem sits in her private parlor facing Sir Naren's fabulous, stern library across the hallway, she hears commotion. Sobbing, maybe a scuffle . . . then the thud of a fall. She sighs, cocks her ear, waits for something more to happen. The sobbing becomes high-pitched wailing. She rings her bell. When the maid comes in she asks what's going on.

The maid says, "It's Roderick *baba*, madam . . . very naughty—he wouldn't give Harish baba his BB gun. They fought and . . ." She stops there.

"Bring them in!" Prem says, suddenly anxious. "What are you standing there for?"

Harish is brought in first—furious, rumpled, scratched.

"What happened?" Prem asks him.

Harish is too furious to be coherent, so the maid explains again.

"It's Roderick baba, madam. He didn't give the gun. Harish baba hit him and then when Harish baba tried to get it . . ."

Prem sees the small bruise on the right side of Harish's forehead and stares at it. The boy is now nearly boiling over, his screams piercing the skies. Then he throws himself on the carpet, bangs the back of his head against the floor, and starts wriggling like a beetle on its backside. The picture of torture.

Prem tells the maid, "Bring Roderick here."

Roderick can't be found. Prem orders a search. Everywhere. Of everything.

Half an hour later Roderick is brought in. At fourteen, he's skinny but too big for his clothes, his long pants stopping short inches above his ankles. He's missing a shoe.

"Why did you beat Harish?" Prem asks. She notices Roderick's mouth trembling slightly. He stares down at the carpet, the manfully wriggling Harish emitting more trilling shrieks, his curiosity to know what happens next getting a little better of his self-pity and righteous rage. Roderick says he can't explain why or how he's done it. The BB gun is Harish's, yes. Harish even has a little pony that he's afraid of, never rides. All that can be gathered is that Harish cocked his BB gun at a bird's nest on a tree, calling its little residents "*Jalian-walla*" and saying, "Fire!" Before he could let fly, though, Roderick ran up to him, snatched the gun away, and knocked him down in the process. Harish hit his head falling and got the bruise.

"It was nice to prevent him shooting the bird, but you shouldn't have let him fall, dear." Prem knows boys will be boys, and Roderick is generally a very good boy, kind to Harish.

"But he was calling the birds Jalianwalla Bagh!"

"He's little, so he heard—"

"No! That's teaching him cruelty. Who could be worse than General Dyer? Harish should never think of being like General Dyer!"

Roderick is crying. Prem looks closer at him. His eyes are reddened; he's been crying a while, maybe . . .

"Yes, I fully agree with you, but Harish—"

"Because of him, all English people look bad!" And finally Roderick's feelings wrestle him down into hiccupping, agonized sobs.

It takes Prem a second to separate the "him" from Harish. Roderick means Dyer. But something more bothers her.

"Now, buck up, my little man—" she begins, as she sometimes hears Sir Naren talk to him.

"I don't want to be the only one in school who has . . . who is . . . English . . . but . . ." Roderick can't finish his sentence. Prem sees that his face is flushed, his throat is tight, and the veins at the base of his neck are prominent, rigid. Instinctively she reaches out to him. He steps back as if she were a snake. Prem's hands freeze in midair, as her heart does inside her. With fear. Regret. Pain. It's no use talking. Roderick is a sensitive boy, more sensitive than most boys his age. Some natures are too tender to romp away humiliation and cruelty.

"You're not the only one, dear boy," she says softly, unsure what to do with her arms now.

"You don't know. All the boys like me are called names. The English boys don't allow us to play with them, and the Indian boys won't talk to us."

After a pause Prem ventures, "But you know they are wrong, don't you? You know you're a special boy, a good boy—"

"I don't want to be special! I just want to be ordinary, like everyone else." His words are steeped in anguish.

Prem understands. She's traveling back to the village, to her girlhood. To being different. Strange. A strange mother. A strange history. Feeling like a pariah and a princess at the same time. She lowers head onto her hands. She weeps unrestrainedly, unabashedly. When she raises her head, there's no one there.

She tells her husband that evening. As she's predicted, he says nothing. If he feels sad, confused, angry, or helpless, he hides it insanely well behind the ever-dignified *Statesman*. She squirms on her chair, waiting patiently like a cat waiting for the owner to wake up from a nap. Sir Naren is keenly aware of her. She knows he is. She waits. After a while he puts the newspaper down, takes off his glasses—a rare thing for him—and wipes them with a muslin handkerchief. Without the monocles his face evokes a plucked chicken, his eyes puckers in naked skin.

"Maybe I should send him away," he says.

"Where? He has no other home."

"Maybe I can find his mother."

Prem was about to speak but is knocked back by this idea, speechless with anger for a while.

"His mother? But . . . he hardly knows her. He wouldn't remember her, and she has never asked for him, so why now? Maybe she's remarried. Maybe she has a whole other family and life. You can't be serious about the idea."

Sir Naren blinks five or six times. Rarely has he been faced with a problem of this sort. Also, he can feel a tug and heaviness in his own heart. Send Roderick away? The truth is that Sir Naren can't imagine that anymore. He can't imagine his life without the boy.

"Maybe then we can admit him to another school, where he won't be treated like a pariah by the white boys."

"Listen, wherever he goes to school he will never blend in or fit in fully. The truth is the truth: he's half of this and half of the other. Roderick shouldn't be moved. He shouldn't feel like a pebble kicked around from here to there. This is all the home he has."

"Thanks to you, madam," comes Sir Naren's ready, piercing reply. And at this double perfidy—knowing well that Sir Naren has long loved Roderick at least as well as he loves Harish, as indeed the whole household knows—Prem's anger crests and drives out her restraint. How dare her husband blame her for a decision that has been nothing but good for Roderick? What other wife would have done this? Or a lot less? Oh, men! Prem could wring her husband's neck. To pretend to be disinterested, detached! While she, who does the real work of living and loving as he twiddles his thumbs, has to bear the entire burden of such decisions. Perhaps Prem can be forgiven for forgetting that nine years ago she essentially gave Sir Naren an ultimatum: if Roderick goes, she goes.

Dinner is announced and the lord and the lady are forced to separate and behave.

CHAPTER 28

Intramural civil war deepens. Harish, who used to worship Roderick, is now sullen, morose, and irate around him. The bruise that was at first on the forehead seems to have traveled and settled somewhere deeper, and he frequently throws tantrums and picks fights about priority and preference. It must be him, not Roderick, riding with the driver in the front seat. It must be him seated at his father's right hand while Roderick has to sit at the farther end of the table, with Roma who fears Sir Naren like an ogre between them. Roderick mustn't be allowed to say the short Christian prayer that he usually says at table. Most shockingly, Harish sings a ditty he's made up.

"Roddy, Roddy, he's no body . . ."

He is threatened with a whole month of having to go to bed two hours early for his bad behavior and manners.

"Is this what the fathers are teaching you in school—to be vindictive? Tell me, is this why you go to such a nice school?" asks Prem—but Harish is nothing daunted.

"You send Roddy to the same school so how can it be such a special school? It's only a school," Harish quips.

One night Roderick asks to be passed some salt and Harish bursts out, "Get your own bloody damn salt, you English dog, for you shall no longer take food away from the mouths of Indians! Gandhi-ji will teach you a lesson . . . and . . . you can't have any!" He somewhat nervously keeps an eye on his father who is apoplectic and immobilized by outrage, but goes on, realizing that his father is temporarily paralyzed.

Talk of salt and the British tax on it has been in the air since the first Indian Congress meeting in 1885. Indians mustn't make their own salt; the British will supply them with it, imported from Britain, at a higher cost. Really rubbing salt into the wounded heart of a country where the popular saying "I've eaten your salt" signifies lifelong loyalty. Eating British salt. Insult added to injury.

Sir Naren finally squeaks when he can talk again.

"Gandhi! Again! Look, look!"—this while looking at Prem who would appear hereby to be the true, prime instigator of Gandhi and his whole Swadeshi or India for Indians movement—"Look at what that disgraceful beggar has created. Monsters! I say, monsters! Madam, I hope you have a fair idea how to quell such disagreeable ideas, madam, because . . ."

Prem stares at her motley tableau, clutching her head with her right hand. Her eight-year-old son a budding nationalist though only recently found shooting Jalianwalla Bagh protesters off a bird's nest in the back gardens. Roderick—"Roddy"? For God's sake! Poor, dear, dear, sweet Roderick!—the whip-cracking imperialist bested at his own schemes by Gandhi. Roma . . . well, Roma's playing no active role here, but Prem has heard the gossip about Roma's pursuit of Roderick's hand in marriage.

Ekbar biday dao Ma, ghurey ashi. Mother, give me leave now so I can get on my way . . .

The plangent notes play jeeringly in Prem's head as she watches this bathetic farce.

What's happening to the children?

Husband's a giant toad and toady of the British.

A great storm is coming. No one to turn to, to ask questions, get some tarpaulin.

In the whole world, not another woman to creep up to, lay down by. Dhai gone. Lilian gone. What woman, what mother, alone, in this way, can ever map the geology of a child's heart—a heart like a newborn planet—with its incessant earthquakes and volcanoes?

Harish has for some time been in the habit of flattening himself against the mahogany door of his father's library, pressing his ear to the warm, gleaming wood. He's afraid of punishment if he's caught, but not afraid enough to stop. In his head is the growing question: Does his father love him?

He hears his father and Roderick talking in the library, a room no one can enter without his father's permission. So if he's invited Roderick in, Harish wants to know why. That he's five years younger than Roderick doesn't stand in the way of his panicked pique.

He wants to know why his father loves Roderick more than him. It is obvious to everyone that Sir Naren loves Roderick. Sir Naren wouldn't himself be able to say how this happened.

Harish has heard that Roderick is his father's son. The servants are not shy about gossip.

Harish wants to know—has his father ever loved him? Or did he stop loving him because of incidents like the bird shooting and the dinner-table salt-passing thing? Has he been a very bad boy? Is there any way he can make up for it?

"History is a noble subject, my boy, a noble subject. All great men must know history."

His father's voice comes across to Harish like this: Blaw blaw. Blaw blaw blaw. Blaw blaw blaw blaw blaw blaw.

His father never calls him "my boy." Always only "ahem," or "come here." He never asks him about school, about history, about anything.

"Well, my boy, and how is school?"

Or, blaw, blaw blaw blaw blaw blaw?

"Fine, Sir."

"What do you like best? Literature or maths?" Insert requisite syllables of blaw blaw.

"I like history best, sir."

"Very well, very well. History is a noble subject, my boy, a noble subject." Standing outside, Harish makes horrible faces miming both of them as they speak, but especially his father's triple-chinned turkey-gobble oration.

"You may go to England after you finish school, my boy. There you'll be able to pursue many different options: doctor, lawyer, maybe even become a judge. Nothing is impossible for a boy who has courage and his wits about him."

So his father doesn't think he has courage or wits? His father isn't going to send him to England?

So he understands. He has to take care of myself. "I'll go to England first," he says to himself that night in bed.

"I'm going to inherit everything," he tells the servants. "You better do what I tell you or I'll throw you out when I'm master."

Nobody tells Prem this.

Part 6:

Bande Mataram, Calcutta, 1928–

CHAPTER 29

It is 1928, the year of the Simon Commission's visit to India. Somehow the children are alive and eleven (Harish), fourteen (Roma), and fifteen (Roderick). Prem is nearing thirty, and she is rather more beautiful than before. And the Simon Commission—seven wise British magi—comes to India. The Simon Commission has been sent from London to decide the age-old question—that tormented Dyer so—about whether Indians can govern themselves. Because the Congress Party, now the single-minded headwind of the nationalist movement since Khudiram's ilk are mostly dead or rotting in jails, declares that India wants complete independence. *Poorna Swaraj.*

There's an old joke that in Calcutta you can get tiger's milk if you pay enough for it. The joke doesn't mention the right price of tiger's milk. It just uses the word 'enough.'

Independence must be like tiger's milk. Day by day Indians feel that the British have set an unknown price on it that is not about fairness or justice. Its only measure is what the empire calls 'enough.'

Alipore is one of the more sedate, stately parts of Calcutta. Indeed, they say that thirty years ago you could hunt tigers there. Old wives' tales, possibly. But even in stately, sleepy Alipore, people—arms raised, fists clenched—march in the streets saying "Go back, Simon." And they chant "No go! No go!" Actually, that last thing in Bengali is *"Cholbey Na, Cholbey Na!"* which the English might translate as something like "That's not cricket! Howzat!"

Poor Henry Babington Macaulay—could he ever have foreseen this day? Macaulay produced the famous Minutes on Indian Education of 1835, declaring all oriental knowledge to be containable within a single shelf of books written in Europe. Naturally—how could one blame his countrymen and women?—the British then decreed that Indians must be taught European or English curricula in schools and colleges, not traditional Hindu or Muslim ones. At some point such educated Indians came to be called 'Macaulay's Children'—Indian by birth, but European by indoctrination and education. And such Macaulay's Children were the founders fifty years later—1885—of the Congress Party that has since led the charge for independence from the British.

This day in 1928, cricket-mad, rights-sensitive, and independence-hungry, Macaulay's burdensome, troublesome sons and daughters scour the turbid, unbreathable milieu of domination with outrage at 'English dogs' very close kin to "Britons never shall be slaves!" But the British are fairly firmly fixed that Indians never shall be Britons! Put it more plainly—Indians never can be Britons. Because then Britons wouldn't be their masters, Hail Britannia! This seems simple and right. But these Indians—burdensome children—are confused about it, and keep saying, "Complete independence! No more home rule! Only complete independence!"

"Where's Roma?" Prem asks at teatime. Roderick and Harish are attending. Roderick says, "I don't know. Didn't she come home from school?" Harish shrugs. His eyes are firmly focused on the jelly biscuits on the platter before him.

"What do you mean? You haven't seen her since you came home from school?" Typically, the children have a half hour to unpack and undress before tea.

"No I haven't," Harish pipes up, then adds, "She's always late."

This isn't true, in fact quite the contrary. Roma is definitely quite a hearty eater; it isn't like her not to show up for meals. So Prem feels anxiety coil around her chest. "Go find someone," Prem tells Roderick, "and ask them where she is."

"She and the driver haven't come back at all!" Roderick returns red-faced and breathless.

The household stands on its side while sharp inquiries reveal that today of all days, when the Simon Commission protests are especially raging on the streets, Roma and her driver haven't returned. Prem storms at the butler, the cook, the maids, the younger gofers, the smallest fry. Everyone looks worried, everyone hangs their head, but no answers are forthcoming. Prem calls Sir Naren at work. "Call the police," he says and hangs up.

Wouldn't you know it. Kanan, last seen at fifteen, flickers before Prem. That broad, unself-conscious smile; wide-set eyes; pale, sallow skin. Those too-large bony feet and hands.

Don't you start now! I've been her real mother!

"Get the Bentley out immediately," Prem orders. She's going out herself to find Roma. It can't be that hard; a fourteen-year-old can't have gone too far. "Madam, outside there is commotion and much trouble," the driver of that car pleads. "Don't go, madam," the butler says. The servants, soundly and incoherently scolded, are standing in a line in the foyer at the front door, eyes wide, faces stricken.

The Bentley barely travels a mile before Prem sees them. Coming toward the car, toward her, like a great wave. Prem has never seen the sea herself but she imagines this is how it might sound, look. A great, blurry, gray line against the sky, advancing with a muffled roar. Within minutes there are people swarming about the car, peering in. Prem shades her eyes, covers her face, aghast and horrified. Others, less concerned with the contents of a shiny blue behemoth that can only belong to rich people, lurch past, holding up flags with arms shooting up to the sky, mouthing the chords and instruments of the one great patriotic aria: "Go back Simon! Simon go back!" Many people believe that Simon is the name of the king of England, the greatest of greatest Maibaps, trouncing whom gives them an unspeakable, exquisite access to power and pleasure. Some are keeping time with the English chanting, speaking in Bengali, "*Cholbey na! Cholbey na! Cholbey na! Cholbey na!*" The car indeed isn't going anywhere. That's what "*Cholbey na*" means, among other things.

Cannot go on. Must not go on. Doesn't work. This empire thing, it won't work.

Sticks and knuckles tap-tap, then clatter on the car's windows. Prem covers her ears but the chanting is even stronger, louder. A few minutes pass, the driver too petrified to speak to reassure his mistress. Prem hears screams outside the windows. "Hey, rich lady! Get out of your fancy car, lady, and join the march! Join the people of your land. Hey! You! No use hiding! Come out! Out!" The Bentley starts rocking. The crowd has found a new toy to smash, a nice diversion to the dull uniformity of chanting and marching and ordering Simon back.

Children, after all. Naughty. They eagerly join the group lending their shoulders to rocking and thumping the beautiful Bentley—soon to be battered, bruised, headlights smashed, fender kicked in, etcetera—until Prem finally cries out and then screams when she sees the murals of brown, maddened faces pressed against every window, windscreen, and back of the car.

The driver would like to run away but he knows he won't get anywhere. He has no choice but to stay, to seem loyal. He does his best. Prem thinks he is protecting her, and is momentarily overwhelmed by such loyalty, before fear floods her again. Her head swims, her eyes feel heavy and burn. "Please," she whispers. "Please. I haven't done anything . . . please!" She will remember later what she whispers now. *Please. I tried.*

And now out of nowhere come a cavalcade of Indian and British soldiers, policemen, constabulary—on bikes, horses, foot—and the crowd, including those watching her as if she's an animal trapped in a cage, pauses and loosens a little. Prem sees the law enforcement approaching, over the heads of the protesters, like a great ship advancing on roiling water. She hears the thick batons called *laathis* before she sees them.

The men in uniform bring down laathis and rifle butts on the heads, shoulders, faces of the marchers. Her windows nearly cleared, Prem watches—her mouth slack, her heart booming, her blood roaring in her head—the laathi-charge. The marchers' slogan has turned into one immense primeval scream. The sound of hard things slamming down on other things can be heard. The sound of a laathi hitting bone is extraordinarily like wood-chopping or carpentry sounds, Prem thinks. Bodies hitting the ground make more of a muffled thud, like wet laundry hitting patient boulders by the riversides where washerwomen work. There are many sounds. Whistles shrill chaotically over the clashing crowd, and the galloping of a powerful horse beats on the brain like canon fire. Is this how war is, Prem wonders. Is this what Jagat heard during his front days, probably his last? That she remembers him just now doesn't surprise her. There have been other times in the past when—overwhelmed by misery or confusion—she's brought his image out, dusted it, held it cupped in her palm for a few moments, then put it back. She's still crouching in the car; the road has almost cleared. She sees an elderly man, his head bare, his arms raised to cover his face and head, stumbling backward and saying something to a mounted officer. The horseman bends down, leaning over the man, and Prem is relieved that this old man will be taken to jail, most likely, where the beatings will be less random and unsupervised. The horseman moves so fast that Prem doesn't see his free arm arcing down from a high point and bringing his laathi down onto the elderly man's skull. The man drops to the street instantly, and doesn't move. A dark, thick stain spreads around his head, snakes outward. The last thing Prem sees before someone squires her car away from the scene is the horseman, dismounted, bringing his laathi down again and again and again on the thing on the ground that doesn't move.

She cannot speak when she gets home. She has to be rushed upstairs to her bedroom because she has vomited all over herself. No one has ever seen her like this. Her head lolls, her eyes are wide and staring, and vomit is drying over the entire front of her clothes. She's helped upstairs by several people, and gently put to bed. There's no doctor to be had at this moment. A senior maid knows where the sleeping pills are kept and makes her take some. Prem doesn't count. She swallows them and stares up until her eyes close and her breathing slows down.

When she wakes up it is late—she senses it from a habit of exquisite awareness of every movement of every day in the family, as if she were a clock keeping time for those around her. Her eyes are glued and puffy. She rubs them and sits up. Her head hurts dully. Sir Naren is sitting next to her bed in an armchair pulled up for him. They look at each other silently.

"I'm sorry," she says after a minute.

He nods. "How're you feeling?"

"Fine."

Then she remembers and feels her breath shorten. "Where's Roma?"

Slowly Sir Naren says, "Asleep in her room, I imagine."

"You mean she came back?"

"Yes."

Sighing, Prem says, "Please, tell me. Tell me everything."

Sir Naren says, his jaw obviously tight, "Well, it seems I missed the most exciting parts."

Prem looks away for a moment, then looks back. "You know I had to do it." *Please. I tried.*

"I said call the police."

Prem waves her hand away.

"My dear," her husband says, still chewing his words, "in the future, you will never go out alone without my permission. Understood?"

"But that's absurd—"

"Understood? Do you know what state the Bentley came back in?"

Is that what he's unhappy about? Wearying disappointment washes over Prem as she leans back on her pillows. Will it never be something else?

"I suppose so," she says, flatly.

"You could have died."

Ah. A secondary mishap.

"When did Roma come back?"

"A young man brought her home around ten."

Prem looks her question.

"Some young college student apparently. I didn't see him, but probably mixed up in protests too. One of those sorts . . . ," says her husband, relighting his pipe. "He found her with a crowd around Esplanade, he said. Something Sengupta. Said she was marching with them."

"What?" Prem says. It's all she can manage. She would never have imagined this. From Alipore to Park Street's Loreto Convent school is about the same distance as Park Street to Esplanade. Roma walked as far as she is driven to school every day.

"No doubt it will be an interesting conversation tomorrow with her," Sir Naren says and rises. "Good night, my dear, and please do not forget what I said about going out."

Had Prem felt less exhausted she would have left the bed and gone to Roma's room right then. But even as she seethes watching her husband recede—he's going to sleep in his library tonight so as to not disturb her is what he said but she doubts that the cause is so charitable—a tidal wave of fatigue overpowers her. She closes her eyes for a few minutes and sleeps twelve hours.

The next morning she summons Roma to her bedside.

The driver who was supposed to pick her up says he couldn't even get close to the school that afternoon. He says he kept driving around trying to find *Missy Baba* until the rampaging crowds started attacking cars and vehicles nearby at random.

"What happened?" Prem asks Roma as steadily as she can.

Roma lowers her eyes and keeps them lowered.

"How did you get lost?" Another silence, and Prem feels a panic rise inside her.

"What happened, Roma? How did you get lost? Did you get hurt?"

Perhaps Roma senses Mashimoni's concern and anguish as much as her anger. Perhaps not. Without looking up she mutters, "I didn't get lost."

"Then how did you end up in Esplanade with the marchers?"

"I left school," Roma says.

Prem doesn't think she's heard right.

"Sorry, what did you say?"

"I left school," Roma says, now louder. Prem can now hear her breathing harder. She reaches out to grasp Roma's hand and Roma skips back just out of reach.

"Come here, Roma!" Prem says. "Or I'll be really angry with you."

Roma manages to sit gingerly on the edge of Prem's bed but still out of her reach.

"I wanted to serve Mother India," she says.

Prem feels as though a million ants have begun crawling under her skin nibbling away at years of hard-earned English flavoring; an intolerable slow burn of indignation makes her coffee cup shake in her hands. She shuts her eyes for a moment. Maybe when she opens them there will be another Roma sitting before her.

"You are serving Mother India by studying and growing up to be a nice young woman."

"No," Roma says. "I'm not."

Prem says, "You are not what? Studying . . . ?" Panic makes her squeeze her eyes shut again only to see clearly the millions of ants under her skin, everywhere.

"I'm not serving the Mother."

"Who told you that?"

"I know. We like the British and the British are draining India's life blood."

"We?"

"Us."

"Us?"

"In this house."

"Who in this house? What are you talking about?"

Roma hesitates, judges the distance between herself and Prem, then says, "In this house we act like the British and we live like the British—"

Prem wants to scream at the girl. "Who tells you such things, Roma?" When Roma doesn't answer she can't hold it back anymore. She shouts, making Roma start and cringe.

"You will never say such monstrous things again in front of me, you understand? Who told you that marching in the streets will make India free? Don't you know what Gandhi-ji says? If you want to serve Mother India, why don't you listen to him? Those marchers tried to kill me yesterday! Do you want me to be killed? You want to march with the people who wanted to kill me?"

The body on the ground flashes up before her. Would that elderly man have joined the marchers around her car, screaming for her blood? And the women she heard screaming? Were they coming to kill her before the police arrived? She knows that she'll never know. She's glad that she'll never know. And now her task is to get this nonsense out of this wayward child's head and bring her back to normal.

"You don't want India free, Mashimoni."

"How dare you!" Prem explodes despite her very best, most strenuous effort. "What do you know about how to free India? Eh? The Congress and Gandhi-ji are having so many meetings with the British for India's independence. You know more than them?"

Oh she should never have secretly brought the *Amritabazar Patrika* into the house. Roderick and Harish have had to learn Latin and Greek at school, but Roma learns Bengali. How careless and irresponsible of her. It's hardly the poor girl's fault after all. She must take her fair share of blame. No more *Amritabazar* in the house.

"Everyone knows Lord Mitter is a bumlicker of the British," Roma says quietly.

Prem stares, speechless. Did the girl just use her husband's name and the word bumlicker in the same sentence? What is she to do now? Should she call Sir Naren in? Should she order punishment for Roma? What can she do and what should she do? Who is this creature? How has she managed to make this thing? Is Kanan laughing at her now wherever she is?

"Go away," she tells Roma. "Go away and wait in your room. There will be punishment for you, and then you will be truly sorry for what you've done. Go! Now!" Her voice cracks as she finishes after the girl has already left the bedroom and closed the door behind her.

Prem rings the bell furiously for a maid to come to her. She needs more coffee. But even the bell makes her remember the whistles blowing the previous day. The ants are now crabs, with vicious pincers and claws. When the maid comes she also brings Prem a letter. It has already been opened, but neatly and surgically, with a pen knife. Sir Naren, of course. Normally he would not open his wife's personal mail. The envelope is clearly addressed to Prem. This is a dare, an insult.

Picking up the letter she can make out the stamp of the issuing post office, the name of her village on it.

The letter inside is from the village estate's head Munshi. Babu-ji has passed away.

CHAPTER 30

Saroj will be made to come live with Prem in Calcutta, in her son-in-law's house. This is unthinkable, an absolute fall from grace. And had her husband been alive, the two would have concurred at least in this. You don't ever go to live in your daughter's husband's house, not beyond the possible customary, sometimes ceremonial, one night or so. After one night, staying on in your daughter's husband's house becomes infamous. Saroj has never stepped foot in her daughter's Alipore Mansion. Neither she nor Manohar Mishra ever saw their grandson. Sir Naren wouldn't risk sending his only official heir to the dirty, pestilential village and the Mishras of course couldn't come to Mitter Mansion.

The same rule doesn't apply to your son's wife's house. In your son's wife's house, in your son's house, that is, you can not only stay longer, but you can even stay long; indeed, you can stay forever.

This is how the strange, unheard of migration happens: Saroj comes to live with her daughter, in her son-in-law's house, because she's in advanced dementia.

She'd been nearly gone from the world around her even before her husband died, of course. But now Saroj has become quite unmanageable, infantile. In the village, people call it being taken by a ghost. Ghost-taken, they say. Sometimes she forgets to wear any clothes. The maids find her sitting naked on her bed, or at the open window on the ledge. They have to wrestle her into her widow's short sari, wrap it around her like a tight wrapper around a hard lozenge, while she screams and curses, demanding to be let go. Sometimes she doesn't eat for whole days because every time the maids bring her food she hurls it away, or sometimes kicks the massive brass plate across the floor—preternaturally strong there—asking how a body can eat again within an hour of eating last.

Then sometimes she demands to be fed every fifteen minutes, whining that the servants are in a conspiracy to starve her to death, it's been so long since she's been given any food.

She still stays up most nights staring out at the cold, rolling fog in the fields, but calls frequently for the visitor knocking at the front gates to be let in, immediately, without roguery or delay, or she'll have the servants skinned alive. Dementia has—perhaps blessedly—released the fury so long packed inside her. Sometimes she cries all afternoon or evening, calling for Munia to come back. There's no one called Munia at the village house. No one knows what she's talking about.

She's become thoroughly hell-bent on tricking the help and going to the toilet anywhere, any time. Just squats, lifts up the hem of her sari, and lets loose. When the maids rush in they see a peculiarly feline gloating on her face, as if she's just dispatched some prey and is smacking her chops. Curiously enough, these days she looks cheerier overall than she ever has.

This is what is called being had by ghosts. Ghosts or a ghost have taken the person who is displaying such symptoms, and are keeping them for their own. A second childhood is the other name for it. Aptly, for it is well known that ghosts are a routine part of children's inner worlds. In second childhood, therefore, ghosts, children, ghosts of children, ghostly children are all one tight-knit family.

No surprise, people say; the woman has been ghost-taken for a long time already. When that maid everyone called The Dusty One couldn't be found one day, Saroj had become hysterical and uncontrollable, demanding she be brought back at any cost. That good, kind husband Manohar Mishra sent out search parties for her but The Dusty One was never found. After that, Saroj got progressively worse in her memory and her behavior. And when Manohar Mishra died, at first she said she didn't know anyone of that name. When they took her to the body laid out in the courtyard for the last journey, they had difficulty getting her close to it. When she finally did, she paid no attention to the departed but looked around wildly and began screaming. Something about an older brother-in-law who was coming for her, and don't let him come near, please don't. . . . Manohar Mishra didn't have an older brother. The doctor had to be called to give her an injection for sleep.

All this the old Munshi writes in his letter to Lady Mitter.

Finally, the old estate Munshi writes Lady Mitter that it would be well, indeed essential, to come get her mother. The farm and ranch help are not what they used to be. The new generation and supply of servants will not easily, loyally, clean an old woman's excrement and effluvia, and tolerate sharp-edged bronze vessels—plates, bowls, glasses, water jugs, anything that's at hand—lobbed at them in screeching, hissing fury. Indeed, maybe some of them will become rough, violent with the elderly woman.

So Prem has to travel with a small entourage to the village. Sir Naren categorically refuses to accompany her or let her take Harish who is in any case too young and too boisterous to be of much help. "Take any or every male servant in the house with you; they will be able to handle the difficulties," is his dictum. She does; with them goes Roderick—gentle, kind, meek Roderick, now almost sixteen—not her blood, but certainly a part of her soul.

Prem faces this journey as one might face the hangman's noose. Why does life force her to return to the village? There she discovered early that neither cruelty nor kindness means anything. She doesn't want to return; she'll be reminded that as long as one doesn't have the power to make, break, take, keep, and throw away things, one might as well be dead. That Kanan's love and friendship, in the end, meant little more than Mai-ji's cruelty. These are not clarifications and realizations Prem wants to renew.

The train ride itself is salty with anguish and ambiguity. With little, half-hearted cruelties. Though she's in a first-class compartment, though Sir Naren's status and money earn her a place in the air-conditioned first class in which whites travel, that she must travel by train is itself a slap in her face, she thinks. Hadn't Sir Naren come in his own automobile entourage to pluck her rose off that hard thorny bush called Bengal-Bihar Province? The way the spongy-nosed Scots, the Irish with pinched faces and slits for eyes, and the shuttered, apoplectic English assess her and Roderick, Roderick's lineage an entire cesspool of speculation no doubt—have elite Indian woman started having liaisons now and resulting Kutcha Bachchas?—and the way white women titter as they sail past her native caravan which is unselfconsciously, cacophonously perched on berths and flopped on the floor of the AC coupe, make her want to hiss: "My husband's bastard—I beg pardon; not mine! Half yours!"

But naturally when the whites flitting past pretend to be courteous by stiffly doffing their hats at her and stretching their tight mouths into cadaverous grins made of equal parts condescension and curiosity, she too nods and grimaces back while sotto voce muttering ripe, homegrown curses she hadn't remembered in decades. Roderick shrinks in a corner of the coupe, his arms folded, his chin dug into the space between his clavicles. It's for him she feels real sadness. She feels rage on his behalf. That the whites shouldn't recognize their own ancestral fingerprints in what they're reducing to a quivering, forlorn mass. *Who do you think you're looking at?* That they have the gall to saunter past, scrutinizing him freely as if he were a freak on display. When she meets his eyes, he returns the intelligent, kind smile so characteristic of him. And a heat starts in her chest and travels up to her temples. *Please. I tried.*

CHAPTER 31

When the train groans and clangs onto the thin strip of concrete that passes for a platform, a torrent of jarring and jangling sensations overwhelms her. There's the hot, sour smell of metal on metal; the smoking and hissing of the train engine; flickering gloom spangled by hurricane lanterns seemingly jigging alone through the air; the hawking of tea and puffed rice to travelers groggy with resignation and sleep; the thwacking and thumping of woven baskets of goods and merchandise hitting concrete and sending up small clouds of dust; the intoxicating over-ripeness of bruised mangoes, guavas, and jackfruit filling some of the baskets; shouts and oaths from wrung wraiths scrambling to keep pace with the timepiece called commerce. Prem has leapt across the chasm called time and landed again in the place called girlhood.

In the whispering, bird-calling dark, Prem and her retinue of retainers, luggage, and Roderick bump and roll along the village road rutted with bullock cart tracks, in a tonga hired for them by the ancient servant—the very one who once ushered Kanan into another horse-drawn tonga with a horse inside it as well as outside—who has come to meet them. Roderick looks around, dazed and silent.

In the plangent moonshine Prem sees small birds dart into the dull silver of a pond and fly away into the dark woods surrounding. She nearly cries out at the sight, the unfathomable mystery of life outside the maze of modern living. When did she last see a flock of birds? She rediscovers a tourniquet of mourning and remorse wound around her heart. Bitterness too. And again, helplessness. It's been more than twenty years. It's not the village she knew and she's not the girl who left it. But again, here, she's helpless. The birds, probably kingfishers, rise again in a hazy murmuration and vanish into the darkening skies like paper kites into clouds. Only silence remains, punctuated by the rattle of metal and wood and the clip-clop of hooves.

Past the creaking balsa wood gates that once seemed massive and magnificent, Prem descends the shallow set of steps into the old courtyard that used to ricochet with noise. There's no one there at this hour of evening, and all remnants of active living and trading are subdued. "Not like it was in the old times; not so many people here anymore," the faithful old servant says. He quietly gestures toward a room at the back of the house, that area into which she so often saw her mother vanish. They are to go there. Clearly, he doesn't want to delay the inevitable. Crossing the courtyard swiftly, they climb another short set of steps toward the back and interior of the house. This lumbering old family home was built around this once vibrant courtyard where lamps burned after dark for hours in recessed sconces as darkness descended like a slow-flowing elixir. No lamps here now. Only shadows in chiaroscuro. Even the moon has gone behind clouds.

They reach a room set well beyond all the others. Prem knows this room well as the room she never knew well.

At the far end of it, near the still wide-open window, sits a silhouette clothed in brilliant white. Prem stumbles slightly over the threshold, even the nervous energy gathered up in the last days gone from her. The figure's cropped head of hair is also nearly all white. In the light of a single oil lamp this much can be made out, but not much more. The silhouette in white is looking outside, through the window, at the darkened fields. There isn't much in the room. Just the massive old four-poster bed, a small table beside it, and a traditional standing rack to hold a few clothes and towels.

"Mai-ji."

The white-haired head turns around, though in this light the expression on Saroj's face can't be seen.

"Mai-ji." Prem stays where she is, doesn't move toward Saroj.

Saroj says nothing. She stares long and hard, not at Prem, but at Roderick.

"Gora?" Everyone can tell who she's referring to. She thinks a white man has somehow slipped into her sanctum sanctorum.

Saroj's voice rises. "Get the gora out of here! Get him out!" There's panic, grit, and suffering in the cry.

"The gora has broken into my house and now my room! Who brought him here? You?" The question is for her daughter.

"And who are you?"

Prem motions Roderick out of the room. He backs out.

But Saroj cannot be stopped. "Filthy devil! Monster! They let him do it! They took everything! Now he's back for what? Who let that man in? Is this still a Hindu household?"

From other parts of the house a few footsteps can be heard heading toward the scene. Prem shuts the door behind her and steps into the room. Saroj comes tripping and swaying toward her, obviously unsteady on her feet. Saroj's eyes are wide, her face hideous in weakness and revulsion.

Then she slumps, quite suddenly, and crumples to the floor near Prem's feet. Prem has taken her shoes off before the courtyard, of course, but still scuttles back.

"Munia? You finally came?" Saroj asks. The eyes of mother and daughter lock and hold each other for what seems like ages but is actually only a few moments.

CHAPTER 32

Prem and her entourage bring Saroj back, semisedated and bundled—opium has regrettably had to be administered in milk—the train coupe ritually washed and purified by the village priest, though Saroj isn't aware of her surroundings in her only semiawake state. A day passes. During them she feeds slowly, submissively from a bowl of rice and yogurt Prem holds to her face, her ire and panic at Roderick and the rest apparently evaporated, her cognition of her surroundings suspended or at least quieted. She looks around the interior of the coupe sometimes, but mostly her face is turned to the window, as if she's siphoning in the land through which the train barrels. No matter in what direction she is placed, her head inevitably swivels toward the window. She stares out. She remains staring for hours, until she becomes drowsy again from the pills given to her, pills she mostly accepts without struggle. Once she asks Prem—whom she apparently now recognizes—if the fair-skinned boy is her grandson. Prem says yes.

And when she is escorted up the great staircase of Mitter Mansion to her own room at the far end of the family floor, Sir Naren emerges from the library and smokes his pipe, looking at her processional ascent. Prem hovers while two maids hold Saroj gently by the elbows and keep assuring her that they are both, indeed, Munia, and that she will see 'him' soon enough. Prem doesn't understand why her mother asks after her husband whom she ignored and avoided all of the time he was alive, but she doesn't really need or want to know. Her duty is done, for now.

The family doctor comes and confirms the village doctor's diagnosis: Saroj's mind is far gone. She's strong and well preserved though, so he recommends a full-time caretaker to control her during her violent outbursts or raging, weeping fits. A full-time nurse is appointed. Maybe because the nurse wears her starched sari the modern way—across the bosom and falling down her back on the left side—and also a severely modest blouse, Saroj never asks her if she's Munia or about 'him.' In any case the Malayali nurse doesn't speak Bengali or Hindi and mostly does her work through signs and cheery expressions. She's a kind young woman and also considers this job easy and a boon, given that usually her charges are moribund or incontinent or completely vegetative.

Then one day in her meanderings Saroj sees Nakul, a servant in the household. He's a good-looking young man, about twenty years old. His curly hair, bleached by the sun of his father's diminishing fields in Bengal-Bihar where he broke his back for eight of his first twelve years, is cut short to the nape of his neck. His eyes are a simmering green that startle especially on his sunburnt brown skin. Saroj sees him and, as the Malayali nurse Mary Joseph reports later, she seems struck by lightning. As if something cuts right through her. She lurches toward Nakul. Nakul is carrying a tray holding cups and saucers. Tea is made and drunk many times in the house throughout the day and almost half the night. It is one of Nakul's jobs to serve tea and take away tea things whenever the bell for tea rings in the kitchen partly modeled on English homes. He sees Saroj coming toward him and tries to step aside, but she won't let him. Instead, she grips him first by the shoulders, then takes his chin between her thumb and forefinger. As Mary Joseph mildly buzzes around her to let the boy go, Saroj peers at him for seconds before saying, "Oh-ho-ho, are you here, then? At last? Where had you gone? How are you, my dearest, my golden one? Why didn't you come sooner to me?"

Nakul is temporarily paralyzed, but only physically. He hasn't served and survived in this great house for years—cuffed and slapped around in the early ones by petty tyrants in the underfoot regime downstairs—without learning to spot the buttered side of bread. Though he doesn't come up to the family floor frequently, like everyone in the house he knows the old woman by reputation, and his quick brain advises him that she being the lady's mother and also 'ghost-taken,' is on a loose rein. He says nothing and allows Saroj to peer, poke, pull, and probe.

Saroj runs her dry, bony hands over Nakul's head and forehead, brings them to his temples, scraping evil spirits off him with her bunched hands and throwing them over her shoulders. She looks fixedly at him and a contented, half smile plays about her mouth. Her eyes glisten. "God listens. God listens.

May God bless you, bless you," she mutters as she repeats her evil-removing gesture. She asks him many more questions about what he has eaten and when he will come up to the bedroom, and only when the nurse reminds her that it's time for her meal—she always and only eats in her room, and Sir Naren will also have it so—does she let go of Nakul's shoulder and arm with one last warm, lingering stroke and withdraws, reassuring Nakul that she will see him very soon indeed, he mustn't worry.

Nobody gets it. When Prem is told about this she listens quietly, a faraway look in her eyes. She says nothing, and gives no orders against Nakul meeting Saroj. Saroj, therefore, sees Nakul here, there, and everywhere and repeats her behavior, asks the maids and Nurse Joseph frequent questions about Nakul's day, food, activities, and health. And at least once a day Nakul has to visit her in her room, or she tears her room apart, Malayali nurse and maids notwithstanding. And Prem says nothing.

CHAPTER 33

Prem is stalling. Prem is balancing, juggling, rearranging—if you will—her crises. Because now it is time for Prem to turn her attention back to Roma, whose reckless revolt has still not been addressed, judged, quelled, punished. This language is of course Sir Naren's, not Prem's. Roma is called in after school to Prem's little court: her cozy, comfortable parlor. Fitted in pink, yellow, and green satin, silk and brocade; shaded by delicate muslin and lace curtains overlaid with blue velvet panels; decorated with gilded and painted porcelain and china—soulfully naked Grecian ladies; miniature Georgian-era high-heeled shoes with oversize gilt buckles; porcelain kittens curled around wool balls; fat, bouncy babies and puny mothers; winged cupids circling a humble cottage— gilt-framed glossy photos of Rudolph Valentino, Gloria Swanson, Pola Negri, Mary Pickford, Douglas Fairbanks, and more; fringed, rococo lampshades held up by embracing lovers in painted wood or ceramic, and so forth. No Joshua Reynolds types here. Hardly an apt site for the dispensation of blind justice.

Roma stands on one foot in a frozen hopscotch, regarding Prem closely.

"Please put your foot down," Prem begins.

"Why?" Roma's face is darker than ever since for a while she's been spending many late afternoons out in the back lawns.

"Because it is not ladylike to do that."

Roma says nothing more. She slowly brings her pendant foot down as if she's balancing an egg on that knee.

"Why?" Prem asks.

"Why what?"

"You took such a horrible risk, and you also put me in danger. Why did you do that? Who told you that you could leave school and join the marchers?"

"My conscience," Roma says.

"Your conscience? What do you mean by that?"

Roma ponders, then says, "I want to serve my country."

Prem doesn't gawk—it would be impossible for her to do so—but her mouth opens a little wider than usual. She recovers, gulps, in a moment.

"I've already said, then become a teacher, a professor or a doctor, and serve your country that way."

"I don't want to become a teacher."

"Why not?"

Roma will not answer this one. Obviously.

"And how does marching in the streets serve the country?"

"You wouldn't understand," Roma says, a little hesitation infecting the bravado of the last syllables.

"Now you listen, young lady," Prem bluffs a huff. "As long as you live in this house, you do what we tell you to do. Understood?"

Roma's head rears and her eyes bore into Prem's. "Well, I'm going to marry soon."

"You will marry when you are old enough, of course . . . ," Prem reasons.

"I'm going to marry Roderick and he will take me away from this horrid house to England." It all comes out as a torrent, leaving Roma visibly panting, her still very level chest heaving hard.

Prem can't believe what she's hearing. She blinks a few times, feeling foolish. She tastes a sudden spurt of bile in her mouth, as if her stomach has just lurched to cast off something venomous. But there's more from Roma.

"And we won't worship the British people like you and Uncle do, but spread the word in England about the horrors of British rule because we are not traitors like you and Uncle, and we will fight the cruel oppressors and when the English leave, people like you will have to beg forgiveness from us and—"

The hard flat sound startles even Prem who doesn't know just when she walked up to the girl and hit her with an open hand. Roma begins to whimper and whine, clutching her left cheek with both hands, and starts backing away. "I hate you!" She shouts as she trips backward, fear dueling anger. "I hate you and your husband and your house and your son and everything and the school and your stupid parties and your stupid friends and all the things you buy for me that I hate, that I, I . . . !" She can't finish her sentence as a huge sob washes over her and her eyes flood. She stands a few feet away, ever ready to run if need be, and screams as she sobs—looking at Prem squarely—drawn-out, tortured screams in which Prem can hear a native malcontent heart twisting to breaking, guts wrenching and knotting themselves up, a savage chorus of boundless grief rising inside the girl and spewing out of her mouth like a tongued inferno.

And at the end of that whole surge of poisonous grief come the next words that could crush what remains of philosophy in Prem's heart.

"I hate you! I wish I had died before I saw you! I wish I'd never been born! I wish I'd died with my mother and never met you! I wish I were dead now!"

It is Prem who runs out of the room, past the cringing but untouched Roma, thinking of a girl who once felt this way, like this one. Yes, very much like this one.

One of the agonies of her situation is that she can't talk to anyone about any of this. Her husband is the last person she would approach. Alone, afraid, she asks herself what is happening. Where has she gone wrong? What has she done wrong?

Hasn't she always tried to do her best? Hasn't she taken in other people's children, practically orphaned, unwanted children? And tried to love them? No, not tried . . . of course she has loved them. Maybe not each one in the same way. But she's certainly tried, tried hard, bruising what's there of her marriage, cracking the foundations of her home, to love each child, each the same amount. Why is this happening? she asks.

The next morning at dawn, the sun meets her pale, tired face, for the first time in years not composed, alert, and fresh. That morning she doesn't leave her room till afternoon, steeling herself to move only because the children are coming home from school.

CHAPTER 34

When Nakul came to the city from his native village Udhampur-Teenteri, he was about twelve. He got off the hot, dirty train at Howrah Station.

There he was, standing on the concrete that smelled of hot metal and piss, already hustled by a group of coolies to carry their smaller loads. At some point he somehow became a teaboy near the huge throbbing station, and then one day he wandered away from that raucous shop full of truck drivers and petty thieves and laborers and sailors, ending up on a wide street with the sun beating down on slippery cobbles looking like the broken backs of a thousand tortoises, the serpentine trams gliding ominously over the rutted tracks going in every direction. He was at a crossroads he'd never seen before. This was the most open space he'd seen in this city. He squinted up to see billboards and marquees three, four stories high, and his eyes ached from the sunlight as well as the brilliant sheen of surfaces with marks he couldn't read. Silently he tried to mutter a prayer, an obsequy, but his heart rang hollow, his true desire mocking him.

A car stopped before one of the larger shops, and a tall man with wispy floating hair and round wire eyeglasses stepped out and hurried into the store. Nakul squatted on the pavement and watched the car, its mudguard and steel handles and the curves of its doors like the lines of a boat at dawn on the muddy Saraju, the yellow-and-black pattern (later he learned these were taxis), and the dancing figure at the end of the bonnet all making him feel empty and quiet inside, though he was also just hungry.

He'd left the stifling tea shop not knowing where to go next, but because he knew that these were not to be his masters. If serve he must, he would make a softer bed for himself elsewhere. He knew that household servants were not cuffed and thwacked as frequently as his master the shop owner habitually dealt these out to him. The city was for hope.

How much time had gone by in this famished reverie he did not know, but the tap of a hand on his shoulder startled him so that he nearly rolled off on his side in his learned hurry to get away from a kick or a smack. Instead, the tall man was telling him something in Bengali and pointing from the shop to the car and back in Bengali, a language he still barely understood. He looked from the man's fingers—jabbing methodically back and forth—to the shop, its large plate glass front keeping the insides a cool, dark-gray mystery. He didn't want this job, whatever it was; he just wanted to sit there and stare at the car, until it went away. But the man kept jabbing, jabbering, breaking into broken Hindi, now that he understood Nakul was not from the city, that he'd brought a sun-dried dusty plain with him, right there between the great buildings of the city.

Nakul remembered that he had to eat, that the tea stall owner who would have missed him since six in the morning, his usual hour of duty, would probably crack his skull open or throw a boiling kettle at him if he went back now, seven hours later. He thought about money: about the few gray, yellow, mossy rupee notes and the sticky, coated paisas that he had seen in the last three months. He smelled their smell and he remembered their power as well as the horror of parting from them for tea, rotis, a little soap. He got up and went into the shop and began bringing out the heavy bundles that the shopkeeper's boy started handing to him. The driver of the car took them from him silently and stowed them into the back part of the car that opened like the beak of a great bird. Then Nakul held out his hand to the tall man who said something else and the driver growled him into the front passenger seat, removing a dirty red rag from the seat to make place for him.

So riding in a motorcar for the first time in his life, Nakul went to Mitter Mansion where he unloaded the monthly supplies for the household for the tall man who was the butler of the house. When the butler offered him the predictable couple of tarnished paisas, he shook his head, pointing into the house and then at his own stomach. The butler looked at these fingers now jabbing methodically from the stomach to the house and back, and understood slowly that the boy was asking to stay. He thought for a second, and something passed like a shadow behind his eyes—perhaps an image of himself oh so many years ago, coming to some Babu's house for the first time—for he broke out into a mild smile.

Thus Nakuldev, Naka, Nakle, Naaku, became another one of the downstairs people and kitchen help in Mitter Mansion.

Nakul then learned how to find money in the pockets of the shirts he had to wash—a twenty-five paisa coin here, a rupee bill if he was unbelievably blessed. Then away he ran after seven to the nearest movie theater, the Star bioscope. Nakul watched the improbable good looks of the pomaded and creamed hero competing with the powdered beauty of the heroine. He joined other boys in the penny seats in the theatre pit who maniacally hugged their own knees and each other, interrupted their craning adoration of the gods onscreen to pair off and imitate the godly couple's dances, doing the male and the female moves, simpering, swooning, and reaching. Their yips and screeches disturbed the decent folks in the boxes and seats behind and sometimes they got cuffed and boxed, dragged out, and left licking their wounds.

But they came back, night after night, some skipping a meal, some skipping a place in the cue for a pavement sleeping slot under some arching overpass. Nakul counted himself very lucky that he had a house to enter through a broken back window every night, however late he stayed out, but generally he did not venture far or stay out late. He had to be up every morning at five or the cook would have his head.

Now, Nakul lights a bidi as he tries to fall asleep. His pallet bed is, as it has always been, on the last landing before the terrace door of Mitter Mansion, and the wrought iron pattern of the staircase spiraling along the inner cavity of the mansion that ends at that landing is as familiar to him as the lines on his own palm. The night is moonless, very dark. He can't see his toes, but he feels a few susurrating movements of his longtime companions: mice and cockroaches.

What's the old woman up to?

CHAPTER 35

Shapes from thirty years ago are returning and circling around Saroj. Sometimes their haunts are dreams, but sometimes they're like daylight robbers who break in and strike her senseless. When she wakes from the blackout, shapes are still streaming in and taking their place until all air and light around her are taken. She begs for a little air, a little light. One by one, only when they're ready, the shapes leave, their gaze never leaving her face. *Remember*, they say as they leave.

She remembers. Her own evening visit to the village grocer. For her 'photooo.' The full-length studio wedding photo with Naveen Chand cut in half wouldn't do the job. The grocer said, slowly chewing paan, "Such business in these mod-eran days needs mod-eran style, clo-jup." Saroj didn't quite understand the distinction, but the grocer took her, half respectful, to the back of his store, and there someone under a dark sheet trained a square box on her that spat out a sharp, fiery blast and then went black again. Picture. Photooo in English. To be sent to the widower in Bengal-Bihar province who'd asked for it. After all, he had the right of refusal. He didn't refuse.

"Nice young thing, *hein?*" she heard the grocer whisper to the invisible man under the dark sheet as she left the hovel of a store. The men laughed. Her body stiffened; blood rushed into her head. Maybe she should just go the barracks after all. With her long, thick, wavy hair, leaf-shaped face, wide-set auburn eyes, and fine, rounded limbs, she was a small woman—with monumental pride—whose beauty deceived men into seeing her as a plaything.

Husks of these memories whirl and whistle around her till she hears a train's agonized, incessant whistle again. And there she is, crawling on the train floor. Her body twists in pain. She's passing out. A face swims before her. A face with beautiful, iridescent sea-green eyes. Twisting, clutching at herself and her belly as if a snake coils and uncoils inside her, she's passing out. She can't see the eyes anymore. On the gritty floor of the snaking train taking her away from everything she has ever known or loved, a widow is made to burn to death that night, after all.

There was once a man who met her at some train station. What was his name again? He exclaimed at some gash on her forehead. She had to tell him that was where she'd hit her head when she slipped in the train bathroom. She stared at the man but couldn't make out his face. Just a blur. A different face, with green eyes, glowed before her.

Someone called Manohar Mishra—she doesn't know how she knows that name—stands looking at her especially long whenever he comes now, though always with the others. Manohar Mishra is a stout, short but erect man with broad shoulders and a broader middle. His grizzled hair is thinning and sleekly brushed back from his high forehead to coil loosely beneath and behind his prominent ears. His face is squarish and heavy, jaws and chin wandering into thick fat. He's lost none of his front teeth but almost all the back ones; his laugh reveals an uneven, squat palisade of bone fencing his generous mouth. He usually wears freshly pressed fine muslin tunics and carefully pleated and creased dhotis. He has small bear paw feet; his polished leather pumps fit snugly over brilliant white socks. He has rounded hands with pudgy fingers studded with yellow gold rings encasing auspicious gemstones like garnets, rubies, amethysts, sapphires, and pearls. His lips are rimmed on the inside with oxblood betel juice. His eyes, under thick gray brows, are small, jet-black, alert and kind. Everyone else calls him Mishra Babu.

One day she will ask him if he can send someone to her old village to look for a woman called Munia. He seems kind; maybe he will do it.

Maybe he will ask who Munia is. She will have to explain that Munia is her personal maid. Supposed to come with her. But somehow lost. Supposed to bring a very important thing with her. "What thing?" Manohar Mishra might ask. She will not tell him the truth though she can see he's not a greedy or needlessly curious man; he just wants to help her. A kind man.

CHAPTER 36

Eight years, Nakul counts. Eight years have passed in this house, and he'll probably live and die in this city. He's never gone back to the village. He tries to remember his mother's face, brown and dry, with deep lines etching her face like the dried riverbeds of summer. He can't. He's never sent money home, even after some neighboring people from villages near his and now working at the tea stalls and shops around sent word back home on the grapevine that

Nakul had been found in Kolikata, working in a Babu's big house. His mother wrote him through the postmaster's hand, the tremulous, twisted letters held before him by the *padhhe-likhhe* servant clawing toward him on a small faded brown postcard, "Send money. Father is ill." When his father died, another smudged postcard arrived to tell him so. He didn't go back. And then "Send money. Sister is to be married." Nakul still can't read, but he knew what the letters said. He threw the postcards into the clay oven of the kitchen, watching them flare for a second before crumbling into incandescent ash. He can't remember his sister's face. Or that of his eight other brothers and sisters. He says to himself, If I cannot remember their faces, who are they to me?

So who does the old hag think he is to her?

He knows better than to talk much. In this house he has three hearty meals a day, and a cup of tea with two Britannia biscuits every morning and evening. Sometimes in the winter evenings, one and a half cups of sweet milky tea. As he grew older, he began to shave in the alley behind the house where the servants bathed and washed, borrowing a blunt razor from some older man. He felt his manhood coming upon him, and he fondled himself at night, finding it pleasurable. No matter how tired he was, usually he gave himself this pleasure. Faint down turned into curling bushes of hair on his chin, upper lip, his pubic area.

The first year in the big house, at *Durga Puja*, he went around for a day with a small allowance—as did all the other servants and jobless youth in the house—to look at the multiple, diverse images of the goddess in great big prosceniums being worshipped all around the neighborhood. He walked and walked, and bought peanuts when he was hungry. He looked very closely at the buffalo demon who lay sprawling in agony beneath the peaches and cream goddess Durga's tiny, rosy feet. He wondered about that. She was so lovely, with her golden-pink skin and large leaf-shaped eyes; her small mouth with the red lipstick on it such as the ladies in mansions like Mitter Mansion wore; and her thin waist and ample breasts beneath the careful pleats of her voluminous sari. He fantasized about touching her breasts, running a finger along where her arm raising the spear joined the swell of her breast. He imagined the soft creaminess of that region, imagined putting his mouth on it, eating it like *Prasad*, nothing like his mother's dry, brown flaps of flesh. He started to sweat, and his legs trembled. The demon looked up at the goddess with lust and rage in his eyes. Nakul knew what he felt. It clicked in his mind suddenly that one might see him as that demon, and the rampant goddess as one of the golden-skinned ladies who lived in the big houses. That as the goddess stood over the demon, the master class stood over him, making him stoop, grovel.

That thought has been returning to him of late, especially since the old woman has arrived and runs after him whenever she sees him, and the way the whole household seems to be in a tight and tacit agreement to look the other way when she does that. He realizes that these people can do anything they like. They can trample over you and just as easily raise you high into the clouds. There's an adage here in Bengal. The love of the great is like a sandbank—one day you are in chains, the next you are on the moon. Whatever they want, they do. And no one can stop them.

The other day he saw something worth money: Lady Mitter slapped that Roma girl tight across the face. When he saw it his own palm itched sympathetically. The girl is a dark, nasty, sulky creature and Nakul has always envied and hated her knowing that she comes from quite low people, and madam adopted her out of pity. She's not all that much better than him, but she acts like the little lady. Missy Baba indeed. She can use a few ells of taking down. Especially shouting at madam like that, saying she hates her, and she and Sir Mitter are 'Dogs of the English,' or something close to that. He's illiterate, but he knows that phrase because these days it's on the lips of so many Bengali Babus on the streets and in the shops, and it's clearly not a good thing.

Madam is weak; he sees that. She didn't even stay to finish the job, but ran out of the room and up the stairs to her bedroom after the nasty girl shouted that abuse she did. Had it been him he would have sent that nasty girl reeling, hitting the wall. But he is only a servant. He doesn't even usually look up at the faces of the big people. It is not encouraged. He is glad, though, that he happened to be the only one near madam's parlor that day. This bit of knowledge is like money. He's going to keep it curled up in his fist so that it grows. One day it might buy him something.

What? He has a faint but rapidly coagulating idea. He's not telling though. He doesn't even tell the old lady when she runs her bony fingers through his hair and up and down his face. As if she loves him—as if she wants to kiss him, hug him. He enjoys the caresses with a large quarry of revulsion. The old lady reminds him of his mother.

No, she doesn't get to know unless he gets something for it. Though of course she's quite ghost-taken, clearly. When she croaks at him, "Come to me, my love, come," he goes at once, sits at her feet on the floor. Poor lunatic! Should be in an insane asylum, really. She frowns and grumbles, says that he should sit on the bed with her, but that Nurse Joseph looks such daggers at him that he hasn't yet quite worked up the nerve to accept that invitation.

Love, the crone calls him. So that's what he is. That's going to come in handy someday. . . .

There are many ways—odd, loose ways. He isn't afraid to try any of them, or all of them. He's been attending the meetings of the Congress Babus. Gandhi-ji speaks and the nation goes into a trance. Everyone becomes a puppet and dances whatever tune Gandhi and the other Congress leaders—Nehru, Sardar Patel, Maulana Sahib—play in the great snake charmer musical of *Poorna Swaraj*. He learns at these meetings how to influence people, how to talk. Himself, he is rather attracted to this new fellow called Omprakash Narayan Srivastava who says a lot about the rights of the masses. It seems some people somewhere in a place called Russia shot off the heads of their king and queen. The demon rose and tamed the gods and goddesses, Nakul thinks. He wants to follow this Omprakash Sahib and throw his lot in with him at a good moment.

And now that this old woman cackles at his sight and tickles and plays with him as if he were a baby or a playmate, Nakul sharpens his senses, waiting for an opening.

And he has one when the servants are called in by Lady Mitter one by one after the Roma-slapping thing. One by one they enter her parlor, close the door, open it after a few minutes and leave. When his turn comes, Nakul takes care to look down at the floor, and pretends to wipe his face with his coarse cotton scarf as if he is nervous and sweating.

"What does Roderick Sahib do when he's not studying, after school?"

"*Memsahib*, I'm a humble servant, what do I have to do with the ways of—"

"Stop. Answer the question. I know you all have a hundred eyes and ears. What do you know about Roderick Baba's friends, his habits?"

"Memsahib, Roderick Sahib is a very, very nice sahib, he doesn't play with any bad boys, Memsahib. He's always studying, studying. Hard. Reading big-big books." He doesn't by any means want to make enemies of the precious boys of this household by telling on them.

"And after?"

"Roderick Sahib never smokes Memsahib"—he considers telling her that Harish already experiments with his father's cigars and the servants' beedis but desists, for that time too shall come when it does come—"never wastes time, just sits on the grass with Roma Memsahib."

"Sits on the grass? They just sit on the grass? That's all they do? Do they play together?"

Nakul scratches his ear, then his head, clears his throat, looks at the wall to his left, then back at the floor. The pause is timed to be long enough to agitate his mistress.

"Well?"

"Only girl boy play sometimes, Memsahib."

"Girl boy play? What do you mean? Explain."

Nakul's head droops lower as if there's something especially intriguing to examine around his navel. Perhaps that girl boy thing, or some part of it. He doesn't answer. Prem knows what he means, and that it's useless to prod him further. No young male servant will mention unmentionables before the lady of the house, the Mai part of the ubiquitous Maibap.

He is told he can go.

CHAPTER 37

Some days Saroj remembers a few things clearly. She tries to store the memories so she can prove that she hasn't lost her mind.

She remembers a young woman saying the wound inside her will never heal. That the bad man has won after all. The only thing he hasn't got is her body. But he's tore out and eaten her heart—also a flesh-eating fiend after all, his holy vegetarian self—and put her on an undying pyre in the end. Saroj didn't know what to say to her, how to comfort her.

The young woman would weep at night and say that the pressure of the stones growing into her heart—her heart was not quite done becoming stone—got worse every day, like when she looked up from the fabrics and glass bangles and scent bottles and plastic mirrors of the chance vendor passing the great farmhouse, and imagined for a second she glimpsed sea-green eyes. But here in Bengal-Bihar—she moaned—the faces were hard, brown; the eyes were clotted with fatigue or early blindness, not pale-green fire and ice like the north country eyes she used to know.

She said no one knows how tired eyes can get from crying, and how tired your arms from cradling loss. Then one day Saroj saw her lying in a room flooded by moonlight, but someone with crazy, tousled hair was lying half across her. She had to close and bolt the door immediately so that no one else would see the young woman and what she was doing inside the room.

CHAPTER 38

Harder and harder, Prem's heart turns on the potter's wheel of rage until shaped into a perfect poison cup.

Roma must, must be sent away. To boarding school. The coming disgrace is intolerable. The danger is incalculable. No more stories of Kutcha Bachchas in this house.

Sir Naren knows nothing of this. Sir Naren also knows nothing of Saroj's turbulent attachment to Nakul. Sir Naren is keeping his eyes pinned on the crucial manufacture of the jute that was made into gunny bags for supplies during the First World War, and that will be made into the rope next year that will hang the militant nationalists Bhagat Singh and Batukeshwar Dutt—Khudiram Bose's dreaded political progeny—for bombing a government assembly and shooting policemen in pursuit.

This time Roma is closer to the bone. "I wish you were dead," she says. And Prem at last turns on her. Totally. Viciously. Heinously. Helplessly.

"You're nothing but the granddaughter of a maid! Of my family's maid. Who do you think you are? What do you think I owe you? You're not like us . . . !"

Please. I tried.

Roma will go to a good girls' school, a convent school run by Irish nuns. New clothes have been bought for her. The maids pack them and each night they find them scattered around the floor, outside her bedroom, in the hallway—where no *objets d'art* are kept anymore—sometimes ink-stained, sometimes stabbed, sometimes ripped through. In their own silent revenge, the maids don't report the state of the clothes to Lady Mitter, just repack them.

The best laid plans.

Like fifteen years ago, one quiet afternoon, while Prem sips the last of her afternoon tea, the front doorbell rings. Five minutes later, a maid arrives, bearing a simple white card made of thick velvety paper bordered by a slender golden vine. Inside, it says, "Madam Lilian Hartfield requests the honor of a meeting with Lady Mitter."

CHAPTER 39

Prem looks at the apparition in her living room in stricken consternation. Her racing thoughts are mainly of Roderick, and whether he will survive life or even contact with this woman. She can only have returned for one thing, instinct tells Prem.

The woman sitting in front of her is solemn, quiet. No rings. Hair trapped in a neat netted bun just above her nape. Stern stockings and excruciatingly practical, ugly black walking shoes.

"Good morning. I trust you are well," the apparition says.

"Good morning," Prem says, wide-eyed, absentminded, her mind still running on shielding, sheltering Roderick.

"I hope my unannounced visit doesn't incommode you."

For this Prem has no answer. Though she knows what the word means, "incommode" isn't a word anyone she knows ever uses.

"That means inconvenience," Lilian explains.

"I know that, thank you," Prem says. "Will you take coffee or tea?"

"Thank you, I'm quite fine. May I see Roderick?"

Just like that. Yes, of course, but still . . . just like that! The old Lilian apparently gone completely, except for this trait.

Prem wants to say No, you may not. You left him here when he was four and I raised him. Now he belongs to me.

She says, "Of course." She rings the bell. A servant materializes. It's Nakul. He's become very attentive lately.

"Ask Roderick Sahib to come," Prem says. A thin mist of sweat overspreads her upper lip. She tries to hold in the strained breathing, the scent of fear. Lilian seems not to mind the tepid, squamous air and light. Nakul nods and withdraws. Soon, light-footed steps come closer and Roderick is at the door.

It's the eyes. Prem sees that Roderick sees and knows. Roderick and Lilian gaze at each other, caught in a preverbal, organic weft. The four blue eyes look at each other, one pair having made the other. Prem's stomach heaves but she won't capsize. Roderick hasn't said anything.

"My dearest Roderick." Lilian's voice quivers.

Natural, Prem thinks. But mothers are made, not born. Bitya . . . Shyampiyari's scratchy voice travels back to her like a sigh borne through time. The tension, the apprehension, are unbearable. Her breath, muscles, and joints are frozen in shock.

"Mother." Roderick's voice comes out of a deep cave or abyss. Momentarily the scene swims before Prem's eyes. The light dims for a moment.

And Lilian Hartfield smiles. Ever so slightly. But she smiles. A mother's smile. The smile of a woman who has successfully given suck.

How can I think I love Roderick more than she loves him? Prem takes the club to her heart already weakened by that invisible potter who too in the end prostrates herself to that earth who fashions all clay and all potters. How could she have imagined Roderick loving her more than his own mother? Birth, death, lineage, all a gyre. How can a foster-mother's love come first? But why can it not?

"Lady Mitter," says Lilian Hartfield, her glowing eyes still fixed on Roderick, "I have come to take Roderick back to England."

"Like hell you have, Lilian," Sir Naren says.

Did someone tell him Lilian had come? He's home early. He's standing at the door to the grand drawing room. He is holding a walking stick in his hand—one of those ancient, tricky, encrusted things he's collected—but he's not leaning on it as he does sometimes. He is standing almost erect, monocles glittering. He even seems . . . a little taller, doesn't he? Prem blinks. She thinks for a few incongruously lighthearted seconds that he seems to know how to be a movie villain—or even a hero—without ever having been to the bioscope. Showing up at the crisis, at just the right moment, and all that marvelous, heady stuff. Prem resigns herself to the shuffling of time, place, order, fidelities. She consigns herself to utter, abject, unfamiliar gratitude. She inwardly kneels to her husband, hat in hand, for the first time. It has only taken him a split second to discern that a Lilian who could become this gray-stockinged thing is what Roderick needs like a hole in the head. She plans to join all her forces with her husband. She prays that Lilian can't exert some old white magic to make Sir Naren think otherwise, to give in.

"The choice is actually Roderick's," Lilian says. "He's eighteen.'"

"And I'm his father still," Sir Naren snaps.

"Are you?" Lilian says.

A hush that feels endless. Sir Naren and Lilian are locked in each other's gaze. Sir Naren breathes slowly, heavily, and has to mop the sweat pouring down his face. Lilian is cool, calm, unflapped.

"What do you mean?

Lilian doesn't say anything, just continues to stare. What was once between these two? Love? Prem cannot imagine it now.

"Madam, explain yourself," Sir Naren says thickly.

"Are you truly his father?"

"So I have been led to believe."

"And you might be a fool."

"Madam! You had best—"

"Don't speak to me that way, Naren! You don't own me as you . . ."

Prem desperately tries to make eye contact with this Lilian who communicates her contumely for the woman—she suggests—Sir Naren does own. The briefest withering gesture, a slicing movement of the head. She looks for any trace of that old, graceful Lilian whom she once nearly loved. For whom—and of course for Roderick—she once battled Sir Naren and won. A pyrrhic victory? Who made this Lilian? How was she made? Who is this? She comes back now, when Roderick is eighteen, to claim the boy Prem has raised?

Outside the room the servants are surely agog.

"You told me he is my son when you brought him here. If you lied, shame on you. And then you are a thieving, cheating rascal."

"The point is, precisely, that you have no way of knowing if he is your son, Naren. But there is no doubt that I am his mother. The birth certificate says so. It doesn't mention a father."

"So is he or is he not?"

Roderick stands a few feet away from them. What must this whole thing mean to the poor boy? How is he holding up against it? How will his heart not break? Prem is desperate with tenderness.

When Lilian speaks again, her voice is lower, grainier than before. "Listen carefully. He is your son because I say so. If I say he's not, he's not. You have no claim to him unless I say so. So he will come with me to England. Because I am his mother."

"Madam," Sir Naren says. Prem's heart stumbles. She sees the old man her tormentor has become. How firmly and sternly he speaks! Maybe the old white magic is all gone. Maybe it doesn't work anymore. Certainly, this prim and harsh woman in the drab clothes and the plodding, sensible shoes does not have that magic anymore. It's been fifteen years. The British overall are no longer the all-powerful sorcerers they'd once been to Indians. Prem nearly smiles at the bits and pieces of nationalist jargon that swarm inside her head. And Sir Naren is no longer wiping off sweat with his handkerchief.

"We shall see. Madam, you will kindly leave us now so we can discuss this matter among ourselves. We will let you know if you may visit again. As to your demand, it is utterly preposterous." Then Sir Naren turns and walks out of the room, no doubt scattering the agglomerated servants listening as though with one ear.

Roderick, Prem sees, takes a step. Not toward her, but toward Lilian. Prem's eyes fill with sudden, stinging tears. Is Roderick leaning toward Lilian, after all? How can her Roderick be so wretchedly ungrateful? Can he forget who, what she has been to him? How? More than a mother—a mother and a father rolled into one. But immediately upon the heels of that comes the vicarious piercing of his imagined pain. Then, immediately again—how can I protect him? Oh yes, I should reach out to him right now and tell him everything will be alright. She tries to make eye contact. He is not looking at her, though. Like a shadow, like an intruder, she must watch. She watches. Lilian is looking straight, fixedly at Roderick. Roderick is walking up to her. Putting his arms around her—woodenly, isn't it?—and, after a moment, planting a (hesitant?) kiss on her cheek.

Prem suddenly feels very cold. And numb. She thinks she might faint. She wishes she could. That would teach them all something. She doesn't faint. She can't faint because she must remain vigilant here, watch what everyone does, says, make sure no one can pull wool over her eyes or her husband's.

Lilian leaves with a curt nod to Prem. She didn't deign to answer Sir Naren. A fact not lost on anyone, surely. Roderick immediately leaves the drawing room. Prem hurries after him, consigning Sir Naren to chewing whatever bitter caustic cuds he must, however he can.

CHAPTER 40

Prem calls to Roderick who is already going up the stairs, and he stops and turns.

It's been a long time since Prem was last at the bioscope, but as Roderick turns to look at her, a lock of his honey-colored hair falls over his forehead, and Prem thinks with a sharp pang—pride and dread sparring brutally—that he looks strikingly like a movie star. Indeed, like that new actor Gary Cooper everyone talks about these days. What a handsome young man he will soon be! She finds it hard to find words with him, for him, for the first time. She looks at him in mute appeal.

"What would you like to say to me, T?" Roderick asks. He sounds hoarse, as if he's been crying. When he was younger, and 'Auntie' didn't stick because the little fellow couldn't manage it and kept saying 'Tanti' instead, it led to an English lady visitor pointing out that *Tante* was in fact French for Auntie, and so why not? And so it was Tanti, and then T in the familiarity of everyday loving, and all these years Roderick has called her T.

"Roderick, dear child, where are you going?"

"To my room, to think, and . . . and . . . maybe to lie down for a bit. T . . ."

Prem almost throttles herself to keep the anxiety from rising and drowning her completely.

"Would you like dinner sent up to you, dear?" She manages in as calm a voice as possible. The boy mustn't be further agitated. Nor should he sense her terror.

Is it at all possible that he might be happy with Lilian, this new Lilian, or at least happy enough? How selfish of Prem to discount the possibility altogether! Isn't she being the worse mother now? She scolds herself righteously, fortified by Roderick's soothing words, his candid look. T. It's easier to be brave when you don't feel completely alone.

"I will come down to dinner as usual, T," Roderick says and goes up the stairs slowly as if boulders are attached to his legs. Prem tries to say something simple and cheerful, but all that emerges is a dry, soundless swallow.

Why is this happening? How can she stop whatever calamity lurks?

In his room Roderick sits down on his bed slowly, as if more vigorous movement would make him shatter. He clutches the edge of the mattress with both hands, willing himself to stay still. Who is this woman who has reentered his life? This person, who he knows is his mother, who's nothing like the mother he remembers—who is she? What is he to say to her? Should he comfort her? Or should he confront her? Should he, for instance, loudly ask, shaming her in front of others, wounding her, "Where have you been all this time,

Mother? What have you been busy with? Why did you abandon me, Mommy?"

Why is she back, anyhow? Why does she want him back? Why England? Why now?

At dinner no one talks. Roderick's face is drawn. Sir Naren clears his throat a few times and glances at Roderick. Harish is simply bursting with curiosity. He didn't see Lilian, but he's heard from Roma, who heard from the servants, that an Englishwoman came today to see his mother. And that his father raised his voice and stamped his stick a few times while talking to her. A very, very few of the servants have recognized her through the cobwebby transmogrification as the once elegant English lady teacher Madam Hartfield.

Harish asks, "Ma, who is this English lady? Is she coming for me? Am I going to have to have more lessons or something?"

He kicks Roderick under the table when no one responds. Then asks Roderick remorsefully if he would like some salt, atoning in part for his misbehavior some years ago, at which Roderick shakes his head gently. Roma focuses only on the plate of food in front of her. Inside her is a growing dread also, a desperation, to know why Roderick is so sad, so silent. This is not like him at all. She looks anxiously from Roderick to Sir Naren to Prem. No one returns her pleading, fretful gaze.

Prem watches this family. Her family. The family she cobbled together from the abandonment of those who should have stayed. She stayed. They left. Having left, why come back? For once she's grateful to Kanan for being plain, downright dead.

After dinner Sir Naren and Roderick disappear into the library. From her cozy parlor across the great hallway Prem can see the heavy, dark door, gleaming and stolid like the lid of a coffin. She considers eavesdropping, but she's too tired to leave her chaise. At one point she falls fast asleep. Her head—on which just faint sprigs of gray are beginning to be visible amidst the dark, luxuriant hair—lolls helplessly on her chest. Fatigue has creased the space between her eyebrows. In her almost childlike repose, the exacting years reveal their rampage on her still gracious face. A little spittle gathers in one corner of her slack mouth.

She jerks awake. She thinks she heard the library door closing again—this time less gently—and footsteps receding. She scampers out of her chaise and goes to the library, pushes the door open without the required protocol of knocking first. She expected to find her husband alone. But father—is he?—and son are both there. Silent, sitting across from each other. Roderick's head is in his hands, his face covered.

In spite of herself Prem rushes ahead toward Roderick. Her hands reach out to touch his head but stop in midair. She doesn't know if she should. Nothing is clear-cut anymore. But Roderick raises his head and face and turns toward her even as he sits, throwing his arms around her waist and burying his face against her midriff. She can feel the hard tightness of his embrace, the rigid way his head digs into her torso as if he's a newborn. Suddenly she remembers a very old thing. When Harish was a newborn he would always sidle up flush against the side of her where he lay (only the first few days of course, before Sir Naren had him removed to his nursery), and she'd wake up to find him boring into her side or into her armpit with his tiny head, as if demanding reentry.

She will not let another child be taken away from her.

Roderick holds her for a long time, and Prem doesn't move. She stands quite still, passing her hands gently over Roderick's head, again and again.

CHAPTER 41

Mary Joseph is bad enough—a Christian blackie being within shadowing distance of a high-caste Brahmin widow—but now a gora mem has been allowed into the house. Saroj hears this during one of her increasingly rarer clearheaded minutes. Whatever her mind expunges immediately otherwise, this thing it holds on to. Was it for this that she did what she did thirty years ago? If goras are to be in the same house as she is, why didn't she just run to the gora barracks instead of letting slip what mattered more than life itself that night of the train to Patna?

Once, she can remember, a new teenage bride was burned down to charred limbs and trunk in some village. A mystery. No mystery, Saroj knew. Every day, another wife or widow in the land was 'mysteriously' burned or beaten or broken into something unrecognizable. No mystery. Men colluding with men. Years before her birth the British Maibap had passed the Widows' Remarriage Act. To end the suffering of Indian widows, they'd said. Passed it promising that glorious day when suffering widows' cries would no longer rise in bitter-sweet, sticky smoke because other men, good men, would step forth to marry them without prejudice and disgust. Because that was the right thing to do.

She doesn't remember the rest, but the night the teenage girl burned, the younger Saroj had looked out at the darkness, muttering. The room became tense with what uncoiled in her; things she herself could not, had rather not, name. She could see things. She saw brilliant eyes. Fire leaping, licking the coal-black night. Voices calling. Come to me, piece of my heart. Oil lamp wicks burning down to velvet soot. Soot from which kohl is made. Kohl, which is eyebright. Lush, black diamond eyebright. Eyebright is for dreams. Dreams and also nightmares like exploding suns. Fire.

This was one of many reasons her daughter Prem, not quite six then, slept in a distant room. So she wouldn't hear throaty murmurs of famished, unfinished reckonings from her mother's room. They frightened her. Saroj too wanted to save Prem from being frightened. Everyone said she was a monster, not a mother. One of those alien women—succubae—who suck the blood of men, of their own children. Very well. Let them. The monster mother would at least try to keep the innocent child safe from herself.

Manohar Mishra, whom Prem treated like he was the young thing—embracing his girth with affection instead of repugnance—would snore boisterously, alone, two bedrooms away. Servants would sleep here and there in the corridors and hallways surrounding the house's heart which was a vast, sooty kitchen and several storerooms. Some nights Prem—the Vine of Love— with little to wrap herself around, picked her way through supine bodies and went to her father's room. Dhai and Kanan slept on where she'd been, but suddenly her heart had begun to ache for the lonely old man. She would go to his room and slept on his great padded bookkeeping bench by the window. Happier there than anywhere near her mother. The slaphappy moon would lurch out of a cloud to pour pale light over her smooth, young face and Manohar Mishra's smooth, older one.

The night of the bride-burning, though, she heard her mother talking. She froze in her tracks in the hallway, quickly looking around to ensure that everyone on the floor was breathing and snoring as required to prove there was life in them. Yes, Mai-ji was talking. She didn't dare approach her mother's room. Who was in there with Mai-ji?

"Burned you down, did they? You couldn't get away?" Mai-ji was saying. Prem clutched her throat but couldn't stop the escape of a small sob. Terror.

"Should have run away, dear. Already. Before. See how it feels now. I know— I'm burning too. They don't see it, but I am."

Prem couldn't figure out why Mai-ji said she was burning. Had something happened? Was it happening now? Set Mai-ji on fire? Shouldn't she go, look? Help? She couldn't. Couldn't move.

"Come to me. Come, dear," Mai-ji said then. "It's what we women do best, child. We burn. Whenever, however, wherever they tell us."

From her room Saroj had seen silver fields and dark, still shapes. The land, always the land. She'd watched the body—shrunken, flesh melting off bone, holes where eyes and lips used to be—coming, still crying, unstoppable, across the field, toward her window. Flailing and scything arms and legs still trying to beat off the flames, the wind—fire's breath—still radiant around her. She'd looked with pity, with resignation. Poor girl. Poor, lovely, small, young, life-hungering girl. Burned for the greed of men for fallow, rich land. A more horrific version of what Older Brother-in-Law, with three children of his own and a crippled, broken wife stowed in a corner room, had demanded of Saroj: *karewa*—the right to marry a dead brother's young, fertile widow and keep the estate to himself.

Brides had always burned easily. Widows even easier. The scriptures said a widow had to burn with her dead husband or she'd go to hell for eternity. But after the 'enlightened' Maibap Widows' Remarriage Act it became much easier to force a widow to yield another way. Tempt them with a second chance at life. The act had made what used to be only uneven custom—where a man enjoyed both the unwilling tastes and cries of his late brother's widow and his brother's share of the estate—law.

Saroj's jaw moved without stop involuntarily as she muttered to herself that night. A hope, a need, for pain had begun spreading through her. Soon, she realized, she must go to her old trunk that stayed under her bed. Almost as good as fire. Bright flash of beaten gold. And a short blade that once kept an evil man away.

The British had essentially told Naveen Chand's evil, lawless older brother: "Go ahead, grab her body and her share of family land." Why? She would have easily given up the land, fair or not. She wouldn't have cared. She'd never cared for the land. She'd never had anything to do with it. But she had not climbed the pyre either.

She had been afraid. Of the agony of burning. Agony like that 'willing' widow's so many years ago, in her girlhood village. And so she had committed the first of her terrible sins.

"Come, girl, come to me."

Prem begged the darkness, the gods, that was not a call for her because Mai-ji knew she was near, listening. She rocked silently on her haunches amidst the sleeping bodies, her clamped hand almost chocking her but not altogether stoppering the long, ululating wail inside. Her mother was a monster. Talked to herself at night, luring victims to her room to feed on them.

Twenty years later, in Alipore, Kolikata, in her daughter's house, Saroj feels alone again, fighting these goras who suck the blood of the dead and the living alike. Who used to pluck women off pyres only to redouse them in the hot oil of shame and return them to the flames again. My God, how many times can one, must one, fight evil men? A gora. In the house.

The night almost three decades ago—how well Saroj remembers all and people keep saying she doesn't remember things—she'd got off the train at the very next station after the village as agreed and looked for Munia. She'd looked in the dingy waiting room, in the murky latrine, behind shops selling paan, beedi, glossy miniature god statues, cigarettes, marigold garlands, vermilion for married women, cheap flashy jewelry, rattles, carved clay animal figures, soap, candles, prayer beads, and much more in hazy lantern light. She'd flitted behind and between the stalls, the cattle, the people, the baggage, and woven baskets on the platform, peered into dark corners and under the benches even. But Munia was not there. Munia didn't come, though the train left only ten minutes late that night. Why didn't Munia come?

After Prem was born Saroj decided to wash her hands of hope. It didn't matter, why Munia hadn't come. That renouncing was practically freedom. Tears dried, leaving just a trace of ashen salt on the cheek. But then she'd started eyeing her second and freely chosen husband's entire household—his servants, his land, their daughter—masked, askance, bitterly. They must be to blame. She needed someone to blame.

Then The Dusty One came. With information she claimed was true. Information that ended all hope, forever. Still Saroj would summon the woman in to her room some days, desperate for something, afraid of missing it by not trying hard enough.

"Tell me where she went."

"I said it. They killed her." The Dusty One's speech was slow and slurred.

She wasn't in the habit of speaking.

"How do you know they killed her?"

"Because everyone knew."

"Who everyone? What everyone? Did you see her? Did you see them do it?"

The Dusty One didn't respond.

"You know where she is, don't you?" The Dusty One remained silent. Saroj begged and threatened her in turns repeatedly to please, please tell her the truth.

"What I have said is the truth."

"Take me to her. You know where she is. Even now she might . . ."

"Mai, no one knows what happened after that, but they killed her. I had to run away with my daughter. They made me homeless also."

Whose fault was it, everything that happened? The sun had not quite set the day the young husband of her heart, her Naveen Chand, walked across a waterlogged field munching roasted, parched grain. This you may not do because it is like insulting the earth that bore you and gave you grain. The earth should not be spurned when she is lying choking, drowning, by your feet made of her own salt walking over her agony. Smallpox. Melting the toes, the feet, the nose and the eyes into each other, making everyone wish Naveen Chand's death would come sooner.

Whose fault was that? That was his fault. But he paid down. And the rest? And now a gora in this house?

And what house is this, now? Why does Munia pretend to be someone else and keep calling her Mai-ji? Acting innocent? Wearing big jewelry, nice clothes? Pretending to be the injured one?

CHAPTER 42

Lilian requests privacy when she comes the next day—a wish Sir Naren grants because, he says, he is not afraid of 'that woman'—so she and Roderick are shut up in the library together. Prem knows her husband is afraid of the woman, very afraid. But of course she goes along with his rhodomontade, his charade of authority, softened by pity for him, and soothed by their unity of purpose for once.

Lilian and Roderick stay inside a long time. Lilian will not be invited to stay back for dinner, Prem has decided. When Lilian leaves, she offers her the use of the driver and car, though. Lilian doesn't say a word about what happened behind closed doors. Roderick has disappeared. As has Sir Naren. Prem feels she has to stand up, stand tall, for all of them. She does her best.

Noblesse oblige is one crutch. "There's a lot of anger outside against English people, Lilian." She calls her by her first name instead of Madam Hartfield. This is not the time fifteen years ago. She is a different Lady Mitter. "You had better take the car. A mob might attack someone they think is English and alone."

Lilian shakes her head, silently retrieving her hat in the entrance hallway. "Please," Prem says. "Sir Naren would also like it."

Lilian now shoots a look at Prem that contains something Prem cannot decipher.

"Yes, Indians have become especially good at attacking and killing unarmed and innocent people. Women even."

Prem knows what Lilian means. Though it was years ago, people haven't forgotten the Chauri Chaura incident of 1922 when a mob surrounded, locked, and finally set fire to a rural police station. Four Indian policemen were burned alive. Since then there have been incidents of bombings and assassinations, or attempts at assassination, of British civilians. Bhagat Singh awaits hanging in Lahore for having set off a bomb in the Legislative Assembly. But her tongue catches fire.

"Innocent? After four centuries of ruling by force you call your people innocent? I don't know where you live, madam, but India is for Indians. So go back to where you came from and no one will attack or bother you."

Lilian simply says, "Goodnight, Lady Mitter. I shall return again tomorrow at your teatime. Kindly have Roderick available." Her voice is black ice.

If Prem could have, she would have remained silent. She can't.

"Please tell me."

"Tell you? What?"

"Please."

"Oh, you want to know if your husband is my son's father! Why should I? Who asks?"

Prem gathers herself up. She will not be at this woman's mercy. Whatever happens it will be a fair fight.

"The person who helped you when you most needed it and took in your boy. The person who's raised that boy with love. She asks, and you will tell her. Is Sir Naren Roderick's father or not? After all I've done, I deserve to know."

As Lilian's heels click-click away, Harish romps down the stairs. Normally he's with his tutor at this time, but today he seems to have escaped early. "Mother, why was that lady here again?"

Prem is holding on to the bannister of the spiral stairs that ascend from hall to upper floors. It's hard to breathe. But then, what does it matter? Will she stop loving Roderick now? It doesn't matter. Roderick is hers, whoever the father is.

"Go back to your room and your studies, Harish. This is for grown-ups. And don't forget to drink your milk at bedtime. I've told the nanny that if you make a fuss, Papa will have to come and make you drink it himself."

Harish makes a face between distaste and appeal. "Mother," he resumes, "will Roderick go away with that English lady?"

"Quiet," Prem snaps, all her indignation and terror about to be poured onto Harish's head, which she desperately hopes to avert by sending the child away. "Always listening in on grown-ups. It's almost your bedtime; what are you doing here?"

Harish can count on his mother's frequent patches of deep tenderness between the rocky outcrops of strict parenting. He makes another face and says, "Do I have to go back to maths lesson with my tutor, Ma? Can't I go to bed now?"

"No, back to lessons, and then to bed, when Mr. Sengupta leaves."

Mr. Sengupta—Gyan Sengupta—is a tall, undernourished, bespectacled young man who is studying mathematics at Presidency College and trying to keep body and soul together by tutoring in the evenings. He applied to the advertisement Sir Naren had placed for a maths tutor for Harish and was found to be exactly what Sir Naren had in mind. Sir Naren also says there's something familiar about him but he can't place him. Sengupta hasn't said anything about that. He walks with a stoop already and though his clothes are clean they are ancient. Prem feels so very sorry for him. Another widow's son. This one came from East Bengal during one of the famines that have become regular and routine in Bengal and elsewhere. People say it's the rapacity of the English and Indian businessman in cahoots that is causing these famines. Lord Winston Churchill of England has said that he wants to know why Gandhi hasn't died if Indians are starving.

"But Mr. Sengupta never leaves unless a maid comes to get me. He will teach me all night if no one comes!" Harish squeals in protest.

"And that's his decision, young man, and stop talking back to your elders. Grown-ups know what's best for you."

As Harish's face puckers into plangent woe, he emits a shrill scream. "Grown-ups! Grown-ups don't know anything! And . . . and . . . some Indian grown-ups are slaves of the British!"

Prem doesn't know whether to laugh or to cry. She imagines these are phrases and slogans now circulating freely among people everywhere, in this dawn of hope that maybe the English can and will be blasted out of India, and certainly the servants are probably repeating them. So Harish may be picking up these things from them, or even at school. The children of many well-known nationalist families attend the best schools in the city, like his. Unwittingly a limerick comes into her head, something she's heard a young girl in the house sing now and again:

> "You grown-ups punish *Khuku*—
> Sure, she broke a pricey bottle of oil,
> But what about you grown-ups
> Who break the country into two soils?"

Yes, that Lord Curzon did it in 1905. Separated Bengal into east and west, and then had to undo it, the reaction was so bad. Really, what are grown-ups up to in this country? And most of all, the men? What are they doing? How can she in all conscience come down on her thirteen-year-old son for pointing out the obvious? Indeed, even in her own house, her own family, what are the grown-ups doing? What is she doing?

She just waves, therefore, at her boy, saying in the calmest voice she can muster, "Off you go now—be a good boy."

For which Harish finds incentive because there's great shouting from the family floor above them, and he races up naturally to see what the matter is, slavery to the British pushed aside in his mind for the time being. And reversing his meteoric ascent there's the rapid near-tumble of a maid who cries, "O madam, madam, please come please come right now old madam has completely lost her marbles!"

It's a scene in her mother's bedroom. Saroj is sitting on her bed, its linens in a ruckus, pillows on the floor, her own sari in disarray, holding Nakul's hand as he stands by her. Saroj repeats to herself, "Won't let him go! Won't let go!" Prem looks at the passel of maids and servants huddling in the room and asks with uncharacteristic wrath, "What happened? Who let this happen? What's Nakul doing up here?"

The oldest retainer present clears his throat timidly, wiping his face with his already drenched, coarse towel. "Madam, we don't know what happened exactly, but old madam called for Nakul to come up and he came and then she said . . . that he would be sleeping in this room, with her, here, because . . . because he might wake up at night and feel scared. . . ."

A stony silence. Prem looks at her mother. Saroj stares back at her daughter. Her hand still grips Nakul's fist like a claw. Nakul shifts from foot to foot. "Won't let him go! Won't let the maids put him to sleep. His eyes! Oh his poor eyes! Look! So tired!"

"Mai-ji!" Prem shouts. "Let him go at once! You are under some mistake. This is Nakul; this is our servant boy. He doesn't sleep here. He sleeps in the servants' quarters, Mai-ji. Do you understand? Do you understand what I'm saying?"

Saroj shakes her head vigorously. She isn't having any of it.

Gradually the story pieces itself together. When Nakul came up as summoned by Saroj, another maid was doing the bed and getting Saroj into it for the night, hot water bottle and glass of almond milk standing by. Saroj told Nakul to come inside and lie down on the bed by her side. For a good night's sleep, she said, apparently.

Prem winces inwardly but desperately invokes composure. "And then . . . and then . . . ," the maid babbles, "she wouldn't let him go, madam! When we tried to separate them, she started throwing pillows at us and ripping off the bed linen."

"Mai-ji, what do you think you're doing?" Prem returns to her mother. But her mother has suddenly slumped. She still holds Nakul's hand, but her grip is loosening, her fingers are dropping like flesh falling off from bone. Nakul still stands there, and Prem turns to him and says, "And you? You imbecile! What were you doing here? Why did you let her grab you?"

"Madam, I . . . I thought . . . old madam is your mother . . . I thought I shouldn't—"

"Go!" Prem barks. "Everyone go, go away!" She knows she's hyperventilating, tries to slow down her breathing.

Saroj is no longer speaking. She has now slumped even further back onto the bed and is lying at an angle on it, her legs hanging off the bed, her torso, arms, and head flat on it. She's looking straight up at the ceiling. Prem goes around her bed and does the best she can to make up the bed linen. She forces Saroj's legs back onto the bed, and pops a pillow under the light, white-haired head. Then she sits down next to her mother and just looks at her.

"Mai-ji. You can't do such things in this house. You can't act like this, Mai-ji. Think of our position. And yours. How could you want Nakul to come to bed here? Don't you understand what he is? And who you are?"

Saroj doesn't speak or move. She is an ashier imitation of her already withered self. Prem sees that her eyes are closed. Her breathing is slow, her chest rising and falling gently. She takes a hand fan and fans her mother's face.

Saroj opens her eyes. She says, "Who are you? What are you doing in my bedroom? Tell me!"

And Prem flings away the fan and runs from the room, gesturing to Nurse Joseph outside to go in, because she's afraid the long, hot needle still inside her since Kanan's wedding will finally puncture her heart and kill her if she opens her mouth.

CHAPTER 43

Maybe the British knew about karewa. Maybe they didn't. Women like Saroj were told the minds and hearts of the mighty—such as Englishmen—were inscrutable, but for the certainty of their boundless, fathomless benevolence, people say. People said, look at what the British Maibap has done—is doing—to free us, our women, from our own shameful, dark superstitions, and prejudice. First the abolition of Sati. Now widow remarriage! What might be next? People didn't know. They couldn't imagine. How could they? Fathomless bounty is fathomless. People didn't then take the leap of talking about the British possibly giving India freedom. How could they? That was not what the fathomless bounty said was good for India. Some day. But not yet. Truly, the British were the saviors of India!

So if the British, who were the saviors, couldn't be reproached, someone else had to take the blame. Manohar Mishra and his household did, mostly. But Saroj had also heard that agitators led by some Bengali pundit had insisted on the law—to raise the status of poor womenfolk, the pundit Ishwar Chandra who'd apparently come to be called 'The Ocean of Knowledge,' or Vidyasagar, explained—and the British had merely graciously obliged. This way, both the British and the educated Hindu men had maintained their reputations as enlightened beings.

Saroj spits into the corner of the room where pundit Ishwarchandra Vidyasagar is standing with the others, not too far from Manohar Mishra and Older Brother-in-Law—now what are those two doing standing so close together?—amnation!—when she sees them. That woman who was shouting at her is gone. Some *firingi* law was supposed to change centuries of the eating alive of Hindu widows? Hai! Goras, like Older Brother-in-Law and Bengali pundits, were obviously cunning about property and stupid about women. But they might have known that men like Older Brother-in-Law would use the 'enlightened' Widows' Remarriage Act to devour their brothers' widows and property? If they had, were they still enlightened? If they hadn't, how could they not have known?

Saroj slowly spins impaled on grief.

She herself doesn't remember, though, exactly when melancholy turned into an intolerable blackness and swallowed her decades ago. She hadn't felt anything so complete even when Naveen Chand died, when Older Brother-in-Law came around sniffing and snarling. When had she started to recoil at the thought of Manohar Mishra touching her, when had she begun to stiffen at his very approach, radiate a scorching freeze incomprehensible to him and to everyone else? So that he would sweat copiously every time he came near her. *For what do you avert your eyes and your path from mine, my beloved Saroj, the one and only lotus in the great reservoir called my heart full of love?* She could hear the man asking silently.

Saroj couldn't have answered, even if she'd tried. Words were stoppered because they were useless. Saroj would have been glad if she could have torn her chest open and showed poor Manohar Mishra the laboring smithy called her heart. Instead of having to speak. Just shown him.

CHAPTER 44

It's been a while since Roderick left for England.

Of course, Roma was not sent to boarding school. After Roderick left, Prem never brought it up again—not with Roma, and not with Sir Naren. She wasn't about to consider letting go of the other child who'd been in her care all these years. Still, Roma is more rebellious and unhappier by the day. When Roderick went away with Lilian, she wouldn't speak to or see him before he left. After, for a week she wouldn't leave her room, go to school, or eat. Well, at least not much. Prem was forced to remember another girl, about the same age, who'd once seen a young man leave, never to return in that case. But she couldn't afford to be soft. She had to, so she threatened Roma with hospitalization—"Big tubes will be put inside you and you'll have to eat and also go to the bathroom that way"—to end her fast.

Fasting is still popular everywhere. Gandhi-ji's fasts come one upon the other like a flock of vultures descending on prey. They nibble, gnaw, and decimate that body, already mostly skin and bones, one that Winston Churchill himself claims to dread and abhor. Churchill calls him a seditious, half-naked fakir. But the eyes in that seditious, cavernous face remain fiercely bright. Sometimes Gandhi-ji fasts to purify the swinish soul of the British government, at other times to purify the hearts and minds of his fellow Indians. And other times to purify himself. There is no end of purification, or the need for it, apparently.

His most recent fast lasted almost the whole of September. Usually the British give in quickly when Gandhi starts fasting. An empire dancing on the collapsed stomach of a sixty-three-year old man. Churchill hates Gandhi and so India is full of velvety love for Gandhi-ji—*Bapu*, or Father, of the nation—when a rumor circulates that asked by some journalist what he thinks of western civilization Gandhi has said, "I think it would be a very good idea."

Roma still ignores Harish's invitations to play. Stays in her room for the most part except for school and the ritual of tea. At the ritual, the empty chair where Roderick used to sit being removed notwithstanding, there's a pall on the proceedings. Roderick has been gone many months, but the empty spaces he used to inhabit are still monstrously empty, like eyeless sockets. Everyone is slower; Harish alone talks, while Roma slumps deeper into her chair and holds a book up to her face as much as she dares.

Prem watches. One of her fledglings is gone. Some mornings, she wakes up disoriented. She isn't sure where she is. She thinks it may be the village, on a Sunday, with the threshing of the rice harvest sounding outside her window. But it's not. It's someone beating and dusting out a carpet on the lawn. Sometimes she wakes up and thinks it's time for her to go supervise the three children leaving for school. There's the sound of a car driving up to the grand portico. She needs to go remind Roderick to wear his cap to school, which he forgets sometimes, and gets punished. Then the car drives away and she realizes Sir Naren just left for office. Roderick isn't here anymore. Some mornings she wakes up and wonders whether she is supposed to be somewhere else, or what day of the week it is, or what time.

Am I becoming like my mother, she thinks, in dread? Am I going to become my mother?

Reminders everywhere. One day she finds a small cruet of salt in what used to be Roderick's cupboard. Deep, in a corner, in a paper bag. And she knows what it is for. It's from that time so long ago when at dinner Harish called Roderick an English dog and declared him not entitled to salt. She clutches the paper bag with the cruet in it to her chest, sits down on the bare floor and sobs till there are no tears left. Not for that day at least.

And Harish is now supposed to be the budding young master of the Mitter household, and a stately young man he seems about to become. While he moped about and was unresponsive to anything and anyone for two or three months after Roderick left, perhaps at some point the thought crept into his mind that maybe now—his half brother and sometime rival gone—he could find his way back into his father's heart. If so, he's never mentioned it aloud, but Prem notices his attempts to please his father, to act the little man around him, to try to anticipate his father's needs. She understands. She knows the ache of the overlooked child who doesn't know why.

She watches Sir Naren as he sometimes interacts with Harish. The hapless old Noddy doesn't know how to communicate with his own son, she realizes. And she grieves for Harish's earnest and urgent efforts to engage his father's mind, heart, or even attention. Sir Naren never speaks of Roderick, not even when the monthly mail arrives from England with Roderick's letters for him and Prem. But Prem doesn't need him to speak for her to know the vastness of the void he feels. And she thinks that perhaps parents don't love their children equally; that sometimes the disinherited might inherit all or most of the love, if nothing else. It's an anguish shared by husband and wife of which neither will nor can speak.

Because Prem has never forgiven Sir Naren for letting Roderick go. Because in the end it was Sir Naren who broke down and granted Lilian's wish, request and, growingly, demand. And finally one day said that it would be no bad thing for Roderick to get a proper English education, no mean ambition for any fine fellow, and blaw blaw blaw blaw blaw.

He let Roderick go. And why did Roderick leave? She never understood it. She never will, probably. And if some day she does, she will already have bled her patience, her forbearance, to death by then. When Roderick declared that he had decided to go to England with his 'mother'—Prem winced though she tried to look sensible, reasonable, ready for negotiations—he looked first at her, of course. His eyes were veiled, dark with something very like shame. But he explained his reasoning well.

His mother had done without him for most of her life. As she'd explained it to him, she'd left him behind in India, but only in his father's house, only after assessing and examining the household and the lady of it, and feeling confident that he would be cared for, perhaps even loved. That she had known that his father's initial coolness could not last forever. She didn't explain how she'd formed this last notion, but she stressed the point. So that, Lilian—her own story went—had never done anything but for Roderick's own good. And Prem didn't accept it, didn't want to hear it, but she had to sit through that entire explanation looking composed and patient.

For how was she going to make a binding claim on Roderick? Who was she to him, in the end, but a foster mother? And if his mother returned, and his father gave her permission to walk away with the young man the foster mother had made from the child the mother had left behind, by what appeal to logic or emotion could Prem possibly press her claim, her case? How?

Roderick himself pleaded his mother's case, in the end. He said that his mother had sacrificed much, suffered much, all alone. Apparently, in England Lilian had turned from a free-spirited woman into a stern enforcer of Christ's message to unwed mothers, God's angry scold for the sinners of London slums. So the stockings, the shoes, and the prim bun. Indeed, that she was in India at all was because the sternly benevolent Charity Organisation Society that she served had supported her travel. Roderick then said that his mother deserved some recompense, some reward, a chance to spend her remaining days with the young son she gave up, before he left home for good as a young man.

So he left, lives with the reformed Lilian in London, and has now entered King's College.

Is he happy?

Prem knows Harish isn't happy. She feels painfully unable to help the children: her son, Kanan's daughter, Lilian's boy. How has it come to this? She hasn't made any of them happy, hasn't kept them happy. Their mélange of unhappiness clusters in her like a canker.

Please. I tried.

Moreover, Sir Naren has recently developed a new, eccentric liking for Harish's maths teacher, the young Gyan Sengupta, in an interesting turn of things. There's no explanation for this. Mr. Sengupta is a brilliant student of maths, clearly, and a very good teacher, but also very clearly secretive, troubled and maybe a troublemaker. Prem hears that he greets people with '*Bande Mataram.*' We worship the Mother. The Mother of course is India. These are dangerous times. These are dangerous words. People are going to jail for dreaming such things. So a young man openly, boldly spouting such words is clearly a malcontent, a disaffected citizen of British India. Yet, somehow he feels protected by something, someone.

Gandhi-ji attends one Round Table Conference after another in London, while some of India's youth seethe at this parlaying with the enemy. Another youngish man named Subhash Chandra Bose is becoming a shining star in the Congress Party. It's whispered that he will supersede Gandhi-ji's nonviolent noncooperation strategies. Subhash Bose, it is said, believes in armed resistance as the only way to overthrow the British. He sweeps the young and impatient off their feet. It's him the impatient youth follow when they greet people with Bande Mataram.

"How can you encourage a young man who says Bande Mataram publicly when you feel as you do about Gandhi-ji and Subhash Bose?" Prem asks Sir Naren one day, in desperation.

Subash Bose, also called Neta-ji, still drives Sir Naren to paroxysms of rage, always. Of Gandhi he has an opinion possibly lower than his for Winston Churchill. He chortles uncharacteristically flamboyantly, recounting that Churchill has begun calling Gandhi the 'Hindu Mussolini,' a rabble-rouser, a new Rasputin. The times are troubled and indeed confused. India is vast, unsettled, fragmented.

"That is exactly it," Sir Naren says, recovering himself after his chuckling during which Prem stonily fights the urge to bop him on the head with his own newspaper. "This country can't govern itself. This country is not ready to be self-governed. This country, I humbly beg your pardon, was never a country. It's never been anything but a loose confederation of warring tribes with power-hungry chiefs." These are also the kinds of things that the British have been saying for decades. The kind of thing Colonel Reginald Dyer, RIP, believed.

Prem doesn't follow the logic. Is there one?

"The Bande Matarams and the Gandhis will, in the end, cancel each other out. And the British will laugh. And that's why I don't see why Sengupta's little hobby should be taken too seriously. On the other hand he is an excellent business manager and accountant!"

Husband, Prem longs to say, you are a fool. And also a pompous ass. And Sir Naren probably reads some of this in her expression. And says, "Ah well, these are young men's follies, flourishes. Gyan has a good head on his shoulders. In the end that's all that counts."

Of course Harish notices his father's predilection for Gyan Sengupta. Now his old maths tutor is the latest competitor for his father's affections. What is his father truly made of, Harish wonders? What is it that makes him pick anyone but his own natural heir and scion as a confidante, a surrogate son? Perhaps this is not quite how it is, but Harish can't but feel that he's been passed over again. And that there is something especially, terribly wrong with this. Sir Naren gives his maths teacher, a stranger, a nobody, a position that should be, must become, Harish's: manager of his entire construction and materials business called Mitter Ventures.

The construction and supplies business is booming. Everyone says there's another war coming in Europe. Hitler and Mussolini are making vicious, tearing sounds, baring their fangs. War is good for business. Sir Naren needs an assistant, a man with a cool head on his shoulders. But Prem thinks this is part of his lengthy, maybe endless, atonement for sacrificing another young man without name or inheritance. Sir Naren aligns himself with strays, because of Roderick. And himself. And doesn't know it.

Prem expostulates. "Your son is ready to join you in your affairs," she tells Sir Naren.

"Stay out of things you know nothing about, madam," Sir Naren grouses.

"I know this for sure—your son feels neglected, and he resents it."

Harish has, rather unfortunately, taken somewhat to a roué's lifestyle. Sir Naren can't not notice that Harish eats and drinks too much because sometimes he's loud and maudlin when he drinks. Rumor is that he's been seen at soirees of certain disreputable madames and socialites in Calcutta, and perhaps even at the *kothas* of *Baijis*. Sir Naren mentions none of this to his wife. This shall pass, he doesn't doubt. He himself was young once. Wild oats and all that.

But Harish's heart is changing as it shatters and regroups. In an attempt to appear canny, insouciant, resourceful, he tells Prem that he will now try to make friends with "Sengupta Sir." Some future day Sengupta might, as an elderly, experienced subordinate, initiate him into the concerns for which Sir Naren now considers him unfit.

He says airily to her, "So I said to him, 'You're behind the times, sir; you're not looking ahead.' I told him he and Papa are both relying on materials and building as though this war will last forever."

Gyan Sengupta apparently doesn't mind being lectured by his former importunate pupil. After all, Harish has no authority over him. He reports only and directly to Sir Naren. Again, closed door meetings in the library. But it's hard to read his mind. Young as he is, and perhaps quite callow in some ways, he has something vulpine about him. As though he moves among people with his claws retracted and loping subdued. A trace, a scent of ferocity always accompanies him.

Meeting him as he pads his way out of the house sometimes, Harish will affect breeziness. Blowing a desperate smoke ring into the charged air around them he will say to his old teacher, "Have you been paying attention to German engineering, sir? I hear they're making wonderful strides."

"Yes, thank you," Gyan Sengupta says, glancing at Harish myopically as though he wonders whence this life form emerged. Then he shrinks a little further into himself and shuffles out of the house.

"Sir, does my father know that you are a member of the Congress Party?"

Gyan inclines his head, almost closing his eyes. This might be the squirming, hooded Bengali style of acquiescence or deferral or deference. Or, it might be a gesture of tut-tutting incredulity. The thing is, one doesn't know with him.

Gyan seems everywhere all the time: at his own office now on Rawdon Street; in Sir Naren's library office; in Sir Naren's office on Theatre Road; at the cement and jute factories owned by Sir Naren; at new construction sites.

CHAPTER 45

There's another well-developed dramatic duel Prem watches, anxiously, hopelessly. It's Saroj and Roma. Roma, to begin with, was entirely indifferent to Saroj. An eighteen-year-old girl who will go around with the mien of a star-crossed tragic heroine isn't likely to be interested in an old woman known to be quite batty. But somehow Saroj has developed a bitter distaste for the girl. And will do nothing to hide it. In her quieter moments she performs an elaborate act of tucking her head into her neck and pretending to look away—like a child trying to appear crafty about its malice—when she sees Roma. In her more rambunctious moments—Nakul is now forbidden to come into her line of sight, but he quite strangely frequently blunders his way into it—when she's been propelled away from Nakul in the wheelchair she now needs, should she catch sight of Roma she bursts forth into a phalange of abuse. "*Ei kahlo bhoot!*" Dark spirits are everywhere, Saroj can testify. One day she says to Roma out of nowhere, "You kahlos should never be trusted. A big mistake. You lowborn people are the creepy-crawlies of the earth!" Another time she sees Roma coming up the main staircase as she's being wheeled off the landing to her own bedroom and sets up an unholy clamor: "*Petni! Petni!* There's a *Petni* here!" Petni means female spirit. Petnis are known to be frighteningly ugly. And dark.

Roma remains kahlo. This is one of her great challenges. Maybe the greatest. After all, in India a girl cannot be considered beautiful if she's not fair skinned. Compared to Prem and even Saroj's still effulgent light skin, Roma is simply, crudely, quite murky. But how, why, and when Saroj has married together Roma's skin and another murky past—a double misfortune no girl can survive—no one can say. Might she remember The Dusty One, or Kanan? Did she ever really even look at them? Notice them? Not as far as Prem remembers. Then how has she put together Roma's complexion and her low birth? No one can disabuse Saroj of an idea once she gets it, and so Prem has long desisted from trying to do so, but there are days she simply wants to pull out her hair and bay.

Like one night thirty years ago she does, unfortunately, ask the darkness around her sometimes: "When will my mother die?"

While Roma seems to go off on a new destructive spree after the Petni incident with Saroj—Prem's cosmetics keep disappearing, things get broken, clothes spill out of dressers and cabinets onto soggy bathroom floors—Prem tastes the bile of her childhood rage, the hammering of her small, powerless heart thirty years ago. And she wonders if, or rather when, Harish will ask the same question about his father. Will she be able to protect even one of the children from this suffering, this curse? Motherlessness is homelessness for girls, after all. And fatherlessness? Nothing short of annihilation for boys, it seems.

It takes her time to summon up enough fortitude to go speak to Roma about the incident. Roma is, as is typical, lying spread-eagled on her bed, her face pressed into the mattress. The girl has grown taller, but she will always be fairly petite. Prem takes stock of her options at the threshold. Truce, she decides. She clears her throat. No response. Well, at least she's announced her intent. Presence. Stepping up to the bed she sees the faint rhythm of Roma's breathing. She sees the wild, wavy curls thrown over the bed, and the slight twitching of the fingers of one hand.

"Roma, my child, my mother is an old woman going senile. She doesn't know what she's saying. You know that. You know how she behaves, don't you?"

To her surprise Roma turns around and looks her straight in the face, a thing Prem has begun to despair of more and more from the children, or from anyone else around her, these days. She perks up a little, like a dying plant suddenly watered.

"But she's right! And that's why everyone hates me!"

"Everyone hates you? What are you talking about, dear? Who hates you?"

"Everyone!" Roma cries out. "You, Roderick, your mother, Uncle, people at school! Everyone hates me. Because I'm kahlo! At school they call me 'Her Darkest Highness!' Because I'm not like you all; I'm the maid's granddaughter . . . ask the maids downstairs, they all say that. . . . Why did God make me dark? Why am I dark when even my mother was at least fair?"

Roma's question, though without an answer, is the question that Prem is aware many young women and girls born in this society, this country, ask, have to ask. It's a bane, a curse to be born dark skinned and female in India. Roma's complexion has lightened slightly over the last years of being cooped inside her room by choice, turning from a drab brown to a strong olive, but she's still darker than everyone in the family. Put it plainly, she's like her father. And Prem doesn't have an answer for Roma's question. Her own marriage was largely possible because Sir Naren was looking for a near-white-skinned bride. During the marriage people said, "Look! Look at the bride's skin! Almost like a Mem!" Yes, that was her most important credential. If a girl's skin is fair it doesn't matter if she has the face of a potato or a princess.

Defeated, Prem retreats. Now she asks her husband again if he will provide for sending Roma away for college or a preparatory academy. She may be happier in a place where there will be many different kinds of girls, where her family history need not be known, where all everyone will know is that she is a member of the eminent Mitter family of Calcutta.

Maybe Sir Naren is unwell that day, or maybe he's unhappy. Maybe he's suffered a big loss in business. Maybe he remembers Roderick. Slowly removing his pipe from his mouth, he looks at his wife for a few seconds. She doesn't like the looks of that look, but looks back at him, steadfast and steely.

Sir Naren speaks, his voice glacial: "May I remind you, madam, that this darkie is the child of a maid's daughter and a peon?"

Prem holds her breath for a few disciplined seconds while the diamond earrings that she wears twinkle as if trying to lighten the situation. "Is that a no, then?"

Sir Naren, saying nothing, is back at puffing on his pipe, but his hooded gaze reconnoiters this woman whose will and fixity of purpose he's come to know so well.

In a calm, even voice Prem continues, "In eighteen years of marriage I have asked you for nothing. You've given me things unbidden, yes. You give me an allowance, and I spend it wisely and carefully. I have given you a son—or rather two, if you really think of it. Something that I think no other wife would have."

Sir Naren chews and spits out his words: "I never asked you to, madam. You did it without asking me."

Prem rejoins, "But aren't you glad I did it?"

What Sir Naren is thinking will never be known. He's not given to flutters and outbursts. He sees life as a series of transactions and barters, hence the language of credit and debit means something to him. His wife knows this. She thinks she will get her way.

Prem also brings up this going away with Roma. The reaction is so unexpected and violent that she has to retreat and take some time to recover.

"So now I get sent away too? See how I said you hate me? See? First you sent Roderick away—now me! Why did you and Uncle even let Roderick and me come and stay? Why didn't you just have your precious Harish live here with you? Why? Why did you do this to us?"

"Stop being melodramatic, Roma!" Prem feels angrier and wearier every day. What's the matter with this girl? What ingratitude! Why such defiance? Where would she have been today without Prem? Married off as a kitchen drudge to some rascal, by that rascal of a father who just wanted to get rid of her! How have the children grown such hard hearts? And toward her of all people! Do they not know what she's had to do to manage Sir Naren, just to keep them?

"Yes, I'm melodramatic, and it's all *your* fault Mashimoni! Because you are the one who took me to the bioscope when I was so small! Why did you do that? Didn't you know that the bioscope is bad for children? Didn't you know Gandhi-ji said they're bad for everyone? That they are like a drug? A poison? You . . . you never think of anyone but yourself, do you?"

Prem wants to howl. She wants to say that all her life she's needed to prove herself worthy of being loved. And her own mother never loved her, and doesn't love her now. And her Roderick is gone.

Trembling with rage she tells Roma, "Then why don't you tell me what you want to do, you stupid girl, since you think you know everything?"

"Yes, I'll tell you," Roma quavers back. "I . . . I want to be an actress."

CHAPTER 46

One day Nakul is found pilfering Saroj's trunk even while she lies sleeping on the very bed above it. She seems to be sleeping very deeply; the commotion doesn't awaken her.

"Out of here!" The old servant Motilal says, glad to finally expel something that has always reeked of mischief at best and malice at worst to him. Saroj seems undisturbed by the ruckus which occurs mostly outside her room. Nakul doesn't resist very much. An odd stubbornness has hardened inside him. He can see a new time coming, a time when these people will regret their doings.

Nakul rises from the pavement outside the gates of Mitter Mansion, dusts himself off, and spits. The spittle glob lands about a foot from Motilal's feet. Motilal has come out of the compound of Mitter Mansion to ensure that Nakul is out, and speeded along on his way. From most of the windows facing the front gravel driveway of Mitter Mansion, faces are peering down. Most of them are indifferent to the matter as such but a few glad indeed to see Nakul go. Mary Joseph among them.

Decades later, when Nakul is Minister for the Interior in Omprakash Narayan-ji's government led by the Janata Dal, the party that will profess to be of the masses, not the spawn of the upper-class Congress Party, Nakul—he'll be Nakul-ji by then—will personally supervise the income tax and fraud bureau investigation of Mitter Ventures and Holdings, have them found directly culpable of wartime appropriations, tax evasions, commercial fraud, and of unpatriotic designs and activities. Also, unsympathetic to populist politics and the interests of the people. He will order the confiscation of all the assets of the Mitters.

That day in 1935, though, Nakul is found stealing—possibly—from Saroj's trunk, kept as usual under her bed. But Saroj wasn't asleep as he was doing this. She was dead. When the first hubbub of discovering Nakul's attempted theft occurs, everyone thinks Saroj is sleeping unusually deeply, perhaps slightly overdosed with sleep medication by . . . who knows, the thief himself? But when after Nakul's expulsion morning rolls into afternoon and Saroj still remains motionless in bed, Mary Joseph raises an alarm. By the time the postmortem is done there are clear indications of asphyxiation by something held over the face and head. By then, no trace can be found of Nakul.

It's wartime, again. The world is in flames again, and this time the fires are also burning in Asia. Who will pursue and bring to justice a mere servant in one of many wealthy households caught stealing, but not caught murdering? The police have their hands full tracing and capturing armed insurgents hastening up Britain's long goodbye to India. Saroj's murderer shall remain forever unpunished.

That night Prem sits in her mother's bedroom. She sits in the rocking chair where Mary Joseph used to sit supervising Saroj, though that dawn when Nakul came in Mary Joseph was fast asleep, didn't wake up, and consequently couldn't say if Nakul had in fact held the pillow over a struggling Saroj.

How could it end like this for Mai-ji? Prem remembers her once dear wish: for her mother to die. She remembers the terrible things Shyampiyari would say about Mai-ji. The fear or another unpleasant feeling Mai-ji aroused in the household. Her solitary existence. Her habit of staying up nights, talking to herself. The day that changed Prem's world forever when she understood, as a girl, that she had once been loved by Mai-ji and then somehow lost that love. Why? She'll never know. Those cuts on Mai-ji's arm.

Saroj's battered, tormented form is laid at rest—finally—in another room. The cremation will be next morning. Maids are taking turns watching by her, guarding her spirit, while Prem takes a little break. Prem has come to this room tonight with a purpose. She's closed the door behind her. The polished floor of Saroj's old bedroom glows eerily in the pale lamplight from the street. Under the bed, the old trunk waits like a horned toad. It's one of those old-time iron chests painted over with a motley assemblage of gaudily colored gods and goddesses. In the patchwork dark, the gods and goddesses have withdrawn from view, and all that can be seen are dented edges and pugnacious corners. Prem gets up from Mary Joseph's rocking chair and squats on the floor, facing the trunk. She grips its metal handle—cool and smooth as snakeskin—and pulls it out. Opens it. Squatting was as natural as breathing in girlhood; now her knees and haunches complain. She settles down on the floor, crosses her legs, feels the cold traveling up from the floor into her body.

There are sundry assorted things in the trunk, as she expected: fabric swatches, spools of thread and twine, a woolen muff, variegated seashells, a lingam on a square base, a small container of vermillion, a few silver bangles. Impatient, she claws deeper. When she did this as a girl she didn't have enough time. Mai-ji had slithered up behind her. Maybe Mai-ji's spirit is now hovering angrily to guard the old armory of her life before the village. No matter. Prem continues to rifle. A little muslin sack containing—wonder of wonders—dirt. A gold *mangalsutra*. As a girl she'd never seen Mai-ji wearing this. Maybe Nakul thought there would be more of that kind of valuables. Then she feels a smooth papery surface. Slowly, carefully, she works her fingers around it and pulls out a photograph.

It's the same photograph that she saw as a little girl. Even in this light she can tell the photo paper has aged in confinement. Its serrated, cropped edges are crumbly. The photo is now blitzed sepia. The streetlamp outside brightens and dims but doesn't go out. Prem can make out the print of that young Saroj proudly holding her baby (a soft tuft of hair tied high up on the right side of the little head with a ribbon, kohl once dark around the eyes). Young Saroj still looking at baby, as if in that moment time stood still forever. Prem feels beneath her fingertips the ridge where the photo is patched up, its halves stuck together with coarse homemade glue. The texture of the joint, glutinous yet brittle, has a distinct sensuousness. Prem feels almost bodily pleasure in grazing the ridge of crusty glue with her fingertips.

With more time now, Prem notices how the baby's sturdy, plump leg grasps the young woman's hip like a warrior riding a steed. Even in the faded print, once luminous eyes swim out to Prem on a river of silver gelatin.

What happened? The old question; old, sharp pain.

She turns the photo around. Behind the photo is a date: 1893. Next to it are the words "*Shirimati* Sarojbala Aulakh and Son Akshaya Aulakh." There's the stamp of a studio with an address in Rohtak, Haryana.

Akshaya Aulakh. Son? Gently, slowly, Prem rubs the surface of the photo with her thumb. Young mother and baby. A precious thing. A sacred thing. The young woman is happy. Prem holds the photo a little higher up to the streetlight. Yes, it's the face of the woman she knew as mother alright. Happy. Holding her baby up to the world. Look, look, see how happy we are. A perfect image. Perfect happiness. A perfect world.

But that baby is not herself. The baby in the picture is a boy. Akshaya Aulakh. Why is it a boy? Who is the boy?

Mai-ji?

She'd almost forgotten. That night all those years ago Shyampiyari had muttered something. "Killing one child wasn't enough for her; she wants to kill this one too."

Her mother had killed this boy, somehow. This Akshaya Aulakh? How? What happened to him? Did he really die? So her own lost baby wasn't the first baby lost?

Prem pushes her hand deeper into the trunk but infinitely gently, as if someone's crumbling bones are in it.

There's another envelope. Another piece of paper. The writing on it is fainter than the stamp on the photo's reverse side. In a shaky hand, in Hindi letters that climb up and roll down hills, are the words in near-vanished ink:

I, Shirimati Saroj Devi, write this in the English year 1903 in hopes someone someday might read this and give it to my son Akshaya Aulakh. God reads my heart. I, widow of Naveen Chand Aulakh who died of smallpox, lost Akshaya when I escaped from my husband's house. My Older Brother-in-Law was forcing me to become his second wife, but I wouldn't. He is a very bad man. My Akshaya was going to come later with my maid Munia to the next rail station by bullock cart. We arranged this to avoid raising alarm if all three of us were found gone at the same time. But Munia never came. My Akshaya never came. I never saw him again. He was only two. Later a woman came to my second home with a girl. She said she was Munia's sister. She told me that Older-Brother-in-Law's men caught Munia and beat her to death. That they took my son back to the house and then my Older Brother-in-Law left the village. I don't know if the woman told the truth. It's too late now. Still, I live with the sin of my son's sacrifice. Had I burned with my beloved husband Naveen Chand maybe our son would have been spared. May the Almighty forgive me. He knows the truth. If anyone who reads this ever finds my boy, please show him this writing. He has green eyes. If God won't forgive me, I still beg my son's forgiveness.

Prem returns the photo, letter, and envelope to the trunk. She lays them down neatly, patting their surfaces, passing her fingertips over them a few times as if reluctant to say goodbye.

Nakul has green eyes. What seemed like an obscene attachment was a woman who never forgave herself believing that at last she'd found her lost son, had been forgiven.

She'd loved the son. She couldn't let herself love her daughter. She'd loved the son and lost him, and nothing else ever mattered.

The cuts. The gills on Mai-ji's forearm. Tales of the demon mother, feeding off blood.

Lies. She was spilling her own heart's blood, wanting to die. Unspeakable grief. Unbearable guilt. Wounds self-inflicted to let out the demons screaming inside.

A drop of water falls on the photo; Prem hastily wipes it away. *Smile, little Akshaya, smile forever in your sepia world. See your mother smile at you, Akshaya. She never stopped loving you; never will.* Prem has to rub her eyes to clear her sight, wipe a face slippery with tears. *Mai-ji, you sleep too. You've earned your sleep. No more nightmares for you. No more staying awake waiting for your son. Now you can sleep.*

There's a smell inside the trunk that reminds her of her Dhai. A musky smell of old cloth and tobacco. Shyampiyari's smell. As if Shyampiyari is also in the room. As if Shyampiyari will at any moment touch Prem's head and stroke it again and again, as long as her Bitiya demands it, until she falls asleep. Prem wants Shyampiyari, right here, now. *Dhai. Do you still love me?* She gingerly picks up an old short blade, dangerously rusted at the edge. Then her fingers graze a bundle pushed deep into the back of the trunk. She pulls it out, unties the rustic knot holding together Shyampiyari's old shawl. This is the source of Dhai's smell. The rough wool-cotton blend reminds her of the old woman's skin. She presses her face into it, breathes its smell deep into her lungs. Holds her breath, tries not to let the smell fade. Opens the bundle slowly, cautiously; the smell must not fade. Inside the bundle there are a few ribbons; a little string of red glass beads long enough to go around a child's neck; a small muslin handkerchief. A rattle; a miniature fan with a Japanese lady on it.

Her girlhood possessions. Back in the village. Now she remembers her father writing that Shyampiyari had left a bundle of things for her when she died. She'd forgotten completely. Neglected to claim the little, humble bequest of the old woman. Dhai had truly loved her. And she left her back in the village and never went back. Why is love so hard to get, and to keep? She clutches the bundle and presses it hard to herself, stuffing it into the new hollow that's opened up in her. *Dhai, I miss you.*

How long has she been in this room? It doesn't matter. She will go back to the room where Mai-ji lies, waiting for fire to bring her peace at last. She won't look again at Mai-ji's scars—little screaming mouths—one last time. That's her mother's nakedness. She will respect it, not examine its tattered remains, not inspect and expose it one last time. She will stroke the white-haired head one last time, say a prayer. *Goodbye. I forgive you, mother.*

She dries her eyes, her face, with the end of her sari. She almost considers looking through the rest of the bundle later, but there's something harder, like paper, inside the old bundle. She decides against exploring, then changes her mind. She opens the bundle completely. There's a sheaf of envelopes tied together by a string. They are of pewter grayish color. They all have AIRMAIL printed on the top, just above the address. They are addressed to *Kumari* Prem Devi, village _____, Zillah _____, Bengal-Bihar. They haven't been opened. There are letters inside. Settling down on the floor, cross-legged, Prem begins to read in the mottled light of that dawn Jagat Pandey's words to her, written almost twenty years ago.

When she has read them all, she replaces them in the shawl carefully. As she is about to tie the shawl back into a bundle her fingers touch smooth glass. An old vial half-full of small dark pellets. She takes the vial out, returns the bundle to the trunk, closes it, pushes it back under Mai-ji's bed. She walks back through the dark hallways to her own private parlor, lowers herself onto her favorite couch, unscrews the lid of the vial, and takes out a single dark pellet. She stuffs the vial carefully under the cushions of the couch. She pauses, takes it back out, takes out one more pellet. Again she pushes the vial back under the cushion. Drops the two pellets into her mouth and lies back. Closes her eyes. Waits for total darkness. Realizes just before it overtakes her that she didn't return to her mother's room, didn't say *Goodbye, I forgive you, mother.*

CHAPTER 47

Now in his twenties, Harish believes he understands a great deal that other people don't. He sees things most people don't see. He understands the power of invisible things to move men, muscles, minds, even hearts. He understands the electricity flowing out of countless invisible fingertips that will bring masonry and machines crashing down like a house of cards. There's news about how Germany has some complex, sophisticated machine called the Enigma that the Poles, French, and Dutch are trying to decipher. How these Enigma machines are now being made in different countries, even by the Italians and the Japanese. That's the kind of future Harish foresees. Admires.

The world is going to change forever. Men like his father and his old tutor Gyan Sengupta are antiques. His father, he's concluded, is a fossil, which is why they have nothing to talk about, nothing in common. Gyan Sengupta is useful as a workhorse. But no imagination, no vision, whatsoever.

This is also why he likes the bioscope and bioscope folks. They're modern. They're visionary, imagining a reality that reality knows nothing of. They're like other new things he'd like to create and run. Like exchanges, banking and insurance companies. Those bring in money in tidal waves, shockwaves.

Though he's only about twenty-two, his disappointments have stamped Harish with a certain physiognomy. His head's starting to look down upon the rest of him; his girth is starting to keep people slightly away. He's inherited his father and his maternal grandfather's physiques, it seems. But unlike his refugee father he's never known what it is to lack a roof over one's head. So the mandarins of Naren Mitter and Mitter Ventures are especially losing access to him. They might resent this as the breakdown of the old way of life. But a new set of young men is replacing them, waving their tall weedy heads in Harish's fantasy dome. They are a new kind of young Indian. They're mostly young, fresh-faced, bespectacled men in drainpipe pants and laundered shirts with sleeves rolled up to the elbows, as if ready at a moment's notice to fish opportunity out of murky waters. Many of them are tired of the political language and events around them. Like Harish himself. Tired of an old-fashioned patriotism. Tired of Gandhi, tired of Subhash Bose, tired of the Raj. They just want to get the best technical education, or at least know-how, available. They just want to modernize. Knowledge is power, they say. They pay no attention to who's right and who's wrong, and all that old-fashioned morality natter. They just want to usher in a new era of progress. They focus on the what and the how, not the why. Whatever government, whatever authority will smooth the path to that, has their loyalty.

Other than his roundedness, Harish is one of them. Enough of revolutions other than technological ones. Born a supply merchant's son—petit bourgeois, really—Harish wants to turn into a 'noteworthy notable' as Calcutta's stately *Statesman* newspaper titles some of these new men, and even a few women. And always, he believes in the disposal of icons that have served their purpose. He's more like his father in this than he knows or cares to think about. He has his father's ability to abstract, detach, excise. Maybe this is why he and his father can't understand or communicate with each other—like repels like.

Despite his landlocked riverine lineage, his heart yearns for the salt sea and sandy gales. Why he can't say. He looks westward, toward Bombay and the sea. Sometimes his friends say—though this mostly on account of his fair skin, inherited from his mother—that there must be some firingi in him, from generations ago when the east and the west embraced and mingled more chaotically in India. Probably cock and bull stories. But it pleases him a little, secretly, to think, and believe, that only truly powerful men, like Napoleon, sprout myths around themselves.

Even from Calcutta he wants to begin investing in the hungry film industry in Bombay, though it may someday bring many other regional industries in Calcutta and elsewhere to ruin. Harish doesn't mind ruin. Those who can't modernize are ruined. As far as he's concerned, it's the Parsis, those descendants of ancient Persian migrants to India, who've introduced the mantra of modernity into India's dreams. Like Calcutta's own adopted Parsi son, J.F. Heeravala, of Heeravala Studios. The talkies have arrived, thanks to that Parsi Ardeshir Irani and his stupendous film *Alam Ara*. The jaws of old-fashioned filmmakers are still struggling to come off the floor after that. Bengali and Hindi directors of the old school are running with their tails between their legs, closing shop, downing shutters. Because they can't modernize.

Ruins foretell another future. And now war is again on the horizon. Out of this conflagration, Harish is convinced, the old order will change, yielding place to a new one, where men like him—and the Parsis of course—will look at the ruins of old buildings, businesses and enterprises, and feel themselves grow out of their fathers' shadows.

One day he decides to tell his father this. That ruins foretell another future. That he respects the builder types and the kind of empire his father has built as a government contractor; making iron, jute, cement, things used to build things. Building things. But the future. That's a different matter.

"A bit *fin-de-siècle*, don't you think, Papa?"

Sir Naren has not been keeping in very good health lately. Lots of rest, the doctor has said. No pipes, cigars, and liqueur for a while. He feels strapped to a life without pleasure by miles of strips of worthless medicines prescribed by doctors like undertakers: for the heart, for the lungs, for the liver, for the eyes, for the circulation. For my foot, he thinks.

Truth be told, Harish has had to come fortified by stronger spirits than just his own.

"Look at the ruins of buildings, Papa! Look at this coming war and what it's already doing to cities, countries, societies, people who thought their monuments would stand up to time. Don't you want me stepping beyond that? Look at the Parsis in Bombay, Papa . . . to what level they've taken commerce and culture and married the two! And here we are in Calcutta, counting beans, eating rice, writing newspaper columns scolding the British—but the British really are all that stands between us and ruin!—and repairing roads that we ourselves built before the rains."

"Is this what you think of me?" Sir Naren asks, dangerously calm.

"No Papa, but times must change and so must we. You may despise the bioscope as does Gandhi-ji"—and Sir Naren must squirm a little uncomfortably here at being put in Gandhi's camp in this regard, which Harish knows and also enjoys a little—"and actors and actresses, but the Parsis have got it right there too. The next age is the magic age of the silver screen and communications, Papa. Oh, people are tired of reality and history, Papa. They need . . . they need a little relief, a little fantasy . . . some entertainment!"

Sir Naren considers his son to be raving. He looks at him. His suit is pathetically too tight for him. He's bursting out of it. He probably can no longer see his polished wingtips if he looks down. Everything bought with Sir Naren's money, of course. And the fool thinks that his bulk is stature. As soon as he speaks of the bioscope, Sir Naren arrives at a firm conclusion. The future is ruin.

"I'm going to become what *The Statesman* calls a 'noteworthy notable.' Papa, believe me, one day I'll make you proud. . . ."

Not just a petit bourgeois supply merchant's son, Brown Baron notwithstanding, Harish thinks to himself and, alas, his father can hear him. Sir Naren's son is going to invest in the scrappy, murky, hungry film industry.

"Not with my money," Sir Naren says simply. He'll remind Harish who's the real ruthless pioneer, the visionary.

"But I have so little money," Harish says. "Sengupta controls everything!" The alcohol in him is now getting restless.

"Leave me," Sir Naren says bitterly. "Please, leave me." His son's damn fool notions make him sick to his stomach, his heart palpitates alarmingly, and the bell has to be rung for someone to bring him a restorative—nonalcoholic—tonic recommended by the doctor for just such occasions.

Harish talks to his mother when something goes especially wrong between him and his father.

"Papa's quite ill, you know. He almost never goes to the Theatre Road office anymore. Sengupta now takes care of everything." He's angry enough to no longer acknowledge the old relationship between him and his maths tutor. The fella is now just a fella, a certain Sengupta.

Prem looks at Harish, weariness pulling down the corners of her eyes and mouth. She's just come from Roma's room and another conflagration. She'd just been considering another black pellet. Harish comes closer. Short as he is, he still looms over his delicate-looking mother who sits on her old, slightly fraying chaise. She pats the seat beside him. He sees suddenly how small, how frail she is, sits down by her, puts an arm lovingly around her delicate shoulders.

"He's taken over a lot of the day-to-day work, Ma."

"You don't want to do that kind of work yourself, right son?"

"Yes, that's true, but we really know nothing about him other than that he says he was a brilliant student at Presidency College and that he's good with accounts and that his mother's a poor widow. . . ."

Absentmindedly Prem says, "Sometimes these things are all true."

"But how do we really know that he is trustworthy, above board? I know for a fact that he is quite active in the Congress Party, actually."

Prem sighs. The winds blowing across the land are bound to enter even this stronghold of those more loyal than the king himself. It will, she thinks. Let it.

"Do you worry a lot?" she asks her son, closing her eyes in simple, utter weariness.

"Don't you, Mother?"

"I have a new worry now, Harish." And she tells him about Roma.

"Didi wants to act in the bioscope?" Harish is genuinely surprised.

It's been some time since that conversation with Prem, and Roma still seems unable to calm down, settle down. To do anything much, really. She seems to shrink on the one hand from the social circles of the Mitters, and on the other hand she seems quite eager to be part of something. Something else, she says, something bigger.

"Something bigger like what?"

"I told you, Mashimoni! I want to be an actress."

Poor thing, Prem thinks and worries. She isn't exactly a head-turner, her Roma. Kanan wasn't a beauty, but at least she had strong features and wheaten skin. Unfortunately, Roma has rather a hard time being noticed at the society parties and galas that she attends. She has, if the sad truth must be told, a shrewish face. Her nostrils flare sharply away from the low bridge of a somewhat flat nose, and her eyes are not beady but not exactly lustrous. They are too closely set, moreover, and her eyebrows are strong and thick. Perhaps hers might be called a face with character. Or perhaps it's just a dissatisfied, self-loathing face. Roma does have a full, wavy head of hair, though, something she's secretly inordinately vain about, and that she tries to keep in continuous heavy-duty maintenance. When framed by that monsoon cloud halo her face isn't pretty, but it can look piquant. Perhaps even lively, mischievous. Maybe I assess her too unsparingly, Prem thinks.

But the look on Harish's face confirms something else. It isn't exactly astonishment. It's embarrassment, consternation. Roma doesn't have the looks to be a successful actress, it says. Not even a minor one, maybe. She's not ugly. She's just too ordinary.

"So there's agitation and rebellion at home, too," Prem says with a wan smile. "Anyway, son, what is your news? Besides worrying about Papa, what else are you up to these days?"

Every day now for a few months Harish has been wanting to confess something to his mother and veered away at the last moment. Even today he can't tell her. The time never seems to be right.

Harish has a secret in his life, one that his parents would rather die than accept. It's partly the weight of that secret that has redoubled his need for his father's approval, his father's validation of his manhood. But it's not a matter that he can bring up easily. He doesn't tell his mother, again.

CHAPTER 48

City of fairy tales, gossamer dreams, or nightmares, Calcutta has begun hearing of a certain Rehana, an Indian nightingale whose recorded voice will, decades after Rehana vanishes, reduce crusty men in their dotage to nostalgic, rheumy tears. Her name right now coils through elite sybarite circles of the city, across races, castes, and religions. She is the beautiful young rising star among Calcutta courtesans. Something of a last great brightness before the extinction of a tradition of entertainment that lived for centuries, since at least the old Muslim and Mughal rule of India. Cosmopolitan, talented performers, graceful and strong dancers, witty, sometimes gifted poets. Declining into their last days of glory, they are a breed yet distinct from prostitutes and streetwalkers.

Trained in the tough classical methods and traditions of generations of such foremothers, Rehana has, besides a voice of stirring purity, a habit of biting her lower lip while smiling at the effusions of her admirers. It drives middle-aged men nearly berserk and old men nearly potent. On *mujrah* evenings she sits on a Persian carpet in brilliant brocaded *ghaghra* and *angrakha*, toes and fingers reddened with henna, draped in the mirrored and sequined jewelry of her foremothers judiciously sprinkled with strands of gold and gems that *Nawabs*, Babus, and Englishmen bestowed on one or another of them, a gold-fringed veil cupping her leaf-shaped face. She sings of patient love and morbid pining, raising that pretty face to her admirers who lounge, long and slump before her on elegant satin and velvet sofas—the mangy rolling on the floor of old princelings, pimps, and hangers-on being a thing of the past, or of penurious infamy.

Love is something Pyari Bai hasn't discussed with her daughter. (Pyari means beloved, but whose beloved, and for what? Questions that give rise to raucous laughter in that house.) Love is also a topic Pyari Bai didn't discuss while closing a certain deal with Harish Mitter regarding daughter Rehana. While Rehana was quite well coached in how the bedroom scene goes—between rape and romance—she's been told nothing about any "happily ever after." In fact, throughout the house, every time the word "love" is uttered there are peals of laughter. Or angry curses, or parodies of whiny film songs where women moan about *ishq* and *bewaafa humsafar* and *behuda duniya*. Her mother and 'aunties' hawk and spit hard and sharp at it. But that doesn't mean that Rehana, only nineteen, doesn't think of it. Fact is, every song she's learned from her music teacher is about love: love for God, love for a faithless man, love for wine, love for love.

But what's this love thing? Where is it to be found? The popular saying is that the brothel is where love is bought and sold. But that's vague nonsense: what's sold at the brothel isn't love but bodies, and sometimes youth and beauty.

Love remains an enigma.

However, Pyari Bai is no fool. She's told Rehana that she prays she won't throw away good fortune when it comes her way, as it surely will. She doesn't really know her daughter very well, actually. She was too busy training and performing when Rehana was growing up. It isn't her fault. She was young then and her best and only years of making money were in full swing. But Rehana grew up here and there in the big house, half the day spent looking out a window at the street below. People, carts, and stray cattle, cats and dogs moving in and past the slick rivulets of filth and more filth. Sometimes she played with some orphan toy, watching other aunties do their preparations for the evening. Sometimes she gawked at her mother—the world's most glamorous woman—singing or thudding rhythmically to the dictates of the *tabla* and the squawking of the dance master.

Everything around is—was—sound, song, color, and flash. There is—was—no center to that world, just pretty frills. The sparkling, packed shops on the street below are—were—never empty of customers. There's always life flowing in the gully below right alongside the constant, faithful filth. Voices and gestures swing, leap between balconies of brothels. Their own enigmatic code Baijis communicate with pitched above the heads and ears of unwary customers already in beds, or on the street making their picks. These customers come and go to and from houses like Rehana's—night and day—just like the rest of the flowing, frothy filth. They come to forget, they come to enjoy, they relieve themselves here, and then they go back to their lives again, wherever those are.

Rehana has known since girlhood that she and her mother are special because they have always had the big room with the old gilt mirror that some infatuated Nawab gave to some dead Baiji, her grandmother or something. It doesn't matter, what really happened. Their lives are not about reality. Rehana has grown up trying to copy her mother—her *latak chhamak* gait of buttocks pushing each other aside as she walked, her gentlemen-maddening songs, her dance movements—before the splotchy mirror in her room. She'd catch a rare glimpse of her mother sometimes as her mother was rushing to the dance hall, or coming out of their room with a departing "guest." Rehana was not to go near the room when her mother had a "guest," or a "friend."

But Rehana has also always known that her mother loves her. She doesn't know her—when has she had time?—but she loves her.

Love has kept Pyari Bai moving through the years and the twists and turns of a dancing girl's fortune. But she's never had time to sit Rehana on her lap and comb and oil her ragged mop and all that. She became a mother at fifteen; Rehana was small during her peak years, the years when she needed to make her money, for the time would come soon enough when no one would ask for her. Rehana has seen it happen to other aunties: teeth rotting, arthritis attacking, tires of flesh wrapping around a once svelte waist. Or worse. Diseases that swell, burn, or rot. Screams from rooms with no traffic for years. It can happen to Pyari Bai too. So she's had to miss her daughter's childhood for the sake of her youth and womanhood. She has focused on finding for Rehana a kind and generous protector while she's still young, pretty. A sort of sole proprietor so she won't change hands much. It's the best the courtesan can bestow on the next generation.

CHAPTER 49

Harish spends most evenings at the kotha. However, tonight, May 1938, there's a party at the Theatre Road mansion of the renowned bioscope producer-director Jagat Pandey. It's the same Theatre Road where once stood a British theatre called the Theatre of Calcutta, burnt down in 1839 and never rebuilt. This night Theatre Road booms and bustles like any other High Street in a British City, but Pandey Sahib's house stands well back from the main street itself. The front garden is in extraordinary bloom. Thickets of English roses jostle, sheltered by Indian banyan, neem and mango trees. A single huge pride of Barbados with flame-curled blossoms towers in a corner of the lawn, looking at the firingi roses with lofty disdain. Countless fairy lights make the summer night look frostbitten.

Pandey Sahib is now close on retirement but he still makes an average of two films a year, and also produces a number.

He treats his actors and stars with respect and consideration—they are his gods and goddesses, bread and butter. His reputation as a filmmaker is tip-top. He's had calls from the siren of the Arabian Sea, Bombay's Hindi film industry. He even made a few films for a few chosen studios, but then he withdrew. His creative needs are not met by those projects and people and, besides, he wouldn't abandon the fine cohort of actors he's introduced, nurtured, and mentored into bright stars in Bengal.

And he's helped, or tried to help, many who've come to him in need. Among those a few he's groomed into stardom. As Heeravala-ji groomed Prudence Cooper Madam. Cooper Madam was a great lady. And a real star. She started as a lowly dancer but real talent won't stay down. A full blow-up photograph of her face, washed in that moonlit silver that was the magic of early the bioscope, hangs prominently on Jagat Pandey's drawing room wall. In the style of those days, she looks like an angel, trapped on earth, gazing up at her heavenly home.

Wars ruin lives. Jagat Pandey remembers Prudence Madam joining Heeravala Studios soon after the Great War ended. Those who lived through those years saw such things. Things Jagat Pandey knows about; other things he can guess at. Such cruelty, and yet such courage. Brotherhood, and also beastliness. Flowers and corpses.

How could women not have suffered too? Women have always fought their own battles. Men say they fight for women, but Jagat has seen women ripped apart and buried by wars they didn't choose. Madam Cooper never spoke to anyone about the years before she came to Heeravala.

That's what the bioscope does. Gives us hope. Makes life possible. Lets us dream. That's what Jagat Pandey wanted to do after he returned from the war. That's what he does.

Love's Garden

Actors are born. They're also made. The best ones are born to be made.

Now, his house is beginning to fill up with guests, laughter, voices. He sits in a dimly lit corner of his drawing room and sips tea. This is one of his so-called quirks. He won't touch alcohol. His mother's face rises before his eyes if he ever entertains the thought. He's a Kuleen Brahmin. But he understands the modern age. His guests are liberally plied with any poison they desire.

People are always impressed and intimidated by the tasteful interior of his house and its grand proportions. There's a grand piano at one end of the drawing room. Light floods in through the wide bay windows. Leafy jade and emerald potted plants stand in silent dignity at well-chosen spots. A bookcase covers one entire wall, holding thick gilded volumes of all sizes and widths, many of which Jagat Pandey has read. He was a schoolmaster, after all. Other than the books, and the great framed photo of Prudence Madam, he's had nothing to do with the things in the house. Bought everything outright at auction from some great family that fell on hard days and had to sell out. There are many such in Calcutta since the war.

Dinner has been announced. The guests begin to stream into the imposing dining room gleaming with silverware. Fresh flowers in tall cut glass vases on the immense rectangle of table. A chandelier spreads a soft glow over the sparkling white cloth covering the table, and when dinner begins arriving the stateliness of it quite overcomes Jagat Pandey himself. Most evenings Jagat Pandey dines alone on a few wheat rotis, some *daal*, and a vegetable of some kind. Occasionally he eats a little chicken—plain roasted. This is one little vice he picked up in France, where he mostly starved otherwise. His cook is a very old, wizened man in a sharply pressed uniform that looks like it's been ironed onto him. Those are not Jagat Pandey's requirements; the cook insists upon this form. No doubt he cooked for some great folks once. Pandey Sahib is told that his nightly dinner is far beneath the cook and is always relegated to some humble assistant.

But his cook and housekeeper know their jobs. The dishes themselves have been carefully curated, or so he's told by the lady married to a top actor, sitting to his right. He can never remember her first name. She always seems dissatisfied and cross. He's tempted sometimes to pat her on the head and say, "Things are not so bad, you know, Mrs. Bonerjee." Unfortunately, her husband and top star of musical romances Utpal Bonerjee, he knows, is having affairs with three different women at the same time. So he can't, not quite.

If he'd had a daughter she might've been about her age. But he never presumes. Especially since he can't remember her first name.

The kinds of people that are never at his table, or in his house, no matter how ill that serves him, are great society folks. He never mixes with Calcutta high society. Those people need too much attention, pampering, lies. He has no love lost for them. He skips the society pages in *The Statesman* newspaper. They invited him to their gatherings and events many times but finally gave up.

He is, above all else, a fervent believer in India's right to complete self-determination. The ravening empire that scooped him up into its maw and then spit him out almost dead, penniless, must go. Altogether. He follows Gandhi-ji like a god. It pains him that Gandhi-ji has forsworn the bioscope, calling it a corrupting influence on the masses. Secretly, Jagat hopes that he will make a film one day that will convince Gandhi-ji otherwise. That Gandhi-ji might even come to see. And change his mind about the bioscope, understand that the bioscope is not the problem, society is the problem. A world of rich, lazy people who want only what lines their pockets and advances their self-love. These people are the problem. That's why he avoids those high society folks among other things. Actors might misstep, but those high society people never do anything but misstep and misspeak. Gossip, lie, and ruin. When Poorna Swaraj, complete self-determination for India, comes—and it can only be a matter of time—these people's heads will be the first to roll. He himself eschews violence, but he knows others won't spare them.

He's getting to know one young man from that set, ironically, rather well of late. His name is Harish Mitter, and he's a dreamer. A bit of a spoiled brat, maybe, because his father is a business tycoon, even knighted by the Raj, but with his heart essentially still throbbing in the right place for the right things. In some ways he's becoming like the son Jagat's never had. Though Mitter's father is some eminent toady of the English, hence unknown to Jagat, this Harish boy has his own ideas. He's confessed to Jagat Pandey how he's fought off his father's attempts to make him study law. Jagat approves of this because the law, he tells Harish, is in any case the law of the English and has nothing to do with justice for India or Indians. It's only to serve the English themselves.

Jagat Pandey makes films that exalt Indian culture, history, and people. Watching the old reels of *Bilet Pherat,* the film that held up a pitiless mirror to that hobgoblin that is the westernized Indian, still reduces him to paroxysms of relieved laughter. But neither Harish nor Jagat Pandey talks about politics, because they have an understanding: Art for Art's sake versus Art for Freedom's sake. The former motto belongs to Harish while the latter belongs to Jagat Pandey, and each knows where the other stands without saying much about it.

The evening passes well after dinner, with a few songs performed by the nightingale of Bengal, Hemlata Sen, and a lively charade by a few of the junior actors who are hoping to make their careers on the good will, good advice, and good direction of Pandey Sahib. More sherry and brandy are drunk, more toasts are raised to Bande Mataram as well as Auld Lang Syne.

When everyone's gone, Jagat prepares to go to bed. He generally sleeps early. But tonight there's a great storm outside. A summer explosion. Looking at the rain lashing the tall trees outside, without invitation or preparation, he remembers. Like a film flashback. After decades. A scene from another life.

A storm shakes the palm fronds and rough thatches of village huts.

Montage: storm sweeping across landscape and camera panning over a great house in the distance.

Cut to a loud knocking on the rickety door of young schoolmaster Jagat Pandey. Jagat is surprised; who would visit, and in such weather?

Cut camera, again. To twenty years later. Now. An elderly man is standing by a bay window; outside it almost seems like daylight when lightning flashes.

Like a scene from another world, the lawn rolling away from his house comes afire in a blaze so white that every last single blade of grass looks like an ice crystal: singular, unique, distinct. It is, as they say, a dark and stormy night. Cliché. Yes. But clichés are at the core of life. They are the framework for complicated, novel stories.

Maybe someday he'll tell his own story. His clichéd story. His own. Not hiding behind mythology about virtuous wives. Lover, fighter, artist, and patriot. Telling the true stories of men and women who've loved and lost. In the language of the bioscope, of course.

CHAPTER 50

"There," says Harish, fastening the rope of gold sprinkled with tiny diamonds around the soft, plump throat of the girl-woman he loves. "Who in this world is like you, *Jaanu*?" What are the moon and stars compared to you?" Rehana regards herself long in the mirror, twisting this way and that to admire herself and the necklace, face radiant.

Bai-jis' kothas wouldn't be on the usual beat of wealthy, westernized men like Harish. But because he keeps company with artistic types—bioscope actors, musicians, poets, and singers—he came to Rehana's song-house and was trapped. This should be a situation where he reigns. It isn't. Instead, like many other bested and tamed imperious suitors, he is the hapless, agonized, tenterhooked prince in an ongoing Thousand and One nights of story, in a song of Sirens over moonlit rocks, a voyager on the mysterious island of Circe, wanderer in the nights of houris and peris. Harish is Selim and Rehana is Anarkali—this from the piercing homegrown grand romance of the young Mughal prince Selim aka Jehangir and his beloved slave girl Anarkali, who was walled alive for her presumption by imperial dictates. Few who come to these publican lanes are dreamers. Harish is one of them.

How can Harish tell anyone, least of all his mother, his secret? If he does, every article, every syllable of his desperate, forbidden passion will be used to write the chronicle of his unworthiness for his father's trust.

He's had to submit to indignities unknown to his kind of modern young man. He has had to regress in time, quite contrary to his views on the glorious modern future. He has 'bought' with a hefty tribute to Rehana's mother—the once coveted and now aging courtesan Pyari Bai—the privilege of 'removing Rehana's nose ring.' Thereby he has symbolically if not actually taken Rehana's proclaimed virginity, and unless he changes his mind she will be his unique property. She might sing and dance for others still, but only he will follow her into her bedroom night after night, or at least those nights that he chooses. Or, in their case, those she chooses.

Every morning Harish wakes up with Rehana she comes to him bathed, perfumed, and bedecked, and coaxes him to sweetened rose water and a princely breakfast, even though she can also be delightfully—modernly—silly at times. She washes his feet in warm, scented water and dries them with her sandal-wood scented hair. It's mostly a charming masquerade, but not entirely. Then she feeds him bits of crystallized, gingered sweets and fresh juicy fruit by hand. "Stop, stop, I'm already fat enough," he stutters in mild protest, but protests end in enough regained heat and steam to fall back into bed and dishevel and dismay Rehana again. Who says this is not "love"?

Now, Rehana knows Harish's father is an important man and rich as Midas. She also knows Harish himself is interested in the bioscope, moves in that world. She isn't hungry for his family's money, but secretly she does harbor a hope that he might get her a role in the bioscope. So many women have done it lately. All those Jewish ladies, and that Nargis, the daughter of a courtesan herself as is well-known. Why not Rehana?

Harish brings Rehana, meanwhile, costly presents, mostly jewelry that her mother Pyari Bai has intimated will be most acceptable of all gifts, except perhaps cash only. Rehana has a generous monthly allowance settled on her, his gifts not included, and she only has to ask for something for him to provide.

Involuntarily, unknowingly, Rehana begins to fantasize. Standing before the mirror while Harish fastens his newest blazing tribute around her elegant neck, she recognizes her beauty in full blaze. The fantasy begins to consume her. Why can't she be a wife? Why can't she leave this place, though the only place she knows as home, and start over again as a respectable woman? As Harish Mitter's wife?

She asks Harish in bed one night, "Will you marry me, Sahib?" She feels a chill when he says nothing but his breathing changes. She props herself up on one elbow and looks at his face, anxious and a little heated. He still doesn't speak, and she asks, as any nagging wife would do, "What? Can we not?"

"It's not done, *Jaan*," he says finally in a small voice.

Tears shoot out of her eyes. "Of course it is," she says, stomping vocally. "Suchitra from next door has just been accepted by her longtime man, and now she lives happily with him in his Bagbazaar house." Pausing, she looks at Harish aslant.

"Happily," he says, as if discovering the word for the first time.

"Yes, happily," she returns it to him like a gingerly held newborn. "Why not? Am I less than her? Because I'm from this swamp, am I less than the fancy lotuses you grow in your vast reservoirs?" She means wives. Then she flounces down on her side of the bed, wrestling with the physical pain she feels. He lies still, staring up at darkness, overcome with remorse. He can't tell her that the man who has taken Suchitra is a petty cooking oil merchant and far freer than Harish Mitter.

One day during this season of discontent she sends down word at Harish's arrival that she is too unwell to admit him. Harish weaves his way out into the dirty street below, clutching his hair, his eyes staring wide. Around him people make way for him as he wanders toward his car, thinking he's a madman or a drunk. He's a lover in pain. But in this neighborhood that's unlikely if not risible. Half his shirt hangs out of his belt and his silk jacket has a rip at the shoulder from him trying to force his way past the stolid doorman who's seen and handled worse. Even standing patrons must be admitted or not only by order. Harish doesn't come for a week after that. Rehana cries herself maudlin. Pyari Bai scolds Rehana to bits.

Rehana cries muffling her face in her loverless bed. Pyari Bai says, "*Oyay!* You listen! Your father didn't marry me either! Hell, he didn't even bring me jewels and perfumes and English-style shoes to wear around the house like Mitter Sahib does."

"Do you even know who my father is?" Rehana screams, then shuts her door for hours.

Outside, Pyari Bai stands, her words died out, her ruined face and incongruously kohled eyes pincered by pain. She tells herself: this is the custom; this is how it is. You know that. You raise a child with the wages of your sin, and then they curse you for the life and fate you have given them. After a while she hobbles away on the arthritic hips of an old dancer.

After that week, though, Harish returns and of course Rehana relents. He tries to please her in other ways. He makes arrangements for her to do a voice-recording of one of her best-rendered *thumris*, and brings her a genuine gold-plated disc of the extended playing record. Pyari Bai's eyes shine with pride as well as greed. A few more of Rehana's songs are released commercially. She also receives more invitations to sing at weddings and follies of Bengali Babus, but Harish asks her not to accept these, and she obeys, still riding a fantastic flowered swing in the cooling breeze of the marriage fairytale universe.

There are men in her drawing room every night far more handsome, just as young, and at least rich enough. Somehow, though, it's Harish she wants to see, waits for. She has fallen in love, it would seem. Pyari Bai scolds her daughter again. "It's the Baiji's biggest mistake: to need the man instead of making sure that he needs and wants only her. Why only a courtesan's mistake, it's the mistake of any woman. Never let a man feel like he can have power if he wants it. Always keep him in beggar mode. The minute you let him think he has power over you, he puts one foot out the door."

But the dream remains, obdurate. And maybe it's the dream that makes it happen, since dreams can be stuffed into the heart through the gashes made by doomed loving. The wound, some poet says, is where the light comes in. And the dream grows into faith, into axiom, into poetry even. Six months into her fledgling modern career of gramophone singing, Rehana discovers she is pregnant. At first she can't be sure, but when the decrepit *Hakim* all the Baijis swear by pronounces her definitely with child, her heart fills with wayward hope.

When she tells Harish his face blazes first, then collapses. She clings to his arm, looking hopefully up into his face. He says very little more that evening, but holds her tighter to himself that night than he ever has. Her heart sinks. But he returns as expected the next evening and seems to be in fairly good spirits. She sings especially sweetly that night, feeling unfamiliar joy despite the uncertainty of the future. From behind the velvety curtains where she usually lolls, smoking her hookah while a maid presses swollen feet peeping out under voluminous ghaghra folds, Pyari Bai watches her daughter with anxious scrutiny and dread. Mixed, as always, with a love so sharp it slices her heart.

Like in the bioscope, there's a great storm that night. Wind slaps the tops of tall trees and palms, sounding like a million hands beating breasts, moaning. Lightning spears darkness; thunder crackles so loud that Pyari Bai sends her reluctant apologies—"*gustakhi maaf*"—to Rehana's admirers, asking them to adjourn and depart for their residences in their assorted Bentleys, Aston Martins, Rolls Royces, Jeeps and even humbler Fiats and motorcycles. They all leave, expressing regret. Rehana was singing so exceptionally well tonight. To no one's surprise, Harish stays back.

The morning after, like the venerable trees and proud palms uprooted and tossed among flotsam and jetsam and an occasional broken animal carcass nauseating the drenched, cowering city, Rehana's hopes and dreams of being married lie blasted and withered.

"It's because I'm Muslim, isn't it? Suchitra's man took her—a nice Hindu man—and she's a Hindu. You Hindus hate us Muslims from the bottoms of your hearts, don't you?"

Harish winces. "Jaan, no Jaan! You know I love you! You know that the whole world could be against you and I'd still love you! You know that, Jaanu. You know I don't and shall never love another!"

"You love me but you can't marry me? How low a creature are you? You can't acknowledge this child? You don't have the courage for that? Who's ever heard of a real lover who doesn't have courage? Did Majnoon have courage for his Laila? Heer for Ranjha? Did Romeo die for Juliet?"

"Don't talk about dying, please, my best beloved," Harish begs. "We are so happy as things are! We can still be so happy! Of course I'll own our child as mine. Of course I'll take care of him and you forever! But how can my parents accept this? They can't. They'll never accept such a marriage. I may be able to persuade them to—"

"Oh ho ho, ai hai hai!" Rehana shrieks. Centuries-old kotha dirge oozes out in the twisted, warped syllables of a beautiful young mouth disfigured by pain. The whole kotha hears, jerked awake. It's another dawn of heartbreak. All the aunties know what it is, at once. Pyari Bai strikes her head with her palm and then keeps pounding it with her fist, pummeling in turns her pillow and her face. Writhing like a woman in childbirth.

"Big lover has come here, hai hai! He can love and he can fuck, but he can't marry! Oh, he can make babies but he can't tell his big daddy what he's done!" Harish clutches his head, covers his ears. Moans, totters out of bed, rushes to the window, pushes his head out, shaking it as if to dislodge the sounds of wounded rage.

"What did I ever do to you but love you?" Rehana howls. "What did I ever do to you? Why are you doing this to me?"

Then. "Did you ever love me????"

Harish will never forget the crescendo of that question. For years, for the rest of his life, the sounds will crash again and again on the borders of his mind, sleeping, dreaming, or waking. He will wonder where she went. Where she took the child.

From the brothel section of Bowbazar, where the kotha is, it's about twenty minutes by rickshaw and a few by taxi to Bow Barracks. Bow Barracks is an old cantonment area where the sweepings of empire have gathered as Anglo-Indians and Christians, where a certain puttering, angled mode of English is punctuated by "*babaa*" and "*come naa*," and so on. In one particular house there, like many others painted red with green shutters, Pyari Bai and Rehana and a single maid put up after the move from the Bowbazar Kotha. Rehana has her baby there.

Then she becomes Jolene.

She does this with the help of Anglo-India and Christian girls of the neighborhood who take charge, knowing her history, one that many of their mothers, and some of them, have lived. Through some of it Rehana is barely aware of her surroundings, of those around her. Only when her son wails she shakes loose a torpor that otherwise mercifully cradles her in its close embrace.

Her hair is bobbed and dyed a bluish black, her eyebrows plucked and penciled into thin arches, *angrakhas*, and *salwar kameezes* exchanged for low-cut frocks and patent leather pumps. When the whole transformation is finished—complete with an education in basic spoken English—Jolene sits back and regards the thing she has created. It has taken almost a year. Then she weeps.

Yes, she's very sentimental that way. She's always loved bioscope music of the sort she'd begun making herself. Far more, in fact, than the kind of *tawaifi* singing that she had to master for a livelihood. She would have liked to sing for the bioscope, but all that's gone.

Then one day like any other Jolene sallies forth into a new world of clubs, dancing, and partying late with officers of the many armies crawling all over British Calcutta. She forsakes the protected dewiness of her past self for something tougher, powdered, and lacquered. The baby stays home with Pyari Bai and gurgles when he sees his mother, but she hardly ever picks him up. If someday she has to give him up for good, it's better this way.

Herself, she will be someone's wife some day and set up house, for real. Naturally, like other lovely women who stoop to one or other kind of folly with men who betray, she imagines love forever massacred in her heart. But a husband, home, and respectability she will have.

Harish glimpses her just once during his increasingly frequent and erratic nocturnes, but what with being blotto and also half-witless in grief most of the time, he doesn't recognize her as once upon a time Rehana. The transformation is an entire success.

CHAPTER 51

It's grim out there. Roma knows. She understands. There's a big war going on. Sometimes she wonders if Roderick is out there fighting. Maybe he decided not to be a sailor. It's been a long time since he's been heard from. If he does send letters, the whole household doesn't get to hear of them as was once the case.

Inside her too there's grimness. Darkness. She doesn't know what will become of her. When Mashimoni dies, who will take care of her? How will she stay on in the house? Won't Harish marry, have a family? Will Harish's wife let her stay? What's it like to be the poor, spinster aunt, and not even a blood relation?

As usual, she storms Prem with her recurrent complaints about life, and the theme of the bioscope. "Mashimoni, Harish knows so many people in the bioscope industry," she grumbles. "He can easily take me to a producer or director for an audition. It's not beyond him. He just doesn't try. No one in this house cares when it comes to me." Prem is so fed up with the whining—her own thoughts wander now in another world and a time she'd been sure she'd rubbed out forever, beyond restoration, and she resorts to a black pellet oftener than she wants to—that she asks Harish to please, please take the befuddled young woman to someone, somewhere, to try to see if she can get a role, any role, in some production, any production, except anything vulgar.

"Didi isn't exactly . . . you know Mother, what I'm saying"—Prem sadly nods at this—"and besides the bioscope world is not in great shape either right now. Raw stock is in extremely short supply; studios are shutting down. It's not that easy to make films these days, or to get someone into films. . . ."

In the end, though, he decides to try Pandey-ji, the one film industry persona he respects and likes, with whom Roma will at least be safe if not successful. Casting couch stories are plentiful, and they're surely not all baseless. He tries not to think of Rehana, for whom once he didn't perform such an errand for selfish reasons.

Roma is beyond excited. The day of her visit—a euphemism for the crass word "audition"—she dresses herself to the gills, georgette and glitter from head to toe, the pages of glamor magazines her main inspiration, but also society figures. She has decorated her buxom mignon of raven hair with jasmines. A little outlandish, or perhaps it's artistic; hard to say for sure. She's wearing a daring outfit—a silver-brocaded, translucent black georgette sari that falls about her feet in soft folds and layers, a somewhat brief white satin blouse with full see-through chiffon sleeves cuffed at the wrist, and a cape of diaphanous shot silk gathered at her throat with a diamond flower pin lent to her for the occasion by a dubious but silent Prem. She can either trail the cape behind her or gather it about her petite form, whichever the director prefers. When finished, the mirror reflects back her sartorial skill.

Roma has learned to dress well. It's an adventurous time in spite of or maybe because of the war. She envies and vies with, in spirit if not in substance, that *belle de jour*, that social butterfly par excellence, Lady Edwina Mountbatten, India's last British viceroy's wife, who's rumored to be having a torrid affair with the princeling of Congress, Gandhi-ji's right hand and ear, Pundit Jawaharlal Nehru, another Inner Temple lawyer like Gandhi himself. In spirit, Roma knows she's the equal of any female Don Juan. Her resources being somewhat limited, she reinvents herself every day with adventuress styles and outfits, little flourishes and frissons that pay tribute to her daring and stylishness, beauty itself be hanged for there's enough of that going around and no one much the happier for it, are they? Look at Mashimoni herself, she thinks.

Pandey-ji has been in the business a long time. Of course he's his eternal gracious, kindly self, but Harish catches at once the regretful incredulity in his gaze seeing Roma.

"What kinds of films do you like, Miss Chatterjee?"

Roma names many. She tells Pandey-ji in a hopeful effusion that she began thinking of the bioscope and acting when she went to see *Nala Damayanti* with her Mashimoni, Harish's mother. She tells him, fawningly, that she idolizes him, always has. Pandey-ji doesn't cease smiling but he looks down at the floor in unpropitious embarrassment. Then he explains to Roma that he wants to usher in a new Golden Age of Bengali Cinema. Create a legacy and remind Bengalis of their own creativity, their heritage, their genius. He speaks as he looks away or down, though, and again Harish's heart sinks. And aches for Roma.

Roma gives her audition.

"A bioscope that will make Bengalis respect—no, worship—women again, and believe in family, love and sincerity. That's my hope and my dream." Those are Pandey-ji's kindly words as Roma and Harish leave. He will review her screen test as soon as pressing business allows him some time. He looks mildly, benignly at Roma and his glasses twinkle.

Roma doesn't know what he's talking about, clearly. She looks anxious. But a shadow comes and goes in her eyes.

"Because for too long we've had tired melodrama, nauseating tear-jerkers and tawdry tragedies. Haven't we?"

Roma nods, uncertain.

Pandey-ji certainly has the gift of the gab. Harish understands that he will let Roma down gently, very gently. He also understands why he's been a great success in the cut-throat, desperado film industry. His poetry is the moving image, and he its keening bard.

Indeed, in a few days Jagat Pandey tells Harish: "She doesn't have any real talent to speak of, my friend. The plainness I could work with, even give her good character roles. But she can't act! I can't do anything with that."

Seeing the look on Harish's face he relents. "I could maybe cast her in a bit part like—you know—sister-in-law, or neighborhood friend. Maybe a nurse or a housekeeper. Yes, that might be possible. She wouldn't have many lines."

Harish thanks him and leaves. Pandey-ji says, "Do let me know."

"What did he say?" Roma meets Harish at the front entrance as soon as he comes home. One look at him tells her that he hasn't exactly come to crown her the new queen of the Golden Age of Bengali Bioscope.

"Didi, yes he said he might have something, but let me come in and cool off, please."

Roma's face falls but she waits with an ill grace. Harish flees to his bedroom and doesn't come down till dinner time, an hour or so later. Roma hasn't been pounding the foyer or anything but as soon as dinner is over she looks at Harish and makes a very slight movement of her head but one that will clearly brook no further waiting. Resigned, Harish leads the way to the informal sitting room, Roma at his heels.

"He could offer you a role as a supporting character."

"What kind of supporting character?"

"Well, someone close to the female lead . . ."

"I suppose that might do to start with," Roma says. "After all, I have no experience. Did he say when I can start?"

"Well, he said he'll let us know . . ."

"What does that mean? Didn't he say he was starting a new movie, something about a Golden Age?"

"That was about a new *kind* of movie, a better *kind* than the dreadful trash being made these days."

"Okay, okay, I don't need to know all that," Roma renews sharply. "Just tell me what kind of supporting role?"

Harish says he has no specific information yet. He has more presence of mind than to mention bit parts: a loose-lipped neighborhood shrew, a sprightly maidservant, a housekeeper. And he feels tremendously sorry for Roma. He sees that she feels that her springtime has come and maybe is about to leave.

He doesn't bring up the subject with Pandey-ji again and Pandey-ji, with innate good sense and compassion, doesn't revert to it either.

Roma goes into a wintry despair. Especially, she refuses to go to the bioscope anymore, for so long her favorite recreation. When Prem invites her she says she has a headache; the movie will be of no interest to her; she's tired. Anything and everything. And she doesn't work on a believability that she knows is not expected. Harish knows she's truly crushed when she doesn't bring up the question of the audition again with him.

Why has she always set her heart on what's thought to be beyond her reach? Dominance. Roderick. Being an actress. She wouldn't know if asked, wouldn't recognize the condition as her own. She doesn't know that she wants to be special; all she knows is that she simply wants her due. The world owes her much. The world owes her something.

But the world is at war, an epic of hatred, rage and suffering. People won't remember it much except those who must, whose lives—as they knew them—are blown apart. Villages torn off the face of the earth. Women raped, then beheaded. Children bayoneted and crushed by rolling tanks as they lie dying. People will later think of the Second World War (again) as "the war to end all wars"—but now all the news is of POW camps. Only the lucky return, stick figures, hollow-eyed, from the edge of the abyss.

1942. Burma is in danger of falling to the Japanese. The Japanese are marching, snarling at India's borders. Sir Mitter talks about the pragmatic Americans and of pragmatism as the reality of life.

Then bombs fall in Pearl Harbor. America joins the war. Sir Naren is stumped and then even more effusive in praise of that great country. "By Jove, what a great country!" he takes to saying. He says it like a child holding a splendid, live fire-cracker in his hands, usually in the company of other stalwart men.

In August 1942 a young Royal Air Force Sergeant visits Mitter Mansion.

Without notice, without announcement, he shows up that sweltering August day. Hard to trace in him the thin boy who was always outgrowing his clothes once. When someone announces Sergeant Hartfield requesting leave to see Lady Mitter, Prem is reading the paper. Her Lady Mitter and Prem parts are especially not talking these days. The world looks very bleak to her. There is no way back to the past, not even to atone for all the mistakes. The past and all its loves and suffering are history. The children she's been spared are unhappy: neither Harish nor Roma seems to have a bright day. Sir Naren is sinking deeper each day into the quicksand of not knowing to whom the next half century belongs, though he's very sure it won't be Indians ruling India. Duffers and peons, he says; how can they? She sometimes wonders what he will do if India does gain independence. In the thick of 1942's great Quit India movement Sir Naren clings to the idea that his lifelong overlords will not only beat the Germans and the Japanese at their game, but also the likes of Gandhi and Subhash Bose.

When the name Hartfield is pronounced it's like a live wire held to Prem's tired heart. One part of her travels back to that morning in 1916 when she first heard the name Hartfield. Lilian came, and Roderick came with her. Losing Roderick scrapes the point of a rusty nail across her heart; it always will. And now a Sergeant Hartfield is here. Wants to see her. In a few seconds she untangles the name Hartfield and the Sergeant part from one another. Her lips tremble while her heart is wrung by joy and fear at once. Roderick? He never wrote to say he was coming. She feels like throwing her arms around blind chance and dancing with it.

A few moments later, blinded by tears that didn't brook decent pause or permission, she's saying: "Roderick! Is it really you, Roderick? Oh my boy, my boy!

"T!"

Roderick helps her down to a chair. She's been taking a few too many of the pellets lately, and she promises herself, in her joy, to stop now.

His face is harder but still boyish.

He's come back. His uniform's ridges dent her face. She doesn't mind.

"Roderick."

"T, how have you been? How are you? My dear, dear T!"

Prem sits smiling unguardedly, clutching Roderick, for the next two or three hours as the rest of the household comes to see him, to exclaim over him, to touch him, to gawk, to rush up and hug him as if they were stealth bombers. Like some naïve, unselfconscious woman from a village many lifetimes ago—some woman who must have made her possible, maybe the foremother who saved the gold anklets for her—Prem grins broadly, dreamily saying to people:

Part 6: *Bande Mataram*, Calcutta, 1928–

"Look . . . our Roderick. He's come back."

Harish comes and grasps Roderick's hand. He can't speak. Roderick folds him in a bear hug.

Roma comes.

Roderick bops her on the head. "What? Still unmarried?" She's already rushed up and glued herself to him. Her eyes are shut tight with all the weight of her bliss.

No one chides him, not even fondly. Everyone forgives him for having been gone. Everyone sees that with him, a new time has come. Everyone forgives him everything.

Roderick was posted in Burma. He only has a few days of furlough now, but soon he will be moved to Calcutta. He will come to Alipore every one of those days, he vows. Men on the fields are dying like flies, he also says. Best make the best use of time, he grins. He and his fellow RAF officers mainly fly supply and aid missions. Night and day, cloud and sun and rain, fresh or near-dead, as long as they can sit up in the cockpit and see, they fly supplies and weapons across the "Hump."

That's what they call the northern Himalayas. Mostly Allied American and British Air Force pilots have been performing incredible feats of flight over them, bringing supplies to beleaguered China from the India-Burma border. Over eight hundred airmen will die in these flights, but between 1942–1945 many thousands of planes fly the "Hump"—scraggy five-mile-high Himalayan mountain ranges—and bring indispensable wartime supplies to the Chinese army cut off by the Japanese occupation of Thailand, Burma, and Malaysia. The "Hump" pilots brave the dreaded Japanese Air Force. The feats of these pilots of the "forgotten army" of the China-Burma-India theater of war will later inspire and educate American, British, Canadian, Australian, French, New Zealander, and South African pilots of the Berlin Airlifts (1948–49) who will fly in supplies to a beleaguered west Berlin blockaded by an increasingly combative cold war-era Soviet Union. But also, whenever they can they bring down the Japanese Sally bombers that buzz at the borders of Calcutta.

The people of Calcutta love their city. It's their entire geography of moth-erland. Defending Calcutta is defending civilization. Unabashedly partisan and salt of the earth, all Calcutta will soon love Roderick.

Roderick never says it himself, but Harish pieces together that he's downed more Japanese Sallys than any other officer in the eastern command. For one, he often flies supply missions over Burmese forests where American and British soldiers are hiding and fighting Japs. Some place called Nhpum Ga, for instance, he says. He's flown over that one often, and recently. Harish feels stunned, awed, irrationally exuberant despite the constant ache in his heart.

Roderick says he has specifically requested to be transferred to the air defense of Calcutta. He wants to fly the most dangerous missions. Normally superior officers don't allow such a young pilot to undertake many flight shifts in quick succession. It's not standard practice. But RAF Sergeant Hartfield is counting on his fervent rhetoric to overcome all objections, ferret out every loophole for permission.

Sir Naren surreptitiously wipes his eyes and determines to pull every possible string to block such orders. His son, just returned, mustn't be up in the thundering skies where no one's a god, and there's no God. Sir Naren is an atheist himself but suddenly he feels weak enough to remember the word.

The week after, everyone is, as always, invited to Lady Sinha's annual garden party. It's always a grand affair ending in dusk to dawn drunken joy and concupiscence for some, and righteous indignation and self-congratulation for those others who leave early. In other words, it's always good fun. At the party there are many beauties with pleasing curves wrapped in glossy, gossamer saris or sparkling frocks; beribboned, be-ringed, gem-fire flashing from their delicate earlobes and slender necks; their dainty feet encased in daintier shoes. Coveted, young, highbred, they move like gazelles—a few bolder ones like lithe, rearing Arabs. Notwithstanding this, this night Roma is resolved to have as many dances with Roderick as possible.

This new occasion sits slightly lopsided with their memories of childhood play and pranks. But she and Roderick dance with each other so much that Lady Sinha, naturally nosy, raises one pencil-thin eyebrow. The little group she's queening over all look at the dancers. And so a pince-nez or two also goes up here and there.

During a brief pause in the music Roderick and Roma sit down, panting.

"Fancy that," Roderick says. He's grinning from ear to ear.

Roma clasps his arm and lays her head on his shoulder. "How much fun this is, isn't it?"

Roderick nods, absent-minded, looking around.

"Roderick! I'm talking to you!" Roma pouts.

"Yes, Mademoiselle, I'm all attention."

"I want not just attention! I want you to be all mine!"

"What? All yours? With all these beauties prancing around? Can't I dance with even a few of them?"

"Roderick, I'm serious. I'm going to have you all to myself, you just see."

"And how will that be done, dear Mademoiselle?" Roderick lights a cigarette and offers Roma one. She would take it but she's afraid of Lady Sinha's eyebrow and also she doesn't think it would suit her as well as the young women with long, pale, delicate arms and fancy cigarette holders. She'll probably look like an earthy beedi-smoking type. She shakes her head.

"By making you marry me, as you promised you would."

"I did?"

At this Roma rises in a huff and walks away, and after a few more puffs of the cigarette Roderick tosses it into a half-drunk gin and tonic nearby and goes in search of her. He doesn't find her, and so he dances with a few other young lovelies who are tremulous to be dancing with this young, dashing officer who's already made a splash and a big name as Calcutta's "knight-errant."

Simpering, one says, "You should be careful Captain Hartfield! We read about all your dare-devil deeds."

Courteous as ever he replies, "Only Sergeant, Miss . . ."

The simperer hastily says, "Roy . . . Miss Roy . . ."

"Ah yes, I beg your pardon, Miss Roy. That's what I do, though. It's what I did when I flew the Hump. That's what I'll be doing in Calcutta."

"We can't thank you enough of course," Miss Roy hastens to say, "but we wish you wouldn't take such terrible risks."

Smiling a mischievously polite smile Roderick says, "You are too kind, Miss Roy. I shall remember that."

Roma looks at herself in a bathroom mirror and frowns. She has a little lipstick smudged around the corner of her mouth and her face powder is patchy. It's such a hot afternoon, who throws a garden party in such heat, Roma grouses silently. She fixes her slip ups, makes a moue at the mirror, and sallies forth, trying to pick up her courage along the way to play the role of the confident frontrunner that she intends to be.

"Ah, there you are!" Roderick says on spotting her. He comes to her with his long arms wide open. Roma can't stay angry. They go back to the dancing at once. At one point during the next bout of dancing her sari's long cascading end falling from a brooch pinned to her shoulder wraps itself around Roderick's trouser legs. It's the closest thing to an erotic embrace she's ever had.

Such happiness. But is it possible to be so happy? How is it possible to be so happy? Roma thinks.

Lines from some poet she read in school come to her: the desire of the moth for the star.

In the Rolls Royce on the way back Roma expects to be soundly scolded by Prem, and indeed gets a little fussing, but beyond that there's something else in Mashimoni's eyes. As if she's just seen something for the first time. She looks very happy after a very long time. Her hand with its heavy diamond ring lies between them on the seat of the Rolls; to her surprise Roma sees her fingers tap as if the music is still playing.

Roderick lives in army quarters in Barrackpore. This is where the allied British soldiers in Calcutta live for the most part. It is swampy, mosquito infested, noisy, primitively supplied, and far from the flash parts of the city like Park Street, the Parade grounds, the Strand, Chowringhee, and Alipore. And from Mitter Mansion. These soldiers will become the Forgotten Army of the China Burma India (CBI) theatre of war even before the war is over. Somehow, what happens in Asia never makes the big news in the annals of world history. The war offices in London and Washington, DC already don't pay these soldiers much mind; they think they have much bigger worries elsewhere.

In some sense the Barrackpore quarters, far and roughshod as they are, are safer for Roderick. This is how Prem and Sir Naren—separately—console themselves for Roderick's billeting. Englishmen, or even Kutcha Bachchas, are more and more often becoming targets of mob rage. The Congress and Gandhi-ji want the British to promise to 'Quit India,' and Churchill thunders at the opportune cunning and self-involvement of Indians. Don't they know there's a war going on?

The Indians say, "Oh yes, we know there's a war going on." This is exactly why we want a promise, now, while the war's going on, and loyal Indians are fighting for the Commonwealth and the King, that the British will leave after the war. The British say, "Nothing doing; just wait!" Even Gandhi-ji is fasting less. The muscle and blood rather than the gastric hollows of India are building momentum. At this point city streets are not always safe for white men.

But from his quarters, Roderick comes most afternoons in his roaring Jeep, like a handsome Bedouin riding out of a dust storm.

Part 7:
Dulce est, decorum est, pro patria mori; Calcutta, 1942–

CHAPTER 52

L ike every year, the Mitters throw their annual ball. Lady Mitter's parties and dinners are popular events. Everybody who's anybody comes to them, and the guest list is highly select. Afterwards people talk for weeks, of course, about the décor, the food, the drinks, the fashions, the debutantes, the music, the dancing. Until the next year, when they are ready to be dazzled all over again.

The night of this party in 1942, Prem stands as customary at the foot of the great stairs in the hallway, greeting guests. She appears queen of all she sees. People may be forgiven for thinking this. People can hardly be expected to know that a desire to vanish lurks in her heart every day, growing a little stronger each day. She has been standing and greeting the world for a long time. That's Lady Mitter's job.

As she smiles, she wonders: Could there have been another life? Another family? Another man? Could she have been that man's wife? She dreams again of the village these days. She dreams of Jagat Pandey. She remembers how thin he was, how frayed his clothes were. How battered his shoes were. All those letters. Never given to her. He never got any replies. Where is he now? Dead? Since the night she found the letters, somehow she thinks he can't be dead. It's a fanciful idea, she knows.

But. This is her real life. Her family. This house. Her creation. She has made all this happen. Of course she is the queen of all she surveys. From mere money, and most of it dirty—she knows this for a fact—she's brought style and beauty into this house. From chaos and suffering she's created a family. Motley, maybe, but happier than the alternative. And now even Roderick is back.

The guests look at her admiringly. She's dressed for adoration. Her still jet-black hair is done in a grand mignon. Mignons are back in fashion these days. Diamonds glitter in it, catching the brilliance of the thousand-piece Bohemian chandelier. She's wearing a deep-blue and silver brocade silk. Her sari covers a silver-beaded satin blouson shirt waist that emphasizes that erect and still slender carriage. She's still a handsome woman.

The letters are in the trunk. The trunk is now in her vast wardrobe. Nothing in it has been removed. She will never open it again. The vial of pellets is under her couch, still almost half-full. There is no portrait of her mother in the house, and she will never again touch the one in the trunk: Saroj Devi Aulakh and Akshaya Aulakh will never be parted again.

But today Harish is already here, and Roma, and Sir Naren is around somewhere, held together with tuxedo, bow tie, pince-nez, pipe, and self-satisfaction. Roderick is coming. This is her life. Not a bad life in the end. She has found love and loved in unlikely places again and again.

Everyone is waiting tonight for Roderick, the uncrowned prince of fairytales in wartime Calcutta. Since Lady Sinha's party, he's flown a record number of times more and chased the Japanese away from Calcutta many times. Prem smiles, momentarily imagining the things people will begin to say when he arrives. A ripple will pass through the room. The swashbuckling Roderick Hartfield himself! Sergeant Hartfield, the legendary slayer of the Japanese bombers incongruously called 'Sally'! 'Knight beaufighter!' Such grand names they've given him. Each one more than well deserved.

Most everyone else of consequence has been announced, greeted and discreetly crossed off the guest list by the professional staff hired for the party. Prem decides to give herself a short reprieve in her private parlor—she's been trying to be very good of late, cutting the pellets into quarters or smaller if at all—until Roderick arrives. Walking past Sir Naren where he stands with a group of his cronies, she hears the conversation and a few stray words. They slow down her steps.

"They don't think or feel like us. Why should the best of society be encumbered by the riffraff, the inferior types and their endless bad tendencies?"

This is the Honorable Mr. Lister, one of the eminent medical men of Calcutta who's just been recognized and distinguished by the Crown. A little knot of pear-shaped grandees is standing around him, some with pipes in their mouths, listening and nodding.

Then Sir Naren speaks. "Indeed! Doubtless! Lives not worth living, I say. As a member of the Aryan race myself I do completely see the worthiness of that approach to our many social problems."

"After all, the Jews have brought it on themselves," another grandee offers.

Though she should sail on past, Prem can't move. Before her eyes once again is the thin body of Jagat Pandey, in frayed clothes and battered shoes. Again, he's eating his lunch of dry rotis, pickle, and a bit of onion or hot chili under a solitary tree, with the sun burning the surrounding grass ochre. She shouldn't say a word but she can't hold it back. She walks up to the gentlemen. Seeing the lady of the house approach, they make vaguely appreciative sounds.

"Are you saying, Sir Naren, that those who come from different classes and fortunes should be eliminated? That the poor are unworthy of living? Or the races are never to mingle? Are you of the party of our modern Satan, Hitler himself?"

She has spoken more ringingly than she'd realized. The sudden silence can be cut with a knife.

Sir Naren partially unfreezes, frowns horribly, and says in his best blaw blaw, "I'm saying, my lady, that certain experiments and actions already in progress in western civilization, to properly classify and rein in the sort of people who reproduce endlessly and cannot feed the mouths they bring into this world, do demonstrate the advantages of distinguishing peons from princes."

In the deep silence Prem and Sir Naren's eyes lock. It's a dare. He knows what she's thinking, and she knows he knows it.

"Certain experiments?"

Everyone knows, really, who Roderick's father is. She has always protected both father and son. Her behavior this evening is quite shocking and she knows it. He knows that she knows it. Still, he is the first to look away.

"And so Hitler is doing the world a favor, Sir Naren?"

A gracious aristocratic hostess doesn't speak like this at a party, least of all at her own. As if she's itching for a fight with her worthy husband. Some people are already wide-eyed, ears cocked for more. But Prem reads newspapers, more than even her husband. Sometimes, after reading a particular report of war losses or news from Germany, she takes a little black pellet to numb herself. But this evening she's absolutely, starkly clearheaded. She hasn't taken one since Roderick's return because she's happy after a long time. On the other hand, Jagat comes in her dreams a lot more since Roderick returned. Dead or alive, he comes. Well, he'd said, "Forever."

The knot of gentlemen loosens, spreads out a little, but lingers, watches. Mouths clamped over pipes and cheroots, paws cupping crystal goblets of cognac and other ambrosia.

Prem finds herself trembling. Someone puts their arm around her. It's Harish. He speaks to her gently, softly, but loud enough that people nearby can hear. "Come Mother, let me get you a glass of champagne. The belle of the ball shouldn't be standing with her hands empty, right everyone?" Some cheer, and the wall of silence crashes down. Silently Prem squeezes her son's hand. How blessed she is in her children at least. This is a thing she must try never to forget. She forces up a smile and walks away with Harish. She can feel the many eyes on her back. She's not sorry for what she just did. Somehow, she feels, she's paid tribute to a poor soldier who loved her, and died not knowing that she didn't get any of his letters.

No sign of Roderick yet. It is eight o'clock in the evening and the last light is fading outside. The lambent greenery wrapping Alipore like a soft Kashmir shawl is darkening quickly into a stony jade. Christmas is only a few weeks away. All over central Calcutta, especially around the military airspaces near Chowringhee and Park Street, lights blaze or twinkle all night. White and black men play jazz into the dark eastern night; sometimes a raucous, strapping woman belts out songs about being blue and in love at Trinca's or Firpo's or at the Ming Room. Customers stagger in and out, GIs and British boys sometimes arm in arm, sometimes ready to cut each other's throat. The immense Christmas tree at Whiteway and Laidlaw's soothes many a young white boy still wet behind the ears who has left his heart behind in Texas or Montana or Yorkshire. Though Christmas is almost three weeks away, the slight wintry chill that Calcutta experiences in December has set in—the air is bright and crisp.

But what is that?

Suddenly noise as though from another end of the city ripples past and around the house. People rush to the large windows to look up and see, unmistakably, that a silent flotilla of aircraft has darkened the sky. The band has stopped and there's shouting in the street. "*Japanee! Japanee! Japanee* coming!" Harish huffs and puffs across the hallway to find the household gathered around the great dining table, someone tuning in vain the radiogram that should have been playing carols and military marches but now fills the room with static interrupted by pops, shrieks, and whistles. The Japanese, despite Chevalier Hartfield's valor and courage, have unimaginably come back to bomb Calcutta, weeks before Christmas. Can this really happen? Of course it can. That's why Roderick is not here.

News comes that the Japs have targeted Howrah Bridge and then raked the Kidderpore docks. Sir Naren loudly, inarticulately curses the Japanese, and Subhash Bose who's turned traitor to his own country and joined the Axis powers. Even Gandhi isn't as great a scoundrel as Bose. Let them all go to hell! Prem looks at the pale faces around her and draws herself up in spite of her terrible dread and panic.

It's her duty to rally the weak and fearful, both as an Indian and as Lady Mitter. More drinks are served, though the band is not inclined to start up again.

Once the raid seems over—no shrieks, rattle, and whistles for an hour or so—the guests leave, go home, go to the clubs, go to the barracks, to the airfields. One by one the house lights that had been switched off hastily and too late in any case, come back on.

Newspapers the next morning report Flight Sergeant Hartfield missing in action. The army looks for him for five days but his body is not found, though his copilot is found in the swamps in the eastern part of the city, stuck in brambles in the jungles off the Hooghly. The copilot's face is unrecognizable. Burnt severely. Looks as though he tried to get away after the crash.

Life goes on. For about a month, little boys will cry for the fallen hero; still, life goes on. The newspapers scream abuse at the Royal Air Force, especially the Alipore Squadron 67; in return civilian grumbling gets soundly thwacked by RAF planes flying dangerously low over the weekend Alipore horse race. A few more bombs fall over Calcutta like burning leaves in a mournful autumn. The children of Bengal—a faithless, spineless Bengal according to the British, ready to turn from the Raj to adoring Subhash Bose amidst rumors of his rising Indian National Army at the drop of a sign from the sky!—still chant during their war games:

Sa re ga ma pa dha ni
Bom felechhe japanni
Bomer bhetor keutey shaap
British bole baap re baap

Do re me fa so la ti
Bombs come from Japan almighty
The cobra springs out of the bomb
The British lose all their aplomb

But life is definitely on pause in Mitter Mansion. Roma doesn't believe the newspapers. Roderick can't be dead. What an idea! And, for herself, if one dream didn't come true—the dream of being an actress—surely the other dream of someday marrying Roderick can't vanish too! This is not a tragic melodrama movie. People don't know how to wait, she keeps telling herself and anyone else who will listen. Roderick will return. She knows it. Maybe right now he's making his way back here. Wounded, maybe, but very much alive. How the whole city can so quickly lose faith in the man they call a hero, she can't understand.

"I don't understand, Mashimoni, why everyone's giving up so quickly. After all, nobody has been found! Why can't people just keep quiet and wait a little longer? This is very annoying!" She blusters to Prem.

CHAPTER 53

It's the sixth day after the crash. Prem looks like a much older woman. Her hair is uncombed and pulled back in an uncharacteristic haphazard bun, loose, untidy strands falling into her eyes and standing up around her head like a faint gray halo. There are deep, dark circles under her eyes, and her skin looks dry and bleached. Sir Naren hasn't even come to dinner since the day the news came. The meals are a funereal affair with Roma, Harish, and Prem sitting at three ends of the table, the seat Roderick usually took empty, again, as well as Sir Naren's seat at the head of the table. Even then Roma frets and gibbers along the same lines, alternating between cheering and scolding the other two.

As follows, one afternoon: "Oh come on now, one would think the end of the world had come from looking at you! Roderick will come back! I'm sure of it. He's an excellent pilot. Excellent!"

Prem's head has been hanging between her shoulders, her face looking down at her knees. Her face is puffy, eyes almost closed. She looks at Roma now. It's just the two of them. Teatime on the sixth day. The tea in the cups has grown cold and filmy. Prem's eyes are dull and glazed, yet full of something Roma will not look at, will not acknowledge. "Mashimoni, buck up!" Roma goes on. "People don't just disappear like that, you know! Roderick is too good a pilot, too clever for that." Prem attempts a nod, doesn't finish it, then gets up and shuffles out of the room.

On the eighth day of the search for Flight Sergeant Hartfield the Army declares it a lost cause and ends the search.

Again, Roma professes derision at this news as well. As the radio announcer drones on about the great tragedy, the terrible loss, the heroic spirit, the tremendous sacrifice etc., she swats the words away like bothersome flies. Roderick is coming back. And that's that. Roderick always does what he says he'll do. So he won't quit. Others might not return. Roderick will.

The clock ticks, the hours turn. And Roma begins to agonize. She abandons efforts to make the others board the dinghy of hope she's on. So she must find an ally, a resource elsewhere. In desperation she makes an appeal to the only person she can think of asking for more help.

Gyan Sengupta is kind to her for some reason. He normally keeps a low profile, and especially the last year or so he has seemed more secretive, more evasive than ever. His work is done meticulously, punctiliously as always, but he no longer seems much available to Sir Naren outside of that. No more long closed-door conferences in the library. He doesn't even come to the house much; says he prefers to keep his work at the office so as to not disturb the family.

"I'm very sorry, Miss Chatterjee," Sengupta repeats several times on the phone. But Roma doesn't want condolences. She needs him to understand that Roderick isn't dead. He can't be. The search for him has been dropped too soon. Will he please, please, use any contacts Sir Naren might have to see if the authorities can be made to recognize their error and resume their search. Doesn't Sir Naren know a lot of people at the newspapers? Surely people can write articles or letters to the editor that will convince the authorities that this search has been abandoned untimely. "Or, if that doesn't work," she says in a lower voice, "perhaps you know some people who may have more local connections, or information about things the police don't know?"

Humans are selfish, but someone else's pain sometimes opens the sluices of one's own grief. Sengupta has grief of his own. He's lost people dear to him too, especially lately, as the violent protests against British rule have grown. Also as Hindus and Muslims are regularly turning on each other, enraged by the separatist politics of the British and the desperate lunging away of the Muslim League from the idea of one India on the one hand, and what to many seem Gandhi-ji's puerile, idealistic platitudes on the other hand.

Sengupta works for Naren Mitter, of course, but there's a greater cause and a higher being he serves. As much as he has no regrets about the death of any English dog, the expression he imagines on Roma's face as she speaks imprints itself on him. It's the expression his mother had the day his father died in the famine that brought them to the city as refugees.

"Of course, Miss Chatterjee—I'll do all I can—yes, yes, no doubt that is true—no doubt further searching will . . . yes, please rest, good night good night. . . ."

A day later Roma calls him again at the office on Rawdon Street. "I'm sorry to bother you, but any news? The papers are not reporting anything."

He asks for another day, maybe two. "I'm sure there'll be some news . . . some good news, I'll see what . . ."

Roma doesn't call again. Rigor mortis begins spreading over hope.

Then she, too, crashes. She closes her mind and ears to people talking about the healing power of time, especially the maid who brings her food in her bed. She hardly knows who or what's around her. She's sure her heart will never mend. She asks herself what curse accompanies her that people die from it. She tells herself that she's lost her final chance at happiness. When she dreams at night, freeing herself with difficulty from the barbed wires of consolation, she hears her grandmother cursing her. She hears moaning. Who moans? For what? It's herself.

Sometimes Roderick floats into the darkness of the dream, reminding her that she killed her mother at birth. She wakes shuddering, babbling in the gray

February dawn, in the light of her new understanding that life does hold terrible mysteries revealed only in suffering, in the discovery that human beings are playthings of chance. She hardly eats, sleeps only in a state of fitful delirium, the tears already pooled in her eyes every time she wakes up.

Her mother also comes in her dreams. She doesn't know her mother's face very well; there is only one faded gray sepia photo that Mashimoni gave her years ago. In the dream she, Roma, married happily to a very nice man whose face is always blurry, takes her mother shopping, buys her nice things: rich saris, gold earrings, a handbag, maybe a Kashmir shawl. Because her mother usually otherwise can be found sitting half in sunlight and half in darkness at the door onto the terrace of an unknown house, fish scales and bones scattered about the dim, murky hallway seen through the door. She sits astride a vertical slicer with a wooden base, the *bonti* Indian women use instead of knives, always chopping, slicing, peeling, quartering, halving vegetables, meat, fish, anything and everything. There's also an awful smell around her; rats scamper about chasing cockroaches with massive antennae. But since Roma, her only daughter, so lucky, so well married, can afford to buy her many nice things, maybe she doesn't suffer so much any longer even if she has to cook, clean, and work so much.

Roma sees in the dream the winking of gold from the fashionable jewelry on her own wrists, her fingers, neck, ears. Though she's wearing the vermillion required of married Hindu women, her hair is cut in a fashionable modern bob, since the man with the blurry face likes it that way.

When Roma is awake, Prem comes shuffling, unsteady, to urge her to eat, to take a shower, change her clothes. Roma refuses, and Prem retreats. She too is so tired. She doesn't have the strength to carry another person on her back anymore. Sir Naren is now seriously ill, completely bedridden. The doctors can't really diagnose the trouble. Prem knows that it's his broken heart. She wishes she too could lie down and never get up again; her heart is so heavy it must be breaking too. But she can't. Because? Well, she can't. It's her duty to stay standing as long as she can.

She hasn't taken a pellet yet. Just in case Roderick comes back. She must be present, awake, alert. It takes great effort not to take out the vial, but she somehow manages. Sometimes she thinks of the hackneyed phrase, 'A hero's death.' Sometimes she wants to bomb the whole lexicon of honor and heroism out of existence.

CHAPTER 54

Yellow isn't a great color in this year, 1942. This is clear to Amherst Ishiru Buck, so-called American Hero of the 'Forgotten Army' of the Allies, in the war to end all wars.

Sergeant Buck does not want to die "a hero's death." He's watched friends and fellows die those.

In the Burmese forest, to distract himself, he invents whole fantasy futures with girls he's never met, girls who probably wouldn't choose him anyway. It's always been like that with him. He's always looked different. Neither this, nor that. But when shelling starts in the forests of Nhpum Ga, and there's nowhere to go from that impossible bluff of mountain—his company, the 2d Battalion of the Marauders, has already been there five days—his heart begins to turn to ash, thinking he'll never be with a girl again, at all. The Japanese are all around, shelling constantly. Heavy casualties. Words that sound just like words until they happen around you.

'Never' too is a word like a bullet with the range of infinity. What can it possibly mean? The 2d Battalion's perimeter—400 by 250 yards on top of a 2,800-foot-high saddle of ground that dominates the surrounding terrain—is filling with shit and gangrene. At night the forest smells like the collective fear and rage of the men marooned on the bluff. That smell will never leave Amherst fully. Also the smell of agony, longing, and vomit. The men sleep and wake fitfully, or not at all. Their suffering feels like airlessness rather than pain.

Then the Japs capture the waterhole. Then Amherst and a few others like him—yellow men, Americans with Asian mixed in—start to be sent out at dead of night to try and bring back water. The second time, Amherst's mate Sterling gets shot down. He has to leave Sterling (father's name Tanaka, mother American, old San Francisco family) at the hole. He just barely gets back himself.

They don't talk about death. Or about relief. Or about home. Or about girls, apple pie, or football games. By silent pact. Among the many pacts that men fighting and dying together make with one another. They can no longer bear it, but there's nothing they can do, they have to bear it. They bear it.

On the ninth morning—Amherst is keeping track of the days for no reason he can name—Robby Mook points his index finger upward at the sky. Deakins, with a foot already turning a mottled, marbled maroon from where he stepped on some shrapnel two days ago, groans and rubs his eyes. Amherst will remember as if it's a movie he watched. Though the sun is barely visible through the trees above, bits and pieces of a leaden sky can be seen, and the occasional plane cuts through the patchy gray-blue like a silver arrow. They've run out of water two days ago. The waterhole is in the crosshairs of the Japanese a few hundred feet away and below, and even if you slither to it like a worm you risk getting a nice, thwacking bullet in your noggin as you try to dip your makeshift water bag into the stinking, crusted water. Sterling and his maggots are keeping guard at the approach. Case in point. His body probably is still there. Has Sterling's blood mixed with the hole's water? Probably.

And then Robby says, "Look, fellas, look!" He tries to buck upward but can't. Keeps pointing up, though, looking as if he's giving the sky the wrong finger.

"Aww, pipe down, would'ya?" Someone a few bodies away grunts. And then the water bags start dropping.

Planes like angels have brought relief; manna has dropped from heaven. Robby Mook is shuddering and weeping, rolling on the wet ground toward the bags as they fall. Stray Japanese bullets from below blow a few bags into silver showers. There's shouting and yeehawing and whooping. There's sobbing and retching.

Amherst can only think that Sterling won't be needing any water . . . he's quite dead. In a few minutes the bags stop falling, the droning and the planes go away, but they're alive and it's morning and they know they might live, at least another day. They are the company to be famous later as Merrill's Marauders. Howdy, goddammit. Some of them say they are the 'Fightin' Aggies.' They say 'whoop' a lot. Still alive on that hilltop. A bunch of men in raggedy clothes, stringy hair, and dead eyes, dancing jigs and back-slapping each other.

And then on the eleventh day the 1st and 3rd battalions break through to them. They find broken men who have aged years, not days, during the siege. Lucky for Amherst and Robby and Deakins; Sterling is just plain ole dead.

Amherst gets back to a Calcutta that is sloppy with rain—the usual. That city has a way of weeping weakly for messy mankind. Huge craters have opened up on the roads. Traffic crawls. He has quite a time shutting out an image of Sterling's face turning into the face of an ancient man. Sterling sort of rolled like a log a few times when the Japanese sniper guard took him down. Amherst can't forget the healthy cream of Sterling's face draining faster than he thought possible. It reminds him of his mother when she was dying. Her skin, too, creased and puckered. Like a much older woman's skin. Gray, not creamy, tired from cancer pain. The colors, smells, the final bloated still shape of death, have never faded either.

In Calcutta, he knows he has to look sharp and keep things going. The city is a wild place. He is a wild man. He tries to construct some sense of a shape of things. In spite of the blur that will continuously creep up. Every day. From different directions. Like an eclipse. Sometimes he just sits. Waits. For darkness to pass. For something to happen. For someone to come. To be called for a meal. Some days he drinks till he blacks out. Some days he stays in bed. The smells and sounds of the Nhpum Ga forest stay with him. Days are still a fretwork of jumping light and shadow, nightmare and guilt. Nights are a primeval forest.

When someone asks him that certain question, with that certain raised eyebrow and smart-alecky face, he says he's Chinese, Chinese American.

He has to live. He must move. Standing before the dressing mirror in his bare billet on Lansdowne Road, he runs his hand through his coarse hair. An old nervous gesture. He's going out. His hair used to be light brown; a nothing color, like his skin. In school he pulled it back with a comb and put a good bit of his mother's pomatum on it so that he'd have a wider, broader forehead. Look more Anglo. Nice. Normal. Now it's sunburnt almost to an ashy bracken.

He has his mother's slanting, almost black eyes, but his face is longer and leaner, like his father's. His father's long face ends in a sharply cleft chin. He has no cleft. His chin is bulbous.

He's not a pretty sight. There are violet hollows under his eyes. His Adam's apple pokes out alarmingly. He also needs a shave. Because he's alive. When you're alive, hair grows. Nails too. He clips his nails. What about Sterling? Still lying there on that alien soil? Is it sunny? Rotting down to bone? Didn't someone say once that hair and nails grow even on corpses? For a while . . .

Why didn't they pick Sterling up when they left? He should've asked. He should've insisted.

He and Sterling used to pretend that they shaved almost every day, like the other fellows.

Mongol. Mongrel. Yellow Peril.

They'd heard those words in school, in the streets, back home. Whispered, flung at them, as they expected. They took them in stride. They were not surprised. That was the key thing. Not to be surprised or look surprised. They didn't talk back.

The teachers wouldn't listen to them. Sometimes even a teacher made fun of their accent.

"Say 'lyrical,' " the English teacher shouted.

"Rirical."

"L-y-ri-cal!"

"Ree-ri-cal."

"Imbecile!"

They didn't talk back in the army either. The commander told them to act like men. "Cuz you fellers are . . . you know . . . Yellers!" And he burst into thigh-slapping laughter at his own joke, giving the cue to the other men.

Today, it having rained a lot, the Calcutta sun feels kind. Moist, warm air feels kind too. These days a few ocean liners still pull in and out of city docks, loading and unloading batches of—among other things—men and women fresh from Britain. Some are already wilted or withered. But fresh young girls from England are still coming, though less and less. Looking for husbands. He has no chance with them.

There are cars everywhere. He sees Baby Austins, Chevrolets, Packards and army jeeps taking daredevil chances. Horns blare. Tires screech as the inevitable pedestrian tempts death. Women in shiny pencil heels traipse in and out of department stores.

Amherst tries to breathe in the day, the light, the air, the sounds—shrill bird-cries of rickshaw pullers, vendors, and the occasional palanquin bearer—as deeply as possible. At Nhpum Ga there were times when he'd stop breathing because he was scared the Japs would hear it. This city, this white Calcutta, is paradise by comparison. But maybe not for too long. The curious, knowing 'black' city prowls right outside. Always has. India for Indians. It's 1942. The Quit India movement leaves streets littered with lathis, turbans, flags, posters, the occasional body waiting to be removed.

And, he notices, more and more people begging in the streets. Their bodies are unusually still, only the hands lifted in pleading. Makes them look like thin, dark birds with long necks and tiny heads.

Today he has an invitation to the Calcutta Club from an old acquaintance. Sunny Roy. He's an 'old' acquaintance because everything before the dank Burmese forest seems eons ago. General wheeler-dealer and playboy from a respectable old Calcutta family. Born Saurendra Roy. Nice fellow, though too fond of the sauce and a fop and, sometimes Amherst suspects, a pansy. He wonders what Sunny Roy's father thinks of his son.

Leaving his taxi, he squints even at the mild midafternoon sun. Things, men, the air itself, are scrubbed into flickering, glassy ghosts. Something has happened to his vision. He doesn't see very clearly anymore, especially not up close. Faces blur and bob as he nears them. Something went wrong in those days of damp, freezing rain, squelching mud, shit crawling with leeches, and fear unlike anything he has ever known. Blinding fear, as they say. Blinding fear in those days when he was always picked for waterhole runs and scouting. The chaps caught glimpses of the enemy in him. He doesn't blame them, exactly. He understands. He never refused. But his eyes haven't readjusted to warmth, food, shelter, and safety. They remain scratchy; his vision remains blurred. Maybe a blood vessel burst. Maybe worse. He accepts it; he accepts most things, never sure of the ground on which he stands anywhere, anyhow. Since a boy he's known not to resist, to do as told.

He hasn't seen the army surgeon in Calcutta. He doesn't want to be told that he's going blind or something. He doesn't think you can avoid suffering. Where's there to go when harm seeks you out? Maybe this is the Oriental in him.

The army was his ticket away from his father. He didn't leave his mother unprotected. She'd died. Finally at rest. At peace. He hopes. She used to say that her life was her fate. It used to make him angry. After Nhpum Ga he's come to see things a lot more her way. There's no escaping fate. His vision's damaged. Okay.

He's seen such things. A man might well put out his own eyes after that. At least he can still see into the distance. Maybe the army will still have some use for him. At least—the sting of this whip is familiar, almost stabilizing—he's better off than Sterling.

CHAPTER 55

He finds Sunny—ever loyal to pleasure-seeking—waiting for him at the imposing entrance to the Calcutta Club. Sunny stands at the club's neo-Palladian entrance, a drink already swanky between his fingers. Sunny is—as always—dressed in the nattiest possible nattiness: seersucker jacket, white panama, the jauntiest of jaunty pearl-gray spats. . . . He'd say a sight for sore eyes, but . . . smiles a little at his own thought.

Sunny's about five feet four, pale and splotchy from habitual drinking and fast living. Probably going a little pulpy inside. Not a handsome man. A *pukka brown sahib.* A crumpled half pack of *Gauloises* is peeping out of his front pocket.

"Passel of smart new gals today in the club, old chap," he says. His voice is a quaver. Always has been.

Amherst feels lustful and lonely.

Such sets will always be exotic, fascinating, and condescending to him. People will take one look at his yellowish-pink complexion, do a double take, and not know what to say or not want to say what they're thinking. Or they'll try to be nonchalant and overfriendly. But Amherst always feels that he can hear them thinking, "Yellow man in American standards!! A Yankee Jap!!!"

He always wants to be invisible till he can tell what kind of reception he will get. Him, half Japanese. There are yellow cowards, yellow fever, yellow journalism. These days there are yellow men, the newest minted and certified menace to humanity. One of the many kinds of yellow peril. Inside the club everyone looks darker, but skin is skin and blood is blood. Those who come to this club also usually have lifelong training in reading pedigree, moreover. Amherst's father is a plumber.

He fears—he fantasizes—that he might be put into the state of mere brute: panting, imbecile, mongrel, neither this nor that, neither friend nor foe, neither brown nor white. In some sort of battle royal. Just a freak. Fear, being shapeless, expands infinitely. At Nhpum Ga or at Calcutta Club.

Sunny introduces him to people who shake his hand warmly. Their eyes shine. Is he a hero then, after all? His father always says a blush is revolting on yellowing cream skin.

He sees a woman sitting at the far end of the Crystal Room at the mahogany bar. She's perfectly poised and sitting quite still. She doesn't stir or change her expression when Sunny begins guiding Amherst that way, a light pressure of his hand on Amherst's elbow. When he's close to her, he looks as steadily and long as he dares.

Delicate ankles disappearing into shiny red high-heeled pumps. Pale egg-shaped calves, a little plump. His imperfect gaze travels up to her pale pink skirt and then the many-ringed hand holding a drink. Her soft white blouse is like that of a schoolgirl, but its low-buttoned front draws men's eyes to peeking cleavage. He feels dizzy.

She's introduced to him as Jolene. Anglo-Indian. Poor thing. One of his sort. While she says hello politely but coolly he wants to reach out and stroke the curve of her cheek.

That night he looks at himself in his tiny bathroom mirror, close and long. He's tipsy, or giddy, or happy, can't say. All he knows is that he's met a girl he can't stop thinking about.

No, it isn't because he hasn't been with a girl in a long while. Or it isn't just that. In fact, he's also never been with any girl for long, but that isn't it. It's her.

They're both mongrels, this girl and he. They know that world of no particular, real roots. They're both despised by both sides of their lineage, no fault of theirs. Suspect, strays by birth. He looks at his poor straight hair sticking up despite all his efforts to smooth it down; his nose—he finds it revolting—wide, flat. He was nicknamed Genghis Khan in school. . . . Suppose his could be the wind-cracked face of that tiny yellow man on horseback in the old paintings where everyone looks like a bird? Slashing at some enemy with a sword as large as himself. Had Genghis Khan's father beaten him regularly when he was a boy? Amherst knows battle, of course. And killing. Sometimes he thinks he should pray for the enemy he's butchered. Rows and rows of Japanese boys— just the same yellow as him—coming at him, at the Marauders. Row after row, mowed down, not stopping. "*Banzai!*" A volley. Again. "Banzai!" And again. The hot, rusty smell of blood.

How people see him or Jolene has so little to do with their real lives.

But he's alive. Sterling isn't.

So next day he calls up Sunny. Asks him if he can come to the club again. The club admission rules are very strict—it's not really a place for people like him. He tells Sunny he'd like to have a chance to see Jolene again. Sunny is all chuckles and guffaws.

"Certainly, dear chap, certainly . . . quite a girl, quite a girl . . . ," he keeps saying as Amherst tries to hang up the coin-operated phone in the drafty, wide hallway of his temporary billet.

So he goes again. She smiles when she sees him, making his heart jump against his ribs. When she smiles it's a slow, almost mocking smile. He nearly turns back, scared by his louche need. That evening he sits with her at the bar, elbows almost touching.

He notices her hair is a dark, almost squid-ink blue. Dye job, he thinks. But a nice one. It's pushed away from her face and clusters in tight curls around her ears. He watches her mouth, her tiny even teeth, the pink tip of her tongue, her neck, her collarbone as she talks and turns her head this way and that, looking at people coming and going, waving at someone in another part of the room. He is fairly sure she's warming under the heat of his frank gaze, his cataloging of her beauty. The side of her neck with a dark mole on it is excruciatingly fragile, unbearably vulnerable. He wants to lick the mole, the neck. Two little gold balls gleam on her earlobes. Poppy-red lipstick.

She seems accustomed to looking, gauging, boring, sizing up. Used to judging closeness, intention, the smallest of movements, moves. He desperately wants to put his arm around her shoulders, to protect her. He guesses that she's had a short childhood.

When she looks him full in the eye, he nearly topples over, her eyes are so dark and he's had so many whiskies on Sunny. Then, just as the back of his head is about to hit the floor, he finds himself swimming in her dark pupils instead.

A group of young women come up to Jolene and begin chattering. They give him not unfriendly looks up and down, almost appreciative. He isn't used to tolerance, leave alone appreciation. It goes to his head where he's already swimming alone like a quick fish in a crater lake at night.

Things are going to turn, he thinks.

"Will you monopolize our Jolene all evening, lieutenant?" one of the women teases not unkindly. Trying to look sober, Amherst grins like an idiot, looks for Sunny, sees him across the room, goes off that way. As he leaves, fighting his stumble, Jolene winks at him.

"Smitten, eh?" Sunny asks him. He has to have several coffees to try and sober up. His heart is galloping.

Sunny doesn't, can't know the half of it.

Some more banter with Sunny. Some men are reading out details of a siege that just happened in Myitkyina. Chaps hacking holes in their pants to let the dysentery flow while they load and fire their guns at the crazy Banzai boys. Chaps falling asleep at their guns from exhaustion and hunger only to have the Japanese creep up to their lines and blow their heads off. Fifteen hundred American boys dead, the count mounting.

He's desperate to find that magic spell again, to put his hands around that crystal ball of desire, that magic globe, like warm paws; keep it safe. It looks like it might begin to disintegrate.

Who am I? he thinks. Maybe he says it aloud. Patriot? Traitor? Who the hell am I?

Just then he sees her walk past, so plumed yet so fragile.

You're lucky, Amherst you scoundrel, he thinks. You got away. You are in the Calcutta Club. Drinking the best bourbon, no doubt a salute to your country for oh so recently joining the fight. In a room with bright light, cool air, plenty to eat and drink. Beautiful women. You are alive, fella. In one piece. A pretty gal called Jolene is here, very close.

But then the sharp twist he felt in his gut when the water-run call came on the bluff comes back. Civilians are excitedly discussing the war and the battles. He is unspeakably lonely. Men of his company have been pressed back into the frontlines, he learns. They must be dying even then of dysentery, cholera, typhoid, scrub fever, gangrene, a shot to the head. Now he imagines, against his will, fighting the images, the Myitkyina men's faces, their hollow eyes. Eyes smoky with hate or rage or simply exhaustion—he can't tell. And Sterling's dead.

But.

He is here.

That's when he makes up his mind.

Why wait? One day the war will end. Who knows what new storm will gather that day? Who knows what that age will bring? Who knows what India will be? Will the British give her independence? Who knows? If not, will India shatter into a thousand pieces? Will Hindus and Muslims hack each other to death?

He'll be gone, surely. Juniper and ash again; the smell of eucalyptus. The sky a tall blue arch overhead. California. The gentle waves of the Pacific, cresting softly, crashing gently. Pale gold, sandy beaches. When the war ends, he doesn't want Jolene to be alone in India. He's seen the black looks people are giving one another on the streets already. He's heard about the killings here and there, everywhere. Gandhi fasts each time killing breaks out, and it stops for a bit. Gandhi sits up, drinks a glass of lemon juice with honey, and the killing starts again.

The English watch, wait . . . waver? They're taking their time.

To free or not to free.

And he's waiting too to be free from his memories, his nightmares. Free to pursue happiness. To not be alone.

Well, he's not English. He's American. He's not going to wait. He's going make a quick call.

Sometimes everything a man feels is absolutely, 100 percent real. Every nightmare is real. Every imaginary whisper is real. Now is his time to make love as if love has been discovered for the first time. This is the way of his times, a time of keeping what one can find. This is love now.

"Hey Amherst! Look sharp, old chap. We're off to play a game of billiards till supper time . . . join us old boy, won't you?" Sunny punches his arm roughly. Sunny's English toff talk amuses him. He goes with him.

When he sees Jolene again—she's sipping champagne from a slender fluted glass—he goes up to her and asks for a dance. She leaves the bar, quite at ease, her hand resting lightly on his arm. The band is jamming something jazzy. They dance. She's quiet. He's nervous. Afterwards they stand smoking in the gardens. The moon is high in the sky and the garden lamps twinkle through the trees. The air is not dull with anguish and pain; it's just the soft, moist breath of the Bay of Bengal.

Time. Of the essence. If he doesn't move fast someone else will snap her up. There are too many men hanging about the clubs, restaurants and bars of Calcutta, pockets clinking, eyes glistening. Pretty girls have their choice.

He asks her to marry him.

"Tell me, Lieutenant. Buck, do you even know my last name?" She says 'Left-e-nant,' like the Brits.

He attempts gallantry. "Won't you be changing it to mine?"

She smiles patiently. His attempt to be fresh. She has surely heard it all.

"But you don't know it. And you're asking me to marry you?"

He gropes, hopelessly, for a witty, gallant retort. He pushes back his hair, rubs his big, ugly nose.

Before it gets too awkward—though Jolene is still smiling at him—sounds of applause come from the club. Louder music comes to them through the club's open windows. The band's playing "We'll meet again, don't know where, don't know when . . ."

The notes of Vera Lynn's cockney contralto fill the air. The audience is singing along. Sunny trots over, pointing out the obvious. "It's a BESA night! What fun, eh old boy?!!" BESA—the Bengal Service Entertainment Association—has been contracted to play tonight at the club as a special treat. Maybe another minor skirmish not gone horribly wrong. Maybe a sudden offhand noblesse oblige of the generals.

Sunny sways from side to side, belting out "We'll meet again . . . ," with a girl on each arm: spritzy, feisty. Unsteady, unsober. Joyous. If his is a gutter-snipe kind of joy, it is uncomplicated, easy.

For Amherst, yellow son of a father furiously disappointed in the consequences of lust, such easy joy is not possible. He was shoved to the frontlines by his father's hot, meaty hand, no questions asked. His father had shoved him also into football in high school where a fall and a blow left him with a ringing in one ear that came back on the bluff. His father marched him up to the war recruiting office in 1941—"'ere's a red-blooded American boy wantsa take out a few Japs"—and saw him off on his battleship.

Mongrel. Japanese Suzie from San Francisco and Anglo-Saxon Ambrose from 'down-deep' Kentucky somehow got together in Los Angeles and brought him into an America that spits him out daily like gristle in an otherwise perfect cut of meat.

He is furious, been furious, all his life. That is why he wants another story. He must have it. He wants a happy ending, two worlds mingling, not clashing.

Sunny—bless his soul—shrieks and whistles at a brief pause in the melody, making the entire room whoop and bellow. Do these people know what they're really doing? What's really going on? For fuck's sake, this is a little war dance, is it? Jolene and he find themselves a few feet to lean on against a wall—now it is standing room only—and listen.

Someday they'll be gone as if they never lived, loved, laughed, or fought. They'll be ghosts staring out of yellowing photos at people trying to imagine—or maybe not—what their lives were like.

He doesn't want children himself but some of them, maybe, will be the children of the dancers and drunks here tonight. Maybe they will or maybe they won't realize that the frail, antique-looking people in the old photos had been real people, quite like them, and also different. That they bled when they were cut. Just like them. That they were flesh and blood. Weak and brave. Maybe they'll even imagine this night of warm Bay of Bengal breezes and lemony-gold chandelier light. This moment. This happy moment! Maybe they who are living in this moment will never truly be dead to the ones to come.

He wishes those children well, and he believes in them. Though that night he can't see their faces, though they too are ghosts of the future, unknown, unborn, he wishes them long life, happy memories, wonder, and delight.

Because there is still magic left in the world.

Like Vera Lynn's song.

The dancers flow around him and Jolene like a flock of swallows. Jolene puts her hand in his at some point, and he holds it firm, sure—and hoping—that there will be blue skies "some sunny day.

Part 8:

Swing Time, Darjeeling, 1943–

CHAPTER 56

Prem goes to Roma's room with every intention of saying the right thing, making the right sense, being wise and comforting. She rehearses her little speech as she goes. It holds together as she goes. Yet, in Roma's bedroom she finds she can't string the words together as she intended. They won't fall into order and hold up the same banner, the same banter of meaning.

So she feels torn between what she has come to say and what she wants to say. She wants to say, "Get up, my girl, and look out your window. There's a new dawn. The light is a slanting caress on the grass. You are young yet. You have loved and lost someone whom it was an honor to love."

Instead she says, "How are you feeling, my dearest girl?"

After Roma turns her head away to that very window, beyond which the sun has risen as usual—wound up by the divine clockmaker, with no choice in the matter for her, as Roma sees it—sitting at the very edge of the bed, near Roma's feet, noticing as if for the first time how scrawny, how petite Roma is, Prem tells her that a marriage proposal has come for her.

For a few seconds Roma doesn't move. Then she turns her head to look at Prem, her eyes clear and wide as if she has just seen the sun rise for the first time.

"Mashimoni, please."

"What, my dear?"

"Please never bring this up again."

Prem stares mutely in anguish.

"How will you live my dear? I won't live forever."

"I don't want to live Mashimoni."

"Don't say that, Roma." Prem leans slightly forward, taking care not to breach too much the distance between herself and Kanan's daughter. A girl she's never fully understood. And always tried to love in spite of it.

"Mashimoni, can't I just stay here the way I am? No one wants me, really. I've been lucky. I've had you, and Harish, and . . . Roderick. But my luck has run out, Mashimoni. Can't you just let me stay? Just the way we are now, the way things are. I don't want anything more, Mashimoni."

Prem lowers her head and fights back tears. Her body—every hard and soft place in it—is weary of crying. She would crash but for the fact that there's no one else to hold up this world she built so painfully. Now she takes a pellet at least once a day. Some of the servants whisper and stare sometimes; she knows. The spine of the great Mitter edifice wobbles as she wobbles. She ignores the stares and whispers; she has to get through the days and nights. Everyone needs her. With the malice of a repetitive injury, grief corrodes her bones and tissues a little more every time she cries. This is why, perhaps, she herself has mostly finished crying. She accepted within a few days that Roderick was dead. But Roma held out so long. She wishes she hadn't allowed that. If only she'd shaken Roma out of that fantasy, then and there.

And if only Roderick hadn't gone and died.

If she could have, she would have offered Roma a pellet. But she can't. She must not.

Please. I tried.

"You can't say that, darling. You're still young. You have so much time ahead of you."

"Mashimoni, please don't say that. Stop saying that. I wish I were dead, Mashimoni. I wish I were dead. I wish I'd died that day when I went out on that march against the Simon Commission. Remember? You scolded me so much that day. Now, if I hadn't come back at all you wouldn't have had to—"

"Can't keep looking back, child—"

"Why not? They used to say I killed my mother; you know that, right? My own father flung me to you when I was small. And I haven't seen him in years, right? See? My own father didn't love me. You think I've forgotten that? You can't ask me not to look back. Now there's no future also . . ."

Roma cries so hard that she hiccups for an hour afterward. Prem, who took a little bit of a pellet before she came, stays seated at the foot of the bed, her head against a bedpost, her eyes half-closed.

That may be the first day in the six months that Roma has refused to leave her room that she really cries. She doesn't cry only for the fallen hero, though she cries for him too. She cries for the what might-have-beens of the life she's lived thus far. For what might have been if her mother had lived. For what might have been if her father, though poor and weak, had loved her. For what might have been, what choices she might have had, if she'd been beautiful, movie star material. If Roderick had lived and they had married.

Because all that imaginary fulfillment, that vindication has turned out to be a purely unattainable dream, like the one in which she's Roderick's wife and taking her poor gaunt mother shopping. She cries from self-pity, from the shock of the violated narcissist, from the fright of seeing the story of her disappointment as the handwriting of fate on the face of an indifferent universe.

Harish comes to speak to her. "Didi, do you want to go somewhere? Let's go to Darjeeling, Didi. We need to leave the city for a while, don't you think?" The first few times he comes and talks she stays in bed, on her side, her back turned to him. But then one day she thinks, Why not? What is here for me after all?

She has looked at the piece of world outside her window coming into focus and going out of it for months. Though she doesn't fully want to admit it, the scene tires her now. She would like at least to wake up to a different picture outside her window. She would like to, maybe, see snow, and mountains, and fir trees. Maybe she would like to walk along winding hill roads. Like a romantic heroine.

And she doesn't know this, but this mood is her salvation. She can live for the imagination of novelty better than for anything else. She can best force herself into activity propelled not by purpose, but by nothing more nor less than boredom. The disappointed grief of Roderick remains wrapped around her senses and her heart like dark, cancerous tentacles, but the only thing that can maybe dull that grinding, choking sensation—maybe—is appetite for a new palette, a new image, a new panorama.

To Darjeeling they go.

Prem is happier than she dares show, for fear that sharing the excitement of this moment might somehow make Roma grow moody again, make her rethink the moment itself. When the car leaves for the airport with Roma and Harish in the back seat and his valise and her suitcase in the trunk, Prem wants to cry for relief. She can't, so she sinks down onto the chaise in her parlor and dozes for a little while.

Darjeeling, the favorite Himalayan summer resort of the British, rivaled only by Shimla further north, is regularly rocked these days by sensational rumors about imminent invasion by the Japanese, but now that America is in the war no one pays great heed to these rumors, the general mood is upbeat, and insouciance and conviviality, a feisty *joie de vivre*, prevails just as the news from Burma and Singapore becomes more and more dire. Thousands massacred. Stories of atrocities committed on civilians, POWs and Buddhist monks alike. The Japanese are building a road to the north to cut off crucial supplies to China and Malaysia, grinding their POWs to death in the forced labor camps where the road is being built.

Maybe the conviviality is a *danse macabre*. Maybe not. It's a strange swing time. Darjeeling's clubs and private bungalows overflow with revelers. Servicemen, tea gardeners, nurses and medical staff, some of the top brass of the American and British armies in the China-Burma war theatre, drink it up and live it down. Jazz and ragtime float out of brightly lit buildings. The buildings are so crowded, gay, that they seem to throb and glow. The liquor is plentiful, thanks mostly to the Americans, and the storied hospitality of tea planters to their own kind is at its apogee. Mixed with the merriment is a thumbing the nose at death.

When Roma arrives here from the relatively ceremonious, staid world of Calcutta, her senses receive a jolt both salutary and shocking. Calcutta, until lately the British capital of India, articulates tragedy as well as everyday life in high seriousness only. For example, Roderick used to play football on the side of the Bengal team—barefoot and unprotected from the punishing cleats of the British teams as the Bengali players had to be, but by his own choice—and the story has done its rounds so many times since his disappearance that it has attained mythic status. In Darjeeling people seem to—at least claim to—live for the day, the night, the moment, the martini. Here all the grandiosity of the Quit India movement's as yet disappointing failure fails to deter most people from drinking to the perdition of Hitler and Mussolini every night, and for some also through most of the day.

Roma and Harish are staying in the bungalow of Chandan Sen, an old schoolmate of Harish and son of planters who own the bungalow. Chandan is in Darjeeling on the ice-thin pretext of learning to manage his family's tea garden. He is a good sport, as the Brits and Americans at the clubs say. He's a charming and guileless member of the exploitative class but the tea garden doesn't do so well under his nominal management. There are rumors about blind intoxication and certain liberties taken with plantation workers' womenfolk. But since these rumors arise from humble shacks and work-hardened organs, it is them against Chandan who, it must at least be granted, is a jolly good fellow. Some youthful indiscretions, yes, the club matriarchs—for there are those even among the Bacchae—concede, but then what young man hasn't sowed wild oats in the past, and what young man in the myriad brave new ages to come won't?

Roma discovers a new pleasure in life: alcohol.

She and Chandan, in fact, grow jolly and chummy over Roma's ability— discovered and trumpeted by Chandan—to drink most people under the table. Harish watches and worries some, but is just too glad to see Roma finally emerge from the darkness of the last year to say much. And in any case they will be returning to Calcutta soon.

Roma is, in fact, a sturdy drinker. An uncharitable observer would perhaps, again, invoke a comparison with that father now lost in the mists of time, but Roma in her cups is guilty of no significant indignities or excesses, at least as of yet. So she dips her sorrows in drink but always swims across to the other shore named survival, and this can only be encouraging and comforting to those who love her and believe her newly gained lust for life to be a ladder, not a pit.

About two weeks after arrival in Darjeeling, Roma announces to Harish that she and Chandan are engaged. Harish, stunned, briefly remonstrates, urges delay. But then he thinks that Didi and Chandan seem well paired, in fact, in many ways. They even seem happy together. Harish sees no reason to demur, to stand in the way, in the end. After all, Didi has suffered enough. And Chandan, wild oats and all, is really a good sport in the end. A week later Calcutta high society learns that Roma Chatterjee has accepted marriage overtures from the rich tea-planter parents of a certain Chandan Sen, Esq., and because Sir Naren has had a third stroke that has left him without speech or movement, his son Harish Mitter gives her away.

CHAPTER 57

The new Mr. and Mrs. Sen live in a house overlooking the Green Valley tea plantation. In morning mist, when smoke rings of clouds fight back the weak, newborn sun, the tiered *terai* beneath looks like the exuberant frills of a green skirt some whimsical girl has left on the hillside. The house was once painted a sky blue, with white trim on the windows and doors. Now its misty grayish exterior blends in with the hills rather nicely. The center of the house, presiding over the terai, is colonial bungalow: the rest of it—servants' quarters, storeroom, packaging room and business office—sprawls languidly on either side.

In the evenings a long shiny car, with many dents and scratches on it, drives up to the bungalow. The little figure at the tip of its bonnet dances ecstatically before it becomes a still piece of metal. Chandan gets out of the car, grappling with the door, especially if he is a bit plastered.

Roma doesn't love him. As to him, what counts as love for him is hard to say. He is an essentially good-natured man. Feckless, terrible with money, sentimental, gullible, but good-natured. But somehow the meaning of married love for him is largely uncomplicated coexistence. He likes Roma's company; he likes her liking for liquor. As to the marriage, in part it is a bargain he has struck with his parents—Roma does not know that—who have been trying to push him into marriage for a while because of rumors that float back to them from the hills. That he gets unruly and sometimes nasty when really drunk, has certainly slept with some of his female workers and who knows who else. There probably are a few unclaimed children fathered by him growing up around the bungalow, in the hills, in neighboring gardens and bungalows. This sort of behavior is not in general unusual among the planters who feel liberated both by distance from Calcutta, and by the whiff of high living and gaiety, and life as either party or auction, as traditional in British plantocracy.

Roma is grateful her in-laws don't live with them. They stay in Calcutta in their flat on Park Street. The flat is rumored to be mortgaged to a rich *Marwari* entrepreneur. But such secret or not-so-secret bankruptcies and mortgages to owners of filthy lucre are not unheard of among high society in Calcutta.

Here in Darjeeling it is a cotton candy pink cloud world; here the line between reality and fantasy is usually blurred by choice. Somehow this suits Roma very well. She likes the feeling of being on a constant high. Drinks at lunch and dinner and until long into the ringing, echoing night; parties every night, sometimes several the same night; apparently enough money to feel unconcerned about the present or the future (the past, now that's a different matter); and an unabashed pursuit of excessive pleasures or perhaps just lazy self-indulgence. She welcomes, even, this low flame existence after the years of smoldering grief. Chandan and she get along very well together. As for love and intimacy, they manage. As every other woman or wife probably manages, she's convinced. She's a respectably, comfortably married woman now, and nosy gossipmongers can just stay guessing if they must poke their heads into other people's business.

Her everyday life here is not that different from that in Calcutta, moreover. There is a continuum of idleness and being waited upon hand and foot between the two places and times that characterizes affluence as well as its ghostly imposter. Dinner at home, though rare, is at eight, with its rituals. There's watery soup, some sort of poached fish or bird, collapsing carrots, peas and tomatoes for vegetables, and some fruit compote for dessert. The sort of food they eat is what the cook—a grumpy old Nepali man—used to serve the English family who owned the place until 1935. It's posh food; English food.

Roma thinks she should try her hand at cooking. Chandan tells her it's *infra dig*; his mother will have a fit if she hears about Roma in the kitchen. Still, since she's got the bee in her bonnet, she persists. She's in the kitchen at four in the afternoon, making the cook's helper grind turmeric and cumin, chop tomatoes, make mustard paste. It's all guesswork, but it comes along. Old Jung Bahadur the cook stands by, his face a study in fury. But that food turns out inedible. The curries are watery, the vegetables soggy, the rice burnt. Frustrated, she grinds the spices herself, chops vegetables, soaks the rice beforehand. The food comes out gritty, full of sand, oversalted. Chandan leaves the table in a huff and drives off to the club, just a slight edge of meanness showing through in him for the first time.

Then Roma realizes that Jung Bahadur is personally tampering with the food before it's served. He's mixing dirt, sand, whatever, into prepared dishes. If she wants to have her cooked food served, she'll have to stand in the kitchen when it's being cooked and served instead of sitting at table like the lady of the house. Jung Bahadur will reduce her to that before he gives up his rule over the kitchen. She fires him. The next day none of the staff come to work. She washes her hands of the matter. She will not let servants' well-known saboteur methods spoil her life now.

Chandan says, "Didn't I tell you?"

Roma, sipping a whiskey sour while turning the pages of a fashion magazine, looks at him, frowning slightly, then decides to say nothing and also wipes the frown off her face quickly because she thinks frowning accentuates her plainness.

From then on they eat boiled and braised meat and fish, tasteless side dishes, and watery desserts to round things out when they do eat at home.

But then, something that might have been expected happens. Over a week or so, Roma feels that she can't really taste anything. And when the unborn child makes its existence known a few weeks later, Roma sobs unconsolably. Chandan isn't elated either; he makes perfunctory motions of solacing her while he sits—for the first time in months—at home, nursing his normally peripatetic bourbon.

And then something strange happens. Roma begins to wrap herself around the unborn child, almost unwittingly. Though she's terrified about giving birth, feeling nearly dead at the very idea, recalling the terrifying things she's heard about it. Her mother died giving birth to her.

What was her mother like? She existed, after all. Before the Mitters, before the newborn universe emptied out, before her own eyes opened, a young, utterly unprepared girl had a baby and died. Roma had supposedly killed her. Will her own child kill her? She asks herself if, as she lay dying, her mother sensed her baby outside her, felt for her even with cold, numb fingers, cried knowing she would never meet her daughter. Her father's mother—the only grandmother she's known—used to say her mother was a nothing, a weakling. Quickly snapped. Easily broken. Will she be like her mother?

She grows heavy with the child, and then surprisingly lighter of heart. She even begins to take morning walks because among the few dog-eared books the previous British owners left behind on a dusty shelf of what was once 'The Library,' she's come upon a certain Thomas Bull's *Hints to Mothers, For the Management of Health During the Period of Pregnancy, and in the Lying-Room; with an Exposure* . . . etc. Very long title. Cracked red leather binding, gilt lettering. Once a handsome book, obviously. Much thumbed. Sometimes she daydreams about the children who might have been born here. About the woman—the women? Englishwomen?—who relied on this book. Victorian Dr. Bull recommends walking. Sleep. Lots of rest. Roma leans considerably on him though of course she has her own living doctor, Dr. Ruggers, who has pretty much brought most of the better sort of hill babies into the world.

Then the day comes. Nothing could have prepared Roma for the birth or the darkness she feels after the birth. When a wailing thing is put in her arms by the midwife, she can barely hold it. "It's a girl," the midwife says. Her not unkind eyes seem to be saying, "What will you do?" Roma can feel nothing. She looks blankly at the splotchy, crunched-up face, the miniscule hands. The tiny twigs of fingers tinged red at the tips as if baby had to claw her way out of her. Which was how it felt.

Everything races. She falls asleep from exhaustion. She wakes to see again this little hatchling—utterly destructible, utterly powerful—next to her. She's taught to give her daughter the breast. It hurts a lot. When she feeds, and when she doesn't. The baby's choice. Roma's bondage.

Terror fills every inch of Roma. She's trapped—but this time she's done it to herself.

Look. At. What. I've. Done! she wants to scream.

What does she do now? Now that this child is the future's weathercock, its key in her tiny nipple-gripping beak.

Chandan sees the baby, squawks, wobbles, and leaves the house; he goes on a drinking spree. Roma is weakly furious. He doesn't return till almost forty-eight hours later. So she gets stuck with this creature that cries every hour or so, that even when asleep seems to want to butt back into her, that needs her body for food every few hours, that 'goes to the toilet' every few hours, that can't speak—can barely open its eyes—that's so tiny she's afraid to lift her, hold her.

She starts having a recurring dream. In her dream she cries out, reaches out, at sight of her mother and runs to her to keep her from disappearing behind a door. Always too late. By the time she gets close there's nothing but a door that opens onto nothing. And then she wakes up to the baby crying.

She attempts baby talk. Don't cry, baby, don't cry! My golden girl, my ray of moonlight, don't cry; there's no one like you in the world. But the baby keeps crying; nothing will stop it.

But what are lack of sleep, exhaustion, soreness, and burning breasts compared to the fear of not knowing who she's become?

What has she done? Really, what is this thing, this motherhood thing?

She doesn't have to wonder long.

The child dies.

In its crib, alone, at night.

This is what Roma can't forget, can't forgive herself for. That the child dies alone.

She worried so terribly that her baby would kill her. But instead the baby dies. All by herself. Apparently she just stopped breathing. When a baby all alone in a dark room feels death coming, does it have memories?

She thinks such things every waking hour and moment after this. She worries about the death of course, but even more about the fact that she wasn't there. She begins blaming herself for sleeping apart, with Chandan, in another room. An adjoining room, yes, but not the same room. Leave alone the same bed.

When she weeps on the trunk call Prem tries to calm her down. "Babies who sleep with their mother in the same bed also die like that suddenly sometimes, Roma. It wasn't your fault; it isn't anyone's fault. Don't cry anymore. It was meant to be." Should she tell Roma about other babies who died? Or nearly died? Or simply vanished? Does she herself believe that all those things were meant to be? She decides not to mention these things to Roma.

"No Mashimoni, there was fault! It was someone's fault! Nothing just happens just like that!! It was the crib that Chandan's parents gave us for her. Why did I listen? Why did I listen to them saying it was the better, modern way? Why didn't I keep my girl in bed with me?"

The girl had been named Rajani—Night—as perhaps fitting for a child of parents who were such boisterously nocturnal beings, but Roma doesn't want to say the name because its holder may have fought for air alone, in darkness, and lost.

Chandan's parents had in fact given the parents-to-be a crib. Within seconds of Roma or the nurse laying Rajani's tiny swaddled shape down in the too-large crib, the baby would let out a splintering wail so full of grief and disbelief that every time, Roma wanted to pick her up and stagger back to her bedroom and lay her down between herself and Chandan, however destroyed she felt. But she would always be held back by the nurse, and often asked by Chandan not to bring the child to bed. The nurse said, "Babies die when parents sleep on two sides. One of them rolls over and crushes the baby. Not safe."

Chandan said, "How can we possibly sleep with the baby in the bed?"

"The way you slept between your parents, that's how!"

"I never did," Chandan said, "That's my crib."

"Oh so your parents didn't even give their grandchild a new crib!"

"Why should they?" Chandan was unexpectedly sharp.

"Because they've given her this one thing, and it's not even new."

And Chandan said, his voice susurrous for the first time with contempt, "You don't know much about tradition and legacy, do you? Of course, how could you?"

This too. He could go wherever he pleased, whenever he pleased, with whomever he pleased, baby or no baby. She couldn't. She had to stay home with the baby. Alone. That was the worst thing. Chandan did often coo at and dote on the baby when he was home, but he still kept the hours he always had, and somehow it was her job alone to be a parent. A parent with a Nepalese Christian nurse in tow.

And it was that nurse who said that babies are safer in cribs. Roma tells her to leave at once. What else can she do? The penalty for the terrible mistakes she has made has to be entirely, remorselessly visited on people who should know better and didn't hold her back from her mistakes. She also has the crib burned before the bungalow in a big bonfire, and forces all the staff to stand around the fire as if it's a cremation. Why did her parents-in-law give her this death trap? When Chandan comes home that night the embers are still flickering, a little ash fluttering hither and thither. Of course the baby has already been gone a few days but this smoldering pyre reminds him so grotesquely, so scathingly, of the reality of the little body's succumbing to fire at the real cremation that he collapses on the wet, dark grass, and weeps.

When he enters the house some time later he hears a sound of something shattering. He doesn't investigate, just blindly gropes his way to the sofa in the family sitting room and falls asleep instantly. The next day there's a semi-expensive china vase in pieces on the floor. Also left behind by the English family. The broken edges don't even slightly hew to the lines of the images on the vase. All is rebellion. What the artist created over months—or maybe even years, who knows—has been returned to dust overnight.

Chandan too breaks into smaller and smaller pieces. One day Roma stumbles upon him nuzzling up against a young maidservant. One hand crushing her breast, the other upon the lintel of the bathroom door against which he has her pressed. Roma wants to look away, to turn around. Instead, she feels rooted to the spot. Standing a few feet away, just around the corner in a hallway that leads to the servants' bathroom, she watches her husband begin to force open another woman. The maid—just a girl, at most eighteen—stares at her over Chandan's shoulder, stricken, dry-eyed, mute. Chandan grinds himself against her, his face in her neck, upon the flat of her chest leading to the swell beneath, like a baby nuzzling, his back to Roma. He reeks even from where she stands.

And though Roma turns and flees from what she's seen, the horror of everything that's happened comes over her again, all at once. The anguish on the girl's face follows her. Anguish is anguish. Whether it's being taken without love by a drunken master, or a dead child, or a vanished hope. Everything burns again in and around her. At night she lies awake, listening to the night pinging softly upon the hills here and there, its language obscure, its expanse unearthly.

Chandan starts drinking from about ten in the morning, doesn't stop till whatever wee hour he comes back from the club, and even then sometimes falls asleep with a tumbler of spilled whiskey rolling on the carpet near him. For weeks she lets him be. She thinks he should come to her. Because she can't. Since it was the crib. One morning, though, she does. She sits beside him on that old, overstuffed couch with its springs threatening to burst and impale the occupants. His eyes open and flutter, then land on her face. After a minute she asks, "Why?"

"I don't know," he says.

"Why won't you stay with me?"

He tries scrambling up, then gives up. The blood in his head is like a thousand drumbeats together. He wants to sleep. He doesn't want to be awake, to know of her need, her demands pressing on him.

Hoarsely, loudly he says, "Because you didn't do enough."

Roma stands up. "She cried for hours before she went to sleep each night. You don't know; you were drunk."

"You were the mother."

"What does that mean?"

"Ahha . . . I wish . . ." And he rolls over, turns his back to her and sinks into the most beautiful oblivion of all. She considers bashing his head in, raining down blows of the lit iron poker in the fireplace on his weak baby face.

One night she wakes up with a shudder. She can't say why. Her body feels something she doesn't know. Her fists are already clenched, fingernails digging into her palms. She looks at the space on the bed beside her. It is prim, unused, grayish—as usual. Chandan hasn't been to this bed for a while.

Nothing is different.

The sun taps on her closed eyes the next morning as, still in bed, she hears confused shouts, commands. The droning of an engine. Heavy steps clambering outside. She wonders what new devastation the cries and whimpers mean, but she doesn't want to leave the bed. It's so warm, so comforting. Then there is a pounding on the door. "Memshaab, memshaab, shaab . . . shaab is . . ."

She squeezes her eyes shut and feels the tears ooze out. Human, only too human. Tears of relief, grief, fatigue. For some reason she doesn't need to be told what's happening.

Outside, Chandan's body is stretched out on the verandah. His full height is apparent. He was over six feet tall. When did he shrink so much for her that she started thinking of him as a small man? A moral pigmy or something. . . .

Whoever cut him open from navel to sternum had to run up the buried knife a foot and then some. Though he's under a blanket, she hears of the nature of the wound from bystanders whispering. One or two make the sign of the cross. Several pairs of eyes are trained on her. They expect her to show sorrow. She stares down at the puffy, broken-veined face of the corpse of her dead husband.

Mostly she feels disbelief. She almost wants to ask, "Why?" Is he really dead, or is he playing possum? Might he spring up as soon as she turns, grip her in a laughing hug?

Yes, Roma is afraid to turn. Things can change very quickly. Anything can happen. To any one, at any time. She knows that from intimate experience. No place is safe. But the corpse doesn't move. She can see that it isn't breathing. Chandan would have to be a great actor to pretend to be so still.

So tiring. All this death.

Chandan's really dead. Her knees weaken as she absorbs this.

The police come. She answers questions blankly, carelessly. The inspector means well; he has a job to do. So many people could have done it. Everyone's a suspect, of course. Even that Jung Bahadur, sitting on the floor, cupping Chandan's head in his hands. The old man looks fixedly at Chandan. Roma thinks it must be bred in his bones to be loyal to a master, any master.

"Madam we will escort you to government guesthouse where you will stay under police guard," the inspector says.

CHAPTER 58

When the train to Calcutta leaves Siliguri, the platform and train station are hushed. It's still dark. At turns in the hills, the Darjeeling Mail looks like a worm with a blazing, smoking head boring through mud.

Recently, this country has been betrayed—by those same English who knighted Sir Naren Mitter—into two independent people. Hindus and Muslims. Indians and Pakistanis. Roma knows about Cyril Radcliffe, a hapless political appointee, an entire stranger to India, no doubt overwhelmed, befuddled, who's drawn a line—wobbling? firm? who knows?—across India. He was told to create a new Hindu-ish India and a Muslim-ish Pakistan. So he's made the inept surgical cut that's bloodied what used to be thought of as India. Like, a cut through a Hindu latrine and a Muslim *dargah,* half of each on one side. The pen is mightier than the sword, after all. There are parallels, too: Chandan, butchered like a pig by an unknown blade; the country ripped like old cloth down its middle; her own botcheries of hope.

She has trunk called Mashimoni and Harish that she's coming to Calcutta. Harish said she shouldn't be traveling alone. She tells him there's no time for waiting. It's true and also a lie. Enough asking. She will just get to the house and everything will be fine. On her end, she wants to make the cut between past and present clean like a precise butcher's expert knife navigating, honoring, the membrane between skin, muscle, and organ. Nothing should bleed into another thing. Yes, everything must be separated purposefully. People die. Other people have to live. Go on.

Didn't she, after Roderick? Did she think of him after the dreams where he haunted, pursued her? No. She didn't. She buried him. Unless he drowned. How can a body just disappear? Or just stop breathing? Well, it seems it can, no use going on about it. She must reach Calcutta, must get home. She must prove herself again.

She's heard, of course, of the troubles in Calcutta. Independence came only a few days ago—August 15. Since then the old ancestral hatreds of Hindus and Muslims have become wildfires. Purges. Savagery. Killing, looting. Once family, community, neighbors, even lovers and kin, now bloody-minded killers, sniffing out the enemy: that one's a Hindu, this one's a Muslim. Mostly. But all this isn't new, of course. Wherever humans go, whatever they do, people kill and die. Live and let die.

She hasn't had a drink in days. She's leaving behind all of that with her time in Darjeeling.

As the train nears Calcutta, passengers get on and off at other stations babbling about terrible trouble in the northwest, in Delhi, Lahore, Amritsar; even in Calcutta. India and Pakistan have been born. The strange freedom birthed by the great Radcliffe guillotine. There are terrible rumors. Corpses the only passengers on incoming trains. No survivors. Death in cul de sacs, at lands' end. Ancestral hatreds have always bubbled, it seems, just beneath illusory comforts, foolish loves.

But Roma doesn't pay any mind. Calcutta is different. Calcutta is, whatever else it is, civilization.

Besides, she has nowhere else to go.

The train is approaching Howrah Junction. Just outside the station it slows down. She looks out. Up ahead she hears bogies uncoupling and coupling, tracks shifting. Clanging and grating. This is normal. At last. Just normal things. Normal sounds. She feels hope spill out as she looks out at that special Calcutta sunset sky splashed with pink, mauve, and yellow on a late summer day.

She feels elated, she feels weak, she feels free, and sentimental. Let's celebrate independence together—she mutters—you and I, my country. Butchered, betrayed, you have survived, whatever you had to let go. I will also survive, just you wait.

I'm sorry, Chandan. Goodbye, Chandan. I wish we'd been given a bit more time, my dear.

There's a sound like chanting or droning, even buzzing, coming from a distance. She can't quite place it. The bogies must now be retracked, because the train begins a slow creep forward. The sound can still be heard over axles grinding on slow moving wheels. It can't be mistaken for the general hum and din of the city. It is something else.

The train struggles into the station. Empty, but it feels as though it has been emptied suddenly, as if prepared in haste for impromptu theater. When the train reaches the covered platform, the sudden extinction of sunlight induces momentary blindness.

When the train finally screams to a stop, Roma sticks her head out her window, looking for a coolie. Surprisingly, no horde instantly surges toward her. No one. The platform is lit only here and there by a sole, erratic bulb. The rest is shadow.

She steps off the compartment and walks a few paces. She sees a pile of what looks like abandoned luggage—sacks, bundles—around a pillar, and despairs. Is there a coolie strike then? It's too hazy to see properly. She feels deeply aggrieved. Is this how independence, hers included, is to be launched? What will she do now? Her two suitcases contain all her worldly possessions and they're too heavy for her to carry. She must find a coolie.

She walks, sourly but doggedly, sore and stiff from hours of traveling, toward the pile near the pillar. As she gets closer she smells a sharp, rancid stench. She goes on, covering her mouth and nose with a handkerchief. Stations are places for squatters, for the poor. So many have been dispossessed. Closer, she makes out some figures on the platform. All sleeping, it seems. Flies buzz around them.

Flies. Black flies, clouds of them, darting about. Why are there so many flies? She feels sad; a sad welcome back to the city. The great recent upheavals have damaged Calcutta. Riots. Refugees. Filthy streets and sewage. Now she has to swat the flies away from her face as she gets closer to the pile. She stumbles over something. Something small. She looks down.

It's a hand. Possibly a woman's. Chopped off at the wrist, fingers cactused, clawing inward as if something has been ripped out of them. The stench is much stronger. She sees dark, reddish splashes pulsating with black flies. Dark smears on the pillar. Around the pillar, bodies. A foot with a sock but no shoe. A head rolled a little away from the heap. A child's head. A face with its eyes gouged out. A woman—young, longhaired—staring wide-eyes at the ceiling. Her breasts are gone.

She only looks back once as she runs. When she looks back she sees dark footprints. Someone is following her. No, those are the prints of her own bloodied sandals. She stumbles, falls. She gets up, runs again. She doesn't look at the ground anymore. The distant chanting is growing clearer.

Later she will hear at least ten thousand people died that night in the city.

Snaking in and out of alleys, corners and shadows. Looking for safety. She keeps thinking she hears many feet stomping behind her. She doesn't know if they're echoes of her own or killers or prey. She tries to race ahead of her feet thudding clumsily in absurd, thin strapped sandals. Her vision dims every other second from sweat pouring into her eyes. She hears her own muffled, regular gasping and hiccupping as she tries to speed up, her eyes torqueing around her as she does. A new, desperate screech of metal against metal. A train has just pulled into a platform a few tracks away. The train's nose nuzzles into the grooved end of its journey. The engine sighs once, loud, harshly. She hesitates. Even stops. People might spill out of that train in seconds. There might be company, safety in numbers.

No one leaves the train.

Only a voice, maybe voices, rises in a keening, broken moan, like a million flies buzzing. A more guttural chanting.

She's reached a battleground, not civilization. On this day in 1947 the city is no more. There's only a very big field of carnage. An epic battle, an endless hunt, souls rising in flames from the slaughterhouse below. This much she gathers from the few skulking wraiths she runs into just outside Howrah Station. Everyone's running, looking for hiding places. As they stumble and scurry they scream at her, into the air, up to the sky, anywhere anyone will listen.

"Hide, hide, or they'll kill you . . . !"

"They" doesn't need to be counted or named. They are uncountable. A riot is in full swing. Hindus and Muslims are butchering one another. Like forever. Like the last decade. The last century. The last hundred years. The last thousand years.

She doesn't know how to get to Alipore, or where to go, or how to hide. She decides to try to follow the Ganges, the city's fluid spine. The arches of Howrah Bridge across the Ganges appear in the murky twilight like eyes from heaven looking at the ripped, bleeding city. Roma doesn't know if she's going fast or slow, if she's traveling toward safety or death. An invisible, furious beast lollops behind her. At one point a truck full of men brandishing swords and large knives rattle past. They shout: "Let's show you how to cut!" The cut they mean is the Partition of India, Radcliffe's carving knife serving up two halves of a country to its people. The "you" the men address, abstractly, are whatever enemy history and the empire have chosen for them, either Hindus or Muslims. She does her best to flatten herself against the transoms of the bridge's arches. Clamps her hand over her own mouth, just in case. The truck passes.

The growingly inky evening comes alive with pistils of distant flares as hate blooms. With every few yards of distance she covers, a long death rattle comes from the city, above the rumble and hissing of traffic, and the stomping and howling seemingly always just around a corner. She sees again, now closer and taller, flames licking the corners of the mottled sky. The homeless wind smells of burning flesh and fear.

Sometimes waves of people come rushing from other directions. Where are they going? Do they think they can just leave the city? A man, his face slicked with blood, shouts at her as they run past. "Don't go that way, lady . . . nothing but dying there, everything burning . . . they're cutting, don't go . . ." She lurches on. Where else will she go?

And then she's completely lost. Hopelessly lost. She's never seen this part of the city. The Mitters would never come to dismal, poor areas like this. The alleys are narrow, filthy. The gutters overflow with sewage. No streetlights. She's most afraid of stumbling on a body again. Dead or dying. Not far away, she can hear voices that sound like women and children. Whoops mixed in. Loud, angry curses. Sounds of hitting, of things being hit. Sounds without sense. She turns half-blindly into another, narrower lane, but suddenly its far end lights up with a bleary, blurry orange glow that becomes jiggling, leaping points of light. Torches approach. They come so fast that there isn't time to turn back. She tumbles into a gutter between two shanties live with a thick, flowing stream. The stench nearly makes her pass out. She squats neck deep in the flow.

The torch-carrying mob thunders past, screeching curses, promising slaughter. Her breath snags on her ragged sobs. For minutes she can't move though she knows she might pass out soon. Her hands shake and her legs threaten to fold but somehow she pulls herself out of the gutter. She lands like a gasping fish on the alley's slippery mud.

The next thing she can remember is stumbling onto a small city square with light from a single tall streetlamp. It's a square in a neighborhood of crisscrossing lanes. Three- or four-story houses stand around it. In the center a spreading tree. Patchy grass growing around it. An ornate metal fence barrier surrounding the trees, the grass. Common enough in the city: a flash of longing for the village, a little tenderness for a little patch of grass. The scene prints on her brain like a frame of a movie. The circular barrier has tall vertical spikes. A variety of body parts crown the spikes. Heads. One seems to be grinning. Maybe a grimace. It's a man's face, small and dark, the eyes wide and interested. Her eyes refuse to leave his face. Almost about to speak. Almost curious. Almost intrigued.

One of the houses surrounding the little square is in flames. On the top floor, shadows dance across the brilliantly throbbing windowpanes. The windows glow like yellow pearls. As the upper floor begins to explode and scatter, the screams become shriller. Then a motley crew of people like a convoy of ants burst out of the house. Toward her.

Again, more frames of a movie. She says to herself, so this is how it ends. Not fair.

But it's a free country now. Free to die. Free to kill. No more white masters. No more patriots. Just killing and dying.

The mob issuing from the house sees her. It makes a sound that cannot be described. Machetes, knives, and swords strike up a new dance, flash.

Rajani.

Roderick.

A car swerves into the square out of one of the dark lanes. The headlights flash once on the crowd—now a tableau in a frame—and then pick out their shapes, outlines. The mob cheers louder, now only a few yards away. The car screeches forward and swerves left between the mob and Roma. A door opens. A hand reaches out. Grasps her arm. She gives in. As she falls into the darkness inside, the door closes and the car begins to drive away.

CHAPTER 59

The man sitting next to her in the back says his name is Arindam Biswas. He was racing home to escape the frenzy on the streets, he says. His driver's face is invisible to Roma and he makes no motion at all. Biswas seems to be saying something. The driver may be watching her through the rearview mirror but she can't see it. Esplanade is roaring past her, some helpless torn thing trailing behind as they hurtle on. Now it's almost dawn. At this hour you can send a taxi through the empty streets like a straight arrow through soft flesh.

She shakes her head to keep herself from falling asleep.

Biswas says he saw her and knew what was about to happen. "I'm happy to have risked my own life to save you, Miss . . . Mrs . . . ?"

Roma has no idea what the man is talking about. She doesn't in fact know what he just asked her. She did hear his name, but hasn't really heard anything since. She still sees the torches, though. Hears the feet. The yells. The burning building. The man called Arindam Biswas gives her something to drink. She sips it—it's whiskey. Its heat sears her parched, raw throat, and travels like a benediction through her. She shakes her head when he offers her more.

The car takes them to the Grand Hotel in Chowringhee. This part of the city is still fairly firmly under British and police control and should be relatively safe, Arindam Biswas explains. In the lobby there are a few Indian and mostly white people standing about, morosely sipping drinks, cigarettes and cigar smoke turning the air inside into a pale imitation of the smoky miasma outside in the streets. Roma struggles to walk and Arindam steadies her, holding her by the arm.

"Madam, what shall I call you?" He asks her again as he leads her through the grand lobby—it reminds Roma of Mitter Mansion, though this is larger—past ghostly men and women standing or sitting and smoking on the lounge sofas and not talking or even looking at anything, and up the spiral staircase to the upper floors. Uniformed and turbaned bearers part aside as they go, as if they too are voiceless phantoms.

Again, Arindam prods her: "Your name, madam?"

Some instinct, some dread makes Roma say, "My name is Mrs. Dutt. Reba Dutt." She herself doesn't know why she lies. Arindam Biswas seems like an average, regular man. And he's Bengali, like her. A middle- or upper middle-class English-speaking Bengali man. She couldn't be in safer hands. And this is the Grand Hotel after all. And this is Calcutta. What are those words she carried with her on the train to Calcutta, and even partway into Howrah Station? Calcutta. Civilization.

Yes. She will be safe in Calcutta, in the Grand Hotel especially. There are many people here, people who are also clinging to the hotel like ants to a spar floating in a flood. Nowhere to go now but forward.

Still, she makes up the name and glimpses—as has become a habit very quickly—momentarily a whole other person, a whole other past and life for this Reba Dutt who doesn't exist. Ideas, thoughts, keep flashing into view like scenes from the bioscope. Words are gone at the moment. This is a relief, actually; she doesn't want to talk.

They are in a room now. The room is cool and dark, and outside sound is mostly inaudible. The air conditioner is humming genteelly. Biswas walks to a gramophone radio on a console and switches it on. Band music fills the room.

He lowers the volume. Now it's like a stream rippling through rocks. He tells her to sit down, be comfortable. She sits. She looks around the room. There's a telephone in the corner. Solid, black, reassuring. She has to make the phone call. She will do it soon. Call Mashimoni at the mansion. But she can't move yet. Very tired. Very, very tired. She hasn't slept for a day and a night. Her clothes smell terrible. It's sewage. She gags once she registers that for herself. Gags and stumbles to the en-suite bathroom and throws up violently, for a long time. She turns on the shower and steps under the cold water with her clothes on. The water begins to wash her, her hair, her clothes, slowly warming up as it does, and she lets it get very hot. Steam is rising around her, out of the shower stall, into the bathroom, misting the mirror. She can see the mist spreading.

"Everything okay, madam?" Biswas asks outside. She has no desire to respond. She doesn't. Silence again outside. The running water drowns out any other sounds there are, and she stands under it for she doesn't know how long.

She steps out of the shower and finds a clean towel on the towel rack. She begins to take off her clothes, then remembers she has no change of clothes. So with the towel she dries her hair, pats her face, her arms, her torso, passing it up below the hem of her sari to reach her calves, her knees, as far as she can. She hesitates to lift the entire lower half of her sari, then does it and rubs hard at her thighs, between her legs, the part of her stomach under her navel. She wrings the sari she's wearing, squeezes moisture out of it, leaving a small pool on the floor. She leaves the bathroom as it is, vaporing, wet, water standing.

She sits down on the sofa near the telephone. She must make a call. She looks at the double bed with the coverlet neatly folded at the bottom. She wants to throw herself on it, right now, go to sleep. But first she has to make the call. It's very important.

Biswas comes near her, solicitous. "Madam can I get you something?"

She says simply, "A cup of tea, please."

"Nothing a little stronger?" Biswas asks. "Not a little brandy to keep you strong?"

She realizes within ten minutes of downing the brandy that she is sinking. And that Biswas is now sitting on the sofa next to her. The radio is playing some kind of jazz. She feels the edges of her vision blur. Her body blurs too; her contour begins to melt and roll down her sides. Arms start vanishing. Feet are dissolving too. It feels good, though, the unfamiliar warm, fuzzy feeling growing in the pit of her stomach as the clear amber liquid—and something else—still works its way down. She tries to swing her legs, feels them swim up to the surface of her senses, and laughs out loud. Biswas is suddenly much closer. His left arm has come up and lies on her shoulder.

At some point, while she giggles and blubbers about how much she loves music, because she loves the bioscope—that they have practically been her only school—she feels his head on her shoulder, as if seeking friendly comfort. Poor guy, she thinks fuzzily, it must be hard to be as ugly as he is. He might even be a little in love with her. She feels sorry for him.

Someone's singing contralto with the popular film music streaming out of the radio in the corner; at some point Biswas changed the station, obviously, after hearing that she loves the bioscope, film music. She hears his voice pouring onto her neck in duet, his rough, smoke-scorched lips rasping on her skin.

He pulls her closer, hip to hip. She hears herself taking a long breath. The small room is lit by a single floor lamp, and everything around the halo of lamplight is fuzzy darkness. She likes that too. It makes her feel light and glamorous, like a bioscope heroine. Back-lighting. No words at all now; only a massive din in her head. In a far corner of her brain she hears an alarm bell ringing, but can't move fast enough. Actually she can't move at all, or so it would seem because the man—she can't remember his name now though she tries hard so she can call it out, shout out—grabs her by the arms, pins her down, and pushes himself upon her, half sitting, half lying. He pushes his tongue, his lips, his thing, into her mouth; she gags on his tumescent organ. His mouth and his hard stumpy thing choke her, cut off her voice. He tears at her blouse, ripping off the back hooks and fiddling frantically with her bra strap. She is flung back hard. She closes her eyes. Let it happen, she thinks, knowing it's a mindless, bottomless thought. She can see, hazily, the man's veined, red-rimmed eyes boring into that bottomlessness. She gasps when she feels him tearing into her and then tearing away inside her. Her pelvis fills with pain. He begins to give great, big thrusts, and a roar grows out of him.

After he rolls off, she doesn't know how much later, she finds she can move her legs though they are heavy, and stiff with pain. She raises herself, tries to stand. Despite her loathing, her fear, she slumps back on the man, though, because her legs give way as she tries to stand. He laughs, lying there limp and exposed, his pants down at his knees, his stubby, hairy thighs pushing up from them like huge worms. Something oozes out of her, between her legs and from her eyes. She closes her eyes. Falls asleep.

She has difficulty waking up to Biswas prodding her with a cup of tea. The pain between her legs and in her pelvis is duller. She can walk. She says she has to go to the bathroom first. She goes. Looking down at herself she finds she's wearing only a bra and a petticoat. *How many more times has he done it?* She touches herself after she sees the thin streamers of red on the white ceramic of the commode. Her fingers have semidried, pulpy blood on them. She tries to turn on the sink faucet and the effort of the torque makes her fall on the bathroom floor that's still wet. She lies there for minutes, or maybe more. This time Biswas doesn't come to the door and ask her if she's alright. She imagines the biscuit-colored skin forming on the tea in the cup and gags. She throws up on the wet, sticky tiles. After voiding her stomach of the sour, glutinous pulp in it, she crawls back into the room, toward the bed, pulls herself up on it and falls in. After that, again, she doesn't remember.

Only in the car later, wherever it's now taking her, she tries to clench her core muscles with great resolve, as someone might who fears limbs, skin, eyes, and mouth ungluing, separating, under the swirling, rushing waters of heavy-lidded self-loathing. She glimpses the tear in the universe gaping beyond this moment, but she can't move or speak very well.

The car stops in a locality she doesn't know. There are many ramshackle buildings leaning on each other, most of their windows showing a woman or two standing or leaning out. She can see better now. The women seem to be dressed colorfully. There are a lot of muddier colors of neglect and decay splotching the brackish outer walls of the houses, some with cracks traveling up several stories from foundations. She's taken inside one of the houses by Biswas and the driver. She is trembling and can't place her steps one after the other, so they semihoist her by her arms through the door, which opens into a passageway with several doors lining both sides. The passageway is narrow and painted a jarring blue, but there's light showing faintly above suggesting a more open space upstairs. She's taken upstairs and lowered onto a bed. Her eye falls on a fat woman sitting on a low cot at the end of the room, smoking a cigarette. The woman says nothing, doesn't move. A tray is brought in by another, younger woman. She sets it down on a coffee table in the middle of the room, between the bed and the cot. The young woman leaves. There's a teapot, cups and a plate of food on the tray. Roma smells the aroma of fried, deep-spiced meat. Involuntarily her mouth waters and her stomach growls. The man called Biswas laughs. He brings her a serving of mutton cutlets on a small plate. She falls on the plate and starts to put the food inside her mouth.

The fat woman on the cot and Biswas watch her. Biswas eats cutlets and smokes and drinks tea at the same time. He gnaws upon the mutton bones and spits out gristle periodically. She can see his teeth now; they are spotted yellow brown and crooked. His searching, piggish eyes rarely leave her. He periodically purses his thin lips and rubs his nose, almost picking it. She sees that he has dirt-rimmed, yellowed fingernails.

Finally, he and the fat woman lean toward each other. They whisper. There seems to be some disagreement, and the woman speaks closer into his ear. His eyes still stay on Roma's face. Now she is lying in the bed, on her back again, her head turned slightly toward them. From this angle it is hard to see them well. *She just wants to sleep. Please. Things can change quickly.*

CHAPTER 60

It's a bleak winter. Harish searches for Rehana. He searches for his son. When the rioting started he began to collapse; had to pull himself together somehow. Rehana is easy prey. Men are going from house to house, neighborhood to neighborhood, picking, pulling out women who don't seem to have menfolk around them, sometimes even those who do. Ordinary folk can't do anything. The men are armed, often drunk or drugged, in the mood for carnage. Then the women don't come back. People go report to the authorities. India and Pakistan are trying to locate missing women and restore them to their families or at least to their countries. There will even be an act passed for this soon: the

Abducted Persons Recovery and Restoration Act. But hundreds of thousands of women are missing.

In every rescue camp in Delhi and Lahore there are thousands of women, they say. Some have babies. Newborns. Or they are pregnant. Their families are contacted but they won't take them back because they are ruined. Because they are carrying the fruits of the enemy's seed. Because they have been raped by Satan and borne his children. Satan's name is Muhammad, and also Ram. Et cetera.

These are the unlucky ones. Survivors. Many of them sit like stones in one place. They don't eat. They don't look at people in front of them. Around them. They don't cry. They don't speak. Some of them hold or sit near babies they don't look at, whom they won't feed, who have to be fed sugar water by small, harassed groups of volunteers who are doing what they can. Which is not enough. The Abducted Persons Act has created living ghosts. Ghosts with babies. Mother India.

Harish goes from camp to camp. Even travels up to the northern camps. Delhi. Rawalpindi. Multan. Nothing. He tries to get permission to enter Pakistan, which is impossible.

In the camps there are also women who cry, who beg to be allowed to go back, to be sent back. Who rage and hurl abuse and sometimes things at volunteers, at the officers and police who patrol the camps. "Who told you to bring us back?" They scream. "Who are you to tell us where to go? We have children on the other side!" They mean the other side of the India-Pakistan border. The new border. The Radcliffe line. They ask why they've been brought back. "Who's going to take me back now?" They shout. "You think my husband wants me back, soiled? What's left in me now?"

And then there are those who are simply missing. Door to door searches have failed to yield them up on either side of the border. Some have died on trains. Some are probably rotting at their doorsteps with no one in the house beyond. Some are lying on the beds of rivers, ponds, wells. These are the lucky ones.

Of course he goes first to the old kotha. Pyari Bai doesn't live there anymore. "Where are they?" He asks beseechingly. "Where is Rehana? Please, I just want to make sure she's alright. This is a dangerous time for everyone, especially for women."

"Hai hai sahib," one of the women says, "You think we don't know that times are dangerous? It's just that for us, for women like us, times have always been dangerous, they'll always be dangerous. So we aren't afraid."

But her companion spits.

The companion is wearing an angrakha-ghagra twice her size and incongruous in daytime. Her hair is a tired, angry red though it is obvious that under the henna dye she must be close to white haired. Maybe once she was beautiful, sought after, well rewarded. Now her face is cracked and darkened with age and her nearly pebble glass spectacles sit crookedly over eyes trampled by birds' feet. Her lips and mouth cave inward over her few remaining teeth.

She spits, then trundles forward and pushes her face right into Harish's.

"Truth is, it's only women like us who are truly safe now, Mitter Sahib. What's happening to all those good womenfolk out there is only what's been happening to us most of our lives. Just that we can deal with it, we have lived all our lives with you vultures around. You see?" Her voice is discordantly booming.

Harish rushes out of the house, runs into others nearby.

Nothing is discovered. No one knows where mother and daughter and baby went. Or they aren't telling. They won't tell. It's the little bit of satisfaction they can get out of their lifelong puppeteers. Look who's crying now, they titter. Look who's dancing at the end of the string now.

In other houses too, no one knows. So many women are being brought, they say. What's the harm if a few have left? Replacements easily available. Peals of laughter drive Harish and other men on similar quests out of the houses.

And Roma never arrives. Prem sends men out on a search. "Go to Howrah Station," she instructs. "Make especially extensive inquiries there. She was supposed to have come by the Darjeeling Mail." Someone must know something.

In the top drawer of her writing desk is a photo of the three children when they were going to school. Her three children. She firmly believes they are hers. Of the three, Harish was probably the least waited upon by the household because she always worried more for the other two, especially for Roma. Though Harish went through his fervently nationalist phase before ten, and heads may have got bumps during that time, there was never any question that he adored Roderick. Though he was also jealous of him. These things can and do coexist.

Why couldn't Muslims and Hindus have coexisted in independent India? In spite of fallings out and jealousies and even rages, why couldn't they? There were so many villages, so many *parganahs* and towns where they had lived side by side, peacefully, for hundreds of years. What happened to drive them at each other's throats? Why did millions of people lose faith in each other, cut the throats of neighbors, publicly rape and mutilate the women they'd once called mother, sister, or daughter? Prem cannot fathom an answer.

The British dealt their hand well. And not just in the last few years leading up to independence. For decades, maybe centuries, they played the gadfly, the ambassadors of hate. Set this Hindu Raja at that Muslim Nawab. Made Muslims in general believe that the Hindu majority was waiting to fall on them as soon as the British left. Made Hindus believe that Muslims were just biding their time to chop off their heads, dishonor their women, and pollute their bloodlines. Stroked and vitiated the monstrous ego of Muhammad Ali Jinnah, the Moses of the Muslim League. Dragged Gandhi around at the end of the rope of Round Table Conferences. A system of divide and conquer. Devil's dice. Till the end.

She thinks these things and also of her own husband. For thirty years she's watched that man live off the leavings of the British. Flatter them, extol them, seek their praise. Turn his back on his country, his people, his duties to his society. The oration he was giving the night of her last annual ball, the night Roderick probably burned to death, returns to her. Nattered on and on about the idea of the natural slave and the natural aristocrat. About the 'peon.' Sir Naren was obviously not a peon, he would have you understand. And for the first few years of her marriage she had believed. Though she'd learned quickly every pathetic weakness of his nature, every calculating *blandeur* in his eyes, she'd given him the benefit of her doubt.

Inequality was nature's way, society's way. He'd said that again and again, throughout the marriage, and she hadn't taken very long to realize that he was a pompous, selfish and cowardly man saying what suited him best to say and even think. Could she go as far as to suspect that maybe he'd always preferred Roderick to Harish because Roderick was half English? The superior sort of mankind, as he used to intone? She shouldn't—she has to pull herself back from that pit.

Harish, she assumes, goes looking for Roma. When he comes home, sometimes after days at a time, she meets him at the dinner table and wants to touch his head, stroke his hair. His face is drawn. He's lost a great deal of weight. She wants to ask him what he knows, what's happening out there. Sometimes he says a few words. Mostly he eats with his head low over his plate, saying nothing. Asking for nothing. Not even for salt.

Poor boy, Prem thinks. My poor boy. I've lost two children and he's lost the only brother and sister he ever had. What comfort is there for him? What can she say or do? She, who cannot herself leave the house because of what's happening outside. And because she's always dazed. She sometimes wants to tell Sir Naren what's happening. She needs someone to talk to, but there's no one to unburden herself to.

Where is Roma? What might be happening to her? She will not let herself ask questions like whether she's dead or alive. She just will not go to that place. Harish has told her that the police are of little use. How many cases will they solve? How many women will they look for? Already there are house to house searches and in most of them the police face angry families, distraught relatives and questions with answers no one can remember.

After dinner he always comes around to kiss her cheek—he's always been an affectionate son—and she doesn't ask the question dunning her. He knows that. He says, "Not yet, Mother. I'll let you know."

He looks for his Didi too, of course. Since the night she didn't arrive his heart has been ripped apart between two geographies of love. And a third. The child he's never seen. He regrets bitterly every waking moment that he turned them loose, that he let Rehana go, because he was a coward. He wonders what would have happened had he had that courage. What was the worst that could have happened? His parents would have disinherited him? He would have been asked to leave? His child would have grown up disowned?

Or maybe none of that would have happened. It's hard for him to imagine being banished by his mother, especially. His mother who had once taken in his father's half-English son. He knows she had loved Roderick truly, dearly. Would it have made that much difference to her that her grandchild's mother was Muslim? Surely his mother had always revealed far greater magnanimity that his father? His father and she had always crossed swords on human worth, on charity, on generosity. Why had he thought that such a mother, such a woman, would have closed her door on a Muslim girl and her own grandchild? Why had he not trusted her? Not given her more credit for who she truly was?

She is mostly semiconscious these days. Sometimes her speech slurs; sometimes she can't be woken from sleep. Maybe it's better that way, at least for now.

He visits his father in his room every night he's home. He wants to be a good son. His father can't speak. He can only move his head slightly in either direction. His wide, staring eyes alone follow someone moving in the room, someone coming, someone leaving. He feels very sorry for his father. The night Roderick's indubitable disappearance was confirmed, his father had his third massive stroke. He has not left his bed since then. The doctors think it is not likely he ever will.

"How are you today, Papa?" Harish asks dutifully each time he visits. Though his father's eyes are blank, still, and clouded, he thinks his father can understand and something makes him think his father wants to ask him something. It's a good thing he can't; there are few answers.

Is he himself a coward? He wonders. Everyone knew Roderick was a hero. Because Roderick was a hero. And he died being a hero. The death of a hero. And what has he, Harish, done? Who has he been? What has he been? Sengupta now almost entirely runs the company, and in fact acts more and more everyday as if he owns it. Harish doesn't doubt that with Sengupta's party connections—of course Sengupta is now a member of the Congress Party and of the West Bengal Chief Minister Prafulla Chandra Ghosh's inner circle—he will no doubt facilitate the nationalization of the Mitter family businesses, especially given the state government's failure to create new industries.

Cassius, Harish calls him privately. Lean, gaunt and serpentine, Sengupta occasionally meets with him to have him sign 'important papers.' Harish has taken to signing the papers without reading them. He doesn't have the strength to envision the coming age. He thinks sometimes of the time when as a younger man he thought his father stood in the way of progress. Now, though only barely thirty, he sometimes thinks he stands where his father may have feared standing. He thinks; he cannot know. His father will not be able to talk about this, or about anything else. Himself, he almost longs for the brutal efficiency of the British: the railways, the prisons, the postal system, the army, law and order. He remembers almost with disbelief and longing the punctuality of trains in his youth. His time, his father's time, was the time of the British, probably. That's why he feels regressed and synchronized with that age, when time comported itself decently, when the British ran the railways like stern gods, no matter if in the avatar of the drunken Irish or Anglo-Indian engine driver. Now, time is a barbarian like the whistling, loutish youth of the neighborhood.

Even Alipore has become an extension of the neighboring dockyards of Kidderpore and its colorful population of sailors, drunks, smugglers, thieves, whores and pimps. Every time he leaves the mansion now in one of the family cars—though the Rolls Royce has been sold by Sengupta who invoked budget shortfalls in the business accounts as the reason for this—he sees all this. He remembers his childhood and youth when the idea of sharing the broad main streets with such people would have been risible to men like his father.

Some of his schoolmates have switched gears to the new age and are thriving. They've become Congress allies and lackeys. They are being suitably rewarded for this allegiance. An old habit of bowing to a master: once British, now Indian. Somehow, he knows he won't be able to fall in the same line and do as they're doing. Oddly, now the past pulls him, drags at him too hard for it. He thinks of the child he never saw. He doesn't know if the child is still alive. He doesn't know if he had a son or a daughter.

What a time that was. Him and Jaanu. Not a thing standing between them, not one serpent in that garden of love. Him drowning in all she brought with her name, her music, her beauty, and her daily tributes of imagination, and she also, she would say, drowning in a lover not hardened and tainted by habitual duplicity and debauchery. What a spring. What hope. She'd begun singing for the bioscope. So happy that made her. And him, seeing how happy she was though he was still cautious, of little faith, worrying for her well-being, worrying about his masquerade. Such a future they might have had. A new empire, even. Of poetry and vision, not concrete and steel. He let it all slip through his hands because he was so afraid. He was mortally afraid. He was afraid of being seen as who he really was. Who he remains. A poet, not a merchant. Not an aeronaut but an Argonaut.

Surely?

He goes out in the evenings. Drinks at the clubs, slumps at cabarets. Comes home so drunk sometimes that the driver has to carry him in, practically. He hates meeting his mother's eyes, themselves reddened and half-open, the next morning.

Prem has finally touched rock bottom. She tried to believe Harish goes out in the hope that he might see Roma one night. See her as what they both fear Roma may now be. Unless she's dead.

Harish goes to the clubs, to the nightclubs and the cabarets not after hope. He goes because he cannot hope, think, anticipate any longer. He's convinced that the worst has happened. He's convinced that all he's doing is counting down to the time when he will no longer be able to pay to get into the expensive clubs for once-rich boys like him. He goes because he just wants to drink, to be left alone.

CHAPTER 61

Late one night a car returning from a film premier collides head on with a freight lorry loaded with steel beams and masonry on Circular Road in central Calcutta. The lorry driver who was drunk dies instantly. In the car, Jagat Pandey's driver dies instantly too. The car engine explodes. Jagat Pandey is rushed to the hospital and dies early the next morning. He's badly burnt and his heart fails.

Harish goes to pay his respects. Jagat Pandey's body lies in the front drawing room in the Theatre Roadhouse. Lovely, patient Damayanti—Jagat's beloved Madam Prudence Cooper—remains gazing upward into the floodlit heaven that is hers forever like a merciful angel praying for Jagat Pandey's soul. Jagat Pandey lies on a white pallet, on a marble floor, with another white sheet covering it, tuberoses shushing and garnishing a violent death, white cotton-wool pads in his nostrils and ears detaining the soul till it can leave the body with appropriate fanfare at the cremation grounds on the banks of the Ganges in Calcutta.

Prem reads in the obituary section of *The Statesman* the next day of "the tragic, accidental passing of the eminent filmmaker and true patriot Honorable J. Pandey, a genius of the moving image who eschewed politics as usual and politicians, but made his bioscope art the vehicle of his deepest, purest love for India and Indians." He began his film career, it is stated, as an assistant director to Jamshedji Framji Heeravala, whose first sensational hit *Nala Damayanti* (1921) changed the course of Indian bioscope. A smallish grainy picture in a longer article about Pandey Sahib shows eminent actors, actresses and film personalities of the day keeping wake around his mortal remains. All Prem can see is a body on a white sheet on a white marble floor, the pallid faces of wake-keepers, a vague impression of tufts of cotton wool plugged into the nostrils and ears of the dear departed so that soul and body are not untimely and irretrievably partitioned.

She feels sad that one of the makers of *Nala Damayanti* has died, and untimely. She suddenly remembers as though it were yesterday the excitement she felt, those twenty-odd years ago, when she went to see that film. Roma had gone with her. She was six or seven. On the way back Roma had lectured her Mashimoni about wifely duties and virtues.

If only everything could be done over again. If only Kanan hadn't married the Kuleen Horse. If she herself hadn't been in a great hurry to marry and leave her father's house, thinking that leaving the village behind was her only way to survive. If, if. . . . If Roderick hadn't died. If Lilian hadn't come back for him. Traveling back in time past is a lonely, painful journey, but Prem can't not linger in it a little. There's so little left to look forward to.

When she and Kanan had made up this little fairytale about their two names she'd believed in a garden where love would grow and bloom forever. Well, she wasn't a very good gardener then—she let many sweet things die— but later she did try to water and shade the little lives that came out of the fairytale, didn't she?

I tried.

She knows that Sengupta is stealing the business away from under their noses day by day. And sometimes she thinks she should do something about it. Harish has clearly lost all interest in the business, and—sometimes her heart twists to think—perhaps in life. And he's lost most of the people dearest to him. And why he's never found a woman to love or marry, she can't understand. And how Sir Naren never understood his little son's heart, never saw how he hurt that boy by openly preferring his older son, whom the boy still idolized.

And how Lilian changed, so completely changed, because of history and the Raj and who knows what else. Maybe just time.

And, above all, how she never replied when they telegrammed her about Roderick's disappearance. How could she do that? *What kind of mother . . . ?* Is she even alive? Prem certainly doesn't expect ever to know.

And then, what is left of the village? After Saroj came away to Calcutta, who took charge of the farm and the property? Does the old head Munshi still do it? Is he still alive?

And what grief her mother kept buried in her heart for a lifetime. The short blade did its work as long as it could, then the blade of relentless guilt and grief cut her loose from the world, and then from herself; set her floating into delirium and then oblivion. She never came back. Maybe she'd always wanted just that, to unmoor and uncouple. And maybe forcing herself to stay moored to an intolerable consciousness was her only way of loving the daughter she didn't want, until she simply couldn't any longer.

And maybe that's all there is. Beyond the promises, and the struggles and the heartbreaks and little and big lies, everyone is just doing what they can, what they're best at. Maybe that's the best everyone can do.

And maybe so has she, Lady Premlata Mitter.

I tried; I really tried.

CHAPTER 62

Harish is having his morning coffee in the library, where he now sits most of the day, like Sir Naren once did. He's not sure how he'll spend the rest of the day. He has nothing to do. He generally avoids crowds now, even where he doesn't know anyone. He has no need to go to the company office on Rawdon Street. Rather, the office has no need for him to come. The Alipore horse races are on, but he is not a betting man, and in any case he has ridiculously little money these days. Doesn't feel like making a pathetic sod of himself with the loaded fat cats of his acquaintance. Friends have vanished with money. Also, in the last years he mostly let his life revolve around his family, his parents, his siblings, and later Rehana. So where does he go?

A note is brought in to him. It was delivered by hand, he's told. The bearer, who left immediately, said he'd not been asked to stay for a response. That the sahib would know what to do.

Inside, Harish reads a brief message in unsteady Hindi calligraphy.

"Mitter Sahib, your son and his mother are leaving for *Umricah* with a white man. She doesn't know I'm sending you this letter. Maybe you can see your son one last time if you make haste."

Harish doesn't answer his mother's anxious questions as he tears out of the library, then the house, and summons the driver to take him to the address given at the bottom of that short note. The driver immediately puts the last remaining car—the Baby Austin—in gear. He stops, blinks and says, "Sahib, not enough petrol in tank." Harish pushes him aside and gets in the driving seat himself. He grinds the ignition key, presses the gas pedal as hard as he can. The great beast of an automobile roars, shudders, and perishes in little, miserable spurts. The gas gauge is in fact empty. Even had Harish had the heart to abuse the driver for his carelessness and negligence in not having the gas tank filled the night before, he knows it is no use. The driver doesn't get enough money in advance to keep the car filled with petrol at all times. Nowadays he's generally given a small sum at the week's beginning and told to manage with it till the end. It's Saturday. The driver has run out of money to buy petrol.

Harish turns out his own pockets, which are empty. He pulls out his wallet and fishes in it, his hands shaking. He has no money. Nothing. He remembers now that his mother asked him for some money a few days ago for household expenses. Since then he's neither needed his wallet, nor used it.

"Go to madam," he tells the driver, "and tell her to send me cash to buy petrol. Tell her it's urgent." The driver runs off into the house. Harish lowers his head on the steering wheel and sits unmoving. The driver returns in about two minutes but he only brings a few paltry notes. They won't be enough. "Madam says this is all there is in the house right now, sahib," he says ruefully.

"Sukhdev Singh, can you lend me some money?" Harish asks the driver.

In shock, the driver withdraws a few bills from his pocket and slowly hands them over to his master. "No, not to me, just go get some petrol to fill the tank and hurry up and then drive me out," Harish says, pushing the bills back toward Sukhdev Singh and turning him around physically toward the gate, and Sukhdev Singh begins walking.

With the petrol Sukhdev Singh buys the car makes good speed. Saturday traffic is light in the mornings. Harish finds himself in this neighborhood called the Bow Barracks, a part of the city he's never been to. The houses here are sturdy and tall, mostly old-fashioned squat structures, painted a fading red on the outside, with dark-green wood-shuttered windows. As the car crawls forward and Harish looks for the house number he sees a mostly sleepy, placid neighborhood, with life stirring faintly. A few bakery type of shops are brewing strong milky tea, and a vendor or milkman cycles past the car ringing the bell merrily and loudly. A few children are playing cricket on the roads, but adults are generally invisible. Washing hangs down almost to the first floors from the balconies of higher stories, mostly European clothes dancing merry jigs in the mellow morning sun. Finally, Harish's eye falls on the number: 12051. The car screeches to a halt though it was traveling slowly, Harish's exclamation causing Sukhdev Singh to hit the brakes hard. Harish gets out of the car.

He's still chubby, and jumping up two steps at a time makes him breathe stertorously, sweat quickly running in rivulets down his temples and face. The address is Flat 43, 12051 Henry Street. When he rings the bell at the door of Flat 43 he feels dizzy, his heart and lungs hurting as if in a brawl with his breath. He thinks he will black out, but this only frightens him enough to stay conscious because otherwise he will miss Rehana and the baby and so lose them for the rest of his life. He presses down hard on the doorbell with the flat of one hand and pounds on the door with the other hand balled into a fist.

The door opens and he nearly falls into the room. Pyari Bai stands before him, then moves out of his way to let him enter. His eyes try adjusting to the darkness of the room. All the windows are closed.

"Where are they?" he asks.

She doesn't say anything for a few seconds. Then, unexpectedly, she shouts, "You come now?"

He stares, bewildered. Their faces mirror anguish but he feels a surge of joy in himself. He will see Rehana. And he will see his son. And finally things will change. He will never ever let her go again. He will shoo away the American, maybe even pay him off. And he will make a very good father, an excellent father, smothering his son with all the love he has missed.

"You asked me to come, and I'm here. Where is she, Pyari Bai-ji?"

And again she says, but this time closer to a whisper, and not as a screaming question, "You come now." Then she raises her face toward the ceiling and shrills, "She's gone! She has left! She didn't stay! They all went away." Covering her mouth with her shaking hands the old, heavyset woman doubles down and slowly slides against a wall till she reaches the floor.

"Bring her back! Oh! Bring her back, sahib! Bring my daughter back!" Her voice, rasping and yet clogged, breaks at each syllable; the words become long, straining howls.

Harish looks around the room. His eyes have now adjusted to the darkness and he sees a low divan, a few chairs, and a low table. He looks at the old woman. As if suddenly understanding what she said he rushes to her side, stoops, tries to lift her, help her off the floor. But she's too heavy, and he's too out of shape. So he sits down by the floor beside her and watches. He's too late. It's over, and he can only watch Rehana's old, wretched mother cry.

"Sahib, why did you let her go? Why didn't you stay? Why did you leave, run away, when she begged you to take her? Why, sahib? Is your heart made of stone?"

Yes, his heart must be made of stone. And the rest of him is turning to stone as well.

Just about an hour before he arrived—probably just as he got the car to run again with the petrol bought with the driver's money—Rehana, the baby, and her new American husband walked out the door, Pyari Bai says, though she threw herself at her daughter's feet and begged her not to leave.

"Umrican soldier, sahib. Took my daughter and the boy, promised to care for the boy like his own. But wouldn't take me. Said Umricah won't let me come."

"And Rehana?"

"I asked her how she could leave, her country, her mother, her whole world, and she just said, 'What's here for me, Mother? You?' "

And so his great love affair has finally ended. Harish watches Pyari Bai cry. Sometimes she looks up at him and begins to curse him anew. She says he's a murderer, a liar, an animal, a monster. She taunts his unmanliness, his spinelessness. She calls him a devil, a thief, an evil spirit. He wants her to do this. He wants to hear her say this is who he is. This is who he is. A coward, a fool, and a beggar. Neither aeronaut nor Argonaut.

She says he hopes he and his family die and rot in hell, while worms eat their insides. Then they will know what it is to lose all hope. To take a miserable, ruined woman's only daughter away from her. To ruin her again, to condemn her to darkness for the rest of her days.

He listens, and hopes that yes, he at least should rot in hell. He wants this to happen. Not to his family. But to himself. All of it. More. All the curses against him and his kind stored up in the heart of this woman and others like her . . . he hopes they all come true. That his life be blighted as hers is.

When the flat door closes behind him, the sun seems to have traveled a good distance. The day outside has aged and is tilting into its decline. It's almost dark. An abandoned woman in Flat 43, 12051 Henry Street, Bow Barracks, Calcutta has cried nearly the day through. He has no comfort for her. She will cry for the rest of her days and sicken and die alone.

Standing right in the middle of the landing on the fourth floor of 12051 Henry Street, Harish looks around. The discolored, mud-streaked mosaic tiles have not been cleaned in a long time. There's litter all over the floor: crumpled paper, cigarette ends, dead leaves, green coconut shell fragments, some animal turd hardening in a corner. My son spent the first years of his life here, he thinks. He realizes now, suddenly, that he doesn't have a photo of the boy. He has no idea what the kid looks like.

There he cries—standing in that glum, lightless landing where the solitary, naked bulb at the end of a wire overhead is a dead eye watching his agony—for the first time since he arrived. He lowers his face into his hands and cries silently, his ample flesh contracting and expanding as he breathes, his body shaking from the violence of his sobs. The door of another flat opens onto the landing and loud voices spill out. One is a woman's voice, the other a man's.

"Two hours, that was the agreement, bitch! I paid good money for this, and you better shell out!"

"Let me go!" The woman screams at breaking pitch. "Let me go, you dirty bastard!"

The man lunges at her, missing her by inches. Harish watches dully. He wonders if this is what happens in the other flats here. If it used to happen in Flat 43. Where Rehana and his son lived.

"Come back!" The man roars. The light from the room illuminates him better than the woman who is half into the landing. He's wearing a sleeveless cotton vest. He's white. For no particular reason Harish looks at the man's feet. White feet, pale and craggy, gripping the mosaic that extends into the flat too. Unsteady, shifting, rebalancing. Feet that couldn't run far or fast.

She should run away now, Harish thinks. The man is obviously blotto. She should take this opportunity and run. She does take a step toward the stairs. He realizes now that she's as drunk as the man. She takes another small, uncertain step and then she falls. She falls like a palette of bricks, without restraint or pattern. She simply falls in a heap, and lies still for a second. Then she begins to try to skid away, her hands clawing at the filthy mosaic, her arms flailing like a drowning swimmer, her body like a snail attempting to hurry away from harm. Harish wants to tell the man to stop, to let the woman be. He wants to help her off the dirty floor, down the steps, hail a taxi, put her in it. Before he can take a step, trying to fight off his fatigue, his lightheadedness and his grief—for this moment, this day, this life—the man comes out of the flat and lands upon the woman and begins to beat her. He beats her as if she were a thing. As if she were a door he's pummeling to be let in. He slaps her again and again around the face. He pulls her head up by the hair and then he slams it down onto the floor. Harish hears a cracking sound.

The woman isn't making any sounds anymore. Harish can only hear the thwacking sounds and the occasional flat-handed slap. And he inches forward, all of him shaking, his muscles refusing this unaccustomed task of bearing a large, crouching body, his heart thudding so hard he thinks it will suddenly shatter, throwing him back into the middle of the landing in a backward arc. But he talks to his heart, his muscles, his tendons, his nerves. "Hold on one moment longer. Just a little longer. Hold on!" And they do, they do go with him, and he travels with them toward where the man is still on the woman and he doesn't know how but he raises his right foot as high as he can and then with one decisive movement brings it down on the head of the man just as the man looks up for a split second and then he hears a sound of bone hitting something hard.

Then nothing. And then he sees, now that he's closer, that the man is holding a bottle in one hand, still, and he leans forward and snatches the bottle from the man and brings it down again on the man's head and hears a shattering sound but it's not the bottle because it's still whole when he brings it back up but there's blood on it.

Now back to the woman. His weak heart is thundering like wild horses galloping, but he can see that she's still moving slightly. He counsels and cheers every step his body allows him to take toward her. Counting. One, two, three, and she's only a few feet away from him. Amazingly, beginning to try to push herself up from the floor.

Are they the only people in the world, or at least in this building? The man on the floor behind him, and he and the woman?

Then he hears glass crunching.

Part 9:

Return to the Village, 1950

CHAPTER 63

"And this is where we made our brave plans for the new future."
Prem shows Roma the precise spot by the pond—it's still there, in thirty years very little has changed at the core of the village—where she and Kanan sat and worked out the future: their children marrying, and life and the century and the rest of civilization and time going on happily ever after.

A little distance behind them can be heard frequent slapping and exclamations. The young servant from Calcutta is experiencing country life for the first time.

"A nice place for dreams, Mashimoni."

The pondside is still what it was, though so much else has changed. The village hasn't quite decided what to do with independent modernity. Areas of it have eagerly adapted to new times and new ways—hopefully better times, better ways—and others have declined as yet. The railway station, some main roads, the post office, have acquired new beauties; a county hospital and a farm affairs bureau have recently cropped up. But the fields, orchards, local and neighborhood ponds and fisheries are still holding out on renovation.

As to the people of the village, in the old village area where Prem's father's farmhouse still stands, they still don't visit each other by invitation. They just walk in and out of one another's courtyards, back gardens, front doors if there are any; women simply walk straight up to neighbors' pantries and kitchens. If it is someone's daughter's wedding, it is still the wedding of a girl who belongs to the tribe and the village.

"Why did you not come back to visit here before, Mashimoni? When we were young? It's so peaceful here. It would have been such a great holiday."

Prem doesn't answer the question. She has no answer. The time for loving and growing is always right now, she thinks. Never forget the right now, this day. Never go back, never live in memory. If possible. She pats her upper left chest. A letter is tucked into her cardigan, there.

They walk on up to the pond's edge, still crumbling, ants and beetles still scurrying away in high serious haste at approaching footsteps.

"We each took one hibiscus flower from a bush somewhere here—it's probably still around, just hidden—and tied it into the borders of each other's saris. And we promised to love each other forever and always be together."

"That is nice, Mashimoni."

"We were simple village girls, you see. We didn't know all the things that city girls like you knew. But we did mean what we said and we did love each other."

Kanan's daughter listens, imagining the fifteen-year-old girl who was her mother.

"Even though my mother was a maid's daughter."

"Even though."

A little later they are back in the farmhouse—the poor teenage boy admitted defeat early and came back some time ago—in the room where Shyampiyari, Prem, and Kanan used to sleep. Saroj's room has been turned into a library, stocked with books from Sir Naren's old library that couldn't be sold with the house. Prem refused to have this room locked up, or to build a private shrine there as the Munshi suggested. "Munshi-ji," she said, a smile playing about her mouth," you knew my Mai-ji. Did she have one single religious bone in her body?"

Prem glances at Roma's face. Roma's left eye is partially closed. The area around it had to be reconstructed after the head injury she got in 12051 Henry Street the night Harish found her. Her assailant—her John for the night in Barracks parlance—was hospitalized and recovered too. At least Roma's vision was saved. Still, hers will now never be seen even as a tolerably passable face though she's still relatively young, only thirty-six.

Roma looks serious but tranquil; it relieves Prem, affirms that she may be doing the right thing. Roma will live here with her; she'll give it a try at least. Kanan's daughter may come home yet. Harish won't, and certainly she can't imagine Harish and Roma ever having married, but there are such precious memories of their years of love to remember not to forget.

And above all, when the grand future she once imagined closed its doors, the past she thought Mai-ji and Kanan stole away has let her back in. A small brick house painted a light sky blue can be seen standing—snug, not lonely—at the spot where a shanty with a thatch roof stood once, home of a poor widow and her softhearted son. When Prem looks at it she remembers a young man who wrote her ardent words of love from a battlefield. She is indeed come home, where her first loves grew and where from the windows of her father's house a little piece of her girlhood still smiles. The ancient Munshi, elated that *Bitiya Rani* is back, promises to help her run the farm and start a mango export business for as long as he lives, which seems likely to be forever. A growing country needs corn, rice, fertilizer, fresh vegetables and fruits. Droughts will come again, and famine will always lurk, but the land is still the land—pure brown gold.

"Well, set yourself up my dear," Prem tells Roma. "You have the pick of any room you like, but choose wisely!"

"Wisely?"

"Choose the spot where the morning sun comes in just the way you like it as you wake up. Where the windows open to the south wind. Where you feel not too far from people but not crowded. And where you can hear me if I fall at night and call you, old biddy that I am."

Roma wordlessly puts her arms around Prem and holds her tight for a long time. She chooses the room next to Prem's, where Shyampiyari audibly whispered tall tales to two girls forty years ago.

"Mashimoni, can we do this?"

"Do what, dear?"

"Live here?"

"Why not, dear?"

"I've never grown anything, Mashimoni. If you think about it, I actually have a long record of breaking and killing things. And you haven't either, Mashimoni."

Since that is not true—Prem grew a life, a home, a family, and three children—Prem only pats Roma on the back.

"Will things grow, Mashimoni?"

Prem looks over Roma's shoulder out the window at the horizon that cradles the land, the fields, and the new harvest. She is her father's daughter too, after all. "Oh yes my dear, things will grow, don't you worry."

CHAPTER 64

Finally, in her old bedroom Prem settles wearily into the old bed freshly made reverentially by the Munshi's daughter-in-law, a smiling, middle-aged woman who can't quite stop gawking at the daughter of this house who became the great Calcutta Lady and all. If Kanan had lived she might have looked like this woman in her middle age.

She brings the letter out from its cradle between skin and cardigan over blouse. Unfolds it. Reads.

Dear Lady Mitter (Or may I use your name, dear Prem?),

You wrote me after Roderick died that you had ever only known mothers who were demons—monsters who bled and devoured men and their own children—and that you were aghast to have to admit, finally, that I was truly one of them. Fair point. In so many ways you were Roderick's true mother. I bore him, but you raised him. We both loved him—you must believe me today when I write that we both loved him—but you loved him harder, closer, hour in and hour out, when you so easily could have abandoned him.

I sincerely grieve that I never got to know your son as you did mine. However, knowing your nature, your heart, I know that he was blessed in a mother who not only was not a monster, but who never gave him a single moment's reason to doubt his mother, to question her love, to feel abandoned. I would have loved him had I known him. Roderick used to tell me such sweet stories of growing up as brothers together with him, of how much your son loved him, yet loved to fight with him. Sweet young boys, ours, lucky to have been together in the glory days of boyhood, when men's lives are sweetest.

But the truth, as you know dearest Prem, is that we make men, and men make wars. Then they take us as prizes or victims. We have both known such men—intimately. But at least we two—if you will allow me the honor of your circle there—can say that we made two of the best kind of men, men who didn't make wars but faced the ones thrust on them for the sakes of the women they loved. Roderick loved his "I" dearly, and in his last letter he told me how deeply he had fallen in love with his other childhood best friend—another little woman!—your very own Roma. Almost my very own. If only I'd had any luck.

I know I seemed hard and selfish—again, a monster—to you the last time we saw each other. In many ways, I had to make myself seem that way, because I was afraid. Afraid that if I didn't behave harshly, imperiously, you and Naren might not have let Roderick come to England with me. And I was afraid Roderick might decline if I seemed wishy-washy. Please forgive me, if you can, Prem. I was lonely. I was tired. I saw that I was getting old and I was afraid of lonely old age.

But Prem, let me say what emboldens me to write to one who can be entirely forgiven for resolutely closing the doors of her heart to me, even should that be the case. I write to you because we are women who know what it is to lose what we have loved best and longest. And to lose not once, but over and over again. You and I—from different worlds but shared histories—know what it is to lose the baby whose skin and limbs we protected from one little scratch or cut. Whose bodies—broken, torn, bleeding—we still had to cradle in the end in our arms or hearts. But I write to you also because you have the biggest heart of anyone I ever knew. You loved and nourished those to whom you owed nothing, not even tolerance. You loved the half-blood child of your husband and his mistress. Thank you, Prem.

My skin is white, and so is yours, but as we both know, our two white skins are worlds apart. We've had to stand looking out at each other across the vast empire that separated us, seeing only strangers, enemies. We had no choice. At least I thought so. But in truth, I now see, all the time we were sisters, lovers, mothers, and allies, and so our causes were the same. We had both hoped to see our sons become husbands and fathers, and live long and happy lives.

Dear Prem, I know you and I will not see each other again in this world. It is my fondest hope though, dearest Prem, that we'll meet again, someday, in another, better one, where we shall see the faces of everyone we loved. And that after that day, we shall never be separated again.

Yours in sincerest affection, forever,

Lilian Nandini Bhattacharya, Exit Row, 2016

Glossary

"aunties": As Rehana would call the other courtesans, her mother's "sisters"

Amritabazar Patrika: A militantly nationalist daily published in Calcutta

arrey, naa: Hindi-Bengali words meaning "oh well," and "no" meaning "yes," mixed into pidgin English

baba: Name for a small boy of privileged background

babaa and *come naa*: Pidgin exclamations and ejaculations

babu: An Indian fop or rake

bah bah: Bengali for "well, well"

baijis: Courtesans, public women, artists, and denizens of the flesh trade

Bande Mataram: The first line of a nationalistic poem by Bengali writer Bankim Chandra Chattopadhyay written in the 1870s; it subsequently became the national anthem of India during the freedom movement

banzai: Japanese soldier's battle cry: "Emperor!"

beedi: Cheap, leaf-wrapped, unfiltered tobacco

beedis: Vernacular for hand-rolled leaf cigarettes containing strong, unfiltered tobacco, usually smoked by the poor

belle de jour: French for the beauty of the day

bheto Bangali: Bhat- or rice-eating Bengali

Bilet Pherat: Bengali for "England Returned"

bitiya: Baby girl

bitiya rani: Queen daughter, or princess

blandeur: In French, insipid pretence of grandeur

bonti: Bengali word for upright steel blade embedded in wooden base that sits flat on the floor, that women use to chop things, squatting. A substititue for a knife

chhoti bahu-rani: Hindi for queenly younger sister-in-law, a term of fealty

chirobondhu: Bengali for "friends forever"

cholbey na: Can not go on

Chor Bazaar: A location in Calcutta; the name means Thieves' Market. Stolen and contraband goods were sold there

daal: Miscellaneous lentil and bean soup

danse macabre: French for Dance of the Dead

dargah: Place of prayer

dhoti: Hindi and Bengali for Indian men's traditional lower garment, a length of seamless fabric wrapped, pleated, and tucked into the waistband

Dulce est, decorum est, pro patria mori: "It is sweet and fitting to die for one's country"—Latin phrase from the Roman poet Horace that served as title of Wilfred Owen's bleak and ironic poem about World War I

Durga Puja: The festival of the great ten-armed Goddess Durga that lasts nearly ten days in autumn

eclat: French for brilliant advent

einh: A plaintive sound indicating "what" or "yes" in village vernacular

fin-de-siècle: Characteristic of the close of the nineteenth century and especially its literary and artistic climate of sophistication, world-weariness, and fashionable despair

firingi: Literally Frank, or French, later applied broadly to most westerners

Gauloises: French cigarettes

ghaghra and *angrakha*: Traditional Indian Muslim women's ceremonial skirts and bodices

gora: Indian name for "white," or "whites," or the English

gustakhi maaf, huzoor: Urdu-Hindi for "beg your pardon, master"

hai hai: Hindi or Bengali for "alas"

hakim: Doctor in Urdu

hein: A vague exclamation

infra dig: English Schoolboy shorthand for Latin infra dignitatem, "beneath dignity"

ishq, bewaafa humsafar, behuda duniya: Love, faithless lover, faithless world

jaan: Life, in Urdu

jaanu: A version of "my life" in Urdu

Jalianwalla: From Jalianwallah Bagh where in 1919 General Dyer ordered indiscriminate firing on a peaceable gathering of thousands of Indians, killing most

jamai raja: Lord son-in-law

ji huzoor:

joie de vivre: French for lust for life

kahlo bhoot: Bengali for black-skinned ghost

Kala Pani: Hindi for the black waters, namely the ocean

Kanan Debi: Literally goddess, but really more like lady, usually used to address married gentlewomen

khuku: The Bengali version of Missy Baba, and a common name for a little girl in Bengali

kothas: Residences

kumari: Miss, mademoiselle

kutcha bachcha: Half-baked baby in Hindi

La Marts: La Martiniere for Boys school, Calcutta

latak chhamak: Sashaying, inviting, explicit

Mahabharata: A fourth-century BC Sanskrit epic telling of a great war in India about a thousand years earlier. It means Great India, or the Great Epic of India

Mai-ji: What Prem calls her mother

manège: French, training of horses, carriage

mangalsutra: Necklace, worn by married Hindu women, signifying their married state

Marwari: Largely an ancient business community originating in Rajasthan in North India, but spread eventually all over India due to mercantile interests

mashimoni: In Bengali, Mashimoni is "mashi" or mother's sister graced with "moni," or gemstone; precious mother's sister

mem: Hindi or Bengali abbreviation of "memsahib," itself short for "Madam Sahib"

memsahib: Short for Madam Sahib

missy baba: A young girl from a well-to-do, westernized family

mujrah: Private singing and sometimes dancing entertainments by celebrated public women, an Indian version of the Salon

nahi huzoor: Urdu-Hindi for "no, master"

nautankis, shikar, and *kusti*: Raunchy female dancers, hunting, and mud wrestling

nawabs: Indian title for princes and potentates who had served under the Mughal emperor, usually in provinces, and whom the British later mostly stripped of all but titular authority and nominal possessions

oyay: A rude call like "you!"

paan: Betel leaf, areca nuts, and slaked lime paste

padhhe-likhhe: "Reading-writing"; literate

parganahs: Districts or zones

pati bhakti: Sanskrit for wifely devotion

payals: Tinkling anklets

poorna swaraj: Full independence

prasad: The food offered to the goddess and then distributed among the worshippers

Presidency College: Elite Calcutta college for Indians founded in the nineteenth century by the British

pukka brown sahib: A deracinated, westernized Indian man. Pukka means solid or fully formed, as in architecture and fruit; a pukka sahib was a colonized person who almost perfectly imitated the English, like Henry Babington Macaulay's predicted race that would be Indian in skin and blood but English in manners and morals

rotis: Hindi for thin Indian flatbread

saal leaf: General vernacular for tree leaves of a beige-brown color when aged

salwar kameeze: Indian women's traditional tunics and pants

sang froid: French for self-possession or imperturbability especially under strain

Satyagraha: Mahatma Gandhi's primary slogan for the anti-colonial movement: Truth Above All

sepoy: How the British pronounced "sipahi," meaning soldier in Hindi/Urdu

shirimati: Akin to lady, or madam

sori chhori: Knife wife

Statesman: Prominent Calcutta English-language newspaper started by the English but still running

Glossary

tabla: Traditional small percussive drum

tawaifi: Complex, semiclassical style of music nurtured and perfected by courtesans from the fifteenth–sixteenth century onward that ended up influencing a lot of Indian film music

terai: Lower Himalayan hillside where tea is grown

thumris: Probably the closest comparison would be as the Urdu version of the medieval French *chansons d'amour*

Umricah: America

zenana: Women's private quarters, though for the working classes such privacy was less common

Acknowledgements

My greatest inspiration for writing this novel is my son Khoka Myers; he knows why. We were misty-eyed and tongue-tied after I read the last chapter of *Love's Garden* in draft out loud to him, and then he nodded Yes. My kindest supporter and prime instigator for doing the work, and making the best of hardest choices, is Leo Hartman, friend and partner. My invaluable ally and life and writing coach Patricia Murphy, a talented novelist herself, showed me that the writing life is possible even as I insisted it was only for others. I have no words of thanks good enough for my debt to these writing teachers and mentors: Chitra Banerjee Divakaruni, Tiphany Yanique, Meg Wolitzer, Joan Silber, Hernan Diaz, Maud Casey, Kathleen Spivack, Mita Mitra, Kristina Marie Darling, Rita Banerjee, and Diana Szokolyai. Nivea Castro, Tori Reynolds, Angela Ajayi, Laurie Thomas, Indira Ganesan, Mia Alvar, Danton Remoto, Shona Jackson, Catalina Bartlett, Marco Portales, Trisha Malik, Alicia Link, Joanna Tam, Mousumi Rao nee Sen, Tazim Jamal, Sarbani Bose, Vivek and Dolly Ahuja, Diana Davila, David Morgan, Susan Lee, Giselle Mora, Renu Juneja, Scott Coon, David Samuel Levinson, Jo Chandy, and my sister Shalini Bhattacharya—you all know I would be nowhere and nothing without you.

My sincerest thanks go to Voices of Our Nation Arts, Sarah Lawrence College, the Cambridge Writers Workshop, the Southampton Summer Writers Workshop, the Vermont Studio Center, the Bread Loaf Writers Workshop, and the English department at Texas A&M University for support and sustenance when I most needed them. My publishers at Aubade—Joe, Vonda, and Cosette Puckett—have been the most fantastic readers, editors, and cheerleaders. I thank you from the bottom of my heart for taking me on. Warmest thanks also to Kristina Marie Darling for being the world's most crackerjack publicist imaginable.

Last but not least, you, my foremothers, who stand behind me in the long, dim hallway of lost time, with love lighting up your eyes and the dimness of forgotten histories, this book is about you and wouldn't have lived without you.

CPSIA information can be obtained
at www.ICGtesting.com
Printed in the USA
BVHW040541191020
591291BV00014B/439

9 781951 547080